LOVE
and
Redemption

JULIA GEORGE

To the memory of my stepmother, Cecilia Klein-Kovacova, and my father, Ivan Kovach.

And for their grandson, Peter.

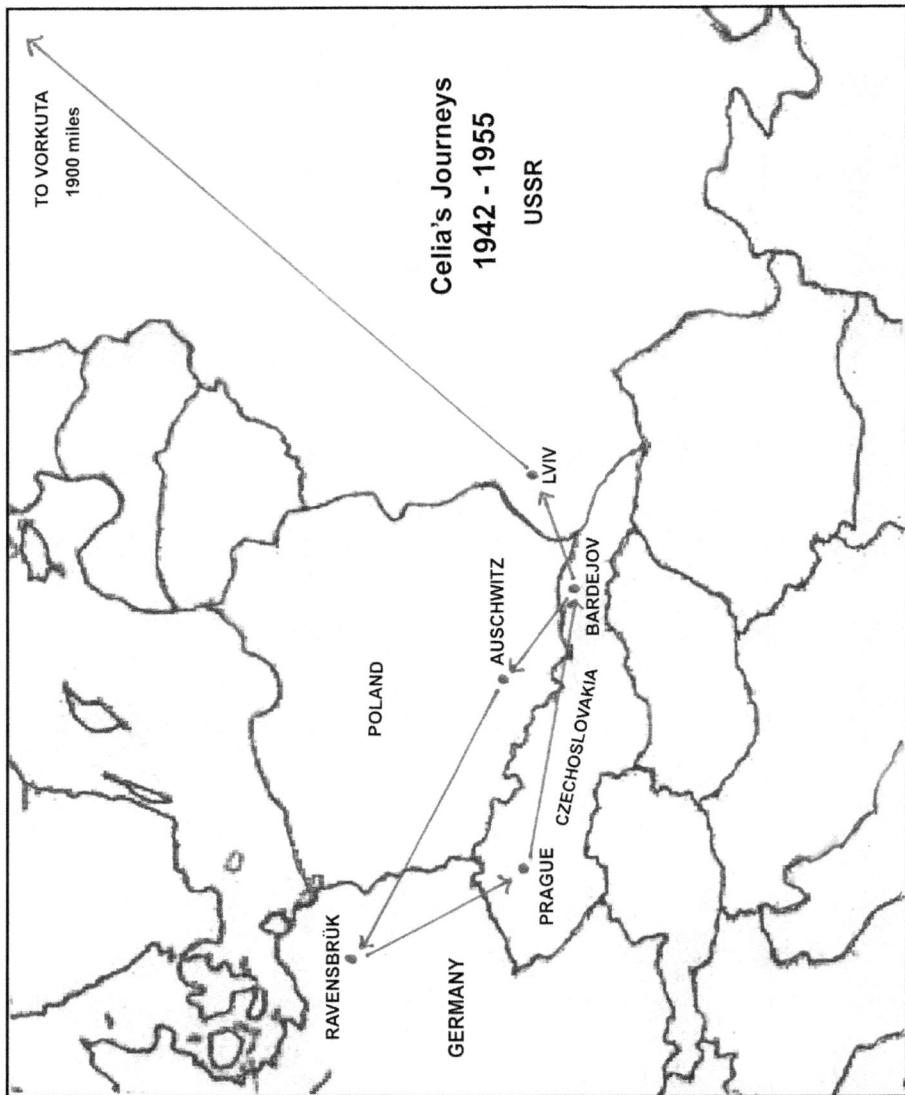

Celia's Journeys
1942 - 1955

TO VORKUTA
1900 miles

USSR

LVIV

AUSCHWITZ

BARDEJOV

POLAND

CZECHOSLOVAKIA

PRAGUE

RAVENSBRÜK

GERMANY

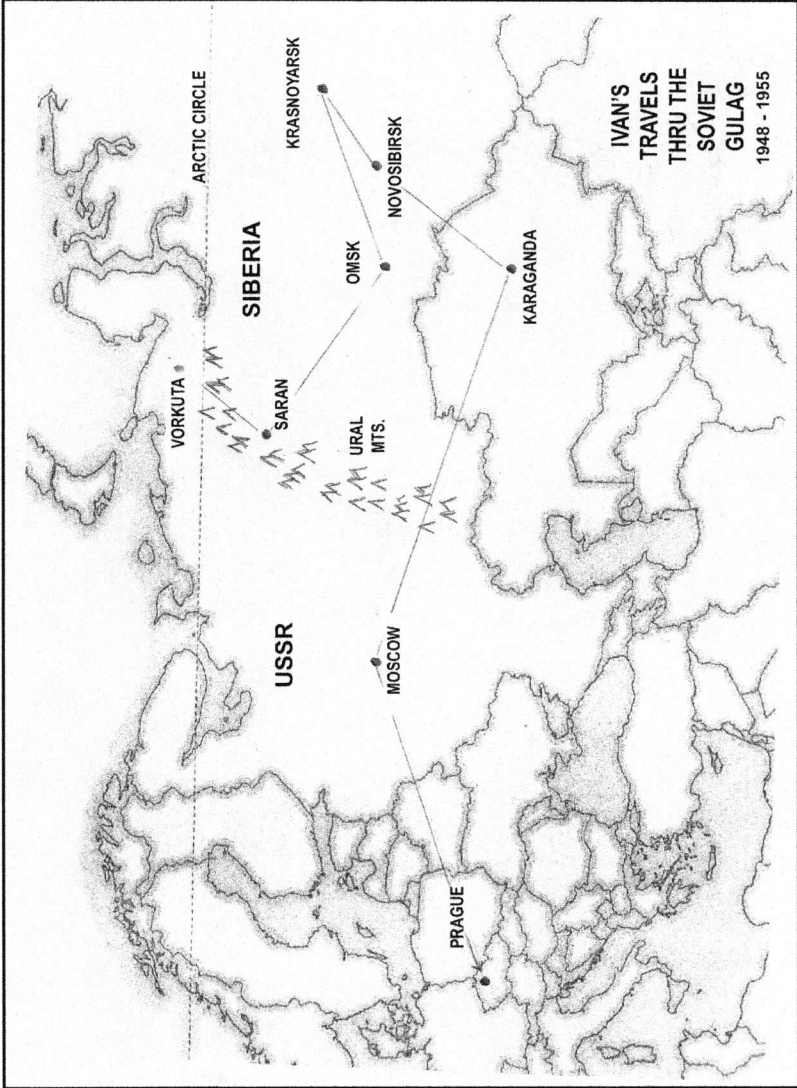

IVAN'S
TRAVELS
THRU THE
SOVIET
GULAG

1948 - 1955

ARCTIC CIRCLE

SIBERIA

USSR

KRASNOYARSK

NOVOSIBIRSK

OMSK

KARAGANDA

VORKUTA

SARAN

URAL
MTS.

MOSCOW

PRAGUE

Author's Note

by George Kovach,
Stepson of Cecilia Klein-Kovacova

Although this book is about real people and events, it is more than a novel based on a true story. The heroine and hero are two people I knew intimately, loved deeply, and respected immensely. They are, in fact, my stepmother and my father. This is the story of their courage, their suffering, and their love and devotion for each other. It is derived from my conversations with them over many years, and from my father's written memoirs of his time in the Soviet gulag.

Love and Redemption is the harrowing story of my stepmother's journey from the hell of a Nazi concentration camp to a new hell in the Siberian gulag. It is also the story of how my stepmother and my father met and fell in love in the last place on earth you would think genuine love between two people could blossom and thrive. And yet, Cecilia Klein and Ivan Kovach found each other and enduring love in this horrendous place. I know this to be true because when I spent time with them; I saw the depth of their mutual devotion and care for each other. It inspired me and I hope their story inspires you.

How many circles of hell can you endure before you become one of the devils?

How often can you reach out for hope before you stop trying?

How long until redemption is impossible?

—CECILIA KLEIN

Liberation

CHAPTER ONE

Ravensbrück Concentration Camp for Women
Germany
April 1945

Fire! Everything was on fire. I ran out of my barracks into the Appelplatz, fear and excitement rippling through me in conflicting waves. A reddish-brown cloud of pungent smoke hung in the cold air. The familiar tang of ashes, bitter and acidic, was much stronger than usual, and different. Ash rained down on me, but this time, it wasn't just from the crematoriums. Across the square, huge piles of clothes smoldered. Clothes taken from the dead. Nearby, masses of paper documents burned brightly. Pieces of charred paper floated up, gaily fluttering in the air before disintegrating into ash. I watched the scene as hope rose in me once more. Hope that had died so many times during the three years I'd been a prisoner, first in Auschwitz and now in Ravensbrück.

Would it be different this time? Could this finally be the end of our suffering? Would the Red Army arrive in time to save us? Or would they be too late, and the SS finally kill us all? You can only die once, and I didn't want to die in Ravensbrück. There were over twenty thousand women and children still in the camp. Twenty thousand testaments to hideous horrors. How could they kill us all? How could they burn that many bodies? It would take too much time to clear away the evidence of their atrocious crimes, the gas chambers, the crematoriums, the hospital laboratories, the mountains of documents, records of their vile experiments. Still, they were horrifically efficient, the Nazis.

It's odd how years of routine abuse make you numb to terror. You learn what to expect, how to act to avoid punishment and death. Just another day in hell. But not this day. Today, chaos reigned in the routine evil world of the camp. That meant the old rules no longer applied. If I were to stay alive until the Russians came, I would have to be very, very careful. I would also have to be strong, stronger even than I had been in Auschwitz. Only the thick-skinned survive hell. For three years I'd taught myself to be hard and ruthless, so ruthless I was someone I no longer recognized. But I had survived.

And I would survive again. Whatever it took, I would escape this hell and live. Because today was different. The devils who ruled us all with such iron will had gone berserk. I watched as guards ran frantically in and out of buildings. SS officers argued with each other, arms waving wildly as if they had lost their wits. Hans, the perpetually drunk associate camp commander, rode around on his bicycle like a madman, laughing and shooting any prisoner in his way.

The devils knew the end was near. Fear, that potent Nazi weapon of terror, had turned on them. Once so cold and efficient, now the Nazis ran around the camp, shouting in high-pitched voices, panic-stricken, trying to destroy the evidence of their unspeakable crimes before the Red Army arrived. They had been so haughty in their spotless uniforms. Such a contrast to us in our filthy striped dresses. Now, covered with soot and sweat, the Nazis no longer looked the Superior Race. I watched them with joy in my heart, even though I knew we were in more peril than ever. Papa had told me once a long time ago: A terrified beast at bay is the most dangerous.

During the last couple of days, Red Army planes had flown low over the camp, but they never dropped any bombs, never landed. Liberation was coming. I could feel it. But was it close enough? Would there still be time for the SS to destroy the most compelling evidence? Evidence with a voice. Us. The women of Ravensbrück.

Recently, the gassing had accelerated to a frenzy. Round the clock, the guards pointed the finger of death at those marked for extermination. Everyone who wasn't fit enough to march. Everyone who was living proof of what they had done here had to be eliminated. Women with swollen legs and protruding bones were gassed. Old women emaciated from hunger were gassed. Anyone who was sick. Women pregnant from rapes. Children too young to march. All were gassed. Day and night, the black, oily smoke choked the sky.

Though I no longer believed in a merciful God, I prayed that time had run out for the Germans. I knew it would. Even for the SS. Time had run out for them before. In January, they'd had to destroy Auschwitz before the Red Army reached it. There was no time then to kill us all, so they had marched us here to Ravensbrück in the freezing cold. Thousands of us died from starvation and exposure on that nightmarish march. They left the bodies where they fell. The dead were not a problem, only the living. But now the Red Army had penetrated Germany itself. Before the Reds arrived with cameras to document the evil, the Ravensbrück gas chambers must be dismantled.

I stood in the Appelplatz now, secretly rejoicing. I turned my face to the smoke-filled sky and listened, every nerve on edge, for the sound of planes. I heard nothing but shouting Germans, sporadic gunfire, the anguished screams of women. The little spark of hope flickered and died.

Slowly, around me, the Appelplatz filled with women for the roll call. This was a routine we endured every day. For hours, we would stand to be counted. If the number of prisoners seemed incorrect, we would continue to stand in our thin clothes in all weather—heat, rain, snow—until the SS officers made the numbers tally and the German passion for accuracy was satisfied. Anyone unable to remain standing was dragged away. Usually to her death. The roll call was a lesson to all. *It is pointless to resist*. We knew what to expect that day as every day.

We were all weak. So tired from hunger and hard physical labor, we longed to just lie down and rest. But that meant death. So, we stood, shoulder to shoulder, supporting each other. Waiting like helpless animals for our fate.

CHAPTER TWO

"Cilka?"

Leah spoke softly and touched me lightly on my arm. She had attached herself to me on the death march when they moved us from Auschwitz to Ravensbrück. On that horrendous march, she told me she wanted to be my friend.

"Why?" I had asked.

"Because if anyone survives, you will."

I had ignored her back then. I wanted no friends, then or now. Cold and cynical as I had become, I might have been a bitter ninety rather than nineteen. Compassion was a weakness that could get you killed. Friendship was dangerous. Feelings of loyalty brought nothing but trouble.

And how could I have any friends? How could I allow someone to care for me? I knew what I had done, and I hated myself. I was unworthy of anyone's friendship. But Leah didn't pay any attention to that. Leah just cared. For everyone. Even me. She was a fool, but somewhere inside myself, I was grateful to her.

"What will happen to us, Cilka?"

Before answering, I looked around to see where the officers were. For now, they huddled in a group some distance away. Good. Talk among the prisoners was *verboten*. I would keep my eye on them. Getting shot so close to salvation would be too bitter an irony.

"I don't know," I whispered. "I think they would like to shoot us all. You know, no women, no problem. But they can't do that."

"Why not?" Leah also lowered her voice to a whisper. "They've killed and killed for years. What will stop them now?"

I shrugged. "Not enough time to get rid of the bodies. The idiot SS blew up the gas chambers and one of the two crematoriums too early. If they murder all the rest of us, it will be too many for one crematorium to handle. It would take them years." I gave Leah a grim smile. "So much for German efficiency. *Heil Hitler!*" I sneered.

Leah looked around furtively. "Then will it be another death march?"

"If the Russians don't come today, I think that's what will happen."

"God help us," Leah murmured. She looked at our fellow prisoners. "The only thing the Russians will liberate is a trail of bodies."

"Not mine, Leah. I refuse to die. If we die, the Germans win."

"Then I'll stick with you. You'll get us home!"

"Stick with me if you want to. I swear I will make my way out of this hell and survive. But I warn you now, as I did in Auschwitz, I take no chances for anyone."

That's what I had become. Practical, cold, ruthless. Like the devils, in a way.

"I wish I had your toughness, Cilka."

I looked at Leah, her tiny body barely discernable in a ragged dress too big for her. Soft brown eyes looked into mine. She was like a homeless mongrel begging for affection.

"Once, a lifetime ago, I believed good things could happen, Leah. Now I know the truth. Life is nothing but suffering and injustice. People don't care. God doesn't care. We must make our own fate. Or die."

Leah's dry, chapped lips curved into a smile. "Courage then. I wish I had your courage."

"I'm not courageous. I'm scared to death all the time."

"Then what is it?"

"Anger. Anger keeps me alive. And hate."

"I don't believe you." Leah's eyes searched my face. "No. I don't believe that."

"You're too good." I looked away. "Goodness in hell is weakness. The good don't survive."

She placed a tentative hand on my arm. "Whatever happens now, I'll stay by you."

"All right," I snapped. "Fine. You can stay with me. But you have to do what I say if you want to survive."

———— ★ ————

I can't explain why I decided at that moment to save Leah. I had cut myself off from everyone. Looking back, I remembered Papa telling me the story of Pandora. After Auschwitz and Ravensbrück, I was like Pandora's box, filled with anger, hatred, fear. But it seems that somewhere deep inside, one tiny good thing remained.

A light spring snow began to fall onto the Appelplatz. The officers came then and ordered us to march. They didn't say where we were going, but no one expected them to tell us. We followed orders as always. We marched, a gray river of human misery pouring out of the gates of hell. I didn't think we could survive another death march, but at least we were leaving. For that alone, I was glad.

They herded us like cattle. I knew we would be driven north, deeper into Germany. The SS were running for their lives. Oh, it felt so good to see them humiliated. It felt good to smell *their* fear.

A bullhorn bellowed.

"Close the gates! Those still inside, shoot them! Then burn the place!"

We froze and turned as one to look back toward the gates, knowing who remained. The sick. The weak. The old. The children. Why shouldn't they have a chance to be liberated and maybe live? We knew why. The dead tell no tales.

We turned around and marched, step by weary step. As if we were of one mind, we followed the same plan for survival. *Keep walking. Don't stop. Don't talk. Don't look around. Don't think.* Do nothing to draw attention to yourself. They were watching, always watching, even as they now walked in fear themselves. I was careful to keep the smile off my face. The joy I felt at their fear and humiliation would keep me walking for weeks. Hitler's Thousand-Year Reich was crumbling in only twelve years.

Now and then, someone would fall to the ground, too weak to continue, and we'd hear a gunshot behind us.

A woman bumped into me, and I turned. I could tell she was older because the shoe-blacking she used to cover the gray in her hair was running down her face. Deep pockets of flesh hung beneath her sunken eyes. I could see by the dark brown shade of her eye sockets that she was so dehydrated it was a miracle she could even stand. A younger woman had linked her arm in hers. She may have been her daughter, but it was hard to tell. They were both so emaciated. The younger woman looked at me, then quickly looked away. But I had seen the fear in her eyes. She knew me.

The older woman spoke, her voice so low and hoarse I barely heard. "Are they taking us to the sea?"

"They'll put us on boats and drown us!" The younger woman was near hysteria.

"Keep quiet," I hissed. "They're watching. You'll get us all shot."

The older woman stumbled then and fell. She struggled to get up, but she didn't have the strength. The younger one fell to her knees and took her in her arms.

"Mama! Mama! No!" She rocked her back and forth, back and forth, her own body shaking with sobs.

An SS officer materialized like an evil spirit.

"Get up! Both of you!"

The young woman looked up at him with such an expression of pain and sorrow, I closed my eyes not to see.

"Get up! Move!" The officer kicked the older woman, then grabbed the younger one's arm.

She kicked out at him. "Devil!" she screamed.

He shot them both.

"Keep moving!" he shouted to the rest of us.

We marched. *Don't stop. Don't talk. Don't look around. Don't think.*

Tears trailed down Leah's dirt-smeared face, leaving pale white lines. Her shoulders shook, but she made no sound. Nothing I could do or say would change reality for her. So, I said nothing.

I knew the pace was too fast for Leah. Sometimes I gripped her arm and dragged her along. I had this fierce need to put as much distance between me and Ravensbrück as possible. It was nonsense, of course. Ravensbrück and Auschwitz would always be with me. You can never outdistance memories.

"Cilka!" Leah yanked my arm. "It's Katya!"

She ran ahead and fell to her knees beside what looked like a heap of filthy clothes. The little fool was going to get herself shot.

"Leah!" I ran over to them.

"It's Katya." Leah looked at me with pleading eyes. "Oh, Cilka, we have to help her. Look! She can't walk anymore. She needs water. We have to save her!"

"You can't save her, Leah." I grabbed her arm and yanked her to her feet. "Come away. They'll shoot you if you try to help. You know the rules."

"No! I can carry her." She fell to her knees again. "Katya. Can you put your arms around my neck?"

Katya didn't say anything, just looked at us. I thought of Bobo, my old family dog who died when I was a child. His eyes had that same hopeless look.

"Please, Katya," Leah whispered. She put her hands under Katya and tried to lift her.

"You can't save her," I growled. "See? You can't even lift her. And neither can I. Even if you could, how far would you get before you both fell to the ground? The SS will shoot all three of us."

I pulled Leah to her feet and slapped her. I shoved her down the road, half dragging her, half pushing her until we were far enough away from Katya.

"I said I would save you, Leah, and I meant it. But I refuse to die. And I refuse to let you die. Keep walking."

Don't stop. Don't talk. Don't look around. Don't think!

"Dear God, Cilka. What have we become?"

"What they've made us. What we've made ourselves. God has nothing to do with it."

We heard the shot then. Katya's suffering was over.

CHAPTER THREE

"*Achtung! Achtung! Alle ins bett!*"

An SS officer shouted the command for bed through a megaphone as his black Mercedes rolled along the line of weary prisoners. Its mud-splattered surface was a testament now to the disintegration of discipline and order so treasured by the Germans.

"He's ordering everybody into bed?" Leah chuckled. "What beds?"

All around us, exhausted prisoners fell to the ground where they stood. Some curled into fetal positions to make themselves as small and inconspicuous as possible. The darkening sky proclaimed the fast approach of night, and I feared what that would bring. We still weren't sure the Germans wouldn't murder us all as we slept.

I took Leah's hand and led her a little way from the ragged line of prisoners.

"Where are we going?" Leah yawned. "I'm so tired. Can't we just lie down with the rest?"

I moved closer to a line of trees near the road and began gathering branches to make a kind of mat for us to sleep on. Leah quickly caught on to the plan, and soon we curled up on a soft bed of leaves and light branches.

"You see," I said as we lay side-by-side. "We do have beds." I pulled some leaves over us. "And blankets, too."

Leah yawned again. "*Alle ins bett*, Cilka!" She imitated the harsh tone of the SS. "They'll probably come around in the morning, like they did in camp, and shout, *Raus! Raus!*" She giggled, drunk on fear.

"Who knows what they'll do?"

We lay awake for a time, looking up at the dark sky sprinkled with stars. It was so vast and beautiful and cold. So unconnected to our miserable lives down here. Where was God in all this? Even if He did exist, which I doubted, He had absolutely no interest in us, or He would have wiped the Germans off the face of the earth years ago.

"Cilka?"

"Yes?"

"I've wanted to ask you something." Leah turned her face close to mine and whispered. "I mean, I'd like to know. What is it that makes you keep going? Where do you get your toughness and courage? So many times, I've felt like just giving up and dying. I'm still here, but I didn't do anything, really, to stay alive. It was just dumb luck, I guess. But I've seen you fight so hard every day to survive. I've seen you do things and make decisions I could never make. Just to stay alive. Why? What for?" She snuggled closer to me for warmth.

I don't know why I shared my personal thoughts with Leah just then. Maybe it was the cover of darkness. Maybe it was the tiny ray of hope of liberation. I'd always kept such a distance from everyone in the camps. Sharing was dangerous. Now, for the first time in years, I longed for friendship.

"I have to survive to get home to my father. My father wasn't taken to Auschwitz when I was. He may not even know my mother and sisters are dead. It's possible he was spared. We owned a good car at home. Town officials commandeered it and assigned my father the job of driving them. He may have escaped the Nazis. He may be at our house in Bardejov right now, waiting and wondering if all his family are dead. We were so close, Papa and me. I was his favorite daughter, and I can't bear to think of him there alone and in despair. That's what drives me. To see him and let him know at least a fragment of his family is still alive. Or, if he's not there, I want to be there waiting for him when he comes home. If he comes back and no one is there, it will break his heart." I choked back bitter tears. "It's not for me, Leah. I fight to survive for him. I must stay alive. For *him*."

"I understand, now." Leah reached for my hand in the darkness. I wanted to pull away, but I didn't. She sighed. "I hope so much you find him. You deserve to be happy."

"Not really. But my father does deserve happiness. I will get home!"

"I have a feeling you will."

"If we can survive until the Russians come."

Leah yawned. "Do you think the SS plan to kill us while we sleep? I mean, how could they do that? We'd hear the shots and run away. Or . . . something."

"Sleep, Leah. Who knows what will happen tomorrow?"

More gunshots rang out in the darkness.

"If there is a tomorrow . . ." Leah murmured. She linked her arm through mine and fell asleep.

Would we ever be free of the constant presence of death? Leah stirred in her sleep and moved even closer to me, wrapping her arms around me like a child. Yesterday I would have pushed her away, but tonight, it was oddly comforting.

I needed sleep, but sleep didn't come. For a long time, I lay staring up at the stars and thinking. Thinking. Until the pain turned into emptiness, and I slept.

———— ★ ————

Leah and I woke to the sounds of fighting. Men shouting, women screaming. We got up and inched further back into the woods.

The SS officers dashed around, frantically throwing off their uniforms and putting on civilian clothes. Some even dressed in women's clothes, the dirty striped dresses that were our own camp uniforms. They tore them off the dead bodies and tried to blend in with the prisoners. Others ran down the road to get as far away as they could.

The women prisoners seemed to have gone mad. They ran around and around screaming, "The Russians are coming! The Russians are coming!" Some women pulled pieces of red material from under their prison dresses and waved them in the air like flags. Leah flung her arms around me.

"It's the Russians! We're saved, Cilka! Saved!" She grabbed my wrist. "Come on! They'll have water. And food! Let's go!"

"No!" I gripped her by the shoulders and held her back. "Wait! Not yet."

Even as she resisted, I pulled her deeper into the woods.

"Are you crazy? We're free. The Russians have come."

"Let's wait and see. Just for a bit, Leah."

"Why?"

"I don't know. I just . . . I just don't trust anyone. Let's see what happens. Then, I promise, we'll go."

I will never forget what happened then. To feel hope die inside you is a terrible thing. Even in Auschwitz and Ravensbrück, during all those years, watching people tortured and murdered, seeing their ashes thrown into the river like dust from housecleaning . . . even then I held onto hope. They say hope lives forever, that it's eternal, but the day the Red Army liberated Ravensbrück, my newly revived, frail hope died another agonizing death.

──── ★ ────

The Cossacks were the first Russians we saw. They rode in like knights of old, dark and handsome in their romantic uniforms, their magnificent horses gleaming in the morning light. Soldiers followed on motorcycles, engines roaring like ferocious dragons. The arrival of the Red Army was a fantastic spectacle. Modern and medieval, even musical. Monster tanks churned up the road. The Cossacks, in their deep black uniforms and tall fur hats, bristled with weapons. Wooden carts, piled high with loot, lumbered along behind, accordion players trailed after, singing and dancing, as though liberation were one grand party! The women cheered and waved their pieces of red material.

Like avenging angels, the Cossacks and soldiers pursued the remaining SS and shot them. They herded the men in women's dresses together and then rode around them, laughing and jeering before they killed them.

Leah and I watched as women ran up to the soldiers and Cossacks. They threw their arms around their liberators and hugged and kissed them with tears of joy. The Russians returned their heartfelt affection with what seemed like genuine sincerity and deep feeling. How could they help but feel anything but compassion for us? We were pitiful wraiths, emaciated walking skeletons, barely recognizable as women.

"Why are we waiting, Cilka?" Leah tugged on my arm. "We should go and show our gratitude. They've risked their lives to save us."

"I'm sure they have, but . . ."

A scream cut through the sounds of cheering. I saw a woman break away from one of the Red Army soldiers and start to run. He laughed, shouted something in Russian, and grabbed her roughly. As Leah and I watched, he threw her to the ground and fell on top of her, pulling her dress up over her head. He raped her right there in the road.

As if it was a signal to initiate action, two other Red Army soldiers grabbed other women and did the same, shouting and laughing even as the women screamed in pain and fear. Terrified women ran in all directions. Some fell to the ground, and the Russians, shouting in their deep voices, jumped on them. I was sorry I understood the smattering of Russian I learned growing up.

"What are they saying?" Leah whispered in a voice choked with fear.

"They're saying it's their reward. That we owe it to them for saving us. You don't want to know the rest."

"But, why, Cilka? Why?" Leah started to cry. "How can they be so cruel?"

"Because they're savages! Just like all the rest."

I took Leah's hand and moved us even further into the woods. We had to melt out of sight if we weren't to become the victims of our liberators. We looked back constantly, afraid they would see and come after us. They were like a pack of wild animals. Gradually, as we moved deeper into the woods, the screams of the women and the cruel laughter of the men faded away.

"How did you know?" Leah's voice, small and trembling as a frightened child, was barely audible.

"I didn't. I just don't trust people. But I never imagined anything like this."

"I feel so sorry for them," Leah said. "For all of us. It's like there's no end. No mercy. Ever."

"Never mind. We're still alive. We have to get to the Americans and the British."

"Why? Why should they be any different?"

"I don't know. Maybe they won't be. But we can't wander forever. We need food and rest."

We trudged on for hours. In the afternoon, we came across a stream and could drink and wash some of the grime from our bodies. Night came on and, with it, a brilliant white moon. The silent beauty of it, cold and indifferent to our suffering, cut into my heart like a knife.

In the distance, the moonlight shone on an old barn. We stopped and studied it.

"Do you think it's safe?" Leah whispered.

"I don't know. I don't like that the doors are closed. It could be a trap."

"What if prisoners like us are hiding inside? They would close the doors, wouldn't they? So as not to be seen."

"They'd probably leave them open. Not to raise suspicion."

"I'm so tired, Cilka." Leah shivered and wrapped her arms around herself. "And cold. So cold. I don't think I can take another step."

"All right. We'll take a chance."

I didn't like it, but I knew Leah couldn't go on.

CHAPTER FOUR

We approached the barn slowly, alert to any signs of danger. The night was so still we surely would have heard any sounds. But all was silent. Even so, I felt as though we were being watched. I whispered to Leah to get behind me as I crept toward the massive doors. One was slightly ajar. I held my breath and pushed hard. The door resisted at first, then swung open on rusted hinges with a loud creaking sound.

Inside, a single shaft of moonlight shone down from a hole in the roof. Dust motes danced in the pale white light.

"It looks empty," Leah whispered. "We can hide here and sleep."

She sounded so hopeful. We crept forward and peered into the darkness on either side of the shaft of moonlight. As my vision adjusted, I saw what looked like glowing eyes. Leah gave a little gasp.

"Animals!" she cried. "But what? Are they dangerous?"

"*Qui est là?*"

I was so startled to hear a woman's voice, I let go of the door. It shut behind us with a bang.

"*Une amie,*" Leah answered immediately and stepped forward.

I didn't speak French, but I knew the word for friend. Still, I would have been a lot more cautious. But that was Leah, always offering the hand of friendship. After all she'd been through, it was incredible naivety.

Slowly and quietly, a group of ten women emerged from the dark corner of the barn and stood in the shaft of moonlight. They were petite, with delicate features and eyes too big for their pinched, frightened faces. Political prisoners? Ravensbrück had many. Somehow, they had escaped the Red Army rape horrors.

None of them spoke Slovak, so Leah translated for me. Gradually, they told their story. They'd been with the French resistance. All from different towns. Two of them were only seventeen. They had been ideal-ists and patriots, risking their lives to help their people in whatever ways they could. Delivering messages and food, providing shelter for fugitives from the Nazis.

Leah smiled. "They are, as they say, *jeunes filles bien élevées.*"

"What does that mean?" I asked.

"It means they are well brought up. Educated in good manners. Of good families." Leah's eyes filled with tears. "When they were arrested, they thought it was just a terrible mistake. They didn't understand how that could happen to women like them."

"None of us did," I said. "The world went mad in a way only the mad can understand."

I looked at the little French women. How these pitiful, half-starved creatures made it to this barn was a testament to their determination and resilience.

"Ask them how they got here."

They chattered to Leah in rapid French. When they laughed and made sounds like sheep, I asked Leah to translate.

"It is so funny," Leah said, laughing. "They sneaked away last night in the dark. They were actually on the other side of the woods we were in. They were terrified the Germans would spot such a large group, but they happened to run into a flock of sheep in the dark. Big ewes. All sleeping in a field. They curled up beside them and then moved off with the flock at dawn before the shepherd came. A German guard walked by during the night but didn't bother about the sheep. They say they are on the way to the Americans and the British just to the north. They invite us to go with them. Safety in numbers."

"It's good we found them," I said. "But we shouldn't stay here. The Russians are all around. Do they know about what's been happening?"

Leah asked them. They said they knew how the Russians were behav-ing. They had heard about it from a few women they met who also had escaped.

Then, all conversation stopped at the noise of a car rattling across the field outside the barn. We listened to the sound of men's deep, drunken voices shouting in Russian. Loud laughter. Car doors slamming. We simply froze, huddled together like the flock of sheep we'd just been laughing about. If the wolf was at the door of our barn, there was no place to hide.

We stared at the barn doors, framed in glowing yellow from the car's headlights outside.

CHAPTER FIVE

With a crash, the barn doors flew open, and a massive Russian stood in the doorway, silhouetted by the blinding headlights. We couldn't see his features, but he was in uniform. The ear flaps of his *ushanka* hat hung alongside his head, and his jodhpur pants puffed around the top of his knee-high boots. A vodka bottle dangled from one hand and a pistol from the other.

We winced against the brightness of the headlights after the darkness of the barn. Then the menacing black shape spoke, gruff and slurred, in sing-song Russian. It was a woman's voice.

"Ahh! Little rabbits. The bear has found you."

She took a swig from the vodka bottle, raised the pistol, and shot one of the French women. Just like that. No warning. No reason. She was either drunk or crazy. I grabbed Leah's hand, threw her into the darkness in a corner of the barn, and dived for cover myself. The French women screamed and ran in all directions. The Russian raised her pistol again, laughed, and shot another.

"*Au secours! Cher Dieu!*" The French women threw themselves to the ground, weeping and crying out in French.

The Russian walked into the moonlight shaft. Coarse-featured, pock-marked, ravaged by alcohol, hers was the face of a true sadist. She smiled and her eyes shone with the joy of inflicting pain and terror. It was a smile I'd seen many times in the camps, a smile to freeze your soul. She spoke to us then, and her Russian was close to the Rusyn dialect I had heard in Slovakia.

"They call me the Beautiful Beast." She roared with laughter. "I am a beast of prey. Are you afraid, little rabbits?" She waved the gun around the room. "Good! In twenty-four more hours, you will no longer be afraid." Her voice lowered to a growl, and she emphasized each word. "*You. Will. Be. Terrified*"

She took another drink. The French women pleaded for mercy again. The Beast fired her pistol into the air.

"Silence!" She turned her head. "Comrades!"

Four Russian soldiers appeared behind her. Wildly drunk, they swayed and leered at the women.

"French, comrades!" the Beast shouted. "Dessert!"

The soldiers, loud and excited, pushed forward like hungry pigs.

"Halt!"

The Beast moved to the cowering French women and ordered them to stand up. She grabbed four of them and shoved them, one by one, toward the waiting soldiers. The women struggled while the soldiers mauled them, pulling them toward the entrance.

"Halt!" The Beast shoved the gun into her belt and snapped her fingers. The four soldiers quickly dug into their pants, handed her some money, and saluted.

"Good. Bring them back alive in the morning or you won't get any more." The Beast jerked her head. "Now get out of here!"

She whipped off her hat and flung it away. Her hennaed hair, the color of dried chili peppers, flew out in a wild red-orange cloud.

"The rest are mine!"

She leered at the remaining women as the four soldiers dragged their women out. The Beast slammed the barn doors and turned. She hadn't noticed Leah or me crouched in our dark corner. Maybe she was too drunk, I didn't know. She took another swig, spilling vodka down her chin. She wiped her chin with her arm, then grabbed two of the younger French women.

"Mama bear loves little rabbits." The mocking sweetness of her drunken voice turned my stomach. She kissed each one and fondled their breasts. "So soft." She pulled them to her in a tight grip. "You want to cuddle with Mama Bear?"

She dragged them into the other corner of the barn and thrust them onto the floor. Then she lay down with them, fondling and kissing them.

The two other French women crawled to the end of the barn with Leah and me to wait out the night. The shaft of moonlight divided the barn like a shimmering curtain, illuminating the bodies of the two dead French women the Beast had shot. Slowly, the moon moved on and the light faded to darkness. The Beast snored. I waited until I was sure she was completely passed out. Then I moved.

CHAPTER SIX

"Cilka? Where are you going?"

"Shh! Never mind. Stay here. Keep the others quiet."

Like a stalking animal, I crawled slowly across the barn toward the Beast. Halfway, she stirred, and I froze to listen. The Beast grunted and rolled onto her side, but she didn't wake. The two French women she'd been abusing stared at me with wide, confused eyes. I placed a finger over my mouth, signaling them to be quiet. If we were to survive this night and make it to the Americans and British, we had to escape this woman. The Beast was as mad as the Nazis and wouldn't hesitate to kill us all just for the sheer joy of it.

She lay there, anesthetized by the vodka she'd probably been drinking all that day. The bodies of the two French women she shot for no reason still lay on the floor of the barn. What I felt was overwhelming fury. As I looked at her, the Beast embodied all the evil I had seen and experienced since I'd been thrown into Auschwitz at age sixteen. Every torture, every rape, every humiliation I and others had suffered. I saw them all in that ugly, drunken mockery of a woman. I think I could have murdered her if I'd had it in me. I wanted to survive. I wanted to go home. I wanted the horror to end. I was sick of it all.

I edged my way next to the sleeping Russian woman and waited, listening to her breathing, watching for any sign she might wake up. I didn't know what I would do if she did. The empty vodka bottle lay at her side. I gently shook her. She groaned but didn't wake. The two young French women cried out in alarm. I shook the Beast again.

"Don't worry," I whispered. "Nothing will wake her when she's like this."

I waited a bit longer, my heart pounding. Then I began to strip off her uniform.

Leah and the rest of the French women surrounded me. I continued to strip the Beast. First her jacket, then her jodhpurs. I stripped her naked while she moaned and muttered.

I held up the Beast's uniform. "We are going to get out of this hell and go to the Americans and the British. I speak a little Russian. I'll tell anyone we run into that I have orders to take you to the Allies because you are foreign nationals."

Leah translated. They all nodded but looked fearfully at the obscenely naked woman who had terrorized us, expecting her to rise up and attack us all. I put on the Russian uniform. It was enormous on my small, thin frame. The jacket reeked and had dark spots I suspected were blood. I grimaced, belted the top tight, and stuffed the pants far down into the boots. The bunched material kept the big boots up. If anyone questioned me, I didn't know what I would do, but I would think of something. *Chutzpah*. I could hear my father encouraging me whenever I was nervous about some new experience. *Chutzpah, Cilka*. Call it gall, nerve, or brazen audacity. *Chutzpah* was what I needed if we all were to get to safety.

I picked up the Beast's pistol and started to shove it into my belt. One of the French women hissed and grabbed my wrist. She carefully took the gun from me, turned it over, slid the safety catch into place, and handed it back to me. I had never held a gun in my life.

Leah gasped. "She said you could have shot yourself in the leg."

"Thank her for me."

We were six: the four remaining French women, Leah, and me. There was nothing we could do about the women the Beast had given to the Russian soldiers. They were on their own. I didn't know how much time had passed since the moonlight disappeared from inside the barn. Time had stopped for me. But it had to be several hours. Soon, the Russian soldiers would return for more "French desserts," and we had to be gone when they did. Quietly but swiftly, we left the barn.

Outside, I looked around to see which way we should go.

"Do you think we should hide in that little forest?" Leah whispered. She pointed to a small copse of trees across the field.

I shook my head. "If I were a drunk Russian soldier bent on rape, that's the first place I would take my victim. No. We won't go there. Ask our French companions which direction they think the American and

British camp is." We were still standing in the open, and I wanted to get as far away as possible as quickly as possible.

Leah spoke softly with them, then turned to me. "They say they heard intelligence in the camp that the Americans and British were to the northwest."

The rapidly lightening sky was to our right. East. West was to our left. The copse of trees behind us was to the south. We headed northwest through open country. Leah and the French women chattered softly together. I couldn't share in their joy of walking freely in the open air. I was constantly on guard. I avoided roads and stuck to the fields. At any time, we might run into a Nazi fugitive or a Russian Army soldier. Both equally dangerous.

We were all cold and hungry. We hadn't eaten in days. We came across a stream, but the water didn't help our empty stomachs or give us the energy we needed. We constantly looked for things to eat. At one point, we found a nest with four eggs and ate them raw. It was still early spring, so berries and fruits weren't ripe yet. We ate some tiny green apples and suffered for it. I knew I had to take action to get us some food. Up ahead, a small farmhouse stood beside a well-tended farm. I could see vegetables in tidy rows—German order amid the chaos. I summoned my *chutzpah*, marched to the door, and pounded on it with the butt of the Beast's pistol.

"*Offen*" I shouted in German. A curtain twitched in one window. I pounded with the pistol again. "Open up! Or I will kick the door in!"

The door opened a crack, and a sturdy German *frau* peered out at us. She made to close the door again, but I stuck my foot in and pushed it open. I pointed the pistol at her.

"Your time is up. The Russian Army is all around you, and the Allies have arrived."

I motioned for Leah and the French women to gather around me.

"These are poor, starving young French women who were abused and tortured in your concentration camps."

The German *frau* waved her hands in the air and cried out, "We knew nothing of that! Those camps. We are not to blame. We didn't do anything. We are just poor farmers. It was that monster, Hitler. You must understand."

I looked inside the farmhouse. A photograph of Hitler hung on the wall opposite the door.

"And yet a photograph of that monster hangs on your wall," I roared. "Enough! You will feed these women who you have starved for years." The *frau* mumbled something about no food to spare. "Shut up!" I shouted. "If you don't give us food, I will shoot you." For effect I added, "I've already killed one person today. I won't hesitate to kill another."

The French women played along, chattering and gesturing. "*Non! Non! S'il vous plaît. Ne tuer personne d'autre aujourd'hui!*"

The German *frau* gave me a look of sheer terror, rushed into the house, and returned with bread, cheese, apples, and cold sausages. She showed them to me and thrust them into a sack. I hadn't seen so much food in years. I grabbed the sack and pointed the pistol at her again.

"You will keep your mouth shut about this!" She nodded frantically. I waved the pistol at the photograph of Hitler. "And get that off the wall!"

As we turned to leave, I heard the door slam behind us and a bolt rasp into place. We took off across a field, scrambled down a small gully beside a stream, and opened the sack. The French women and Leah tore off hunks of bread and cheese, cramming them into their mouths. Half the sausages disappeared in an instant. One of the French women choked. I slapped her on the back and grabbed the food from her hands. I shoved the rest of the food back into the sack. As the women shouted in protest, I closed the sack and confronted them. Leah translated for me.

"Your stomachs haven't seen food like this in months," I said. "If you eat too much too fast, you will be sick and throw up everything. I have seen it happen. Stop now. Who knows when we'll get any more food. Drink some water from the stream and let's be on our way again. When we get to the Americans and the British, there will be plenty of food."

They reluctantly agreed, and we got underway. My success with the German *frau* had boosted my confidence in my disguise. From now on, we would follow a road and make better progress. The sun had risen in a clear blue sky, and the air was crisp but not freezing. The food had marvelously revived our spirits. The French women laughed and twittered like birds.

I don't know how far we had walked when I noticed a car in the distance, coming down the dusty road toward us. It could be anyone. American, British, Russian. Even German, I supposed.

A muddy jeep pulled to a stop beside us. The lone driver was a Russian Army officer. He gave us a narrow-eyed look, and I clicked my heels and saluted. He saluted in return, but still studied me.

"That's an irregular uniform, Sergeant." He raised an eyebrow.

He didn't look like the brutish Russian soldiers who went on the raping rampage yesterday. This officer was thin, around forty, with a weatherworn face and piercing gray eyes that looked me over with suspicion. I pulled my shoulders back and saluted again.

"Yes, sir. Sorry, sir. It's the best I could find."

"A bit large." He frowned. "How old are you?"

"Nineteen . . . Sir!"

The ghost of a smile curled his lip. "And still alive. Good for you." He eyed the blood on the jacket. "Seen action, have you?"

"Yes, sir." I hoped he wouldn't question my Rusyn accent and simple speech. "This uniform belonged to a friend. Killed two days ago. I had to get rid of my own uniform." I grinned. "When I took it off, it started walking down the road . . . Sir!"

He laughed. "Yes. The lice are the real winners in this war. Where are you taking these women, Sergeant?"

"They're French. Sir! I'm ordered to take them to the Americans and the British."

"You're headed in the right direction. The Free French are there as well. Turn them over to them. It'll make us look good."

"Yes, sir." I took a chance. "We need that right now. From what I've seen."

He took off his hat and dragged his hand through his dusty hair. "True, Sergeant. We're not looking so good right now. All this raping is a damn headache."

"Yes. Sir!"

"What do the Americans and the British want? We won the war for them. Over twenty million Russian men and women have died. Some of my men have fought over four years on the Eastern Front. Out of twenty Germans, we killed nineteen. The Americans and the British have no idea what the Nazi beast has done to Russia. Damn them! What do they expect? A tea party to end it all?"

I held my tongue and saluted. "Sir!"

He gave me a crooked smile. "Sorry. Good luck, Sergeant." He revved his engine. "But I have to say, the Americans make good jeeps." He ran his hand lovingly along the side. "I love this jeep. More than any woman I've ever known." He laughed. "And she'll never betray me."

He spun the tires and took off down the road in his American jeep.

CHAPTER SEVEN

The sun climbed high in the sky. We stopped once to eat the rest of the food. This time, the French women showed exquisite manners and ate slowly, like ladies instead of ravenous animals. The road climbed, and Leah and the French women breathed hard with the exertion. I hoped we didn't have much farther to go. We didn't see any people until we reached the top of the hill, where a lone soldier sat beside a truck, facing away from us and smoking. Smoking! The French women twittered excitedly, and the soldier turned around and jumped up. He looked astonished to see us.

"Wow! Where'd you come from?" he said in English.

Two French women understood enough English to find out he was American.

"From someplace called Detroit," Leah told me. "His name is Mila."

"Mila!" I exclaimed. "That's a Slovak name."

He caught the word Slovak and asked me in my language if I was from Czechoslovakia. I smiled and said yes.

"Wow! We're landsmen!" He held out his hand.

I shook his hand. "Cecilia Klein," I replied, then asked him where he was from in Slovakia.

He laughed. "I was born and raised in a small town called Hamtramck, surrounded by a big city called Detroit. Where they build all the cars. And now tanks. But my grandparents came from a farming town near Bratislava."

He was young, not much older than me. He spoke pretty good Slovak with a funny kind of drawl.

"That's a Russian uniform," he said. "What's the story?"

"I found it in an old barn." I didn't tell him about the Beast. "We're trying to get to the American and British camp. I speak a little Russian and thought we'd be safer if I pretended to be a Russian soldier."

"Yeah," he said. "I've heard some pretty lousy stuff about those Russians. Supposed to be our friends and allies. Sound like a pack of wolves to me. Nasty. Especially to women."

"Yes. We've seen some terrible things. We were in the concentration camp they liberated at Ravensbrück."

"Gosh! I heard about those camps. Never seen one. Can't believe the stuff I've heard. I mean, gassing women and children and burning them to ashes. Is it really true?"

I knew then it would be a long time before the world would believe the horrors inflicted by the Nazis.

"It's all true," I said, then changed the subject. "Do you know how far away the Allied camp is?"

"Not far. Just up the road. You all look pretty beat. Tell you what. I just took a cigarette break, but I'm supposed to deliver this truckload of food and stuff to the camp. I'm not a fighting soldier. I work in the Quartermaster Corps, taking care of food and supplies. Napoleon or somebody, I forget who, said an army marches on its stomach. He got that right. Anyway, you ladies can ride along." He slammed his hand against his forehead. "Jeez! Where are my manners? You must be starved. You want some chocolate?"

He threw the rest of his cigarette away, dashed over to the truck, and came back with a whole box of Hershey bars. One of the French women rushed to pick up his half-smoked cigarette. The women passed it around, each of them taking tiny puffs to make it last.

"You wanna smoke?" Mila asked us. He shoved the box of Hershey bars at me and ran to the truck again. He came back with a long box filled with packs of cigarettes. "Here. Take the lot."

The French women squealed in delight, threw their arms around him, and smothered him with kisses.

"Wow!" He grinned and blushed. "They'll never believe this back in Hamtramck."

He opened a pack, took some matches from his pocket, and lit cigarettes for the French women. They inhaled deeply, blew the smoke gently into the air, and cooed like doves. Mila offered me a cigarette, but my mouth was already full of Hershey's chocolate. He laughed.

"Good choice. Hershey's is the best!"

He hurried to the truck and shoved stuff around in the back to make room for us to ride.

"Hey, girls!" he said. "I want you all to see something. Might cheer you up. C'mon."

He walked to the edge of the hill, and we followed.

"What do you think of that?" Mila pointed over the hill. "We just captured an entire German army!"

From where we stood, the hill dropped steeply toward a vast valley. Spread out below us were thousands of German soldiers. They sat or lay on the ground while American soldiers moved among them, handing out food. Farther on were tanks, trucks, and cars. It took my breath away. No one could imagine the joy we all felt at the sight.

"*Allez-vous tous les tuer?*" a French woman asked hopefully.

Leah translated and Mila looked at her in shock. "We don't do that kind of stuff. Nah! We'll probably spend weeks processing them, give them some money, and then send them on their way back home. A lot of them are just kids, you know. Hitler chewed up men by the hundreds of thousands. Recruits kept getting younger and younger. What a waste." He turned away. "Let's go, girls."

Leah and the French women piled into the back of the truck, and I sat in the cab with Mila while he told me in Slovak what it was like living in America. He was looking forward to going home now that the war was almost over. I told him I was going home too.

The first thing I saw when we rolled into the Allied camp was mountains of supplies. Boxes and crates stacked sky high beside mounds of potato sacks. The Free French had raised the French flag in their section. Almost before Mila stopped the truck, the French women jumped down and rushed toward their countrymen, crying out with joy, and carrying Leah with them.

"Come with me," Mila said. "I'll take you to see my colonel. He'll get things organized for you."

He smiled and linked his arm through mine like we'd been friends forever. I wondered if all Americans were this nice and informal. It was so different from the Germans and Russians. The colonel's headquarters was in a commandeered German house. Tables filled the former large living room. An army of secretaries, men and women, sat at the tables, busily typing. The women looked fresh and clean in their neat uniforms, with lovely coiffed hair like they'd just stepped out of a beauty parlor.

"Wait here," Mila said. "I'll pave the way for you."

He ran up to a closed door, rapped on it, and walked right in. When the door shut behind him, the clatter of the typewriters came to a sudden stop. All the secretaries looked up to stare at me. I knew I was a shocking sight in my filthy, blood-splattered Russian uniform. It hung on me like a bizarre dress-up outfit on a child. My hair, matted and lice-ridden, stuck out in all directions. I still had the Beast's pistol shoved into my belt. I wondered what they thought. It seemed an eternity until the door opened and Mila waved to me. As I walked into the colonel's office, the typing started up again with a vengeance.

CHAPTER EIGHT

"Good God, you're just a kid!"

The American colonel stood and came around his desk. He was a much older man than I expected, tall and wiry, with salty gray hair and a deeply tanned face that was a road map of experiences. Arctic blue eyes studied me.

"Here! Mila!" The colonel waved a hand. "Get Miss Klein a chair."

Mila jumped to the command. The colonel took my hand and gently guided me into the chair. It was so strange to be treated with concern and respect.

"From what Mila tells me, you've been to Hell and back, young lady." He frowned. "I'm afraid I don't speak anything but English and a bit of high-school French." He waved at Mila again, and Mila translated for him. "Well, we're here to help, so let's figure out how we can get you set on your feet again. Mila, get Miss Klein a cup of coffee, and I think there's some cake left."

Coffee! I hadn't had coffee in over three years! When Mila set the cup in my hand, I closed my eyes and breathed in the fragrance. The taste brought back mornings with my father when we would have coffee and toast and discuss what the day would bring. Mila broke the spell with a piece of chocolate cake. I think that cup of coffee and the chocolate cake was the first time I felt that the war and the horrors of the Nazi camps were truly over. That the world had a chance to be normal again. That I could go home. That maybe my father had survived, and we would have breakfast together again and help each other forget. Tears came to my eyes and I brushed them away.

"There, there, my dear," the colonel said. "You're safe now."

"I'm just so grateful," I said. "Thank you so much."

"You're welcome," the colonel replied. "I know the power of a simple cup of coffee in wartime. I wasn't too much older than you when I fought in the first one of these damn wars. The War to End all Wars." He sighed. "They got that wrong. Let's hope the world gets it right this time and comes to its senses. Mila, I think this young lady needs another piece of cake."

I didn't say no to a taste of heaven.

"Now. First things first." The colonel smiled. "I'm sure you want to turn in that bloody Russian uniform for something a bit more stylish. I'm afraid we only have WAC uniforms to offer, but I hear the Free French brought a load of dresses in their supplies. You can take a Frenchwoman out of Paris, but you can't take Paris out of a Frenchwoman. Mila will tell them to set you up after you've had a nice long shower and washed the grime of war out of what looks like a lovely head of raven locks."

"I can't tell you how good that will feel," I murmured.

"Well, that's just for starters. Mila says you want to go home to Czechoslovakia. Ordinarily, that would be a real arduous trip since most of the railroads have been bombed to smithereens. But you're in luck. We've got a convoy heading to supply General Patton's Third Army, which is just entering Czechoslovakia. The convoy leaves this afternoon."

I jumped up, excited. "If you can get me to Czechoslovakia, I can make my way home."

"Good. You're going to need some money." He pulled out a drawer in his desk, took out various paper bills, and handed me the money. "Here's twenty-five dollars. The American Dollar is king right now, so that should get you out of any difficulties. The German Reichsmarks won't be worth the paper they're printed on in another week, but they may be useful in some cases. Here are some French Francs as well."

I looked at the money in my hands. It represented freedom, security, protection, things I hadn't known in such a long time. "How can I ever thank you? You've been so kind."

"No need. We're here to help in any way we can. I wish you a safe journey. I've got a daughter just about your age back home. I miss her a lot. I hope you find your father. He'll be glad to have you back."

He raised an eyebrow then and asked, "Do you want to keep that pistol? You can if you feel safer with it."

I'd forgotten about the Beast's pistol. I pulled it out of my belt and handed it to the colonel. "No. You take it. If the Russians found that on me, they'd probably arrest me as a spy and send me to Siberia."

He laughed. "Oh, I don't think they'd go that far, but they might ask a good many questions. Best now to just be a nice young woman on her way home." He took my hand and held it. "Good luck, Miss Klein. Mila, help this young lady find the showers and some clothes and see she gets on the convoy."

— ★ —

How often I've wished I could wipe all memories out of my mind. In Auschwitz and Ravensbrück, memories of happy times brought only pain, and I struggled to push them back. The horrors of camp existence were an everyday reality to be endured or avoided by any means possible. Those horrors were ever-present memories, never to be forgotten, never to be erased. Stepping into the small shower that day, I felt such a rush of fear and revulsion, I almost turned around and fled. Showers would forever be rooms of death. My mother and sisters. Hundreds of women I had known by name. My hand paused before turning the faucet. Water? Or poison gas? Who could ever have imagined such a question?

I shoved the memory away and savored the feel of hot, clean water over my body. There was real soap! It even smelled nice. Real shampoo and something to get at the lice in my hair. For the first time in so long, I felt truly clean. I wrapped myself in the towel hanging on the wall and peered out the door.

"Cilka?" There was Leah, looking fresh and clean herself, waiting for me with an armful of clothes. "The French brought so many nice dresses. I picked out the two I thought were your size and colors. Try the yellow, flowered one. It will look nice with your hair."

She joined me and helped me dry my hair, fussing like a mother hen. I put on the dress. It had tiny white flowers sprinkled all over and a white lace collar. I stroked the fabric. It was unbelievably soft. I'd become so used to my coarse striped prisoner's dress, I felt strange in civilian clothes. Like I was wearing a disguise.

"I chose one with long sleeves," Leah whispered. "Covers the tattoo."

"Thank you." It was thoughtful of her. She, too, wore a dress with long sleeves. The tattooed numbers would always set us apart, provoke questions we didn't want to answer, mark us as strange, or victims, or worse.

Leah put her hands on my shoulders and turned me to face the long mirror on the opposite wall. She fluffed waves into my short hair, gently curling a lock behind one of my ears.

"Look at yourself, Cilka! You look beautiful. Just beautiful." Leah's soft brown eyes glistened with unshed tears.

It had been over three years since I'd faced my image in a mirror. This thin young woman with haunted, dark-rimmed eyes too big for her face was a stranger to me. A pale ghost of a girl. Where was the young girl with the rosy cheeks and sweet smile?

"These shoes are about your size." Leah handed me a pair of brown slip-on shoes. "I picked ones with low heels in case you have to walk far."

"Thank you." I put on the shoes, wondering about the journey ahead of me.

Leah picked up a small, battered leather suitcase. "I gathered some things from the French you might need on the trip. You know, underwear, a toothbrush, an extra dress. That sort of thing." She handed it to me with an encouraging smile.

When we stepped outside, Mila was waiting to take charge of me. His face lit up when he saw me. "Wow!" He gave a long whistle. "All I have to say is, Rita Hayworth better watch out! You look like a million bucks." He took my arm again. "C'mon! For the sake of goodwill among nations, I have to share you with the French guys."

The Frenchmen lived up to their reputation. They smiled appreciatively and complimented me and kissed my hand. No one had ever kissed my hand before. I didn't know what to say, so I just smiled. I wasn't used to feeling feminine or being treated like an attractive woman. I had been tough and hard for so long, I felt like an impostor. These charming young men saw someone who didn't really exist. Suddenly, I was eager to leave.

"Time's up, guys," Mila said. "Have to get Miss Klein on the road to home."

Leah came with us to the convoy to say goodbye. "I'll miss you, Cilka." She wiped away tears. "Thank you so much for saving me and protecting me. I know I was a trial sometimes, and I'm sorry for that. I admire you so much. I hope someday I can be as strong and brave as you."

"Don't, Leah. Be yourself. Always. You're a truly good person, and I admire you for that."

She threw her arms around me and hugged me tight. I returned the hug.

"Visit me in Amsterdam soon," Leah said with a bright smile. "I just found out that my brother survived. I'm going home to live with him. He would love you." She gave me a piece of paper. "Here's my address. Say you'll come . . . soon."

"I will. And you can come to Slovakia. My father would welcome you as a daughter, I know. He was . . . is . . . the kindest of men. I just hope . . ."

I couldn't go on. I hugged Leah one last time and turned to get into the convoy truck.

"Hey!" Mila grabbed my hand and pulled me into an embrace. "Best of luck to you, Cilka." He tossed my little suitcase onto the truck, turned back, and handed me another piece of paper. "Here's my address at home. Write to me. And, when you get to America, look me up. When my buddies in Hamtramck see you, they'll only be able to say one word."

"Wow!" Leah and I said together and laughed.

I climbed into the truck that would take me home. I looked back as the convoy moved down the road. Mila and Leah stood there, waving. I waved back. The smaller and smaller they grew, the more alone I felt.

Home

CHAPTER NINE

Bardejov, Slovakia
June 1945

I stood under a tree across the street from the two-story house. As I traveled across Czechoslovakia to reach Bardejov, I constantly suppressed the idea that our house might have been destroyed during the war. It might have been left to ruin. It might have been bombed. But there it was across the narrow street. It looked just the same, as though time had stood still, waiting for my return. A modest house with a small front yard. A neat little fence with a swinging gate. I wondered if that gate still creaked. The lace curtains in the windows looked new, but maybe they were only freshly washed. The flower boxes under those windows glowed with bright red geraniums. Someone had cared for my house. Hope flickered again at the thought it might be my father.

I wiped the tears from my eyes and crossed the street. The little gate opened without a sound. Someone had oiled it. I walked slowly up the short path to the door and knocked. A curtain twitched in one window, but no one came to open the door.

"Papa?" I called and waited.

Slowly, the door opened, and a woman stood there, staring at me, trying to decide if she knew me or not. But I knew her very well. Mrs. Bartos, the wife of my father's foreman at the factory. Their daughter, Sofi, had been my childhood friend. My father must be alive. But maybe he was ill, and Mrs. Bartos was taking care of him. Why didn't she know me? Of course. I must look nothing like the young girl she remembered.

"Mrs. Bartos." I smiled. "It's me, Cilka. I'm back. How is my father?"

She gasped and covered her mouth with her hand.

"I survived," I said softly. "I'm home. Where's Papa? Is he all right?"

She just continued to stare at me, frowning. I knew then that my father wasn't there. If he had been, she would have welcomed me with joy. Now she would have to be the one to tell me he was either dead or missing.

"It's all right, Mrs. Bartos. Please. May I come in?"

I felt strange asking to enter my own house. Mrs. Bartos must have felt strange, too, because she quickly stepped to the side. "Yes. Yes, of course," she said in a rush. "Come in."

— ★ —

I walked into a world of memories. It seemed to me as if nothing had changed. I stood in the entryway and breathed in the familiar smells of beeswax furniture polish, Persian carpets, books in leather bindings, fragrant flowers in a vase. The house was so quiet, the only sound the ticking of the grandfather clock from where it had stood since I could remember. In the silence, I fancied I could hear my sisters' laughter, my mother singing, my father's deep voice.

Something drew me to the parlor my father had turned into a library. There were the bookcases with their glass doors to protect his collection of books. I opened one and ran my fingers over the carefully preserved leather bindings. Embossed titles winked at me, silently reminding me of the books I had never had the chance to read. I took out our copy of *Anna Karenina.* My bookmark was still there. I opened it to find that Anna was still trying to decide if she should go to the ball. With a lump in my throat, I put it back and closed the doors to the case.

I turned. The ghost of my father stood by the upright gramophone. He wore his white gloves, as he always did when handling his precious record collection. Which opera would he listen to today? Slowly, he lowered the record onto the turntable. Carefully, he placed the needle into the groove. The table turned. The overture to *Madama Butterfly* filled the air, and I could hear my father humming along. I turned away and quickly left the room.

Mrs. Bartos still hovered in the hallway, nervous and agitated.

"We didn't know if anyone had survived," she said. "We moved here not so long ago. To take care of the house. In case . . ."

I turned from her and walked down the hall, stopping outside the dining room. More ghosts. Soft candlelight. A white lace tablecloth. Our best china place settings. Sparkling wine glasses filled with deep red wine. Soft *matzo* on a plate, waiting for the blessing. Passover Seder. Papa in his neat, dark suit at the head of the table. Mother in her best dress with the lace collar. My sisters in crisp white blouses. And Papa, telling the story of the Exodus in his clear baritone voice, making it come alive as if it were happening just then. Escape from slavery to freedom. God's divine liberation of the Jewish people. The imaginary *matzo* became ashes in my mouth, and I turned away from the ghosts.

The sound of feet on the stairs made me look up. I caught my breath at the sight of Sofi leaning over the railing. The girl I remembered had become a lovely young woman, her blond hair framing her perfect heart-shaped face in soft curls.

"Mama?" Sofi's cornflower-blue eyes held an eager expression. "Who's here? I heard someone come to the door."

I stepped cautiously into her sight, not really knowing how to greet her, unsure of what she knew or felt about my family's fate. She stared at me for a moment in confusion. Then her face lit up in a brilliant smile.

"Cilka!"

She ran down the stairs. I was ready for her to fling her arms around me like she used to, but she halted at the bottom of the stairs and looked at her mother, a tiny frown on her face. I glanced at Mrs. Bartos and saw both a warning and disapproval in her expression as she quickly shook her head at her daughter. I hadn't lived through what I'd experienced without recognizing the signs. Mrs. Bartos's expression was a warning to me as well. I was not welcome in my own house. I was not wanted here. I was a serious problem, and serious problems require solutions.

My happiness at being free had blinded me to the truth. Mr. and Mrs. Bartos had taken over our house when we were deported to the camps. They may not have known everything about those camps, but they knew enough to feel certain we'd never return. So they moved into the house that had belonged to my father, Mr. Mikulas Klein. A much better house than the one they owned. I had heard about this in the camps. Properties of Jews confiscated by non-Jews. Even before we were taken away, the town authorities confiscated my father's business. He was asked to stay on for a few years because no one knew how to run the factory. Not even Mr. Bartos, his foreman. Maybe Mr. Bartos felt it was justice to take our house. Maybe he hated Jews too. If he did, he had hidden his hatred well during the years I'd known him. Did Mrs. Bartos hate us as well? And Sofi? Over three years had passed since we were taken away. Now they saw our house as their property, their home, their right of ownership. How did they see me?

CHAPTER TEN

Mrs. Bartos picked up my little suitcase. The air was charged with suppressed tensions. I wondered if she would ask me to leave and find another place to stay. The way things were, the authorities might support her claim to the house. After all, my whole family was supposed to be dead.

Mrs. Bartos handed Sofi my suitcase. "Take Cilka up to your room. I'm sure she'd like to freshen up a bit."

"Of course!" Sofi relaxed and the little frown faded from her face. "Come on, Cilka." She grabbed my suitcase and marched up the stairs.

Sofi's room turned out to be my old bedroom, completely transformed. New wallpaper dotted with pink flowers replaced the blue stripes that had been mine. New, pink-ruffled curtains hung on the window. All the natural wood in the room had been painted white. A hooked rug with big pink roses woven into the pattern lay on the floor. But the bed was the same one I had slept in. A new pink and white chenille bedspread covered it, and a frilly doll rested against the pillows. I wondered where they got the money for all these nice things.

I felt like a stranger. A guest. Like I had traveled back in time to a gentle, forgotten past from a future ugly world of violence and death.

Sofi stood by the window, holding my suitcase, looking at me.

"They told us to move into your house," she said, turning away. "The authorities told us to. Papa took over as factory manager when your father . . . disappeared. There was no one else." She looked back, an apology in her eyes. "It hasn't been easy for him. Running the factory, I mean. He's always upset. Nothing ever seems to go right for him." She gave a little shrug.

I said nothing. What could I say? That my father was a superb manager and her father had never held a position beyond foreman and didn't have the skill or the knowledge?

"I missed you," Sofi said, putting my suitcase on a narrow white bench. She smiled at me. "You look different." Her hands flew up as if to ward off a blow. "I mean, so do I. We're nineteen now. Grown up."

"Yes."

"You look . . . you must be tired."

"I am."

I couldn't think of anything more to say. I doubted if Sofi knew anything about what had happened to me. The Jews disappeared from Bardejov when she was sixteen. What was she told? Where did she think I'd gone? To work in Germany? If she guessed, or was told, the truth, she probably didn't believe such a thing could be possible. I had lived through it, and I still had trouble believing people could do such horrific things to other people.

"I'm sorry, Cilka." Sofi hugged herself. "I took your room. I didn't know . . ."

"Don't worry, Sofi. It's all right."

She brightened. "I saved some of your dresses. I wore them. I hope you don't mind. They were so pretty."

I walked to the window and looked out on our small garden at the back of the house. The ghosts of my sisters were playing tag and laughing. I thought of them torn from me in Auschwitz and sent immediately to the gas chamber. A cloud passed over the garden and their laughter died.

"If you want a bath, there's still some of that lilac soap you had. I only used it occasionally. It smells heavenly."

Lilac. My mother's favorite flower. She would fill the house with bowls of them in the spring. "My God," I murmured. "How can I stay here? This house is filled with ghosts."

"I'll move to the guest room," Sofi said quickly.

She gathered up a few things. A nightgown, robe, slippers. Finally, she took the doll from the bed.

"I was wondering . . ." She hugged the doll. "When is Magda coming home?"

I couldn't do it. I could not pretend everything was *just fin* . That hell on earth had not happened. That we could all just pick up where we left off and go on with our lives and be cheerful and happy and filled with hope. I turned away from the window and faced Sofi.

"Magda's never coming home. Not Magda. Not Olga. Not my mother. None of them are coming back. Ever! They were killed with poison gas and their bodies shoved into an oven. Their bones were ground and thrown with their ashes into the Sola River. You can go there. You can swim in the Sola. But the truth is you'll be swimming with the dead! Millions of them."

Sofi's face went white. "I . . . I'm so sorry . . . I . . ." She clutched the doll tighter and backed out of the room.

I closed the door. Why had I said those things to her? That was a terrible thing to do. Now she would ask questions and get answers that would give her nightmares. But I couldn't be silent. The ghosts deserved the truth. I was a ghost too. The Cilka that Sofi had played with was dead, never to return. The new Cilka was a creature no one knew. Not even me. And my truth was, I could never escape her.

I leaned against the clean white wood of the door and sank to the floor. I rapped my head against the door over and over. Then I drew my knees up and wrapped my arms around them. Shaking with silent sobs, I gave in to the tears I had held back for so many years.

CHAPTER ELEVEN

A bird sang outside my window the next morning. The sun filtered through the frilly pink curtains, giving the room a rosy glow. It had been good to sleep in a proper bed, not a pile of straw or branches as I'd done on the road, or the hard boards of the camps. I hadn't gone downstairs after Sofi left me yesterday. I couldn't face her again. And I did *not* want to see Mr. and Mrs. Bartos. They must have felt the same, because they didn't seek me out. I had taken the bath Sofi suggested, crawled into bed, and lay there, thinking. Finally, exhausted from travel and emotion, I had fallen asleep.

That morning I had to do something about my situation. I knew I could not live in this house with the ghosts. I would have to find someplace else to wait and watch for my father in case he came home. I would also have to find work. The money the American colonel gave me wouldn't last forever. I would go into town and see if any shops needed someone to help. Most of the shops in town had been owned by Jewish families before the war. I knew the authorities had given them to non-Jewish Slovaks. But even though they weren't Jewish, they were people I'd known. I had gone to school with their sons and daughters. They must remember me.

I was hungry, having had nothing to eat yesterday except some bread and a piece of cheese. I still had a couple of Hershey bars left from the ones Mila had stashed in my suitcase. I lifted the lid of my suitcase, unwrapped one bar, and ate it. I couldn't wear either of my French dresses if I wanted to apply for work. They were a mess from my journey. I opened my closet and there were all my old dresses. Ghostly memories rushed in once again. My father taking me to a restaurant for my fifteenth birthday, telling me how nice I looked in my new blue dress. A year later, almost to the day, the Nazis took me away to Auschwitz.

That same blue dress still hung in the closet. I chose a different one and put it on. The dress that fit so well when I was sixteen hung loosely on me. I cinched the sash tighter. My shoes were lined up in a tidy row on the closet floor. I'd forgotten that Sofi wore the same size. They looked so dainty. I finished dressing and stood in front of the mirror that hung on the closet door. The young woman with wavy raven hair and big dark eyes looking back at me was someone other people saw. I stared at my image and wondered how I could look so normal.

It was still early, so I thought I'd get some breakfast in town. I remembered that the Red Army controlled Bardejov now, and I had seen enough of Russian liberation to be cautious. I hid the dollars and francs in a dresser drawer. I had also picked up some Slovak Koruna along my way home, so I put a few in the pocket of my dress and left the house.

Bardejov looked a bit shabby, but its medieval fairy-tale charm lingered still. I wandered through the old town square, feeling the familiar cobblestones under my feet. The only vehicles in the square were a couple of jeeps with Red Army soldiers standing around. American jeeps again. The Soviets must have taken over the Old Town Hall in the center for their headquarters. Soldiers in black NKVD uniforms, the fearsome secret police, stood guard on either side of the main doors. A sleek black ZIL was parked in front, and two higher-ranking officers in black dress uniforms and peak hats stood by, talking. They looked me over. I couldn't tell whether they thought me attractive or suspicious. I pretended I hadn't noticed them and walked on.

The pretty pastel colors of the old houses surrounding the square had faded, the paint peeling, the walls dusty and cracked. When I was a child, those houses were cared for like treasures. Nearly all of them had been owned by Jews before the war. They had their shops on the ground floor and lived above. Most of the shops were still there, but now they were a painful reminder of what had happened here. Many still had anti-Jewish slogans painted on the walls and windows, as though the town was proud of its hatred. The kosher symbols and Jewish stars were crossed out, often with red paint, the former owners' names painted over. Mr. Halberstam's shoe store, Mr. Grünberger's bookstore, Kunitz Jewelry and Watches,

Horovitz Haberdashery. It was as though they had never existed. All the owners and their families were probably dead. Bardejov had become a town without Jews. But the town could never paint over or erase the memory of the horrors those Jews had suffered. The town knew what it had done to us, no matter how much it wanted to forget.

I knew this from the strange, nervous expressions on the faces of the people I passed. I recognized some of them, and I could tell they recognized me. But they didn't speak to me, and I didn't speak to them. I wasn't wanted here. I was not a person to them anymore. I was a symbol of their guilt, fear, prejudice, whatever had driven them to collaborate with the Nazi exterminators. If I stayed here, I would be an unwanted ghost haunting the town.

Still, I had nowhere else to go. I walked to what used to be Mrs. Mandelbaum's coffee shop and tearoom. It wasn't as charming as I remembered. Gone were the crisp tablecloths on the little round tables. The ruffled curtains in the windows were dingy and limp. It used to be so cheerful, with little vases of flowers on each table, the air filled with the aroma of freshly ground coffee. The war had taken its toll on teashops, it seemed.

A woman appeared from the back of the shop. I didn't recognize her, but she seemed to know who I was.

"You've come back." She looked annoyed. "You're the first one I've seen."

I tried not to react to her dismissive tone. "I'd like a cup of coffee and a piece of toast, please."

"Can you pay for it? I don't take any foreign money."

"I have koruna." I put some money on the counter. "This should be enough."

She poured me a cup of bitter coffee and put a couple of pieces of bread into the little toaster. "There's no cream and no butter," she snapped. She put the toast on a chipped plate and set it in front of me. "I guess there's a little jam." She ladled a teaspoon of red jam onto the plate.

"Thank you." I took the coffee and toast to one of the little tables and sat down.

She followed me and hovered, impatient, hands on her hips.

"Do you know anything about the Mandelbaums?" she demanded. "Are they coming back too?"

So that was it. Like Mrs. Bartos, she was worried the true owners of the shop and house would return and want their property back.

"I know nothing definite," I said, then took a bit of revenge. "I think they may have survived." I smiled. "It might take them some time to get back, but I'm sure they will do everything in their power to get home. Like me."

"Hmmpf!" She turned and marched back behind the counter. "Just my luck! Of all the Jews that disappeared, *mine* would be the ones to come back."

Her Jews? I sat in silence and took a long time to finish my toast and coffee. *Let her worry. Let her feel uncomfortable.* I didn't care.

"Are you going to want something *more?*" the woman asked. "Because I have a lot of errands in town, and I always lock up the shop. You can't stay here."

"I'm finished. Thank you," I said, then walked out.

Two women across the square looked at me coming out of the tea-room, then looked away and began talking to each other. I walked on down the square. Although there were more people around now—shopping, chatting—no one spoke to me. If our eyes met, they would quickly stare at the ground or turn away. I felt utterly alone. There was no point in trying to find work. No one would want, or dare, to hire me. What in the world was I to do? I had to think. I walked to the end of the square and into the entrance of the tower of Saint Giles church. I wondered if someone would stop me from climbing the tower. A Jew in Saint Giles? But there was no one around the church and I mounted the stairs alone.

I had no problem being in the church. Our family had not been orthodox. My father kept a few holidays—Passover, Hanukkah—and ensured my sisters and I understood our religious heritage. But he always saw himself as cosmopolitan. He had been born and raised in Hungary in what was then the Austro-Hungarian Empire. He'd been to Vienna and Budapest. He was a great reader of history and philosophy. He spoke German and Hungarian and a bit of French. He was a man of the world, not just Jewish. And although the Jewish community knew and respected him, we didn't live in the old Jewish quarter but in a house in town with neighbors who weren't all Jewish. We felt assimilated, part of a community.

I was only thirteen in 1939 when discrimination against Jews in Bardejov began. I remember hearing my mother talking to my father about it. She always felt it was a temporary thing, that it would pass like discrimination against Jews had passed before. My father, as always, tried to keep the worst from me and my sisters. And, like all young girls in their teens, I was wrapped up in my own experiences—little triumphs, little troubles. I didn't see how painful it must have been for my father to become an outcast in his community. I felt his pain *now*.

If only I could see him again. So many things I needed to tell him. He'd had so many plans and dreams for me. I would go to college. Maybe I would become a doctor. He had wanted to be a doctor when he was young, but his family had guided him into business. Why hadn't I read more of the books he wanted me to read? Why had I spent so much time fussing over silly things like whether I was pretty, which new dress to buy, which boys were cute? My father tried and tried to expand my education, to pass his knowledge on to me. And then, before I could grow up enough to appreciate it and make use of that opportunity, I was taken to Auschwitz, my education cut off. Now, at nineteen, I was as ignorant as I had been at fourteen.

"I will change that, Papa," I whispered. "I will spend the rest of my life trying to become a daughter you can be proud of. I promise. I have lived through the worst, and I am still alive."

From the tower top, I looked out over the town and countryside. Such a beautiful country, my homeland. Rolling green hills surrounded the town on all sides. They looked peaceful, like they were untouched by war and death. From this height, the little town looked so normal. Surely, the people weren't all angry or filled with hate. There must be kind people even here. I just had to find them.

The tower wasn't so high that everything below was tiny. I saw the tearoom woman hurrying down the street. Another woman came out of a shop, and I recognized her as Mrs. Bartos. The tearoom woman clutched Mrs. Bartos's arm. They talked together, animated, waving their arms and shaking their heads. No doubt the tearoom woman was telling Mrs. Bartos about me, and Mrs. Bartos was bemoaning her distress with me. I had returned to bring her trouble. *Her Jew.*

I sighed and descended the tower steps. As I entered the square, the clock on the tower chimed three. I had been wandering and thinking for hours. I knew there was a small park just outside the square, and I thought I'd go there to sit in the sun for a bit. At the end of the square, I saw a shop I remembered. Before the war, it had been Mr. Zachik's ice cream shop. He had been one of the few non-Jewish shop owners in the town square. All the children loved him. His round, jolly face seemed made for dispensing sweets and ice cream. The door was open, so I went in.

"Hello, young lady. What can I do for you?"

There he was, Mr. Zachik, looking just the same. The same roly-poly shape, the same big smile with the same twinkle in his eyes, the same soft wisps of gray hair floating out from under the same white cap. I just stared at him, wondering if he would recognize me. Ripples of concentration appeared on his forehead as he studied me, searching his memory. Then his smile faded and the twinkle in his eyes dimmed. Conditioned now, I waited for him to turn me away. As I watched him, the ripples smoothed, his face softened, and sadness filled his eyes. It lasted only a moment, and then his smile appeared once again, brightening the little shop.

Mr. Zachik wagged a finger at me. "I know you, young lady. Now, don't tell me. It'll come to me . . ." He snapped his fingers. "Cilka!" He came around the counter, grasped my arms, and held me a little away from him, studying my face. "I see a bit of trouble there. Yes. Trouble." He patted my face with his chubby hand. "Don't you worry, little Cilka. You've survived, and that's what counts. Things will be better now. You listen to old Mister Zachik, hmm?" He took me by the hand and walked to the counter. "We'll start with some ice cream, shall we? Vanilla ice cream was your favorite. I remember."

He opened the little freezer, took a small cone, and put a big scoop of vanilla ice cream into it, tamping it down so it would stay put. He handed it to me with a smile.

"Cones aren't quite as big as before the war." He shook his head. "No . . . not nearly as big." He sighed. "And the milk isn't quite as rich. But I do the best I can." He pointed to a metal box behind him, reached out and patted it. "Just got this electric machine a week ago. Been hand-cranking before that. This lasts longer." He smiled at me again. "Glad you're back, little Cilka. Terrible times we're in. Terrible thing to happen. Pretty girl like you. Just terrible." He came back around the counter and put his arm around me. "I have a feeling things will be better now. People . . . people will be better. Have to be, don't they?"

"I hope so, Mr. Zachik."

"That's the spirit! Hope." A little frown clouded his cheery face. "We have the Russians here right now for a while. Order and everything. But that's just temporary . . . yes . . . temporary." He brightened. "So, don't you worry. We always have ice cream, don't we?"

I gave him a smile. "We do. Wonderful ice cream. Thank you, Mr. Zachik." I reached into my pocket.

"No, no, no. You just keep your money, young lady. Ice cream is on me. You need it. Looking a little thin. Come in anytime. Anytime. Fatten you up."

I thanked him again. As I walked toward the little park, I looked back. There he was, standing in the shop doorway. He waved. I waved back. Just like old times.

I sat on a bench in the sun. The ice cream tasted delicious. A little dog came and sat by the bench, hoping for a treat.

"You can have the cone," I said to him.

I felt almost happy. I had found one kind person—Mr. Zachik. There must be more. I leaned back and lifted my face to the sun. I closed my eyes and drifted back into childhood and summer days, friends and family, fun and laughter. And ice cream.

A cold shadow slid across the sun, blocking its warmth. I opened my eyes. A young man in an NKVD Russian uniform stood looking down at me. He smiled.

"Are you Cecilia Klein?"

My heart raced, but I kept my voice steady.

"What do you want?" I asked.

He smiled again.

"Your ice cream is melting. Let me take it for you." He took the cone from my hand and threw it to the little dog. "There you go, doggie. Now Miss Klein, we'd like you to help us by answering a couple of questions. That's all. If you could come with me to the station, it will only take a few minutes."

CHAPTER TWELVE

The NKVD colonel behind the desk didn't even look up when I was escorted into his office. The young officer who brought me placed a chair a few feet from the desk, took my arm courteously, and sat me down. Without a word, he saluted the colonel, turned on his heel, and marched from the room, leaving me in uneasy silence. There was a window directly behind the colonel, and the afternoon sun poured in, casting long bars of golden light across the floor. With such brightness behind him, the colonel was in shadow, and I couldn't see his face, just the top of his head as he studied the papers on his desk, turning them over one by one. With nothing to do but wait, I focused on the colonel. His dark green uniform with gold epaulets and rows of ribbon medals looked uncomfortable in the warm, stuffy room, and the rigid formality reminded me of the SS. Anxiety crept in and I shivered despite the heat.

I told myself I had nothing to fear. *I've done nothing wrong. I'm just a young girl returning home.* But as the minutes ticked by and he still didn't look up, the old, familiar dread crept over me. I shifted nervously in my chair. Then he spoke.

"*Warum besuchen Sie Bardejov, Fraülein Klein?*" he asked without raising his eyes.

I answered quickly, "*Ich besuche nicht. Ich kehre nach Hause zurück.*"

Even before he looked up at me, I knew I had made a serious mistake. His uniform reminded me of the SS, and his German was so perfect I answered automatically. I watched him arrange the papers into order and put the neat pile to the side of his desk. He sat up straight, steepled his hands together, looked directly at me, and smiled.

"Your German is excellent, Miss Klein."

Hard eyes the color of steel didn't match his smile. I waited in silence.

"Where did you learn such good German, Miss Klein?" he asked in Slovak as excellent as his German.

Wherever he got his training, it had been thorough. I would have to be careful. This was no boorish Red Army soldier or uncultured, low-ranking border guard. Still, I had done nothing wrong. The Soviets could have little interest in nineteen-year-old Cecilia Klein, survivor of Auschwitz.

"I was in a German concentration camp for three years," I replied. "Understanding German was necessary for survival."

"Understanding, yes." He lowered his hands and crossed his arms. "Speaking as well as you do, however, is . . . unusual. Don't you think so, Miss Klein?"

"I also learned some German in school. Most of us did here, before the Nazis . . . before the war."

"Ah, yes . . . before the war." He chose a paper from the stack and studied it. "It says here your father was Mister Mikulas Klein, born in Hungary. Is that correct?"

"Yes."

Why was he interested in my father?

"I see he was the manager of a factory here in Bardejov. Is that correct?"

"Yes."

"It seems he was well off. He owned a car."

I didn't comment. What did it matter that my father owned a car? Several people owned cars in Bardejov. My father used it for work. Occasionally, we went for a drive on Sundays.

"Your father owned a car," he repeated. "Is that correct, Miss Klein?"

"Yes."

"Your family lived in the non-Jewish area of town?"

"Yes. We were not orthodox."

"In other words, your father saw himself and his family as cosmopolitan. Remnants of the old Austro-Hungarian Empire, perhaps. Well-off, educated, and sophisticated members of the bourgeoisie."

My wariness must have shown on my face because he narrowed his eyes at me.

"Would you say that was correct, Miss Klein?"

His voice had an edge I didn't like. As if he was trying to accuse my father and my family of something. I tried and failed to keep a growing irritation out of my answer.

"I don't know what you mean by well-off bourgeoisie. We were not any more well off than most families who earned a living, or owned or ran businesses in Bardejov. My father worked extremely hard to provide for us. We lived in a modest house like most people. Bardejov is not a sophisticated metropolis. It's surrounded by farms with little industry, mostly in the town."

"So, in a small town surrounded by farms and farm laborers, your well-educated, cosmopolitan father manipulated capital to run a successful business, owned a car, and lived in a pleasant house in town." He raised his eyebrows and tilted his head a bit. "That is correct. Is it not, Miss Klein?"

I didn't know what he was after, but I was tired of bullying and harassment.

"Since you know this much about my father, then you also know the Nazis took over the business he ran, commandeered his car, arrested his family, sent them to a German concentration camp, and murdered his wife and two of his daughters. Then my father disappeared. The truth is my family was destroyed. What does it matter who or what we were before the war?"

"And yet . . . you have returned to Bardejov."

He had so much information that I wondered if he knew anything about my time in Auschwitz.

"Yes," I said. "I have come home to find out what happened to my father. I see nothing wrong with that. It is a perfectly natural thing to do."

"You are a very outspoken young woman, Miss Klein. From what I've seen, most of your people returning from the camps are reticent to speak at all."

He opened a drawer in his desk, and I watched in growing anger and alarm as he took out the two dresses I received from the French soldiers, a handful of money from the American colonel, and some of the chocolate bars Mila had given me. He arranged them in an orderly row on the desk and studied them like curious exhibits in a museum, fingering the dresses, examining the money, and smiling a little at the chocolate bars. There was only one way he could have come by these things. Mrs. Bartos had taken them from my room while I was in town and brought them to the Soviets. If she could discredit me with them, perhaps I would be driven from Bardejov, and she would keep possession of our house. What had she told him?

"These are very nice dresses, Miss Klein." He held one up, and it shimmered in the sunlight coming through the window. He examined the neckline. "It has a French label. That's very interesting. I doubt they gave you French dresses in Auschwitz. Where did you get French dresses, Miss Klein?"

I gritted my teeth and answered him. "When I was liberated by the Americans, the Free French were also there, as well as the British. The clothes I was wearing were filthy and lice-ridden, as you can imagine. The French soldiers had thoughtfully brought some dresses with them to give out to the French women who survived Ravensbrück. They kindly gave me two."

"These French soldiers simply gave them to you? Free of charge?"

"Yes!"

"You gave them nothing in return?"

"No! It was a gesture of kindness. We had nothing but the prisoner clothes we wore in the concentration camp. They were in tatters."

"How gallant of them," he said with a touch of sarcasm. "The French are so . . . civilized."

He put the dresses down and picked up the money, fanning the bills like a hand of cards. He pulled out a couple of German marks.

"Nazi Reichsmarks. Worthless now, but I'm curious why you, a former prisoner of the Nazis, would be interested in keeping them. Nostalgia, perhaps?" He crushed them in his hand and dropped them into the wastebasket. "So much for the Thousand-Year Reich!" He eased out a couple of French Franc notes. "French again." He waved them gently under his nose. "I detect a trace of scent. Did the French soldier give you some perfume, perhaps? Not surprising. You're not a bad-looking young woman and the French are, shall we say, frivolous and romantic." He gave a dry little laugh, tossed the francs on the desk, and held up the American Dollars that remained. "Last but certainly not least, we have American dollars. Two tens. Twenty dollars. That's a lot of money, Miss Klein. Particularly now, when the dollar is king, as they say." He held them with two hands and snapped them a couple of times. "Solid currency, American dollars."

He rose, walked around the desk, and stood towering over me. I forced myself to look up and tried to keep a rigid indifference. He was tall, surely over six feet, with a commanding presence. There was no smile on his face now. His brow creased and he looked at me with hard, penetrating eyes. My palms grew damp with an old fear, and my mouth went dry. He was suspicious and trying to intimidate me into admitting to something. What? Was it a crime to return home? What had Mrs. Bartos said to him? I told myself to stay calm and not give in to fear.

I have done nothing wrong.

"Where did you get all this money, Miss Klein?" he demanded.

I raised my head and looked him in the eyes. "The American colonel gave it to me to help me get home."

"An . . . American . . . colonel? I am curious, Miss Klein. Why would a high-ranking American officer give you a significant amount of money?"

"I told you!" I took a deep breath. "To help me get home. I had nothing."

"I have seen Displaced Persons camps, Miss Klein. They are filled to overflowing with former Nazi prisoners. Did this American colonel give *all* those prisoners money to, as you say, help them get home?"

"I don't know. It was kind of him."

I struggled to keep my voice even, but he'd put me on the defensive.

"So," he drawled, "among all these former prisoners, this American colonel singled you out and gave you money to return to Czechoslovakia."

I answered too quickly. "He didn't single me out. Mila . . . I mean . . . the young soldier who brought us to the camp took me to the colonel."

He reached into his pocket, pulled out a scrap of paper, and read aloud, "Mila Janich. Two-six-three-three, Holbrook Street, Hamtramck, Michigan." He thrust the paper in front of my face. "Is this, perhaps, the young soldier?"

I clenched my hands into fists to stop them shaking. "Yes." I didn't know what to say that he wouldn't twist somehow.

"Mila Janich is a Slovak name."

"Yes." I sighed in frustration. "He was nice. We spoke Slovak. He gave me his address in case I ever went to America. He was close to my age. He was just . . . friendly." I knew I was telling him too much, but I wanted him to see how innocent it all was.

He looked at the paper with Mila's address, folded it carefully, and put it back in his pocket. He fixed his eyes on me again.

"Hamtramck is a city surrounded by Detroit. Did you know that, Miss Klein?"

"I don't know anything about America. I've never been there, and I will never go there."

"Detroit is the center for the manufacture of military arms and weapons for the American army. Do you expect me to believe you knew nothing about that?"

"No! I mean . . . yes! I knew nothing about that."

"What did you promise the American colonel in return for the money he gave you?"

"Nothing! He didn't ask for anything in return."

"What did Mila Janich tell you about Detroit?"

"Nothing!"

"Why are you in Bardejov?"

"I told you! It's my home. I'm looking for my father."

"What did you give the French for the dresses?"

"Nothing!"

"Why do you still carry German Reichsmarks?"

"I don't carry them! The American colonel—"

"Miss Klein!" he snapped. "Do you expect me to believe this fantasy? First, you are sent to Auschwitz, a Nazi extermination camp for Jews, for three years. Your family is killed in the gas chambers, but you survive. You also spend time in Ravensbrück, an extermination camp for women, and you survive. The Red Army liberates, but you make your way to the American DP camp where a young American soldier, who lives near the center of a military munitions factory in Detroit, Michigan, takes you to an American colonel. This American colonel gives you a significant amount of money, which you say was an act of kindness. Then, a young soldier gives you his address in Hamtramck and invites you to visit him when you go to America. French soldiers give you two expensive French dresses and French perfume, for which, you claim, they asked nothing from you in return. You make your way to Bardejov, where your father worked as a well-off, bourgeois businessman in an agricultural area of farms and farm laborers. You return, even though you know your father's business was confiscated, your home was given to one of your father's exploited workers, and your town is now under the protection of the Soviet Union. Yet you claim you are simply a young woman returning home to find her father."

He heaved a great sigh, shook his head, and returned to his seat at the desk. The way he told it, my story was highly suspicious. But I had done none of the things he implied. It was such a lie! I'd had enough of lies.

"What did Mrs. Bartos tell you?" I demanded. "She was the one who brought you all these things. It could be no one else. She went through my closet, drawers, and suitcase to find them. I deserve to know what I am accused of."

"Mrs. Bartos didn't accuse you of anything, Miss Klein." He spread his hands as if I were the one fantasizing. "She was worried about what all this meant. She was only doing her patriotic duty as a concerned citizen. During this period of post-war chaos, the Soviet Army is the guarantor of law and order. These are difficult times, Miss Klein."

"Yes," I replied bitterly. "And Mrs. Bartos is happy in my house, the house that belongs to me by right. The property of my father."

"Property is a complex issue, Miss Klein." He picked up one of the chocolate bars and looked at it. "The Americans think they will conquer the world with Hershey chocolate bars. We'll see about that."

"What are you charging me with?"

"I haven't charged you with anything yet, Miss Klein. Your case is complex. I will report to Moscow, and we will see what develops."

"Then, if you have no more questions for me, I would like to leave now."

"I'm afraid you will have to remain under my protection until I've heard from Moscow." He reached under his desk for something. The door opened and an NKVD officer appeared. He wasn't the young officer who had brought me. He looked like a thug, and he didn't wear a smile. The colonel waved his hand.

"This young woman will stay here while her case is being reviewed. Show her to a cell."

The NKVD officer grabbed my arm and jerked me out of the chair.

"You can't keep me here!" I cried. "I've done nothing wrong! I am a Czechoslovak citizen!"

"Cecilia Klein"—the NKVD colonel didn't look at me—"don't make this any harder than it has to be."

The officer marched me from the room in silence.

I never saw the colonel again. For three days I sat in a cell at the NKVD headquarters in Bardejov, under continuous interrogation. Sometimes it was an NKVD officer. Other times just a soldier. They kept asking question after question. The same questions. I would answer and they would ask again. Over and over. Where did I get American dollars? How did I come to have dresses with French labels? Why did I have a note with the address of a man in America? How many workers did my father exploit in his business? Why did my father own a car? Why did I come back to Bardejov? What did I promise the American colonel in exchange for the money? What did I give the French soldiers in exchange for the dresses? What information was I to send to Mila Janich in Hamtramck? Was I a spy for the Americans? Exhausted, I would fall asleep, and they would wake me and start over with the same questions. Every time, I would tell them the truth. Every time, they would repeat the question as though I had lied.

At the end of the third day, they put me in a truck with two guards and drove out of Bardejov.

Prisoner

CHAPTER THIRTEEN

"Prisoner Klein! Wake up!"

Rough hands grabbed both my arms, jerking me out of a deep sleep and hauling me to my feet. At first, I didn't know where I was. Instinctively, I fought to get free.

"Prisoner Klein! Stop!"

The two guards shook me hard, and I remembered I was in a truck. I stopped resisting. It was dark and the truck smelled of onions. We seemed to have stopped moving.

"Where are we?" I rasped. My throat hurt and my tongue was dry.

"Quiet!" They shook me again.

The back of the truck opened, and a Red Army soldier looked in at me and my guards.

"Just one?" he grunted.

"That's it."

"We held up the train for one?"

"Nothing to do with me."

"Come on, then. We're behind schedule."

One of my guards jumped out of the truck while the other guard shoved me out the door, where I fell. They yanked me to my feet again, pulled my arms behind my back, and pushed me forward. We were parked behind a building. As we passed it, I looked up at a sign illuminated by a single dim bulb. *Poprad*. We were at the train station in Poprad! The same station the train for Auschwitz left from over three years ago!

We rounded the station building and there was the train. I stared at the black engine towering over me, its smokestack puffing clouds of steam into the night. It might have been the same exact train, except instead of a swastika, it had a grimy red star on the front. Looking at the long row of boxcars behind the engine, I shuddered in revulsion. Nausea rose in my throat. I did not know why I was here, but I knew I couldn't get on that train. My legs collapsed and my body slumped. The guard holding me swore. The second guard took my other arm and together they dragged me alongside the train. Somewhere down the line, officers were shouting orders.

We stopped. A soldier pulled open the door of one of the boxcars. I panicked and my ears rang as dizziness washed over me. The butt of a rifle prodded me in the back. Rough hands lifted me off my feet and shoved me into darkness. And there it was again, the familiar smell of heat and fear and human excrement. The same heavy door shrieking along the groove, slamming shut with a thud. The same bolts clanging into place. The scream of the whistle.

Dear God! No! Not again.

The car lurched as the train started moving. I fell to the grimy floor and crawled away to crouch against one of the walls. There were others in the car. In the darkness, I couldn't tell who they were or how many. All I knew was that I wanted to be as far away from people as I could get. I drew my knees up, wrapping my arms around them, and tried to stop my uncontrollable shaking. My lungs strained with each desperate breath, but I couldn't get enough air. My life had become a recurring nightmare, a circular hell, a place where I was doomed to relive the same horror over and over.

The sounds and smells of the Soviet train faded into blackness. Reality shifted, and I was back there again. On the train to Auschwitz. The same station platform. The same locomotive. The smell of coal and steam. And the ghosts. So many ghosts. My mother and sisters dressed in nice clothes. Clean. Neat. Respectable. Each of us carrying a small suitcase. My sister has her arm around me, and I hold my mother's hand, not to be separated. The SS soldiers in their black uniforms shout at us to move faster, prodding us, shoving us. They herd us like cattle into the stinking cars. Darkness. Slivers of light through the wooden slats of the car. Too many people. Bodies shoved against each other, swaying and lurching with the movement of the train. My mother falls and I kneel to help her. Someone steps on her hand. I look up and the man winces an apology at us. I pull my mother into a corner and wrap my arms around her. The doors slam shut. The car shudders and begins to move. Once again. Into an all-too-familiar unknown.

The ghosts retreated into the dark past. My present fear remained. The same fear. Only sharper this time because of what I knew.

"Please! No! I can't do this again."

I pounded my hands repeatedly against the wall. "Why? Why?" Tears I couldn't control streamed down my face as I rocked back and forth, sobbing, pleading with the God I'd rejected.

"Forgive me. I had to do those things. I had to live. I know it was evil. I hated it—hated myself. Punish me if You will. I deserve punishment. But not this again. Please! Not again!"

Why did I bother to plead for help? God, indifferent to my suffering, had pointed a finger at me once again and determined my destiny. I was to be an outcast. Thrown away like unwanted rubbish. Diminished to nothing. Just as before. A prisoner. For life.

I didn't know where I was being taken this time. My brief glimpse of hope had vanished. I would never see my father again. He would never know I survived. I pounded my head repeatedly against the wall as though I could knock some sense into this. I heard the shuffle of feet as the other people in the car moved as far away from me as they could. I didn't blame them. No doubt they thought I was crazy. Possibly dangerous. The sense of isolation was overwhelming. I was totally alone now. More alone than ever. More rejected. An object of suspicion. An object of fear.

The rocking of the car and the monotonous *clack-clack* of the wheels on the track gradually lulled me to sleep. When I woke, daylight had filtered into the car, and I saw who journeyed with me. It was a much smaller group than in the cattle cars to Auschwitz. There were maybe fifteen people. All women. They stared at me in silence.

I didn't speak to them. What is the point of human contact when you've lost the desire to live? I saw nothing ahead but suffering and abuse. I'd had enough of that. I felt nothing. I didn't care about survival anymore. Let the Russians kill me. I was tired. So tired. Tired of people. Tired of life.

Finally, the women stopped staring at me and went back to talking among themselves. I was the subject of conversation for a short time.

Who was I? Was I crazy? Would I do something violent? Gradually, since I didn't move or speak, they talked about themselves. Most of them were from Czechoslovakia. A couple were Austrian. Some were Russians who had been in the Red Army and captured by the Germans. Now they were considered traitors. They didn't understand it, thought it must be a terrible mistake. Someone would discover this soon. They would be released and sent home. I could have told them they were dreaming, but I didn't care anymore. Let them hope. What did it matter?

The drone of their voices and the swaying of the car were hypnotic, almost soothing. I curled up in a ball on the floor and escaped once more into sleep. Dreams came and went. Familiar visions of hell. The train lurched to a stop, and I woke. The women rushed to gather by the door, chattering.

"They have to give us food now. We've had nothing since yesterday."

"And water! I'm dying of thirst."

"Do you think they'll let us out here? Maybe this is the place."

I had been cramped into a ball for so long it was hard to straighten my legs. I stood up and leaned against the wall. The other women looked at me, decided I wouldn't do anything crazy, and focused on the door again. I heard the bolts draw back. The door opened with a scraping sound, and I looked out on a sunny day. The sign on the station said Lvov.

"We're in Ukraine!" one of the Russian women said. "Now they will see the mistake. We'll be let go." She pushed her way closer to the open door.

I looked out on a country landscape. Trees. Cottages. In the distance, a large city. The station was a small, rundown wooden structure with no platform. We must be on a sidetrack, probably to avoid the train stopping at any regular stations. I peered down the length of the track, expecting to see armed guards lined up all along the train like I remembered whenever a Nazi train came to a station. But there was nothing like that here. To the left of the station, some guards stood with two young women. The uniforms of the guards looked strange, accustomed as I was to Nazi order and precision. These guards wore faded tan uniforms, jackets carelessly tucked into crumpled jodhpurs, boots covered in dust. They looked scruffy and unwashed. What was our train carrying? Surely a train loaded with angry prisoners required many more guards to keep order and prevent revolt.

Two guards approached our car with a sack of bread and a bucket of water. One guard dumped the bread on the floor of the car and backed away, pointing his rifle at us. The women crowded around, holding out their metal cups for water. The other guard poured it out in a rush and the women had to be quick to fill their cups before it was gone. As soon as their cups held any water, they retreated into the car. The two Russian women shouted at the guards.

"Take us to your commanding officer. We are loyal members of the Red Army. We are here by mistake."

The guard with the rifle told them to get back. Then he saw me. I watched his eyes rake over me. A little smile curled his mouth.

"You!" he shouted.

I pretended not to hear.

"You!" He pointed the rifle at me and motioned for me to come closer. "Here!"

I don't know why I went instead of just letting him shoot me. Some instincts, like the will to live, are impossible to control, no matter how indifferent we think we are. I edged my way to the open doorway and stared down at him. He came closer and spoke in a low voice.

"This dress . . ." He fingered the hem of my dress, pulling at it.

I stiffened. What did he want? I continued to stare at him in silence.

"There are no parties where you're going, girl." He grabbed my arm. "Come with me! Now!"

I heard the women behind me take in hissing breaths. They knew what the outcome of this would be. If they felt anything for me, they didn't show it. Better me than one of them. The guard pulled me roughly out of the car, catching me as I fell.

"You're as light as a feather," he muttered as he set me on the ground. Then he marched me ahead of him into a small storeroom in the run-down station house and shut the door.

I didn't want to show fear, but I couldn't control my shaking. Had I escaped all the raping of the Russian soldiers during the liberation only to be molested here in some godforsaken station in Ukraine? I folded my arms tight and eyed him warily. He was shorter than average and gaunt, with dull brown hair streaked with gray. His faded, frayed uniform seemed too large, like it had once belonged to a more robust man. I stared at him, my eyes riveted on a large burn scar that covered the left side of his face, from his hairline down to his neck. It was deep blue-black and shiny. What did he want?

He set his rifle carefully against the wall. I tensed but said nothing.

He held up his hands. "Don't worry. I won't harm you." He moved closer and I edged backward. He reached out and touched my dress again, rubbing the fabric between his fingers. My shoulders gave an involuntary nervous twitch.

He looked up and frowned. "You're already cold and it's only Lvov." His voice grated like sandpaper. "Do you know where you're being taken?"

I shook my head.

"I didn't think so. You're going to Siberia—Vorkuta! That's one-hundred-sixty kilometers above the Arctic Circle! Near the Ural Mountains. You'll be digging coal in deep mines. You'll die in two days dressed like that." His eyes held mine with a haunted look. "I should know. I was there."

I cringed. If Siberia truly was our destination, he was right. I would freeze to death. The dress I wore, the dress he seemed to be fascinated with, was the summer dress I had on when I was taken to the NKVD office in Bardejov. I had seen people freeze to death at Auschwitz, suffering in pain and fear as their bodies slowly shut down, piece by piece. I was indifferent to whether I lived or died, but I was not indifferent to the way I died. My entire being revolted at the thought of freezing to death. I felt a surge of my old defiance and growing anger at this new injustice. The NKVD had sealed my fate. The question was, why did this Soviet guard care what happened to me? As I glared at him, I thought I saw a flicker of sympathy in his eyes. They were gray, deep-set, and etched round with lines that spoke of pain and hardship.

"You should be angry," he said. "Vorkuta's a hell of a place." He dragged a hand through his dusty hair. "I suffered six years there. Got caught up in one of Comrade Stalin's collectivization purges. I was just a farmer, but I had a cow. That made me a *kulak*, an exploiter of the people. Nineteen-thirty-five, that was. Should have been in Vorkuta for twenty years, but Stalin needed more fodder for the army, so they released me and *promoted* me to soldier. Like most prisoners, they sent me to a punishment division. To the front lines. We were the first in. Fought for Mother Russia for the last four years. Few of us survived." He rubbed the side of his face with the scar. "Got this as a souvenir. At the end of the war, I was free but still under suspicion and sent to this forsaken outpost to serve the State and repent of the crimes I never committed."

I couldn't figure out why he was telling me this bitter story of Soviet injustice. It did nothing to ease my mind. He turned away, flipped open a bin, pulled out a pair of woolen long johns, and held them up like a salesman in a clothing store. They were bright red.

"Listen. I've got a deal for you. It's going to get a lot colder in that boxcar as you head north. The dress you have on is useless against that kind of cold. These long johns will serve you a lot better on the way to Siberia. Give me the dress in exchange. I have a daughter just about your age." His eyes softened. "She was only three when I was sent to Vorkuta. Her mother was arrested, too, but I never heard what happened to her. They put our daughter in an orphanage for children of enemies of the state. I was lucky to get her back after the war. She hasn't had any nice things. We're getting reacquainted in a way, and your dress . . . well . . . it would make her happy."

If I wanted to survive, I'd be a fool not to make the bargain. I removed my dress as quickly as I could and left it on the floor. I grabbed the red long johns from his outstretched hand and put them on. I buttoned them all the way up to my neck. They were clean but scratchy. Nevertheless, he was right. They were comic-looking but warm. I started to kick the dress toward him. I still didn't trust him.

"No!" he barked. "Don't kick it!" He reached down and picked up the dress like it was a precious treasure. "What is this fabric?"

"Rayon," I muttered.

He held the dress up to his face and rubbed it along his cheek. The one without the scar. "It's so soft," he murmured. "I've never seen anything like it. Maybe when we've finally built true socialism in this country, our wives and daughters will have dresses as nice as this."

He was the strangest guard I had ever encountered. I figured I reminded him of his daughter, and that was why he was being so nice to me. A lump of pain formed in my chest as I thought of my father. Papa would be glad I'd given this man my dress. *Never pass on the chance to do a* mitzvah, *Cilka.* A good deed? Dear God! What would Papa think if he knew how I had survived Auschwitz? I buried the thought and watched the guard carefully fold my dress, put it in a rucksack, fasten the top, and place it on a shelf. I didn't think exchanging my dress for warm long johns qualified as a good deed, but I could imagine how happy this guard's daughter would be.

The guard turned back and asked abruptly, "What was your crime?"

"Nothing!" I raised my chin. "I committed no crime. The NKVD colonel thought I was a spy because I understood and could speak some German. It was stupid. Nearly everyone in my town spoke some German."

The corner of his mouth lifted in a skewed smile that didn't reach his eyes. "Quotas."

"Quotas?" What was he talking about?

"Your NKVD colonel is required to find and arrest a certain number of spies every month or risk losing his job and maybe ending up in a Siberian concentration camp himself. You fit right in. By the time he finished his report to Moscow, you probably also had a short-wave radio and communicated with Winston Churchill daily. Nothing personal. Just fulfilling the quotas. You'll understand better when you get to Vorkuta." He moved to pick up his rifle. "It's time I got you back. The NKVD takes over your train from here on. They don't like delay." He moved to open the storeroom door.

"Wait!" I pointed to a pair of boots in a corner. "I want those boots over there too."

He laughed. "You've got nerve. Good for you." He picked up the big rubber boots and held them out. "Here! They belong to the State anyway, so I don't care. Take them."

I grabbed the boots and clutched them. "They're not going to shoot me because these long johns are red, are they?"

He laughed. "No. All the party big wigs wear red long johns." He looked me over again, this time with a quiet smile of regret. "You've got spirit as well as looks. Bewitching. I think you might survive."

"Why?" I was curious.

"Small."

"Small?"

"Shorter prisoners require less food and don't lose weight as quickly as the big ones. The big ones usually die the first winter. Being short is one reason I survived."

"Great," I grumbled. "I guess I'm lucky."

"Could be. Like I said. You've got spirit. It makes the difference between life and death in Vorkuta. Take my advice. Stay strong and fight. Make your father proud."

The train whistle sounded.

He grabbed my arm. "We've got to go. They've added the new prisoners by now. There's only one carload of you on this supply train. Summer in Vorkuta." He raised his eyebrows and laughed. "Not as many dead workers to replace."

He opened the storeroom door and took me back out into the stationhouse. He poured some water into a metal cup and handed it to me with a hunk of bread.

"Here," he said in a gruff voice. "I made you miss your food ration. And keep the cup. You'll need it."

I was starving. He watched me devour the bread and gulp the water. When I finished, he grabbed my arm again and marched me out to the train. The door to the boxcar was still open, and some of the women were looking out. They quickly drew back when they saw us. The guard lifted me into the car, then stepped back and gave me a mock salute.

"Good luck to you. Little witch."

He slammed the door shut and bolted it. The train whistle screamed, and the car lurched as we started. My future looked the same, but something had changed inside me. The guard had been sort of kind. Like Mr. Zachik, the ice cream man, he had seen me as a person and not just a Jew or a worthless member of a hated class. In a world bent on cruelty, I had run into two kind people by chance. Maybe there was a reason to live after all. The guard had told me to stay strong and fight. I felt my old spirit reviving. Whatever they threw at me on this train, I was now determined to survive the journey. What would happen when we got to Vorkuta? I didn't know. Maybe anger and hate would serve me there too. Maybe my father would return to Bardejov and hear of my fate and know I was alive. Maybe, like the guard said, I would make him proud.

CHAPTER FOURTEEN

The two new women, who were put on the train while I was with that guard, studied me with nervous eyes. No doubt I was an alarming sight in those dingy long johns, clutching big rubber boots. All the women retreated cautiously to the other end of the cattle car and watched me in total silence. I faced them, bold and defiant now.

"I know you all think I'm crazy," I declared. "I'm not, so you can stop worrying."

They continued to eye me warily, like I was a snake poised to strike.

"Do you know where we're going?" I demanded.

A tall girl with short brown hair and angry eyes took a step toward me. "They told us we're going somewhere to work," she said. "It must be a terrible mistake. They'll let us off at the next station and send us back to our homes."

I looked her in the eyes. "I've got bad news for you. That's not going to happen. It isn't a mistake. You're going somewhere to work, all right, but it's not what you think. You are now no better than slaves, and you're being transported above the Arctic Circle to Siberia to work in the coal mines of Vorkuta. The guard at the station told me. You may never go back."

The women began shouting, crying out in fear and outrage.

"They can't do that! It's against the law."

"We'll die there!"

The tall, angry girl called out, "But we're Czech citizens."

"Not all of us," another woman cried. "I'm Austrian."

"I'm Polish," someone wailed. "This is outrageous!"

A fragile blond girl whimpered in a trembling voice, "What have we done?"

They continued crying out together. I pounded the boots against the side of the car.

"Quiet!" I shouted into the din.

They stopped immediately and stared at me, shocked into silence, unsure of me again.

"We haven't done anything," I said. "They don't care who we are or where we're from. We are slaves of the State now. We are no longer human. We have no identity or purpose other than working until we die."

Some of the women began to cry. Tears, denial, anger, fear—I knew them well. One thing Auschwitz had taught me was that people did best when they faced a desperate situation as a group. And a group with a forceful leader did best of all. I doubted any of these women had been in a Nazi concentration camp. They were too well fed. Their eyes didn't have that haunted look that spoke silently of unimaginable horrors. Probably horrors lay in the future for these new Soviet slaves, but right now they were as naive as they were innocent of their so-called crimes. The three years I spent under Nazi persecution had molded me into the kind of leader they needed. Not because I was compassionate, but because I wanted to live. Why? I still didn't know.

"What is, is," I barked. "The sooner we accept that and fight for what little we can get, the longer we survive. If you want to get through this nightmare, we have to work together."

"What do you know about it?" the tall girl said. "Maybe you're one of them. That guard gave you things. Why?"

"A purely selfish motive. He wanted my dress for his daughter. It was a trade."

"Where is Vorkuta?" the fragile blond asked.

"North of the Arctic Circle, the guard told me. Way north. Near the Ural Mountains."

Her voice was almost a whisper. "How will we survive when we get there? I don't know anything about mining."

"Who knows how we'll survive?" I shrugged. "Like I said, if we work together, we have a better chance."

The tall girl snapped at me. "Who are you to boss us around?"

"No one," I snapped back. "Just a woman like you. But I know what I'm talking about. Total control over us is what they want. To get that, they will do everything to break our spirits."

Their general protest was loud and desperate.

"Listen to me!" I shouted. "When we arrive, they will make us strip naked and shave all our heads. If we complain, they will beat us. If we cower, they will win. You have to fight if you want to live."

"Why should we believe you?" The tall girl glared at me.

"Because I've seen it. Never mind where. We'll face what happens when we get there. Right now, we have to get practical, or many of us will die in this cattle car." I picked up a tin can from one corner of the car and held it up. "By now I think you've noticed this is their idea of a Ladies Room."

They groaned and a couple of them laughed. The car already smelled of urine and feces. I knew from experience it would only get worse. Fortunately, this car, with only twenty or so women, wasn't nearly as jammed full of people as the cattle cars to Auschwitz. Bile rose in my throat just thinking about it again. One hundred fifty people, wedged in, body to body, relieving themselves where they stood. The suffocating smell . . . the filth . . . the shame.

I held up the rubber boots. "These boots will be our latrines. It's better than living in our own piss and filth for however long this trip takes. We'll dump them when we stop for food and water."

Again, the tall girl cut in. "Who elected you the boss?"

"No one. If you don't like what I suggest, don't do it. It doesn't matter to me. In this car, you're free to go your own way until they drag you out."

I put the boots in a far corner of the car along with the tin can. Either they would follow my advice, or they wouldn't. I really didn't care. It would be easier if we got along without antagonisms, but I understood their mistrust of me. They didn't know my experience with situations like this. I sat down again at the end of the car with my back to the wall. The women shuffled their feet for a bit but kept their distance. Eventually, the little blond girl came over and sat beside me.

"My name's Anichka." Clear blue eyes smiled at me. "I'm from Slovakia. Bratislava. Where are you from?"

She reminded me of Leah. She didn't look a thing like her, but she radiated the same basic goodness, not judging but simply offering friendship. How would she ever survive Siberia?

"I'm from Slovakia too," I answered. "Bardejov."

"I was there once." Anichka beamed at me. "When I was a little girl. I remember the town. It was like a fairy-tale village. I expected to see dwarves or a witch or something. Silly, wasn't it?"

"Not really. Bardejov is very old. From the Middle Ages."

"What's your name? If we are all to work together, I think we should know each other's names, don't you?"

It was a start. "Yes," I said. "My name's Celia."

Anichka brightened. "My best friend's sister's name was Celia. Everyone called her Cilka. Shall I call you Cilka?"

"No!" I snapped.

I never wanted to be called Cilka again. The memories were too painful. My mother crooning my name with a musical lilt. My sister Magda crying out to me as they separated us at Auschwitz. Women in the camp furtively whispering my name. No. Whatever the future in Siberia held for me, I was determined to leave Cilka behind.

I took a breath and spoke more softly. "No. Just Celia. Cilka was a nickname from my childhood. I'm no longer that little girl."

Anichka tipped her head to one side like a bird. "I think I understand that." She held out her hand. "Hello, Celia. I hope we'll be friends."

I took her delicate, soft hand and shook it. "Thanks." I didn't know what else to say.

"Don't worry." Anichka nodded toward the others. "They're just scared. Even Branca. You know, the tall one who seems so angry? I know her. She's from Bratislava too. I'll get them to come around. I know you're right. We have to stick together. There's safety in numbers. Especially when we're on a journey to the unknown. We'll pretend it's an adventure. Then it won't seem so bad."

I watched her go back to the group of women and start her campaign of solidarity. If anyone could unite this group, it would be someone like little Anichka. Her adventurous journey to the unknown was a journey into hell, but I didn't have the heart to tell her.

CHAPTER FIFTEEN

The train moved relentlessly on. We viewed the changing landscape through the small, barred window hole in the cattle car and the glimpses we got at the various stops when they opened the door to shove in a few more women or bread and water. Mostly, we traveled through the flat, bleak country under gray, cloudy skies. We saw no houses, no evidence of human life at all. It was as if the land was uninhabited.

Our number leveled off at twenty women. Anichka had a hard job convincing them to trust my ideas about how we should get on. Gradually, as day followed day and their hope of release died, they realized the truth of what I had said. Some became so depressed they didn't even have the will to eat. This had to change. We didn't need women dying of starvation or dehydration in this small space. It wasn't easy, but with Anichka's optimism and my suggestions for survival, we made progress. Most of the women finally accepted the facts. If they were to survive working in mines in Siberia, they would have to stay as fit as possible in mind and body. Even so, Branca still had a chip on her shoulder about my taking charge of things. She called me Comrade Celia, the NKVD Persuader, and never stopped grumbling. Her resentment annoyed the other women, and they left her alone. Soon, only two others remained in her camp.

Our train made slow progress. We were the least important train on this track, constantly moving to sidetracks to allow other trains to pass us. Sometimes we would wait hours or even days before continuing.

I started a daily exercise routine to keep the women from losing strength due to sitting in the car day after day. Each day, a different woman led the routine. Anichka enjoyed it, even though she was the most petite and delicate of all the women.

"It's time for our strengthening," I said. "Anichka, you lead today."

"Everybody on the floor!" Anichka barked like a platoon leader.

All of us, except Branca and her two allies, dropped to the floor to do push-ups and sit-ups while Anichka called out the number of reps.

"This is stupid!" Branca griped. "You're just exhausting them when they're already weak. What are you, Celia? Some kind of sadist?"

I ignored her and kept doing push-ups and sit-ups. We then formed a line and marched from one end of the boxcar to the other to complete a half mile. I was still in such poor shape from Auschwitz and Ravensbrück, I was out of breath before long. But I kept going with everyone else. I gradually learned that none of the other women in our car were Jewish and hadn't been in a Nazi concentration camp. They were picked up in their towns and villages for various reasons, snatched abruptly from everyday family life. I wondered why. Were they also considered spies, like me?

Anichka confronted Branca while we marched. "We have to be stronger in order to work in the mines. If we're too weak to work, we are useless to them. What would they do with us then? Why would they feed useless workers?"

"That's nonsense, Anichka," Branca grumbled. "I'm sick of all these rules and jobs. Clean the floor! Use the boots! Exercise! Comrade Celia, the NKVD Persuader, is crazy!"

I stopped marching and confronted her. "If you don't like it, don't do it. Your choice. But together we are stronger. Something I learned in a different circle of hell."

"Yeah? If you're so smart, Comrade Celia, figure out how to get us some bread. In case you didn't notice, we didn't get our rations at the last stop."

"I did notice, Branca. My stomach's been shouting loud and clear. You're right. It's time to take action."

"Like what, Madame Persuader? Next stop, we hop out, overpower the guards, take over the train, and steam on to freedom?" She gave a bitter laugh. "Good luck with that."

"A nice fantasy, Branca, but not likely. No. We need to get their attention."

"And how do we do that?" she jeered.

As I thought it over, a crazy idea materialized in my imagination. "By scaring them."

Branca rolled her eyes to heaven. "With what? You have a hidden stash of weapons, Comrade?"

It was hard, but I held my temper. "What's the worst thing that can happen to a train?"

Anichka jumped in. "Derailment! I know that. My father was a train engineer."

"Exactly," I said. "If we work as a team, we could derail this train."

"You're crazy!" Branca sneered. "How?"

"Stop the march!" I shouted. Everyone halted where they were. I moved to a side wall of the car and looked at the other side. My idea seemed possible. "Here's the plan. We run from one side of the car to the other as a group. If we keep doing it, back and forth, eventually the whole car will rock. The guards will feel it all down the train. If we get it rocking enough, it could slip off the tracks."

"Mmm . . ." Anichka murmured. "We don't want to derail the train because then they might shoot us. But the rocking should scare them enough to make them stop the train, and that's when we make our stand and demand our rations."

Anichka walked over to Branca and put a hand on her shoulder. "Come on, Branca. It's worth a try. What have we got to lose?"

Branca shrugged but made no objection. I thought the idea interested her. For all her grumbling, she was smart and tough. I figured she was a survivor like me. She just hadn't accepted her fate yet. When she did, she would be a valuable ally.

"Okay, girls," I said. "Let's rock this thing!"

All twenty of us formed into a tight group on one side, ran to the other, turned, and ran back. We did it again and again. The women laughed and shouted at each turnaround. Gradually, the cattle car began to rock. The faster we ran, the more it rocked. We were so excited about our success that we linked arms and made whooshing sounds as we ran. Some of us fell down as the car swayed precariously from side to side, but we picked ourselves up with good humor and began again.

The sound of squealing brakes signaled the success of our efforts. The train slowly came to a stop, and we heard the shouts of guards as they ran along the track to our still-rocking car. They pounded on the door, and we all stopped.

"Everyone get in a tight group by the door," I said. "When they open it, we shout together. Food! Water!"

"Right!" they all agreed.

We were working together now, and our force was in numbers. I hoped this crazy scheme wouldn't backfire and make the guards so angry they'd shoot some or all of us. The door flew open, and we looked down at a group of six soldiers with rifles. It was enough to frighten anyone, but we chanted together.

"Food! Water! Food! Water!"

We kept it up, stamping our feet on each word. The soldiers waved their rifles at us, but we didn't stop. We might as well die shouting for food and water as anything. In this case, Soviet orders were on our side. The soldiers knew they had to deliver a certain number of prisoners or there would be dire consequences. They couldn't shoot us all as we stood shoulder to shoulder with arms linked. We were fresh workers for Stalin's coal mines. They wavered, lowered their rifles, and tried to calm us down. That was the main difference between the Nazis and the Communists. The Nazis just wanted to exterminate their enemies, or the Jews. The Communists wanted to work us to death.

"Girls! Girls!" I called out. "Quiet down! Don't shout."

A senior NKVD officer appeared. The soldiers snapped to attention and saluted.

"What's going on here?" The officer looked from them to us. "These are only women. They could not have caused this mechanical problem. Why are they shouting?"

"Sir!" One soldier bravely stepped forward. "Somehow, they caused the train to rock. We don't know how. They are shouting for food and water."

"Why? Rations were supposed to be handed out at the last stop." The NKVD officer glared at the soldier.

"Not to us!" we shouted again in unison. "Not to us!"

"Is this true?" The NKVD officer turned to the soldiers. They shuffled around and one produced a piece of paper. The NKVD officer grabbed it from him and looked it over. "Car number six is the prisoner car and designated for rations." He pointed to the number clearly painted on our car. "This is car number six. Get this taken care of!"

Immediately, three soldiers took off and returned with water and more sacks of bread than we had yet seen. We also received five sausages. The NKVD officer looked us over and scowled. We glared back at him.

"Because of you, this train is now behind schedule," he said. "I should have you all beaten for this. However, I must make up the time and I have to deliver you in fit working condition. You have your food and water. There will be no more insubordination. Next time, I will take the time to punish you as you deserve." He marched off but turned back and gave us a tight smile. "You're either exceptionally courageous, or you're crazy." He took a bottle out of his jacket pocket. "Here! Good vodka!" He threw it to us and Branca caught it. "Good night, ladies!"

No bread, water, or vodka had ever tasted so good. We may have been prisoners, but we had fought together, and we had won! Our shared fate forged a bond between us all. We were no longer strangers. We were a team.

A festive mood prevailed in the boxcar that night. Someone started singing softly and others joined her in a popular tango song. Two women danced with each other, laughing over the steps. Spirits revived. We talked for hours, telling our individual stories of home and family. I spoke only of my childhood. Nobody pressed me for more, seeming to understand I didn't want to talk about later years. We all spoke of our arrests and the injustices inflicted on us. When the singing and dancing ended, most of the women fell asleep. Branca, Anichka, and I continued to talk late into the night.

"Anichka?" I reached out in the darkness and touched her arm. "Do you have any idea why you're here? I mean, you're barely out of school. What could you possibly have done to come to the notice of the Soviet authorities?"

Anichka gave a little sigh. "I think I'm guilty by association."

"What?" Branca scoffed. "Don't tell me you were part of a resistance cell in grade school. What a joke. Although I wouldn't put it past them to come up with something just that stupid."

Anichka giggled. "That would be a stretch, because the worst thing we did in my school was lock our math teacher out of the classroom."

"So," Branca pressed, "what dastardly person did you associate with to bring the wrath of Stalin down on your pretty little head?"

"My father."

"Oh no, Anichka!" I knew well how painful that must be for her.

"Bastards!" Branca snarled. "What did they accuse your father of?"

"Collaboration with the Nazis. I told you my father was a train engineer. When the Nazis took over, they forced him to continue to run the trains. It was do that or be shot. He was afraid my mother and I would either starve or end up in a concentration camp if he didn't obey the Nazis." She paused and wiped tears from her cheek. "After liberation by the Red Army, the Communists arrested him as a collaborator and shot him. My mother was sent to prison. They just took her away. I didn't even get to say goodbye. I don't think the Soviets knew what to do with me, so they just arrested me as well. I don't know what happened to my mother. Do you think she might be where we're going? In Vorkuta?"

"Who knows?" I took her hand. "Maybe you'll be lucky and see her again."

"Sure," Branca grumbled. "And hell could freeze over." She laughed. "But not before the bastards burn to a crisp! I hope."

"Why were *you* arrested, Branca?" Anichka asked.

"A story of tainted blood and long memories," Branca answered. "My family has its roots in the landed gentry of Imperial Russia. In fact, my father was a general under Czar Nicholas and fought with the White Army during the Revolution. As you know, that didn't end well. Not for my family, and not for anyone, as far as I can tell. Anyway, when the Bolshevik writing was on the wall, my family fled Russia to settle in Slovakia with many other Former People, as the Soviets called anyone connected to the nobility."

"So you're Russian?" I asked.

"By blood, yes, though I was born in Slovakia and never set foot in Russia until now. But I grew up hearing my father's version of history and he had no love for Bolsheviks, or Communists in general. That was fine for a while because our circle of friends were all Former People. We despised totalitarians, which included Nazis and the Soviets. I even joined the Partisans during the war to fight the Nazis." Branca laughed. "Like father, like daughter. General Branca."

"Why did the Soviets arrest you?" Anichka puzzled. "You were fighting a common enemy."

"Ah, that's where the long memory comes in. When the Soviets moved into Czechoslovakia, a lot of us Former People who fought with the Partisans couldn't just disappear into the woodwork. My name came up, and some older officer recognized my father's name. He must have known him, probably as a young Bolshevik during the Civil War. Anyway, for some reason, he had a personal vendetta against my father. Of course, my father was dead by this time, but that didn't matter. I was alive, the same blood ran in my veins, and I was just as militant against crazy governments as my father had been. So here I am. Tainted blood. Who knew?" She put her arms around Anichka and me. "Let's forget about all the whys. What do they matter now? We're here, we're in this together, and we've scored a victory today. My father would tell us to fight one battle at a time and never give up."

CHAPTER SIXTEEN

The train pressed on through unending forests of fir and pine. The stops for fuel and water for the engine were simple wooden huts with a water tower and a pile of coal nearby. Beyond, the forest spread for miles and miles. Sometimes at these stops, the officers and guards let us out to stretch and relieve ourselves outside the filthy cars. I guess they thought it was safe. Who would be crazy enough to try to escape into that wilderness of wolves and bears without food and water?

Even though it was late June, the nights were getting colder the farther north we went. Some of the women had the good fortune to have held onto a jacket or coat. A few had scarves. But most had only light dresses. I was grateful for the red long johns, even though they were scratchy and now filthy, and made my skin break out in a rash. At some ration stops, we demanded to keep the burlap bags our bread rations came in. The guards at those stations probably knew where we were headed. Besides, what did it matter to them? The State had piles of burlap bags. We used them as shawls for the women who had only dresses. A woman could wrap herself in one bag. Sometimes two women, if they were small enough.

One day, the train pulled off onto a siding in a clearing in the forest. We often pulled off like that to let larger freight trains pass, watching them through the small window and broken slats in the car. They carried coal from the mines in the north. Coal was our future, but we had no idea what mining would be like. None of us had ever thought about where coal came from, much less how it was taken from the earth.

On this particular day, we experienced a small miracle. The soldiers thrust the door to our cattle car open as usual. We crowded into the doorway and stared out at a massive clearing in the forest. On the barren ground, weird pillars of rock stood around like stone warriors. They must have been a hundred feet high. Just beyond the train, steam rose into the air from a natural hot spring. We looked longingly at three pools of blue-green, mist-covered water. The NKVD officer appeared and addressed us all.

"Wash time! Everybody out! You will keep your underwear on. Do not go beyond the pools, or you will be shot!"

Why he allowed this, I will never know. Our boxcar full of women, the only car with prisoners on this supply train, was a headache for him. I like to think our act of defiance in rocking the cattle car inspired his respect. He watched us with interest as we all climbed out. The soldiers shoved us toward the pools. For a time, we just stood and stared up at the rock pillars. They seemed like remnants of some lost civilization. The silence of the place was broken only by the occasional puff of the steam engine and a gentle bubbling from the pools. We approached the pools with caution and felt the water. It was hot but not scalding.

"Soldiers! Form a ring around the pools!" the NKVD officer commanded.

The soldiers spread out, and we found ourselves surrounded by them. We didn't move. We had no control over a situation like this. Would they be allowed to attack and molest us? Already, there were smirks on their faces. A few mumbled suggestive comments. With all the prisoners unloaded, there were more of us than of them, but they had guns.

The NKVD officer took out his revolver and barked a command.

"Anyone who touches a woman will be shot!"

He gestured to all of us with the revolver.

"Move! Wash! You have twenty minutes."

We took off our dresses and cautiously moved to the warm blue pools. The first thing we did was wash our clothes clean of dirt and lice. We spread the dresses and my long johns on the rocks and stepped into the pools. Wet bras and underpants clung to our figures, and the guards watched us with hungry looks and suggestive grins. Why wouldn't they? Most of the women were not as undernourished as I still was. They had enough flesh on their bones to give these guards a tantalizing glimpse of forbidden temptations.

We didn't care. The warmth of the water was delicious. The feeling of being clean at last was so invigorating it revived our youthful spirits to the point that we almost forgot we were prisoners and relished the freedom of being in the open air. We became giddy, plunging under the water and jumping up into the cool air, laughing and splashing each other like children. Maybe it was the minerals in the water, or the strange rock formations, but we felt like we were all in a mystic, enchanted place, a fantasy Eden where nothing bad could happen. We grew bold and began flinging handfuls of water at the guards while they laughed and taunted us. Our behavior, on both sides, was a bizarre parody of light-hearted flirtation.

"Time's up!" the NKVD officer shouted. "This isn't a picnic. You may leave your wet clothes by the train to dry until the coal train passes. Stay inside the car." He focused on the ring of guards. "You men! No talking with the women. Any man caught having any unauthorized contact with the prisoners will be left in Vorkuta to work in the mines with them."

We toweled off with the burlap bags, gathered our dresses, and did as he commanded, draping the wet dresses on the ground behind Car Six. By now it was late afternoon. The coal train must have run into trouble up the line because three more hours passed without sight of it. A hazy dusk descended. The rock pillars took on a ghostly aura in the mist rising from the mineral pools. I had not retrieved my long johns yet because they took so long to dry. Still in my underwear, I went behind our car to get them. When I heard a couple of guards coming down the track, I crouched low so they wouldn't see me. They stopped next to our car. I couldn't see anything but their boots from underneath the cattle car. They kept their voices low.

"That was torture today, Vasya. I thought I was going to burst." The guard spoke Russian with a strange accent, like he was from one of the Central Asian republics.

"Me too, Osman. What a waste."

They must have lit cigarettes because I smelled the smoke. A burning match landed on the ground, and one guard stamped it out with his boot.

"Why shouldn't we get some action, Vasya?" Osman laughed. "Give them a few thrills before they hit the mines in Vorkuta, huh?"

"I bet half of them are virgins." Vasya grunted like a hog. "We could show them what they'll be missing."

They both laughed, and Osman said, "I saw the commandant break open another bottle of vodka today."

"Oooo!" Vasya whistled. "Something's eating him for sure."

"Probably the same as us," Osman said. "Women! But he can't do anything about it."

"Poor bastard. He'll be out cold in an hour. I say we move on the women then."

"What about the coal train?" Osman asked.

"Who knows when it'll get here?" Vasya didn't sound worried. "Tracks up north are always under repair."

"Which beauties do we pick? Can't have them all."

"So many choices, so little time," Vasya chuckled. "They're a bunch of feisty little bitches. Remember the rocking?"

"Yeah," Osman growled. "They should be good for some real action. There's a little blond I was hungry for all during that washing business."

"She's yours, pal."

"But what do we do about their screams, Vasya? This lot won't submit quietly."

"What do you think we've got guns for? Besides, this car's far enough from the commandant. If they scream, it won't be for long."

Osman threw down his cigarette and stamped it out. "I'll meet you here in an hour."

"Right. And bring four other guys. It'll be more fun with help to hold them down."

I waited until I was sure they had gone, then rushed around and rapped on the side of the car. Branca opened it quietly, just wide enough for me to get in.

"We've got trouble," I said. "I overheard a couple of guards planning to come here in an hour to rape us. They're bringing four more with them."

The women all cried out at once.

"Oh, God! I knew it would happen."

"It was stupid to taunt them at the pools."

"How can we escape it now?"

"They'll kill us if we resist. God help us!"

"We've got to do something!" Branca cut into the general chaos. "We can't just let them rape us."

"But they've got guns," Anichka said.

"I don't think they would shoot us," I said. "They'd be afraid. We're the property of the State. Remember the quota."

"You're right," the woman from Poland called out. "We have to fight back."

The Hungarian girl started to cry. "If we do, they'd probably beat us as well as rape us."

"For sure," Branca snapped. "There's nothing against delivering us bruised. The bastards!"

"Wait!" I called out. "Let me think."

"Make it quick," Branca said. "We haven't got much time."

I paced around and around, trying to think of something that would stop them before they could even get into our car. If they got in, we would be at their mercy. Then an idea came to me, so outrageous I wondered how I had come up with it. The question was, could I get all the women to agree? It would only work if we all took part. The other problem was, did we have enough *ammunition* to pull it off? I turned and faced them.

"I've got it! It's a wild plan, but it's our only hope." I motioned for them to gather around. "Here's what we're going to do."

CHAPTER SEVENTEEN

They were right on time, even a little early. Six of them. They pounded on our cattle car until it shook. Two of them sang a crude song, their words slurring, while the others laughed. One of them called out, "Rise and shine, ladies. It's time to party."

They dragged open the door to our cattle car and stood below, swaying on their feet, passing a bottle of vodka around. They had stupid grins on their faces, seeing ten of us lined up in the opening, looking down at them.

"Rejoice!" Another spread his arms wide. "We are answer to maiden's prayer."

We all shouted in unison. "Piss off!"

They laughed.

We smiled at them and raised our skirts. We wore no underwear. They were immediately silent, staring at us in surprise. When their expressions turned from surprise to lust, we did the unthinkable. We let go with a shower of urine. When one of us had given all she had, another would come forward and take her place. The urine rained down on their upturned faces. We shouted again.

"No one messes with the Pissers!"

It was wonderful to see their expressions change from greedy lust to shock. They cried out and covered their faces. Branca and I brought the latrine boots to the open door and flung that load of excrement down on them too. They groaned, slammed the boxcar door shut, and bolted it. We heard them swearing and shouting in disgust as they ran away.

"I can't believe we did that!" Anichka covered her face with her hands.

"I can't believe we got away with it!" Branca added.

"We're lucky they're drunk," I said. "If they'd been sober, they might have been more eager to take revenge."

"Let's hope we get to Vorkuta before they get another chance," Branca said.

Anichka's smile lit up her little face. "No one messes with the Pissers!" She raised a fist into the air.

We all raised our fists and shouted, "No one messes with the Pissers!"

Miriam Saves Me

★

CHAPTER EIGHTEEN

Vorkuta, Soviet Union
July 1945

After enduring the circles of hell I've passed through, I learned that sometimes Fate intervenes and throws a lucky chance your way. Until we arrived in Vorkuta, I had ceased to believe in luck. As far as I knew, Fate could care less about me or anyone. We make our own luck by taking action, good or bad, to endure, to change, or to save our lives. But in order to take that action, you need an opportunity. Fortunately, opportunity awaited us as our train, with a grinding screech of metal, pulled slowly up to the buffer stop in Vorkuta.

They thrust open the boxcar door before the train stopped. The women of Car Six crowded around, more curious than fearful. I understood it. They were young and still in good health despite the hardships of the journey. They hadn't lived my life. They had no previous experience with what to expect when a train filled with prisoners reaches its destination. Memories of my arrival at Auschwitz flooded in, and I approached the open doorway with every nerve in my body tight with apprehension.

"Snow!" Anichka turned to me in wonder. "It's snowing in summer!"

"And it's damn cold too," Branca said, hugging herself.

We learned later it was one of the freak summer blizzards that often occurred in the region. The air swirled with a dingy mixture of snow and coal dust. We had arrived at night, but since the Arctic sun never completely sets in the summer, Vorkuta was cloaked in a dismal gray. What we saw was chaos. It seemed everyone in town was running up the muddy street, away from the train. Prisoners, soldiers, guards, camp bosses, women, all carrying shovels and picks, all shouting. We watched them pass and waited for someone to take charge of us and give us orders. A guard appeared and shouted at us.

"Down! Now! Form a line. Don't move beyond your car."

We climbed down as we were told and stood shivering in the cold, waiting for guards to herd us off to whatever nightmare awaited new prisoners. I racked my brain for ways to deal with it. On the journey, we'd managed to control our fate through sheer luck. That would not be the case here. We were helpless to resist the brutality that surely awaited us.

A man carrying a shovel ran past, and I shouted at him, "What's going on? Why is everyone running?"

"There's been a collapse in one of the mines. We need everyone to clear the rubble and bring the bodies out." He hurried off up the street.

Suddenly, I saw our opportunity. I turned to the women of Car Six. "Pissers! This is our chance. I don't know what kind of official reception prisoners get in Vorkuta, but I'm sure it isn't a good one."

They nodded in agreement and looked fearfully down the track. Guards moved slowly up the line toward us, checking the supply cars first. Luck was with us.

"You heard the man," I said. "There's been a mining accident. If we voluntarily offer to help, we may escape the welcoming committee. If we stick together, we might pull it off, in case they give us trouble. We might even become heroes!"

The women agreed, and we started up the muddy street in a tight group. We made an odd sight, twenty of us marching through the blizzard, dressed in summer clothes, me leading in my now-grimy red long johns. We had no idea where the collapsed mine was, so we followed the crowd for what seemed to be a mile into the bleak tundra that surrounded Vorkuta. Finally, we came to low concrete buildings, mining machinery, and piles of coal. The snow started to stick, dusting the dirty buildings and machinery with a frosting of white.

Just before we reached the mine, a loud explosion nearly knocked us off our feet. A massive cloud of black dust billowed high into the air ahead of us. Women screamed and men shouted. We ran toward a crowd of male prisoners standing near the mine entrance. A camp boss shouted and shoved at them while the prisoners pushed and yelled back. All of them were black with coal dust. A mass of debris blocked the mine entrance.

"Get moving!" the camp boss shouted. "Clear this blockage!"

"We're not going in there!" a prisoner shouted back. "There's methane."

"It'll blow again, sure as hell!" another added.

The camp boss shouted back, "And more of your comrades will die if you don't get them out now! Unnecessary deaths are against camp policy and a waste of State resources."

"There's not enough room for a dog to squeeze in there now," the first prisoner said. "The shaft is blocked."

The second prisoner stood his ground. "We're not going in! Shoot us if you want. Better that than crushed or burned alive when the methane lights up."

I looked at the bodies already carried out of the mine. Some were clearly dead. Others lay moaning on the ground. They looked like they were sculpted of black stone. The snowfall covered them as well. I looked again at the mine entrance, a chaos of rock, coal, and broken timber posts. Black dust still drifted slowly from the interior.

The camp boss turned and noticed us. "What are you women doing here? Why aren't you in regulation clothes?"

"We're your fresh batch of workers." I pointed down the road. "We arrived on the latest train. We were never registered. Your problem with the mine explosion is more important than sorting out a bunch of women."

He looked back down the muddy road and frowned as if he didn't know what to do with us and didn't want trouble from his superiors.

"Get back to your train and go through the proper procedures. We can't be bothered with you here."

"No!" I said with as much *chutzpah* as I could muster. "You shipped us here to dig coal, and build socialism. We might as well get on with it. Better than standing around and freezing to death, waiting for someone to get organized. Workers are dying in there, and no one here wants to risk death to save them. We're willing to try."

I turned to the rest of the women. "Right?"

Anichka, bless her, stepped right up. "Right. And we're small. We can get inside easily."

"I always wondered why they were starving us," Branca mumbled sarcastically. "Clever."

"Hell!" the camp boss grumbled. "I'm not authorized to—"

"Do you want to save those men still inside or not?" I demanded.

The camp boss looked again at the stubborn prisoners, then back down the road, as if he expected the camp commandant to appear with a firing squad to take him prisoner.

"Send the women in," one prisoner growled. "They aren't registered yet. If they die, you won't have to account for them. We're not going in, and that's that."

The camp boss shrugged. "All right. Someone has to go. It may as well be you."

I turned back to the women. "Stick together. Let's go, Pissers. Show them what we're made of."

The male prisoners stepped aside, clearing the way for us. As we passed, they handed us picks and shovels and old acetylene lamps to wear like a headband.

"Women are crazy," one of them muttered.

"Good luck," another called to us. "You'll need it. You don't have a hope in hell."

CHAPTER NINETEEN

The men watched us as we formed an assembly line to move the rocks and timber from the mine entrance so we could get in to help those trapped. None of them, prisoners or guards or soldiers, lifted a finger to help us. I wasn't surprised. By volunteering to take on the dangerous job they refused to do, we had branded them cowards. Their hostility fired up our competitive spirit, and we worked with an energy we didn't know we had. Twenty women, unused to lifting heavy objects, found hidden strength. We paired up to shift the posts and enormous chunks of rock and coal. The camp boss showed us where to deposit the rubble away from the entrance. He seemed amused at our efforts. Maybe he hoped we would shame the men into helping.

We cleared the entrance and found the rubble lay farther into the mine than we'd thought. The assembly line continued as the smaller of us made our way in and passed debris out. Gradually, our path cleared, and we understood why the men had refused. There was so much rubble on the mine floor that we had to crawl on our hands and knees, and sometimes on our bellies, to make any progress. Anichka and I were the only ones small and thin enough to make it farther in.

How can I describe what it was like inside that mine? My father once told me a frightening story about an ancient labyrinth, an endless nightmare of twists and turns in dark passageways, with a monster who preyed on those who got lost trying to find their way out. I thought I had lived through enough horrors to be immune to fear. But the utter darkness inside the mine, the strange, sweet smell, almost like flowers, the coal-dusted icicles dripping black water onto the rubble, and the groaning echoes of the trapped men chilled my soul. I shook, not from the cold because, oddly, the inside of the mine was warmer than on the surface. I trembled with a nameless terror, an ancient animal fear of being trapped forever in darkness, of dying underground, buried alive.

Anichka and I stopped when we reached a place where the passageway split into two. Here was a pocket of colder air coming from some source deeper in the mine. I was afraid a sudden draft would snuff out the weak lights of our safety lamps, but they continued to burn. I told Anichka to stay put while I probed into one passage. When I heard her scream, I turned back so abruptly I banged my head on the low ceiling.

"Rats!" Anichka screamed again. "Rats!"

I heard her lamp fall to the ground. I bobbed my head up and down while the lantern cast points of light and shadow on the floor and walls. Small dark shapes ran through the light. Rats. I found Anichka trembling and taking deep breaths to suppress the terror. A larger dark shape leapt from the shadows. We heard a shrill, terrifying squeal and then nothing. As I moved the lantern around, it illuminated what looked like a giant rat but turned out to be a black short-haired cat, a dead rat hanging from its mouth. The cat padded softly over to Anichka and laid the rat at her feet.

"You have a champion, Anichka." I swung the lantern around the area. "I don't think the rats will come around for a while. The cat brought you a present. If you pet him, maybe he'll stick with us."

Anichka reached out, and the cat nuzzled her hand. "Good kitty," she crooned. "Thank you." She put her lantern back on her head. "I'm all right now. Which way do we go?"

"Who's there?" The voice was faint and came from the left passageway. "Help me. Please. Can't move. Post on my legs."

"We're coming!" I called.

Anichka and I made our way into the left passage. Soon, the space grew in width and height. We couldn't stand upright, but we could move forward, bent at the waist. The man lay with his back against the side of the tunnel. One of the wood posts used to shore up the tunnel had fallen in the blast and lay across both his legs. He groaned when he saw us.

"Oh, God! Not women. Useless!" He threw his head back and groaned again.

"We're the only ones who could get in," I said. "We'll get you out."

The post was around five feet long, thick, and heavy. I grabbed one end and Anichka the other. We couldn't lift it.

"Maybe we could roll it off his legs," Anichka said.

"No!" The man threw his arms out to stop her. "That would crush them, you idiot!"

"All right!" I snapped. "Let us figure it out."

He let out an exasperated sigh. "The post is waterlogged from the summer thaw. It's half again its dry weight. Both of you take one end. That way, you might be able to lift it enough for me to slide my legs out. If they're not broken."

"Do you think they are?" Anichka worried.

"I don't think so," the man mumbled. "But I can't be sure because they're both numb."

We did as he suggested, straining with the weight of the heavy, water-logged post.

"We should have done more strengthening exercises on the train," Anichka gasped. "It's not moving."

"It will," I said. "Let's count. One. Two. Three. LIFT!"

We groaned with the effort, but slowly the post rose off the man's legs.

"Hold it there!" he shouted with surprising force.

We stopped lifting and held the post a few inches above his legs, our muscles straining until we thought they would tear from the stress. My arms quivered, as Anichka's must have. If he didn't get his legs out soon, our arms might fail and the post fall on him. It seemed like an eternity as he slowly dragged his legs from underneath the post.

"Drop it!" he said.

We let it fall to the floor of the mine. Our hearts beat fast with the exertion, and we sat on the ground to catch our breath. The man probed his legs, squeezing and kneading them with his hands.

"Are they all right?" Anichka asked. "Not broken?"

"No. Damn it!" the man growled. "If they had been, I could have gotten time off."

"Let's get you out of here before there's another explosion or col-lapse," I said. "Can you crawl, or should we drag you? The passage nearer the surface is tight."

He made an effort to stand, but his legs buckled under him, and he sank to the ground with a curse. In the end, we half-dragged, half-pushed him to the mine opening where Branca and the rest of the women had cleared more rubble. They pulled him out the rest of the way, and a faint cheer erupted outside the mine. Some, at least, were glad he was safe.

Anichka and I went back in to hunt for more survivors. Deeper in the mine, the air smelled of rotten eggs. Was that the methane the men were so afraid of? The open-flame lanterns on our heads worried me, but what could we do? The cat appeared again and followed us. He didn't seem affected by the smell, so I figured we were all right. We took the passageway to the right this time and soon found two more miners. They appeared to be asleep but woke when we shook them, then stared at us in wonder.

"Angels," one of them muttered.

The other lay back down and closed his eyes. We couldn't take both at once, so we roused the groggier one. He had a broken arm but could use his legs. We helped him through the difficult passageway. Nearer the opening, he seemed to revive with the fresher air.

He stared at the cat, rubbing against his legs. "Vanya!" He laughed. "Hello, you old rat-catcher. Glad you survived. Used up another one of your nine lives though. Stay alert, old fellow."

"Anichka." I touched her arm. "You can get him out now. The others will help you. I'll go back and get the other one. The gas is stronger. We may not have much more time."

I hurried back into the mine and down the right passage. The other man stared at me with wide eyes and a strange, twisted grin.

"You came back." He licked his lips and gave a low moan.

"I don't have any food," I said, unsure what he wanted. "I'm here to help you."

"Don't want food from you. Got a different hunger. You can help that for sure."

I had a bad feeling about him. Something about his voice and the way his breath came in short, quick gasps. I was sure the gas was affecting him. I was feeling lightheaded myself.

"We have to get out of here fast," I said, moving toward him. "The passageway is cleared enough now. The gas is getting stronger. Can you walk?"

"Then we'll have to be quick," he said as he lunged for me.

He took me completely off-guard. Under any other circumstances, I would have recognized the signs, but not under the current circumstances. A trapped man, facing death in a collapsed mine with deadly gas building up to a potential explosion, was looking to rape a woman who had come to save him. He pawed and tore at my filthy long johns like a rabid dog. I fought him with fists and knees and feet, yelling curses and finally screaming for help. I didn't think about if anyone could hear me this far into the mine. I fought with fury at the depravity of human existence in these forsaken places.

I thought I heard Branca's voice calling me. Other voices joined in. I shouted as loudly as I could.

"Shut up, you damn bitch!"

I felt something hard on my head. I heard a ringing far away. The mine lit up in orange and yellow stars of bright light. Something like thunder sounded inside my head, and the world turned black.

CHAPTER TWENTY

I woke to a whiteness so blinding it felt like needles stabbing into my eyes. I closed them, but the stabbing continued. I opened them again, very slowly. The blinding light gradually came into focus as a white circular pan with a brilliant bulb in the center. I tried to remember where I had seen it before. I knew. The interrogation room at the NKVD headquarters in Bardejov. I waited for an NKVD officer to appear. Nothing happened. I became aware of something soft under me. *Not a hard floo , then. A bed?* My eyes searched the room, moving from the blinding light across a white ceiling to where it met a white wall. *Why is everything white?* My eyes still had trouble focusing as they moved down the wall until they passed over a cabinet and stopped. I stared hard at it, trying to make out what I saw. It was tall and narrow, made of metal, with glass doors. Inside were what looked like bottles, small and large, with labels pasted on them. *Medicine bottles?* My vision cleared. There were glass beakers, a stack of bandages, metal instruments. I knew now where I was. I cried out in panic.

"Mengele. No! Please! Not Mengele."

"Mengele?" a soft female voice asked. "Is that your name? Mengele?"

Her face materialized close to mine. She had dark hair showing around a white scarf. She wore a doctor's white lab coat, instruments in the breast pocket, a stethoscope around her neck. *Dear God! No! I've got to escape. I know what they do to women.* I pushed myself up on the bed. She grasped my arm, and I pulled away and rolled to the other side of the bed. She grabbed me just before I rolled off and held me down, gently but firmly.

"It's all right." Her voice was soothing. "You're safe here. No one will hurt you. This is a hospital."

I know about hospitals. I know about soft-spoken female doctors. I struggled to get up.

"Please lie still," she said. "You've had a severe blow to your head. I feared a concussion because you were unconscious for such a long time."

I sat up and immediately lay down again. The pain in my head was excruciating.

"Who are you?" I whispered, fearing the answer.

"I'm Doctor Miriam Eliashvili. In charge of this hospital."

"How did I get here?"

"You had an . . . accident. The camp boss brought you in."

Memory flooded back. "The mine! That bastard!"

The doctor smiled. "Good. You remember. I would like you to answer a few questions for me. Just to see how well you're recovering."

I watched her go over to a table and get some sheets of paper. She moved slowly, with a slight limp. Offhand, I wondered what injury she had, how she got it. She pulled a chair next to the bed and sat.

"Where are you?" she asked.

"In a Soviet prison camp in Siberia," I grumbled.

"Very good."

"Not really."

She smiled. "A sense of humor is encouraging."

"I wasn't being funny."

"How did you get here?"

"In a filthy cattle car." I struggled again to get up. "Anichka and Branca! Where are they? Did they get out before the explosion?"

"Are they the two girls who got you out of the mine?"

"Did they do that?"

"Yes. There was no explosion. You were hit on the head with a piece of rock by the man who attacked you. Your friends gave him more than a few bruises."

"Good for them. Are they all right?"

"They're fine. Don't worry. I'll tell them you're feeling better."

Suddenly, I didn't feel better about anything. We had worked so hard to bring the men out of the mine, and what was our reward? Assaulted by one of them. And what was our future? Attacks by men little more than beasts. Work in those hellish mines until we all died.

"Feeling better," I said with real bitterness. "Until the next time and the next."

The doctor said nothing, just filled in the form and asked, "What is your name?"

"Celia Klein."

"You're not Russian." It was a statement, not a question.

"No, I'm Czechoslovak."

"Then why are you here in the USSR?"

Her questions were becoming stupid. Did she really think there was a reason?

"I guess Czechoslovakia didn't have any prison space for me." I glared at her. "Or maybe the USSR needed more slaves, and my government obliged them. I've stopped trying to understand the ways of men and governments, Doctor. I'm here. That's enough."

She was so patient.

"You must have been accused of something. They usually have a reason."

"Fine. They accused me of being a spy. For the Americans, because I had some American Dollars and a couple of American chocolate bars. For the Germans, because I had some worthless Nazi money. Oh, and I was a spy for the French, because they gave me two dresses with French labels when mine was in tatters."

"You speak German?"

I couldn't resist the irony of that question. "Oh, yes. I was privileged to attend a very select concentrated German language course for nearly three years."

"In a concentration camp called Auschwitz?" she asked in that soft voice of hers.

I instinctively drew my arm behind my back.

"I'm sorry," she said. "I saw the number when I was examining you."

I wondered if it really mattered in this desolate place above the Arctic Circle. I had noticed all the prisoners around the mine had numbers on their clothes. They may not have numbers tattooed on their skin, but they were numbered just the same. Numbered. Like cattle.

"I guess it doesn't matter here," I said. "At least the Communists don't tattoo a number on you. Careless, don't you think? The Germans are much more thorough." I wasn't sure about the answer to my next question. "The Communists don't gas you either. Right?"

She sighed. "Right. This is a place of *slow* extermination. They simply starve and work you to death."

"Not very efficient," I said.

"It depends on what your object is."

"What is the object?"

She said nothing and returned to the form. "Your mother?"

"Dead."

"Father?"

For some reason, I didn't want to tell her my father might be alive. Or maybe I didn't want to hope anymore. My sentence was ten years in Siberia. If he weren't dead, he would be by the time I was released—if I *was* released. If he heard of my fate, it would probably kill him.

"Dead."

She made a note. "Brothers and sisters?"

"Sisters. Dead."

"Any other relations?"

"I would guess all my relatives are dead. German efficiency, remember?"

She nodded. "How old were you when they took you to Auschwitz?"

"I had just turned sixteen."

She didn't ask another question. Just waited for me to go on. I knew what she wanted to ask. Why was I still alive? She was intelligent enough to figure that out for herself. I hadn't seen much of Vorkuta, but I'd seen enough to know it was another hell, where you either burned to death or became one of the devils. What did people do here to survive? I shivered to think of the future.

"What you want to know is how I survived." I felt Cilka coming back. How easy it was to resurrect her. "I survived because . . . because I was useful to them. I became what I had to become and did what I had to do. They made me what I am, Doctor. The world is nothing but lies and hatred and greed. I learned that lesson well. I will never be that young girl again. She died in Auschwitz."

The doctor just smiled. I didn't understand it. Why?

She continued with the form. "I see you went home after being released from Auschwitz."

"I did. Back to my family home." I realized I *wanted* to tell her what happened, not for sympathy, but because it was proof of what I said about the world. "People we knew . . . before. They had taken it over and were living there. I was good friends with Sofi . . . their daughter. I thought they would be glad I survived." I laughed then. "I was so stupid."

"They didn't want to give up your house, is that it?"

"It wasn't just that. They had come to hate Jews. I don't think they did . . . before. But now they do. The whole town is like that. People I'd known all my life wouldn't even look at me. It was like I was a total stranger. Like someone with a disease. Someone to shun."

"You said the NKVD had money and dresses of yours. How did they come to have those things?"

"I don't know for sure, but it had to be Sofi's mother. She must have gone through my few things when I went out to walk around town and look for work. She probably reported it to the NKVD. They arrested me only a day after I came home." I looked the doctor in the eye. "I told you. Lies and hatred and greed. I trust no one. Never again."

She got up, folded the report, put it in her pocket, and looked down at me, considering. "You've suffered more than anyone should, Celia. I understand your anger and bitterness."

"You mean bitterness at visiting hell not once but twice?" I laughed and finished it coughing. "And the best part is I'm still young. Tell me, Doctor. After my ten years here, how many more circles of hell can I visit?"

"I can't answer that," she said. "But none, I hope."

She had the kindest eyes. Kind eyes in Vorkuta! How did she do it?

"But I can say, given your health after Auschwitz, you won't survive a week in the mines."

"Who cares? What's the point of living anyway?"

"There is a point, and I'm going to give you a chance to figure out what it is. I'm giving you a job in the hospital. I need a full-time assistant nurse. Knowing your history, I'm sure you've seen worse cases of physical and mental abuse than even this hospital sees. I can tell you're strong-minded and strong-willed. What you see here won't shock you." She smiled that little smile again. "But a nurse's job is helping and healing others. Giving them hope. Who knows? You might even find some hope yourself."

"Hope in hell?"

"Yes. Even there. I want you to rest for a week. I'm doubling your rations during that time so we can fatten you up a bit."

"Don't waste your time on me, Doctor."

"We'll see. Now rest."

She walked to the door. I stopped her.

"Tell me, Doctor. Why are you here? In hell, I mean."

She turned back. "A tale of revenge is not an appropriate bedtime story." She turned off the light. "Good night, Celia. I'll see you tomorrow."

She walked out and quietly closed the door. I lay there in the dark, wondering what had inspired her to save me. I knew she was right about working in the mines. I would be dead in a week.

Ten years in Vorkuta.

I wasn't sure I wanted to be saved.

CHAPTER TWENTY-ONE

I awoke with a crushing headache and a deep depression. The energy that had sustained me yesterday through the rescue of the men in the mine drained away like sand in an hourglass, leaving only the empty reality of the ten bleak years of life ahead of me. The only experience I'd had with evil had been Nazi concentration camps. The things I had done to survive those camps at sixteen changed me completely and still haunted me, day and night. Liberation had finally come, and with it, the return of hope. A hope founded on the idea that I could bury the past three years and become someone I thought was dead. The old Celia—Little Cilka. My father's darling. The girl with the bright smile and loving heart.

What a fool I was. She was dead. As dead as all those others with bright smiles and loving hearts I had seen murdered. But the Nazis hadn't killed my father's darling.

I had.

I lay in the white hospital room, staring at the dingy gray window. Outside, tiny snowflakes still fell, blown by the Arctic wind. Snow in summer! I couldn't escape the feeling that Vorkuta was my punishment. Why had I been condemned to live? I didn't know what I was expected to endure in this new hell, but I already knew I would not be allowed to escape by dying. The doctor with the kind eyes had seen to that. I was not to work in the mines. I was to learn to help and heal. I was to find hope in hell for those condemned. And maybe for myself.

She was either a saint or a fool. Or both.

The door opened, and she walked in.

"Good morning, Celia."

I started to ask what was good about it, but she stopped me.

"I'm sure your headache is still intense, but you have a visitor this morning who can't be kept waiting. The camp commandant has something to tell you."

In my experience, camp commandants only visited prisoners to deliver bad or fatal news. I could imagine what he had to tell me. I hadn't waited to follow orders when we arrived in Vorkuta. And I had taken twenty women with me. We may have been a help at the mine, but we had also acted *independently*. They do not tolerate independent behavior in an authoritarian society, Fascist or Communist. Follow orders, stay with the group, don't think, don't act. I wondered what punishment I would get. Not that it mattered.

The commandant was not what I expected. The ones I remembered from Auschwitz embodied the precision and efficiency of Nazi Germany in their smart uniforms. They had a vain obsession with neatness and order. Their jackets were crisp, their jodhpurs well-fitting, their boots mirror black, every button and emblem polished to a shine. Even the NKVD officer who had interrogated me in Bardejov had been neat and precise.

The commandant of Vorkuta was shabby by comparison. His ill-fitting uniform, faded and worn, had seen better days. It hung on him as though he had lost weight. His face was weathered, like dry leather. He might have been thirty or sixty. He looked tired, but his posture was upright and solid. The odd thing about him was his eyes. Clear blue, sharp as Arctic ice, they missed nothing. And yet, they seemed to carry a spark of surprising humanity.

"Prisoner Klein." His voice rasped, hoarse and gravelly, probably from years of shouting into the fierce winds of Siberia. "I've come to apologize for what happened to you in the mine yesterday. I have dealt the prisoner who attacked you a harsh punishment he won't soon forget. I congratulate you on your service to the State in selflessly rescuing those men."

He waved a hand, and Anichka and Branca came into the room. They wore regulation camp clothing, padded jackets and pants to protect against the cold. Oddly, their heads were not shaved, as I had noticed on other women when we marched to the mine yesterday. I wondered why. They both smiled at me. I was glad to see them.

"I have also congratulated your friends here for their bravery and quick thinking," the commandant continued. "The State has awarded them extra rations and sturdy winter clothes. I have housed all twenty women of your group in a separate barracks in honor of their teamwork and as an inspiration to other prisoners to work collectively for the good of all. The USSR will always recognize loyal builders of the Socialist State." He came to the bed and shook my hand. "I wish you a speedy recovery."

"Thank you," I whispered.

Doctor Eliashvili spoke up. "We all thank you very much, Commandant, for taking the time to apologize to Prisoner Klein."

"It has been my pleasure." He smiled, then turned and left the room.

Anichka and Branca looked at Doctor Eliashvili for further instructions.

"You may stay with Celia for another ten minutes," she said. "I am required to stay in the room with you, but feel free to talk. I do not report conversations among patients."

Anichka and Branca came to the bed and looked down at me with concerned expressions.

"Will you be all right?" Anichka asked. "We were afraid you were dead."

"We gave that bastard what he deserved," Branca said. "He's got a couple of scars to remind him too."

"Yes." Anichka grimaced. "But he was furious. He swore he would take revenge on us as soon as he could."

"I wouldn't worry too much," Doctor Eliashvili said. "The fact that the commandant put all of you in your own separate barracks means he's aware of the situation. He will probably also order the guards to watch for trouble near your barracks. Not that you shouldn't be on the alert yourselves."

"You can bet on that," Branca said. "The other miners weren't too happy either. We showed them up. And we're new women. We've already learned enough about how things are here to keep all the Pissers on alert."

"They better not try anything." Anichka made a fist and punched the air. "No one messes with the Pissers."

"Will they make you work in the mines?" I asked, dreading the answer. Anichka wouldn't survive any better than I would. And she would be constantly terrified of the rats.

"I don't think so," Branca said. "A camp boss came around last night and told us we would start in the clay yard. I guess that means working outside, digging clay, and forming bricks."

"We might work in the brick factory too," Anichka said. "They have to dry the bricks and it will be warm inside." She shrugged. "At least I hope that's where we'll be when it's well below freezing."

Branca held out her arms and turned around. "How do you like our new outfits? The very latest. I doubt they're wearing them in Paris this winter, but I have to admit they're warmer than I hoped for." She raised her leg to show a thick gray felt boot. "They call them *valenki*. They're actually quite warm, at least for now."

Anichka went to stand beside Branca. "We look a little like stuffed teddy bears."

They both laughed. I wondered how quickly they would lose their good spirits.

"Oh," Anichka said. "I found out about Vanya."

"Vanya?" I asked.

"The cat who saved me from the rat. I hoped to bring him out of the mine and keep him as a pet, but the workers wouldn't let me. They said Vanya must work too. He's important for the collective because he always over-fulfills his quota of rats. That makes him an *udarnik*, a shock worker. He's famous in the camp." Anichka smiled. "And he eats very well."

Doctor Eliashvili said, "I'm afraid you will have to go now. Celia needs to rest, and you must be in your barracks when the morning rations are finished and it's time to report for work."

"Can we come back sometime?" Anichka asked.

"We'll see," Doctor Eliashvili said, giving a ray of hope where there was probably none.

They hugged me goodbye. After they left, the doctor checked me over.

"You are to avoid any sudden or unnecessary movements of your head. I want you to eat anything I bring you and to drink water whenever your glass is full. You should be ready to begin training for hospital work in a few days."

"The commandant," I said. "Does he really believe all that stuff about the State?"

"Yes and no." She paused. "He's not a bad person, really. Even though he carries the title of commandant, it's the head of the NKVD who has the final say."

"You sound like you know him."

"I do. The commandant is the reason this hospital has sufficient supplies and medicines. Do you think all camp hospitals are this well-cared-for and clean?"

"I wouldn't know. In Auschwitz, a hospital was the place they put you to die or be experimented on. Fresh paint was not an issue. But how do you know the camp commander?"

Doctor Eliashvili sat on the end of the bed and looked at me.

"When I first came here, this hospital was my worst nightmare. It was filthy, falling apart, and stocked with nothing more useful than a couple of bottles of alcohol and a few gray rags. Rats lived inside the walls, and you could hear them running around at night. It was a place to get infected instead of healed. I had worked in an up-to-date research hospital back home in Georgia. Outraged, I complained day after day to no purpose."

"In other words, no one cared," I said.

"Exactly. Until the commandant's five-year-old son came down with typhus. Little Sergei was extremely sick, and the terrible climate here in Vorkuta complicated the illness. The commandant begged me to find a cure. We had no medications that would suffice." She shook her head. "Vorkuta is dead last on the list of medical needs in the USSR. However, I was from Tbilisi. Georgia is the center of bacteriophage therapy research. I had seen what it could do, and I used it on little Sergei. He recovered with no lasting ill effects. His grateful father promised me anything I wanted. He even offered to give me my freedom."

I sat up so quickly the room spun. Doctor Eliashvili gently pushed me back down.

"Good God!" I moaned. "Why didn't you take it?"

"Perhaps I should have," she sighed. "But there was nothing for me back home except isolation. As an enemy of the State, I would not be allowed back into research in Tbilisi. I was looking at the most menial of jobs. If I stayed here, I might make a real difference in suffering. I asked for a good hospital here in Vorkuta. I demanded medicine and instruments. The commandant said he would do what he could to give it to me." She looked proudly around the room. "I think we did all right. Don't you?"

"I would have gotten out of here. No matter what. You're too good, Doctor."

"I'm not, Celia. I'm just a woman whose passion is medicine. If this is the only place I can practice, then this is the place I will stay." She smiled at me. "And you can call me Miriam when we're alone. Not in public, of course. It would get both of us in trouble."

"Miriam. That's a Jewish name."

"The sister of Moses and Aaron. Yes, I'm Jewish. That's another reason I'm sympathetic to your plight. Our people have a long history of persecution and struggle. You have had more than your share. And at too young an age. I can't change your unjust sentence, but I can mitigate its damage. Call it a *mitzvah*."

"Don't waste your *mitzvah* on me."

"A *mitzvah* can never be wasted, Celia." Her eyes softened. "What are we here for but to seize the opportunity to help another when the need arises?" She got up. "I'll leave you now. Someone will bring you some breakfast. Be sure to eat all of it. I need you to do me a *mitzvah* and get well enough to help me help others."

She went toward the door, and I stopped her. "Miriam? You never told me how you got here. The bedtime story of revenge."

Miriam paused with her hand on the doorknob and then turned back.

"I did the unforgivable, Celia. I insulted Comrade Stalin."

"How did he find out? Did someone inform on you?"

"Probably, but it wasn't surprising. I made copies of a joke in the form of a poem about Comrade Stalin and left them in as many places as I could. It was foolish. But I was furious."

"Why?"

"Because a significant number of my esteemed and talented colleagues and close friends in Georgia disappeared without a trace in a very short time. The poem poked fun at Stalin's physical attributes. It wasn't very nice. And it accomplished nothing."

"And for that, they sent you to Vorkuta?"

"For twenty-five years."

"Twenty-five years?" I thought nothing could appall me anymore. "Good God! Why?"

Doctor Miriam smiled again, but it was a bit off-center. "Some people just don't have a sense of humor."

She turned and walked out the door, leaving me again wondering how she could be so calm and caring. She was no fool. She *was* a saint. I felt profoundly unworthy in the face of her patient endurance.

Ten Years in Vorkuta

★

CHAPTER TWENTY-TWO

I fell from one circle of hell—Auschwitz—to another. Vorkuta was a place of living death. The agonizing cold, the gnawing, never-ending pain in empty stomachs, the constant fear of punishment by the authorities or persecution by the criminals, the depressing darkness for half the year, and the mind-numbing monotony of labor with no end or reward bred a desperate hopelessness that seemed eternal. How can I recount the despair of those who worked for years in the darkness beneath the earth, sometimes digging coal with their bare hands for want of tools? Or reveal how starvation and hard labor reduced once intelligent and talented men and women to pitiful creatures whose thoughts focused only on their next piece of dry bread or watery soup. Men were transformed into savages by a system that gave power to criminals and sadists. Women struggled to live in an environment of abuse, where submission to the most primitive appetites of human nature was the only means of survival.

There was no escape. Those who tried were shot in the attempt, dragged back, and beaten, or, if they got far enough, froze to death on the merciless tundra. Some simply went mad, which was a kind of escape, I suppose. The horror was endless, death the only release. But death took a long time. In Auschwitz, death for most was immediate because the goal of the Nazis was extermination. In Vorkuta, the goal of the Communists was to squeeze every last ounce of work out of prisoners before they died. Doctor Eliashvili was right when she said Vorkuta was a place of *slow* extermination.

Those ten years I endured seemed endless, and many times, I was in deep despair. But human beings have an incredible ability to find something to ease the burden of their suffering: friendship, humor, creativity, faith—things you would think impossible to find in such a place. But I did find them, and each time my anger and despair lifted for a moment, I felt almost free.

I had turned my back on friendships long ago. Nearly all my friends from the time before I was sent to Auschwitz were dead. The few who were still alive, like Sofi, felt estranged because of what had happened to me, because of their guilt, because of prejudice. And there were people I had betrayed through actions I would never have dreamed possible before Auschwitz. Actions I was driven to by a fierce desire to live. In the bizarre world of the Nazi camps, those who formed friendships walked a treacherous path that could lead to death. With sadistic pleasure, the Nazis exploited the simple emotions of love, compassion, and friendship. They seemed to enjoy forcing people into impossible choices, like deciding which of your friends would live or die, your own life in the balance. They conditioned you by twisting compassion into a disobedience that was severely punished, a weapon of torture.

This wasn't so for me in Vorkuta, but it was because Doctor Miriam had saved me. If I'd had to work in the mines, or the clay pits, or any of the other physically destructive labors, I would have shunned friends as I had before. But my job in the hospital demanded I care for the sick, the battered, the dying. Compassion was necessary, not something to be feared.

Having friends I cared about, and doing what I could to help them, relieved the dreariness. In those moments, I was a normal young woman. Until the moment passed, and Vorkuta closed in once again. Despite the bleak darkness, the bonds I had formed with Anichka and Branca endured. I lived at the hospital because we were always overwhelmed with patients. Anichka and Branca lived in the barracks assigned to the twenty of us, whom Anichka liked to call, the Pissers.

The three of us vowed to get together at least one or two Sundays a month. Strange as it was, everyone got Sundays off in Vorkuta. Perhaps on the theory that a little rest would prolong the working life of the State's slaves. Whatever the reason, our Sunday get-togethers kept our friendship alive. I often brought some extra bits of food from the rations left over in the hospital by patients too sick or depressed to eat. We made do. We talked mostly of our lives in Vorkuta and tried to help each other in any way we could. Sharing these little things made life more bearable.

We plotted strategies together, commiserated together, cried together. And more often than I could have imagined, we laughed, desperate to squeeze every drop of humor we could out of life. When we were with each other, we no longer felt like slaves. When we laughed together, our spirits were free.

There were scarcely any interesting events in our lives to relieve the routine suffering. Whenever one of us heard of some unusual incident, a bit of curious gossip, or an amusing story about one of the prisoners, we would eagerly await our Sunday meeting to share the tale. Moments like these were rare. Unusual happenings took on a larger-than-life quality.

The strangest event I witnessed was that of Anichka and the criminal bosses of Vorkuta. These bosses were not political prisoners but men convicted of ordinary crimes. They were murderers, thieves, and common thugs that the commissars used to keep all the political prisoners in line and working through intimidation and beatings. For us, striking a bargain with the criminals was almost impossible. Even if a prisoner managed to, the criminals would often turn on him just for sport.

Many of these criminals in Vorkuta came from the Indigenous peoples of Siberia, and they brought their tribal beliefs and customs with them. They were highly superstitious, believing in the supernatural world of benevolent and evil spirits, in animal spirit guides, and in the power of trance and storytelling. They tattooed their bodies with symbols of these spirits and wore amulets and other crude jewelry made from scrap metal, stones, animal bones, and even coal. When things went bad for the criminals, they would seek out a spiritual guide they called a shaman.

The shaman of the criminal group in our camp had recently died, and they were on the lookout for the person they believed would house the wandering spirit of their dead spiritual leader. Why they chose Anichka is one of the most unusual stories of my ten years in Vorkuta.

CHAPTER TWENTY-THREE

The *Shamanka* of Vorkuta

Branca, Anichka, and I arranged to meet in the *zemlyanka*, an abandoned dugout earth-house by the cemetery. We didn't know how old the *zemlyanka* was. It was dilapidated but well camouflaged, perfect for our private meetings. In summer, grass stubble, blackened by the eternal coal dust, covered the mound of earth. An old wooden door, rotting now, shored up the entrance. It leaned precariously, as if it would cave in and bury anyone who might venture inside. The rest of the year, the entrance was just a small black hole in a mound of snow and ice. It was the only relatively warm, secluded place in the interminable winter where we could be private. The guards hardly ever went near the cemetery unless there was a burial. Although burials happened often, they rarely happened on a Sunday. The criminals and their bosses also stayed away from the cemetery, mainly because they believed the angry spirits of dead prisoners hovered there, waiting to take revenge on any of their former tormentors who had the misfortune to pass by. We were always watchful for discovery on our way there, but once inside the *zemlyanka*, we were hidden. There was no reason for anyone else to go there. The place was dirty, cramped, and dark. We didn't care. It was our secret gathering place.

One winter Sunday during the second year of our time in Vorkuta, I waited inside the *zemlyanka* for Branca and Anichka. I had brought a little food from the hospital. A patient had died, and Miriam had given me the patient's uneaten rations to share with my friends. I also had two candles, which I hoped would provide not only some light but also a feeling of heat.

"Anichka!" Branca's voice carried in the quiet air outside. "I thought you weren't going to make it today."

I could hear Branca stomping through the snow, and I peered out of the opening. Anichka stood clutching a bundle of rags. Branca helped her over a couple of logs and pulled her into the *zemlyanka*. She drew our makeshift door of brush and old pieces of wood over the entrance and crawled inside to crouch by me at the back of the tiny space. The *zemlyanka* wasn't big enough to stand up inside. We were like three moles.

"Candles!" Branca exclaimed. "What luxury! I can actually see you for a change."

"I also have a little food from the hospital," I said, handing a hunk of bread and a thin piece of cheese to Branca and Anichka.

"Cheese!" Anichka exclaimed. "What a miracle!"

"Careful, Celia," Branca teased. "You're going to get a reputation for being bourgeois."

Anichka sat down on the branches we had laid on the dirt floor to protect against the cold. She hugged the bundle of rags and looked at us with a bright but hesitant expression.

"I have something I want to show you." She unwrapped the rags.

Two lumps of coal lay in her lap. What could she find of special interest to us in lumps of coal? Every day, we tripped over lumps of it, kicked it aside as we walked, breathed its dust in the air, struggled to get its blackness off our hands and faces. Had Vorkuta finally worked its evil spell on Anichka? Was her mind slowly becoming unbalanced? Anichka studied the coal lumps, a little frown creasing her brow. Then she chose two and held them out. Branca and I each took one.

"Please look at them and tell me what you think," Anichka said.

At first, I saw only a shiny black hunk of coal. It was hard to see anything special about it. I held the object nearer to the candles and inspected it. In my hand, the figure of a small black bear stood on four short legs, his muzzle raised as if smelling the air, his ears bent forward to hear the slightest sound. I could see his beady eyes, the shape of his nose, his slightly open mouth. Random scratches on the surface gave the impression of fur. The little piece of coal was a work of art.

"Anichka!" I exclaimed. "It's beautiful."

"Do you like it?" She bit her lower lip.

Branca moved closer to the candles as well. Her little coal figurine was a howling wolf, sitting with its bushy tail curled around. The detail was so lifelike that I could almost see the cold moonlight and hear the howl echoing across the tundra.

I wasn't a woman given to flights of imagination. Auschwitz had killed whatever creative soul I had as a young girl, made me a fighter, not a dreamer. The only imaginings I had were visions of torture, sickness, and the gas chambers. But I had changed since coming to Vorkuta and working in the hospital with Miriam. The change had not come easily. Gradually, I learned not to scold, not to speak harshly, not to overpower patients with my will. Miriam's example taught me the healing power of a kind word for the suffering. Smiles were difficult to produce. I worried sometimes that I had lost the ability to smile, but Miriam said it would come in time.

I had a rare smile on my face now as I turned back to Anichka.

"Did you carve these?"

"Yes. It's so bleak here. I couldn't find anything beautiful to look at. Even the snow is never allowed to be soft and white. It's always gray and black with coal dust. But the coal itself has a beauty of its own. I love the shine, the blackness of it. I like the way every lump has a different shape. I found myself just gazing at the lumps I picked up and trying to find different animals or objects in the shapes. These were two lumps where I saw definite animals. I had such an urge to carve them into a little bear and wolf." Anichka held her hand out, and Branca gave her back the little wolf. "I'm afraid of wolves. I know they don't get into the camp, but I've heard them howl out there on the tundra. I thought if I turned a coal lump into a wolf, I might feel less afraid."

"We never knew you could do anything like this, Anichka," Branca said. "You've been hiding your talent under a bushel of coal, as the new saying goes. I wish I could do something half as special as this. Where did you learn to carve so well?"

"When I was in school back home," Anichka said softly. "Before all this, I had a teacher who thought it was important that each person try to see if they had any creative skills. She had us try different artist things. Musical instruments, painting, acting, sculpting. I liked sculpting best of all. She said I had a gift for it. I used to carve all kinds of things out of all kinds of different materials. I liked wood best. But there's no wood here, just scrub bushes. So I tried coal."

I handed the little bear back to her. She held both figures in her hands and studied them.

"I was going to ask you something about these," Anichka said. "I was wondering if I could trade them for extra food or clothes. I know they don't have any real worth. I mean, you can't eat them, and they won't keep you warm. Still, I think people need something special, particularly here. A man in one of the barracks draws pictures for one of the guards. He draws whatever the guard asks for. I've heard they're not very nice pictures. Mostly of naked women. With big breasts." Branca and I laughed. "The guard gives him extra rations for each one."

"I've seen some of them," Branca said. "The guard gave a couple to one woman who works in the clay pit. He visits her a lot. She laughed at the pictures. Said he could fantasize all he wanted, she wasn't going to do anything like that. They were disgusting."

"Well, Anichka won't sculpt anything disgusting," I said, hugging her. "Trading them for things is a good idea, but the prisoners are not your best customers. They have nothing themselves and even less to give away. The criminal bosses might be a good choice. They've got lots of food and clothes, and even money. But . . ."

"Oh, Celia!" Anichka gasped. "I could never approach the criminal bosses. They're so mean and brutal. I would be scared to death. And what would they want with little figures of animals?"

"Celia's right," Branca argued. "I've heard stories about the criminals. A lot of them come from Siberia, tribal guys who just went crazy and committed crimes. But I've heard they're superstitious. Supposedly, they believe that everything around is occupied by some supernatural being. Rocks, trees, animals. Who knows, they might want your little coal animals for some superstitious reason, like protection or something."

"Branca, I couldn't go to them." Anichka shivered. "I just couldn't."

"I'll go with you," Branca offered. "I'm tough. Besides, you need someone to negotiate the price for you. They're used to being paid, not paying others. I'll find a way to arrange a meeting outside somewhere. You just carve a couple more animals you think might be powerful spirits. We can talk about how lifelike they are and how we think they hold some kind of magic. One thing I've learned here is to never pass up an opportunity. Even if they say no, at least you tried."

"All right." Anichka didn't sound enthusiastic. "But only if you're with me."

"I won't leave your side. You think I would throw you to those wolves? No! They'll come to reasonable terms, or they'll have to deal with me."

We all laughed at Branca's bravado, but not without a level of fear. The criminals were a terrifying force in the camp, especially for women. They took what they wanted and were often vicious just for the sport. Why had I ever suggested such a thing? It wasn't like I didn't know what they were. I had had several encounters with the criminals at the hospital. Knife wounds were the usual reason they ended up in our care. Fights over old tribal animosities and vendettas. When one of them landed in the hospital, a couple of his buddies always came with him to make sure we did our job to their satisfaction. Their physical appearance alone was frightening.

The three of us didn't meet again for an entire month. The weather turned nasty and the hospital was overwhelmed with cases. When we could get together again, Branca and Anichka were waiting for me at the *zemlyanka*, with an amazing story to tell. I felt bad because I couldn't bring any food this time. But I brought candles again. In the warm light, I could see Anichka's big smile. A necklace of bones hung around her neck, bones of varying shapes and sizes, separated by oddly shaped pieces of metal.

"Celia!" Anichka's eyes glowed in the dim yellow light. "We have sausages! Real ones. Not sawdust!" She pulled two sausages from her pocket, tore off a piece, and handed it to me. "You were right. The criminal bosses love my carvings." She dug again in the pocket of her jacket. "I have bread too. Not stale!" She laughed. "We can have a real sandwich."

"What did they say?" I asked. "What did they *think*?"

Anichka gave Branca a hunk of bread. "Branca was great," she chirped. "She got one of the guards to arrange a meeting between us and one of the criminal bosses. I don't know how she did it, but I'm glad that guard was with us. He was just as big and tough-looking as the criminal boss. Taller too. I think he made the boss pay attention."

"A guard?" I looked to Branca for an explanation. Her eyes rolled up to study the ceiling, such as it was. I guessed it was a story she wouldn't share, so I didn't press her. "That was fortunate."

"Yes," Anichka chattered on. "The guard's name is Vlad. He told the criminal boss I had something that might interest him, and he was to listen to me. I was so scared. The boss had tattoos on his face. Stars. And an enormous spider that looked like it was crawling from his chin to his forehead." Anichka shuddered. "It was disturbing. I don't like spiders. He stared at me for a long time without saying anything. I looked him in the eyes because I just couldn't look at that spider. Then he laughed and grabbed my face in his two hands and forced me to look deeper into his eyes. He had high cheekbones and a low forehead, so his eyes looked like they were lodged in a dark crevasse. They were the color of ice. White, with blue rays. The pupils were so small you would have thought he was blind. He never blinked, just stared into my eyes. I could not look away, and . . . strange as it sounds . . . I didn't want to. The longer I looked, the safer I felt. It didn't make any sense."

"It made no sense to me either," Branca grumbled. "I wanted to grab his hands and tear them off your face. Such an ugly beast of a man. I threw a few looks at Vlad, but he just shook his head. Next thing I knew, the ugly guy grabbed Anichka by the shoulders and shook her. Not hard. Almost like he was happy, if that's possible for someone like him. Then he ripped her *ushanka* off her head and sort of played with her hair, feeling it, smelling it, and mussing it with his hands. It was *bizarre*."

"Anichka," I said. "You must have been terrified."

"I should have been, but by then I wasn't anymore. Something about my hair pleased him. Vlad said later it was because it's such a light blond color—platinum. It means something to the native people where the criminal boss comes from. Not that I have a lot of hair after the last head lice shaving. Anyway, he told me his name is Yogush, and he's the highest rank of all the criminals. He asked my name, and I told him. He asked for my little figures. I gave him the bear and wolf, but also an eagle. He took each one separately, warmed it in his hands, smelled it, held it to his ear, closed his eyes, and listened for something. I didn't understand any of it."

"By that time, Vlad was getting impatient or bored," Branca said. "He told Yogush to speed it up. Yogush growled at him and Vlad growled back. It was a very amusing power struggle."

"Will the criminals buy your little statues?" I asked.

"Yes! Yogush said they're powerful, and he will get requests from his fellow criminals for the animal spirits they want. And then he told me he had decided that I was the new shaman! I didn't know what he was talking about. He explained that his criminals had a shaman, sort of a witch doctor or native priest or something. This man died recently, and they were trying to find out where his spirit had gone, who it was inhabiting now. Yogush said he saw that old shaman in *my eyes*. He declared I was now *Shamanka* for the criminals of the camp. He said my head was never to be shaved again, nor my hair cut. He said he would contact me after he told his fellows."

"Can you believe this?" Branca said. "Yogush arranged with the authorities for Anichka to deliver her figurines to their barracks whenever she finished them. I told her she would be crazy to go there. But she insists they aren't dangerous to her now that she is their *Shamanka*. Maybe you can talk some sense into her."

Anichka smiled and shook her head. "There's no need. I've been there. They like the animals I make for them, and they give me extra food, like these sausages. And one of them always walks me back to our barracks so nothing bad happens to their *Shamanka*. Yogush says my figurines protect them, so he and his men are honor-bound to protect me."

I reached out and touched the strange necklace she wore. "They made this for you?"

Anichka fingered it gently. "No. It's the old shaman's necklace and will be passed on to the next shaman when I die." She fingered one of the bones. "It's the symbol of my office. As long as I wear it, all the criminals and guards know I'm not to be molested. I never thought they could be like that." She looked up with a bright smile. "Everyone has something decent in them. Sometimes it's just hidden."

That was Anichka—always looking for light in the darkness. I could never buy it. But if the criminals wanted to believe Anichka was their sacred *Shamanka*, I wouldn't argue with them or her. Protection wasn't easy to come by in Vorkuta. Anichka's naive soul and arresting beauty made her a target. Now, however bizarre, it looked like our little dove had found an unexpected refuge in a nest of vultures.

CHAPTER TWENTY-FOUR

The Matchmakers of Vorkuta

Serious injuries were an everyday occurrence in Vorkuta. I moved quickly from assisting Miriam with office details to caring for patients and even helping with more complex procedures. I worried that each time a new patient arrived, it might be one of my friends from Car Six. When I found Branca waiting for me in one of the rooms, I was relieved her injuries were relatively minor, by Vorkuta standards. Still, the burns on her hands were severe enough, even though she made light of them. Typical Branca, more concerned about her friends than herself.

"I'm worried about Anichka," she told me.

I applied a salve to the burns. "You should be worried about yourself." I gave her an exasperated look and tied a knot in the bandage. "This is the third time you've burned your hands so badly they sent you to the hospital. I know the brick kiln is ancient, but you've had plenty of experience with it. Why do these accidents keep happening?"

Branca tried to make a fist and flinched. "I'm trying to get shock worker status like Vanya the cat." She laughed. "Being an *udarnik* would mean more food and maybe a better jacket. One that isn't ragged, with the stuffing so worn it no longer keeps the cold out." She grinned. "Mine is *sooo* out of fashion."

"Do you think working so fast you burn yourself is a good way to get the brick boss's notice?" I snapped. "It's more likely he'd accuse you of trying to injure yourself to get time off work."

Branca thought about that for a minute, then tossed the idea aside in her usual fashion. "No, I don't think so. I'm a Pisser, remember?" She laughed again. "We still have a bit of a reputation for grit and persistence. But, seriously, *udarniks* are rewarded well for over-fulfilling their quotas.

I could share any extra rations with the rest in our barracks. We're not getting any fatter."

"Sadly, no. The hospital has had an increase in malnutrition cases over the last few months. Doctor Eliashvili is frustrated to find a solution."

"Hah!" Branca shouted. "I can make a good guess. Probably someone near the top of the food chain is stealing and stuffing themselves with the pilfered food. There's nothing I can do about that, but I can use my brain to come up with a more efficient way to increase our brick quotas. I thought I had found a quicker way to get the bricks out of the ovens and onto the pallets to speed up loading the kilns, but I burned my hands yet again." Branca heaved a deep sigh. "If only I had thicker gloves."

"Why were you handling the hot bricks with your hands at all? Don't you have paddles to move the bricks around?"

"Yes. But I was trying to get the bricks out so fast I took too many on the paddle at once. They were so heavy I dropped the whole lot before I could get it to the cooling area." Branca closed her eyes and scrunched up her mouth in an expression of self-scolding. "It was so stupid! And then I felt embarrassed and tried to fix the problem by picking up one of the bricks. What was I thinking? Making the pile more orderly? What a joke. All I knew was I didn't want the brick boss to see the mess." She looked down at her bandaged hands. "Some shock worker," she said in disgust.

"Maybe you should find a different way to increase production." I sighed in exasperation. "Something that doesn't get you burned."

Branca threw her bandaged hands in the air. "I don't even know why we're making bricks in Vorkuta. From what I've heard, the best places for brickmaking are in the hot parts of the country. They can dry them out in the sun instead of using so much fuel to fire up kilns. Seems stupidly inefficient and wasteful." Branca shrugged. "Especially since there aren't a lot of forests around to supply the wood. The tundra's just permafrost. Try to grow a tree in that soggy mess! They have to ship the wood up from the taiga. Imagine what that costs!"

"What did you want to tell me about Anichka?" I asked, changing the subject before Branca went off on a tirade. "You said you were worried. Is she all right? She's not sick, is she?"

"No. She's thin as a rail and has a persistent cough, but she's still as sweet and lively as anyone can be in this God-awful place. The problem is she's always wandering around the camp to deliver those little amulets and carvings she makes for the prisoners. I've warned her it's just a matter of time before some sex-starved prisoner goes after her. She seems to think she has a magic shield." Branca shook her head. "Sometimes I think she believes this whole *Shamanka* thing."

"I can see why," I said. "I'm amazed. The criminals see her as a kind of living amulet or human good luck charm. And she's such an innocent."

"No kidding. Anichka's like a child still. Can you believe it? She told me the criminal bosses ask her to tell them stories. I mean, why not? Most of them can't read, and even if they could, where would they get any books?"

"You mean Anichka spends time in the criminal barracks? That's forbidden."

"Who's going to rat on the criminals?" Branca said with a knowing smirk. "No one is that crazy."

"What kind of stories does she tell them?"

"Fairy tales of all things! All the stories she heard and read as a child. Romantic nonsense. She says they *love* them. Seems these goons never heard them as children and, just like kids, they want to hear them over and over. According to Anichka, they sit in a circle around her and are perfectly quiet. Can you picture it? Dozens of tattooed thugs listening to stories about Cinderella and Sleeping Beauty and witches and dwarves. I would give anything to see it, but I'm not invited." Branca rolled her eyes.

"If the criminal bosses walk her back afterward, who protects her when she's delivering the amulets?"

"No one. That's the problem. They don't know when she can come. I mean, there's no schedule for that. It's just whenever she finishes an amulet. That's why we have to find a man to . . . you know . . ." Branca trailed off, not wanting to say what she meant.

"By some miracle, Anichka has been spared rape in Vorkuta. You know what you're suggesting, don't you?"

"Yes. But I don't see any other way. At least if we approached some man with the proposition, he might treat her like we ask."

"Now *you're* the one telling fairy tales."

"Yeah. I guess. But there's this guy just arrived in the camp. Civilized. From Poland, I think. He's young. Some kind of political. But tough. Worked for an underground paper of some sort, or so I've heard. Got arrested for printing anti-Soviet propaganda. He's condemned for twenty years. I've seen him. He's not bad-looking. And he's fresh, not perverted yet."

"A prince charming for Anichka?"

"Why not? It's better than the alternative. She'll get raped at some point if we don't do something. Why not have it be sort of consensual? She's lovely, Celia. He'd be a fool to refuse. I was thinking you and I could talk to him and, well, convince him to kind of court her. Am I crazy?"

I had to laugh. "Probably."

Branca cleared her throat and looked away. "I've found a man, who looks after me . . . I mean . . . well, you know I haven't been spared like Anichka. I didn't tell you, but I was desperate to find some protection. Vlad, one of the guards."

"The guard who negotiated with the criminal boss for Anichka?"

"Yep. He's not the most romantic guy in the world, but he's tough and he's the jealous type, if you get what I'm saying. Not so tough with me for some reason, thank God, but the rest of the men around don't mess with Vlad. And they leave me alone. It works."

That didn't surprise me. Random rape was common. Women formed sexual relations with male prisoners and guards for protection.

"If this Polish man is, as you say, fresh and not perverted, what makes you think he can intimidate the other men?"

"I don't think he'll have to. If the criminal bosses think Anichka has fallen in love, like in the stories she tells them, they might support the union." She looked at my skeptical expression. "What? It could happen." She frowned. "At least, that's what I'm hoping."

"Perhaps you're right. Anichka's criminal bosses seem to be an unusual combination of brutal and fanciful." I shrugged a question. "Are we just going to go up to this young Polish man and put it to him?"

"We could . . ." Branca frowned. "But now that I think about it, I have a better idea. I'll get Vlad to do it. I told him about Anichka and my fears for her. He seemed sympathetic—if a Vorkuta guard can feel anything remotely like sympathy. But even Vlad sees something ethereal in Anichka. Like she's a spirit or something."

I smiled. "Maybe Vlad's not as unromantic as you think."

"Oh, sure." Branca gave me a saucy look. "Or maybe I've got potent methods of persuasion." She laughed. "I can't believe we're talking about romance in Vorkuta!"

I thought about the unrelenting hideousness of Vorkuta. "All of us," I said, "even men, at times, long for an escape from all the ugliness and brutality. Look at Anichka's criminal bosses. Fairy tales? No one would ever believe it, but there it is. Does Vlad know this young Pole?"

"Of course. One of Vlad's duties is to process new prisoners, and he says it's important for guys to have women. Gives them a needed physical outlet. Makes them better workers! So he and all the other guards turn a blind eye to rapes and couplings. It's crazy. Vlad told me the Pole hasn't taken any women yet. Vlad was concerned about that. Wondered if the guy was interested in men or something and would cause trouble. Probably because he's slight and good-looking. Vlad's the beefy type. Used to be a boxer before he got sent here."

"Then I think you're right. Let Vlad act the role of matchmaker. I'm sure his powers of persuasion will convince your young Pole of the advantages of the match."

"I'll have to get Vlad to let me talk to the guy before he approaches Anichka, though. I want him to go about it slowly, get to know Anichka, make her feel special."

"Depends on who he is, or rather who he was. Before they arrested him and sent him here."

"Well, he looks the part. And you know, I think Anichka is ready for something like this. If it's done the right way."

I helped Branca get her padded coat back on over her bandaged hands. "Let me know what happens."

"You bet." Branca raised her eyebrows. "Happily ever after?"

"Not in Vorkuta," I sighed. "How about safely ever after?"

———— ★ ————

It was four weeks before I saw Branca again. A storm rolled into Vorkuta and the temperatures dropped to negative forty. The three of us had no chance to meet at the *zemlyanka*, even though I was eager to hear what had happened with Anichka and the young Pole. As soon as it stopped snowing and the temperature warmed to just bearable, we arranged to meet. It was still dark as night, and I was glad for the perimeter arc lights. I moved in and out of circles of light as I waded through the snow to the *zemlyanka*. I found Branca huddled in a corner, flapping her arms back and forth across her chest to generate some heat. An old kerosene lantern sat in the middle of the space, shedding welcome light. I wondered where it came from. At the same time, I noticed Branca had a newish padded jacket and big padded gloves.

"Branca! Did you get shock worker status? I'm so relieved you have those gloves. I worried your burns wouldn't heal right without enough protection."

"No, I didn't make it to shock worker. All I got was a reprimand for dropping the load of bricks and causing a *disruption in production*. The brick boss is such a bastard! He cut my rations. Said I lost work time because of my hands. At least he didn't accuse me of sabotage. Just being stupid."

"I'm sorry. Then how did you get a new jacket and gloves? And this lantern?"

"Love is in the air." One corner of her mouth twitched. "Or whatever you call it."

"What are you talking about?"

"Vlad got me the jacket and gloves. He saw the burns on my hands and turned into the big male protector of the little woman. Came to visit me one night with these clothes and a sausage." Branca winked. "I was going to make a joke, but he looked like a big shaggy bear with a guilty conscience, so I made nice. But you know what I think, Celia? I think he got so into his role as matchmaker for Anichka and Jan, the Polish guy, that he softened up."

"I told you I suspected a romantic side to your Russian bear."

"Yeah, well, we'll see how long that lasts." Branca picked up the lantern. "Gave me this, too. I told him about our meetings. He didn't like the idea of us in the dark." She blew out a quick breath. "Who knew my Vlad would aspire to be a gentleman?"

"Thank your lucky stars. So, tell me what happened with Anichka and . . . you say the young Pole's name is Jan? Is it okay? I mean, is Anichka okay with the arrangement?"

"From what I can tell, yes. She doesn't talk about it, but I've caught her smiling to herself more than usual. Like she has a secret. I saw her talking to him once outside. They stood really close together. He pulled her *ushanka* down to cover her head more and tugged her jacket closer around her neck. It was touching. Maybe we'll get the full story today."

We heard the crunch of footsteps in the snow outside. As always, we stopped talking and waited to see who was there. Nothing in the camp was totally secret. Certainly, other prisoners knew we met somewhere. We always worried some guard would take an interest and use our meetings as an excuse to inflict punishment on three women.

The makeshift door scraped aside and Anichka edged her way in. She unwrapped the rags covering her face to keep out the cold, and I marveled again at how young she looked. The ravages of Vorkuta, cold, hunger, sleep deprivation, the grueling forced labor, these things aged women in such a cruel way. But not Anichka. It was almost as if she walked through the camp in a different reality. I could see how the superstitious criminal bosses associated her with the magic of their shamanistic beliefs. Her childlike innocence enveloped her in a protective cloak. I wondered if this sexual relationship with Jan would change her.

"I've brought treats!" A shy smile lit up Anichka's face. "You won't believe what they are." She dug her hands into her jacket pockets and brought out two lumps wrapped in newspaper. She carefully unwrapped one, and we gazed at a perfect round of light brown bread. Its crust was shiny and studded with something that looked amazingly like currents.

"It's called a *babka*," Anichka whispered, as if it was a secret. She held it out. "Smell it."

Branca and I leaned over, our noses close to the tantalizing bread.

Branca took a sniff and gasped. "It smells like lemon and orange!"

Anichka broke the little loaf in half. The inside was soft and crumbly, tinted pale yellow and studded with tiny currants and bits of candied lemon peel. I hadn't seen such a treat since I was a child in Bardejov.

"Where did you get this?" I breathed in the fragrance once more.

"Wait!" Anichka unwrapped the second packet and held up two foil-wrapped bars of what could only be candy. "They're called *Prince Polo*." She beamed at us.

Branca and I simply stared at her, our faces two big question marks. Anichka's cheeks turned a rosy pink, and she lowered her eyes to the treats in her lap.

"I have a new friend," she murmured. "He's Polish. His mother sent these to him because it's near to Easter. He . . . I told him how the three of us were on that train and all the things we did and he . . . he thought you'd like these treats too." She looked up with sparkling eyes. "His name is Jan. He's a political. I don't know why they let him get these from home."

I hesitated to pry. "He must like you a lot," I said. "I mean, to give you his mother's gifts." I had a feeling Vlad had something to do with Jan actually getting to keep the food from Poland.

Anichka's eyes softened. "Jan is very nice. We're . . . I guess you'd say we're lovers. At least that's what he says. I was worried about the criminal bosses when Jan and I first started to see each other. I was afraid they would want to protect me and maybe hurt him. But it was the funniest thing. They think it's like the stories I tell them—romantic." She laughed. "As if you could find a prince charming in Vorkuta."

But the soft, rosy glow on her cheeks and the sparkle in her eyes suggested that little Anichka had a fairy godmother looking out for her. Actually, a fairy godmother and godfather. Branca and Vlad. The Match-makers of Vorkuta.

The Vorkuta Art Theater

I was thankful for my work in the hospital. It gave me focus and some meaning to my existence. There was no reason for me to be in this grotesque hell. There was no reason for any of us to be here except that the Soviet Union needed millions of slaves to build the workers' utopia. The mines of Vorkuta were essential to that purpose because they provided much of the fuel for Leningrad. The town of Vorkuta, which grew up in relation to those mines, served as an administrative center and home for the guards, the commissars with their families, and former prisoners who had finished their sentences and had no place else to go. Living and working so far above the Arctic Circle, where half the year was in total darkness and the other half continuous light, was not normal. Even though the residents of the town had more food, warmer clothing, and better living conditions than the camp prisoners, they, too, were trapped. You didn't just write to Moscow and request a change of job location. I often wondered why our commandant was assigned to Vorkuta. As a loyal Party member, he should have had a job in Moscow or Leningrad. My guess was he wasn't ruthless enough in the Stalinist view, and Vorkuta was a not-so-subtle form of punishment.

Nevertheless, the commandant understood that if Vorkuta was to function efficiently, both the people in the town and the prisoners in the camps had to have some relief from the grueling monotony of life in this harsh and unforgiving place. To that end, he saw to it that evenings of entertainment were held in the town theater and included plays, opera performances, and music.

It was no surprise that artists, singers, actors, musicians, poets, and writers were among those swept into slavery by Stalin's paranoia. They were all political prisoners, of course. Some had worked in the resistance in their home countries; others, who were Russian, had simply said the wrong thing, performed in the wrong plays, or been friends with the wrong people. Vorkuta got its share, and these artists were eager to perform for townspeople and prisoners alike. Especially since the performers got a bit better food and sometimes better accommodations.

Not just the professional artist-prisoners benefited from the entertainment. Regular prisoners could volunteer to help make costumes, build sets, even take roles in the productions. And the commandant often allowed regular prisoners to attend in order to fill the theater with an appreciative audience. The time off from labor and the ability to escape into the world of make-believe helped distract these prisoners from the harsh conditions. Performers and audience members favored classical plays, both comic and tragic. The ability to cry or laugh made everyone feel like they were still human beings in an inhuman world.

★

"Celia!"

I stopped in the doorway of Miriam's office with my arms full of clean bandages. Well, as clean as could be expected. Bandages were always a depressing gray color. Like the sky. Like the snow. Like my spirits that day.

"I have some good news." Miriam's eyes sparkled. "They're setting up a new production at the theater in town, and it's one of my favorite plays by Shakespeare. *A Midsummer Night's Dream.*"

"I've never seen a play before." I hugged the bandages. "We didn't have a theater in Bardejov while I was growing up. My father once took me to the theater in Bratislava as a birthday present. It was a ballet about a swan maiden. I dreamt about her for weeks."

"This play is about dreams. It's a comedy with silly lovers and fairies and strange magic. You'll like it."

I laughed. "Do I have a special invitation or something?"

"The hospital does. *A Midsummer Night's Dream* requires a lot of imaginative costumes and sets. The commandant asked me to send as many of our patients as we can to work on setting up the production. I'm putting you in charge of them. Pick the ones who are in good enough shape. You'll take them to the theater every day to build the sets and costumes."

"I don't know how to sew costumes or build anything. What if I can't figure out how and nothing's ready on time? I'll get everyone in trouble, and you know what that means."

"Don't worry. You'll have help. Moscow is sending a professional director and designer to oversee this production."

"Sending them? Don't you mean they're new prisoners?"

"No. They're not prisoners. They haven't volunteered, exactly. They're ordered to come, but they go back when the show closes."

"How strange. I don't understand. Why?"

"From what the commandant said, there are some high-ranking officials coming from Moscow to check on the town and assess the efficiency of the mining system. Naturally, everyone's nervous and wants to make sure they're treated well and shown Vorkuta's best face."

"They picked the wrong time of year for that," I jeered. "Vorkuta's face is covered in filthy snow and ice. I can't believe Moscow officials will be impressed with anything. Especially after they feel how cold it is here. A lot colder than Moscow, I bet."

Miriam nodded in agreement. "You're probably right. If you've never experienced this kind of cold, you can't imagine the impact."

"Let's hope they don't stay long enough to see how sick and emaciated their slave laborers are. That wouldn't give them much confidence in the efficiency of Vorkuta."

"Oh, they don't care about the conditions of the prisoners. They won't even go near the mines. They'll meet with the commandant and other officers and receive reports on production and quotas. Everything tweaked to look good. They'll wine and dine in homes in the town and attend an entertaining production of Shakespeare. Then they'll go back to Moscow and give a positive report."

"And nothing will change for the slaves in Vorkuta."

"Exactly. Except that *you* will have the fun of working on the production of a play. You'll get to see the rehearsals as well. I've heard two rather famous actors from the Moscow Art Theater are prisoners here in Vorkuta."

"Prisoners?"

"Unfortunately, yes. I'm afraid artistic talent is no protection for those who have offended the State. Maybe you'll get to meet them and hear their stories."

"I hope so." I put the bandages on a shelf. "I'll round up my crew of patients. I know of five who have recovered enough to do light work. Do you think that's enough?"

"Yes. Make sure you have a mix of men and women. I doubt our male patients have any sewing skills."

"I don't know about that. You'd be surprised what people can do when they have to."

"That optimism applies to you, too, Celia. Good luck. I'm eager to see the production."

★

The next morning, I dropped my little crew off at the theater workshop and went in search of the director and designer. I entered the theater to the sound of a woman weeping and a man begging.

"Valentina! Darling! Please!"

I stopped in the shadows, not knowing exactly where to go and not wanting to add to what looked like trouble. The man, wrapped in multiple layers of sweaters and scarves, knelt at the feet of a beautiful auburn-haired woman sitting on the edge of the stage. Even though her figure was extremely thin and her complexion as pale as the moon, she had the kind of classic beauty that even the ravages of Vorkuta couldn't destroy. Tears glistened on her face like ice drops on snow.

"Valentina," the man crooned. "My sunshine. I know how terrible this is. If I could take your place, I would gladly throw my life away to save your beauty and talent from this enslavement. But darling! We are pawns on the chessboard of life!"

"I am not a pawn, Sergei!" Valentina dashed the tears from her face and glared at him. "I am a queen in exile. A queen! Do you understand?" She lowered her voice to an angry hiss. "That monster in the Kremlin is as evil as Richard the Third. He is a Caliban! He is Cassius and Iago rolled into one." She flung her head up, eyes closed, her hair tumbling down her back. Then she cried out.

It was the howl of an animal in torment, and it sent a shiver through me. I had never heard such a voice. It was deep and pure, resonating throughout the space, sensual and yet feminine, her anguish heart-rending. She stood abruptly and began pacing back and forth across the stage, stopping at intervals to speak directly to the man I guessed was the professional director from Moscow. No one in Vorkuta would have possessed such nice sweaters and scarves.

"I am supposed to be the Queen of the Fairies." Valentina turned slowly with her arms spread. "Look at me, Sergei! I am skin and bones. I have no breasts at all anymore. How can I play Titania with a body like this? Oberon would shrink away in disgust."

She sank dramatically to the floor and covered her face with her hands.

"Valentina. My beautiful swan." Sergei climbed onto the stage and took her in his arms. "You must focus on the joy your performance will bring to these people forced to live in this wasteland. Think, my angel, what a ray of sunshine you will bring into their darkness."

"You idiot! My audience of slaves will not have the strength to even applaud my performance. They are starving, Sergei. Starving! Do you understand?" She took his face in her hands and focused her furious eyes on his. "Each day, they get a chunk of black bread, a miserable cup of *kasha*, and a bowl of soup not even fit for pigs. On this, they work around the clock in utter darkness, their lungs choking with coal dust. They are human beings! Not animals!"

Sergei pulled her hands away and held them. "Darling. They assured me they did not treat you like this. That you were taken care of."

"And you believed them?" Valentina laughed and pulled away from him, her eyes glittering in their dark sockets. "What a craven creature you've become, Sergei." She sighed. "What does it matter? I don't blame you. Grovel to them as much as you need to escape this place of creeping death."

"Did they lie to me?" A worried frown appeared on Sergei's face.

"Lie to you? Not as they see it. It is true—I receive a few morsels more to eat than the other prisoners. Well, you can see for yourself how ravishingly healthy I am." Her voice trembled with loathing and scorn. "Oh, I am pampered for sure. I sleep in a room with only six other women instead of thirty or forty. Sometimes, if I have given a particularly moving or amusing performance, I might be invited to dine with one of the camp officials in the town." Valentina smiled. "But there is a price for the stroganoff and hot port wine."

"Valentina!" Sergei groaned.

"Oh, don't look so horrified, my dear. Those men are never brutes." She shrugged. "I feel rather sorry for them. They are so bored! There is nothing for them to do in Vorkuta after they've finished their work in the administration. There are no clubs, no restaurants. Nine months of the year, you can't even go outside to take a walk because your face would freeze before you got to the end of town. And in our one month of summer, if you just stick your nose out the door, you're bitten to death by flies. So I don't complain if they demand to know more of me than my performances."

"This is outrageous!" Sergei stood and paced the stage. "That these peasants should make a prostitute of the brilliant Valentina! I will speak to them. I will tell them—"

Valentina's laugh filled the little theater. "How beautifully melodramatic!" She wiped tears of laughter from her eyes. "Thank you, but you have no grasp of reality. Save your breath. I will survive."

"Darling! You are so brave. So stoic!"

"Hardly stoic, but I have realized I have one special advantage denied the other prisoners. Because I am blessed with the talent to entertain, I am allowed, during the two hours' traffic of our stage, to breathe the full air of freedom. To be transported to another time and place. To be a real woman with a mind and soul of her own." Her beautiful face fell. "But, in the end, they are only characters in fiction."

Sergei sat beside her again. "Darling, I am desolated." He stroked her hair. "It is small consolation, but I am ordered to give you a message of love from your fellow artists. We all miss you at the Moscow Art. You are loved still. Everyone abhors what they did to you."

Valentina gave a dry little laugh. "Miss me? I doubt Varvara cares a kopek about me. All my starring roles are now hers."

Sergei shrugged an apology.

Valentina edged closer to him and lowered her voice to a vibrant whisper. "Listen, Sergei. None of that matters. It is nothing to me compared to what I have learned here. I was a believer. You know that better than anyone. Well, my eyes are opened at last. How I ever believed in such an evil system is a mystery to me. Look around you! You are living in the town, it is true, but surely even there you can see the truth. These people. My audience. Many of them are fine, talented, intelligent people. They have done nothing wrong. Nothing! And they are treated worse than animals. Animals, Sergei! And I am one of them."

"Hush, Val." Sergei glanced furtively around the theater.

"Oh, yes. Do be careful," Valentina whispered. "You could be next. No one is immune. They are listening, always listening. But I no longer care."

I couldn't stop a cough, and Valentina peered into the dark corner where I stood.

"Who are you?" she demanded. "Come here!"

I walked to the stage and stood silently before her. She seemed larger than life, so powerful was her presence.

"I work in the camp hospital. I've brought workers from the camp to help with the setup for the play. We're ready to do whatever you need. Make costumes, build sets, furniture. Whatever we can do."

"How nice." Valentina smiled at me graciously, just as though we weren't inmates in a camp of the walking dead but good friends and members of a renowned theater company. "This is Sergei Kozlov, our director from Moscow. We are lucky to have such a distinguished and talented man here in Vorkuta. He has sacrificed much to come to our little theater on the tundra. Under his guidance, our *Midsummer Night's Dream* will be an event to remember." She beamed at the director. "Won't it, Sergei?"

He cleared his throat. "How could it be otherwise, with you as inspiration, Valentina?"

She ignored his compliment and focused on me. "This is a comic fantasy," she said. "There will be fairies, and kings and queens, silly lovers, magic love potions, funny rustic characters, and even a woman who falls in love with a donkey." She winked at me. "Which happens more often than you might think."

She was amazing. All traces of her former anger and frustration had vanished. Her eyes sparkled and her voice vibrated with excitement. Exhausted as I was, some of her enthusiasm rubbed off on me.

"I'm afraid my crew and I don't know much about building costumes and sets," I said.

She waved an airy hand. "Oh, don't worry. I have lots of ideas for costumes. And Ilya, our designer from the Moscow Art, will show you what to do. He is a genius. Although it will be a challenge for him to create a pastoral Arcadia in an Arctic hell. I can hardly wait to see what he comes up with." She took my arm. "Come with me. I'll introduce you to our genius." She raised her fist in the air. "We shall overcome!"

— ★ —

And we did. It was the most fun I'd had since before I was torn from my home in Slovakia. We made wigs out of cotton wool from the hospital. We crafted lace from medical gauze. We used civilian clothes, taken from prisoners on arrival, for the young lovers. We took apart common prisoner clothes, so worn they were thrown away, and turned the matting into a velvet-like cloth. Ilya, the designer, had brought as much from Moscow as he could. Things he figured we didn't have in Vorkuta. He was amazingly cheerful, never complaining about having so little to work with. He hunted out as many prisoners with artistic, acting, and musical talent as were to be found and put them to work painting and rehearsing.

When the day of the final rehearsals drew near, my little crew and I had only one costume we couldn't create. The ass head for the character of Bottom was simply beyond our abilities. It was the funniest thing in the play. We sat on the floor, surrounded by materials, worried we had let everyone down, when we heard the most awful groaning, braying noise. We jumped up and turned. On the stage, Ilya pranced around wearing the head of an ass.

"Hah!" Ilya shouted. "*I see their knavery: this is to make an ass of me, to fright me if they could. But I will not stir from this place, do what they can. I will walk up and down here, and I will sing, that they shall hear I am not afraid.*"

Valentina appeared from behind a rock and put her arms around him. "*Out of this wood, do not desire to go. Thou shalt remain here, whether thou wilt or no. I am a spirit of no common rate. The summer still doth tend upon my state. And I do love thee.*"

She kissed the very lifelike ass head, and we applauded.

"Darlings," Valentina said. "I told you Ilya was a genius. He brought this wonderful mask all the way from Moscow. What would *Midsummer* be without Bottom's ass?"

The play was a big success. Many more prisoners got to see it at the special request of Sergei Kozlov and Ilya. And although, in the end, our midsummer dream returned once more to a midsummer nightmare, we had escaped for a time.

I will never forget it.

CHAPTER TWENTY-SIX

Miracle in Vorkuta

On a bitterly cold, dark November morning in 1950, I sat brooding over the fact I had served only half of my sentence. Five more years loomed before me. Five years as monotonous and unforgiving as the barren tundra stretching for miles on all sides of Vorkuta. Looking back, it seemed incredible. Five years had already passed since I arrived in that cattle car, a bitter, angry young woman of nineteen years. I was angry still, but the fury no longer flamed. Instead, it burned as a nest of glowing coal burns through the night, staving off the cold of despair. Anger was as necessary to me as food and water, because it gave me the will to survive until I could be free of this hell on earth. What I would do then, I didn't know, but I knew it was best not to dream. Dreams had a way of turning into nightmares.

A nurse appeared and my dark thoughts slipped away.

"Someone wants to talk to you," she said, urgency in her eyes. "She's waiting outside. She said her name is Branca. She's at the side door."

"Thank you. I'll be right there."

I ran to the door. Branca stood in the snow outside the hospital, stamping her feet, either to keep warm or with impatience. Icy flakes swirled around her, sticking to her eyebrows and lashes, the only part of her face visible beneath the wrapping of rags.

"You have to come to the brickyard!" she said.

"What's happened?" I asked. "Has there been an accident? Let me get my outdoor gear on and grab some medical supplies."

"No accident, but you must come and see anyway. There are three nuns being tortured. They're forced to stand outside in the freezing cold and wind on the hill above the clay pits. The NKVD guards put them there yesterday. At the end of the day, they came to get them. I think the guards expected them to be near death by freezing, but when they pulled them to their feet, the nuns just walked away with them as if nothing had happened. I saw it with my own eyes, Celia. Today, the guards brought them again but took away their gloves and caps."

"This is one of the coldest winters since we came here. They'll die like that."

"That's what everyone thought," Branca said, "but this is nearly the end of the second day and the nuns are still alive. The guards brought them early this morning when work started, and the three nuns have stood there since, motionless, just like yesterday. But nothing happens to them."

"Why is this being done to them? Why aren't they working in the clay pits instead of standing on the hill?"

"I asked Vlad. The story is that when the nuns first arrived, NKVD guards assigned them to work in the brick factory. They refused to do any work for the Communist regime under compulsion. They said it was working for the devil and they were servants of God, not Satan. I agree with them that Stalin is the devil's henchman, but no one I've ever heard of has refused to work and lived." Branca kicked at the icy snow. "Vlad says they've been here for days. Fed nothing but rancid soup and a hunk of black bread. And Celia, Vlad told me the bastards have tortured them in horrible ways. The NKVD put them in strait jackets, with their hands behind their backs, and tied with a rope from their wrists to their ankles. They pulled the rope so tight the nuns were wrenched into a backward bow. It's inhumane."

"Inhuman behavior from that group isn't a surprise. What happened to the nuns?"

"Vlad says they didn't scream or anything. They just moaned and then lost consciousness. The NKVD guards repeated the torture again and again. For two hours each time until they passed out. But they finally stopped it because they were afraid the nuns would die."

"Typical! Stalin wants slaves, not corpses. At least not until he's leeched years of hard labor out of them. Did Vlad see all of this? Was he part of it?"

"No. He isn't NKVD and not high up enough to be ordered to be a guard of any special prisoners. I'm glad. Vlad's not a prince among men by any means, but he takes care of me. I've gotten to know him in a way, and from the way he described what he heard about the nuns, I think he would have trouble doing that to them. Odd as that sounds about a gulag guard."

"It's to his credit."

"Will you come? There's something strange about these nuns. The prisoners, and even some guards, are getting superstitious about it. There's muttering about judgments and miracles. You have to see for yourself."

"I'll come. Let me just tell Doctor Eliashvili. I'll bring some supplies just in case they need attending."

"The guards won't let you near them. And, strange as it is, I don't think they need help."

★

The sky was leaden, and the wind had real teeth in it. It was exceptionally cold. Minus twenty degrees. The fierce wind blew across the tundra, and as we neared the clay pits, the full force of it nearly knocked me over. I hated the pits. My anger rose every time I saw the miserable women prisoners, six of them crammed into each pit. Five-foot-deep holes in the ground, like animals in traps. All day they chipped away the hardened clay, sometimes with their bare hands, to make bricks for buildings in the town and the surrounding camps. The guards standing over the pits swore at the women and grumbled at the cold. Today, however, an eerie silence hung in the air. The women continued to work, but I heard no groans of pain. Only occasionally would a guard swear softly under his breath. Every now and then, both the women and the guards cast furtive glances at the hill above the pits.

I followed their eyes to where three small figures stood motionless. They wore no gloves or caps, just light scarves on their heads. Their basic cotton jackets and pants were nothing against the full force of the bitter wind on that hilltop. The women laboring in the pits wore heavy padded clothing and the warmest regulation boots for winter work, and still it was barely enough to keep them from freezing. I had seen too many cases of frostbite coming from these pits.

From where I stood, I couldn't tell how old the nuns were. They might have been thirty or seventy. I could see no evidence of suffering on their faces. Their wrists were bound in front of them, palms together. They were perfectly still and appeared to be gazing serenely at the scene below, prisoners and guards alike. I was sure they were frozen. Then, as I stared at them, they all three raised their bound hands in prayer and knelt together.

"Mother of God," a woman whispered in the pit nearest to me and crossed herself.

"Shut up!" the guard hissed. He shuffled nervously, stamping his feet on the cold ground.

A strange murmuring rose from the pits. The sound didn't build, just remained steady. The women were muttering prayers as they worked. Or maybe they were incantations to ward off evil. I didn't know. The guards said nothing, which was surprising. It was as if no one knew what to think or do. I sensed fear in the air.

"Here come the NKVD guards," Branca said. "It must be the end for today. I need to get back to my station at the brick ovens. You stay and watch what happens."

The guards stomped up the hill. They bent over the nuns and peered at them, then gave them each a shove. The nuns toppled over as though they were statues but immediately righted themselves and awkwardly tried to get up. I saw the guards talk to each other for a minute. Then they yanked the three women to their feet and marched them down the hill and away.

"Get back to work!" the guard near me shouted over the pits. "You have one hour more to meet the quotas."

Every guard in the pits repeated the order. The prisoners went back to work, still crossing themselves and praying. I returned to the hospital and told Miriam what I had seen.

"Why are they alive?" I finally asked her. I still couldn't understand it.

Miriam sat at her desk, thinking for a time before answering.

"The human mind is a mysterious thing," she said, "as difficult to control as the wind. When I started in medical school, we naturally focused on all the organs of the body. One day in class, a student asked the professor about the difference between the brain and the mind. Were they separate or the same thing? Was our mind trapped in its physical home of neurons and cells, or did it have a life of its own? Could it transcend the material world? Was it the only thing that outside forces could not control? Was it free? Our professor was terrified of discussing anything remotely connected to individual thought or action. He went on as if the question had never been asked." The corner of Miriam's mouth lifted in a rather wry smile. "The student was arrested several days later."

"I'm not surprised."

"But to get back to your question about the nuns. Before you came here, I encountered a prisoner who had been to Tibet. Stalin sent him as a spy. The prisoner had failed to give a satisfactory report because he became a Buddhist while he was there. So naturally, he ended up here. I treated him for severe wounds. He wouldn't tell me how he got them. He talked a lot about Tibet and the monks. One story is oddly similar to what you just told me. He said the monks could meditate for hours and abstain from food for days. And he observed a ceremony where the monks were wrapped in wet, cold sheets and placed in a room below forty degrees. Most people would suffer hypothermia in such a state, but he said the monks were able to generate body heat through deep concentration. He saw steam rising from the sheets within a few minutes, and after an hour the sheets were completely dry."

"That's really hard to believe. Are you sure he didn't just make it up?"

"He told the story as if it was something profound, not just a tale of strange customs. I believe he had a spiritual awakening there that changed his life."

"And landed him in the gulag."

"Unfortunately. But he had an inner peace I hadn't seen before."

"Strange. I'm going back to the clay pits tomorrow, Miriam. Will you come?"

"I'll try."

★

Miriam couldn't go with me that day. It was the third day they took the nuns to the hill, and this time they also took away their scarves. They stood bareheaded, without gloves or caps or any clothing protective enough against what turned out to be the coldest day we'd had so far. News of the miraculous nuns ran like fire through Vorkuta, quickly becoming the chief topic of conversation. When I got to the clay pits, there was a crowd of prisoners, guards, even hardened NKVD men. They all found an excuse to come by the clay pits near the brick factory. At the end of the day, the bareheaded nuns were taken away once again. They had no trace of frostbite, and people began murmuring that God had brought a miracle to pass in Vorkuta.

Miriam and Anichka both came on the fourth day. The three nuns stood on the hill as usual, their eyes lifted toward the gray skies, snow falling softly around them. This day, they sang hymns in perfect harmony. The women digging clay in the pits continually crossed themselves, and the area hummed with the sound of mumbled prayers. I could feel a nervous energy in the air, like before a storm.

"It's like God is sending us a sign of hope," Anichka whispered. "Reminding us not to despair."

"That's a tough sell in this place," I said.

Anichka looked at the nuns and sighed. "I know you're right, but you can't deny what you see. Their faith is so powerful. How else can it be explained except as a gift from God?"

I knew Anichka believed God cared for every person. Her faith had seemed to grow rather than die during her time in Vorkuta. My faith died in Auschwitz, where I had imagined my anger rising to God in the smoke from the crematoriums. I wondered if Anichka would have felt the same under those circumstances. Probably not. She would have found little rays of light in the darkness. Vorkuta was different from Auschwitz. Here, death came not from a gas chamber but from continuous grueling physical labor and starvation. Was it better to be exterminated quickly or by the slow death of twenty years in a labor camp? How do you compare two unspeakable horrors? I couldn't. I just turned my back on God and hoped He felt at least some guilt for His indifference.

The murmuring in the pits ceased, and all we heard was the singing of the nuns. All eyes turned toward the hill where the commandant appeared with Colonel Baranov, head of the NKVD in Vorkuta. I had never had any personal encounters with the colonel, but I heard everyone feared him for his ruthlessness and cruelty. The commandant may be strict out of the necessity of his position, but Colonel Baranov, they said, took pleasure in inflicting pain.

"I wonder why the commandant is here?" Miriam whispered.

The nuns stopped singing and fell to their knees, heads bowed in prayer. Colonel Baranov moved to drag them back to their feet. The commandant stopped him with a single sharp command. The commandant himself went to the nuns, took each gently by the hand, and raised them to their feet. Then he turned to the assembled crowd by the clay pits. Prisoners, guards, criminals, and people from the town all waited to hear what would happen. The commandant's authoritative voice, strong and confident, resounded over the area.

"It is the will of the Soviets that these women have suffered their full punishment and will be put under special guard from this time forward. They will not be tortured. They will be taken off punishment rations. They will care for themselves in special confinement, preparing their own food and making their own clothes. They will be treated with respect. There are some here who are prey to fear of powers not of this earth. That is superstitious rubbish. Some have flatly refused to touch these women or have anything to do with them. That is nonsense. There is no witchcraft or divine power at work here in Vorkuta. Return to your work. The drama is finished."

Colonel Baranov, looking anything but pleased, led the nuns away. The commandant stood for a while, watching the prisoners in the pits and the guards, until all muttering ceased and work returned to normal. Then he turned on his heel and walked away.

Miriam watched him, amazement on her face. "I never thought to hear such a pronouncement. The faith of those nuns is incredible and inspiring, but what you just heard from the commandant is the *real* miracle in Vorkuta."

Anichka smiled. "I think God won a quiet battle today. Maybe there will be new hope and even a return to religion by many prisoners, even some guards, through these nuns. That really will be a miracle."

The nuns remained in Vorkuta. They never did one day of work for the Communist regime. The men who guarded them did so with respect and even awe. They were still prisoners, but they were spiritually free. No one in the Soviet Union ever had that kind of freedom of worship.

Discovering Ivan

★

The days followed one on another, ever more slowly, it seemed. In winter, the sky blended in with the earth, creating a vast whiteness scarred by the mines and the ever-growing number of wooden crosses in the cemetery. Spring came and went in the blink of an eye, as though it didn't want to stand in the way of summer with its partially blue skies and warm weather. Of course, with summer came the hordes of insects that drove men crazy, but when your world is excruciatingly cold for over half the year, you'll endure anything for the light and warmth of the sun.

It was during this time that I waited for something new to happen. Prisoners came and went in the hospital. Gradually, I learned the art of healing. I learned the power of a kind word or look, the power of being quiet and listening when my patients needed to talk, the power of a smile to lift the spirits of a dying man. I learned to focus outside myself, to put my anger and bitterness aside. What did it matter what I thought? It was hell in Vorkuta for every exploited slave of the State. However different we were, we were still in it together.

And then, eight years into my sentence, a day came I had never dreamed of. A turning point and the beginning of a new life. The day an unusual man arrived in Vorkuta.

— ★ —

"We have a new patient this morning, Celia." Doctor Miriam looked up from a paper she was studying. "He arrived late last night from a camp in Central Asia. According to this report, he was beaten on his arrival here, in a brawl with other miners. Officially, he is a well-documented saboteur and wrecker. Accused of smuggling and stealing, among other crimes. Rather a celebrity in the camps, it seems."

"Sounds like a typical member of the criminal set." I shrugged. "I'm not surprised they beat him up on arrival. It's a way of showing him who's boss in Vorkuta." I heaved an exasperated sigh. "I hope he won't be disruptive. Our patients need rest."

"That's why I think you should look after him today. See what you can do. I gave him a sedative when they brought him. He's been in and out of consciousness most of the night."

"All right, Miriam. I'll do my best, but I've had my fill of Soviet criminals lately. Seems like they're always finding ways of getting hospital time at the expense of prisoners with genuine needs."

"I agree. But he isn't a Soviet. He's a Czechoslovak. From some town called Kosice."

I caught my breath. "Kosice! Why didn't you say so? That's near my hometown."

I hurried to the door. I don't know what I thought. That he would have news of home? That was ridiculous since he'd been a gulag prisoner long enough to have an official reputation as a troublemaker.

"Wait!" Miriam called out. "I didn't tell you why he's a celebrity. It looks like he's the lawyer who's been getting prisoners released from camps using Soviet law against the Soviets. And he has a bad habit of organizing prisoner strikes. You may have heard of him."

I *had* heard of him—most of us had. News of what he'd been doing had spread throughout the camps, even in a place as far removed as Vorkuta.

"Is he the Ivan Kovach prisoners talk about?" I asked.

"Yes, he is. I was told to put him in the confinement room. Treat him well, Celia. He may not have much time left. The NKVD officers who brought him in were eager to have him back."

"Bastards!"

I flew down the corridor and stopped myself just in time from rushing into the confinement room. The last thing I wanted to do was startle or upset this man. I opened the door and walked softly up to the bed. I don't know what I expected, but it wasn't the dark-haired, good-looking man who lay there. I had never heard a physical description of Ivan Kovach and just assumed a lawyer with the skill he had would be much older. At the very least, he should have had gray hair, if only from suffering in the camps. But here he was, battered, cuts and bruises from last night's beating all over his face, but looking like a hero after a battle. Or maybe I was indulging in a romantic fantasy because he was Slovak. I stood there watching him, and a strange new emotion I had never felt before surged through me. As if something I had been waiting for had just happened. I felt energized and . . . absurdly . . . happy.

I gathered some clean cloths and a basin of water. His eyes were closed, and he appeared to still be out from the sedative. I soaked one cloth in water and began sponging the cuts on his face. Why had he been beaten up immediately on arrival here? Had he said something and the other prisoners took offense? It seemed unlikely based on his reputation as someone who helped prisoners. The NKVD had brought him into the hospital. That was also odd. Usually, the camp bosses were the ones who took care of trouble between prisoners. Of course, if he'd been involved in strikes, the NKVD would be interested in him. He must have slipped up somehow.

"Too clever for your own good, I suppose," I murmured, dabbing at a bloody cut on his chin. "Stubborn too, I bet. A strong chin usually points to a stubborn personality. And too handsome for your own good, too, Mr. Ivan Kovach from Czechoslovakia."

Why was I talking to this man like a bossy sister? Worse, why was I calling him handsome? Thank goodness he was unconscious. I wrung out the cloth in cold water again and laid it on his forehead. What on earth had he been doing? Had he gone into one of the mines to sabotage it? Is that why he got beaten up? He was a mystery. I was eager for him to wake up, to find out more about this fellow countryman of mine. Why? What was the point? If the NKVD wanted him, then Miriam was right. He probably had little time left.

"You don't know it," I whispered like a fellow conspirator, "but we're from the same area. We might have passed each other sometime. In Kosice, or maybe Bratislava." I smiled. "Would I have taken a second look?"

Where did that come from? Who was I to take a second look at anyone? But something about him touched me in a way I hadn't felt before. Flirtatious? It was nonsense. Thank goodness he was unconscious and would never know. I leaned closer and murmured, "Even though you're at least ten years older than me, for sure I would look."

His eyes flew open. I pulled back immediately, embarrassed. His eyes swept slowly around the room and came back to me.

"Am I in heaven?" he murmured.

I hesitated, unsure of what to say. "Not yet. You probably just missed it, though. Heaven, that is."

"No. You're wrong," he said in a voice as deep as a well. "Everything is so white." His eyes crinkled at the corners, trying to focus on my face. "And a beautiful angel is ministering to me. I *must* be in heaven." He smiled and then winced with pain. "Does my angel have a name?"

I felt so embarrassed. How much of what I said had he heard? Had he been pretending to be unconscious the whole time I had been talking to myself? I dabbed energetically at his chin. "Behave yourself, Prisoner Kovach!" I snapped.

"Ah," he said. "I've learned something. Angels have tempers."

"What a ridiculous thing to say." I frowned at him. He looked around the room again.

"I'm curious," I said. "What landed you in this hospital bed?"

He ignored my question. "I still can't get over how white and clean everything is. Paradise." His eyes came back to me, and I saw a gleam in them. "And, of course, how beautiful you are. My very own angel."

"Oh, of course," I said with sarcasm. I dipped the cloth again and put it back on his forehead. "You didn't answer my question."

He gazed around the room again. "What landed me in heaven? Nothing much." He looked at me. "I made the old mistake of speaking truth to power." He raised an eyebrow. "Could happen to anyone. My comrades of the NKVD disagreed with me, and I told them they were sadly wanting in a sense of humor. They didn't agree with that either. We engaged in a brief *bagarre*—very brief since there were four of them and only one of me." He smiled. "I lost."

"Well, I'm not surprised if you used a word like that."

His laugh ended in a cough, and he winced again in pain.

I changed the subject. "You're from Czechoslovakia. So am I."

He tried to sit up, and I pushed him back down.

"We're landsmen!" he said with a smile. "Landswoman, in your enchanting case."

"Do you never give up?" I tried to sound annoyed but couldn't hide my pleasure. No one had ever flirted with me in such a way.

"Be patient with me, my angel. I have been six years in Hades. I'll be good. Where are you from?"

"Bardejov. Have you been there?"

"I have! A charming town. For a charming—"

I put my hand over his mouth. "Now stop!"

He grasped my hand and kissed it. A shiver ran up my arm. What was wrong with him? I tried to pull away, but he held my hand tight. His eyes looked straight into mine, and I could feel my face burn. He kissed my hand again and released it. I felt lightheaded, happy. I turned away to fuss with another cloth. I had to get these sensations under control.

"Forgive me," he said. "That was better than a tonic. I've learned something else. Angels can blush."

This time, I ignored his comment and carefully folded some bandages into a neat pile. "Where are you from?" I tried to sound casual. I had never dealt with anyone like him before.

"Kosice," he said. "Have you been there?"

"Once . . . when I was nine." I shook my head at him. "I've learned something too. Famous heroes don't always behave as they should."

His eyes opened wide at that. "Famous hero? Who told you that tale?"

"Everyone knows. You're the man who got a prisoner released from the gulag using Soviet law. That has never been done. And you also led a successful strike of prisoners. You're famous." This time I frowned at him. "What I really want to know is this. If you're so smart and tough, how did you get sent to the gulag in the first place?"

He nodded with a sage expression. "An excellent question. I spent a good few months in prison, pondering the answer to that. I've also spent years seeking enlightenment from various members of our ruling class."

"And?"

"They didn't tell me. It doesn't matter. I know the reason. Ambition, my angel. Ambition. I should have remained a hardworking lawyer in a tiny office in Kosice. But I sought a bigger stage. I became a politician." He raised his eyes to the ceiling. "Never become a politician."

"Were you a poor politician?"

"The worst. My platform was too simple. I pledged a government with no masters or slaves, no bribes, no obscene gifts, and especially no court jesters." He shook his head. "What an idiot! And I had received a first-rate education. You'd think I would have learned something from it."

"But didn't you?" I couldn't understand how anyone like him would not have benefited. The Nazis had deprived me of an education.

"I did. Just a little too late."

"What did you learn just a little too late?"

"That the world's not fair and you can't make it so. Get on with your life and stop complaining and scheming. Or, as Voltaire opined, cultivate your own garden."

"If you talked like that, I can see why the NKVD beat you up."

"Ouch!" He gave me a crooked smile. "That pompous, am I?"

"For Vorkuta? Yes." I shook my head. "Where do you think you are? In parliament?"

"No. I should have been in Moscow today, negotiating with the prosecutor general."

"Oh, naturally!" I was becoming as playful as he was. "And I should be in Paris shopping. You must still be suffering from a concussion. You're delirious."

"Do you think you could get me a pen and some paper, my angel?"

"Hah! You know perfectly well that prisoners cannot have pen and paper without the permission of the authorities."

"Ah. Yes. The authorities."

"What are you writing? Your memoirs?"

"Someday. But not today."

I stared at him, the truth becoming clear. "You're writing to the authorities in Moscow!"

"You're quick, my angel."

"That would get us both in trouble."

"Or set us both free."

He was serious. I understood why the NKVD wanted him. He was too determined. I picked up and held his wrist, pretending to check his pulse. "Not physically sick." I made a face at him. "Just a mental case." I could have added stubborn to the point of dangerous.

This time he took my hand gently and held it to his cheek. That strange sensation of lightheaded happiness flooded into me again. I felt like we were old friends who had been parted and reunited. He was so much older and smarter than I was, had seen and done so many things, had been so many places before they arrested him for his courage in speaking truth to power. If I'd been thinking clearly, I would have been completely tongue-tied in his presence. But the way he talked to me as though I was his equal, his joking, his smiles, made me want to answer him the same way. I gave his cheek a playful slap and pulled my hand away. I had never felt or behaved like this with any man in all my life. I didn't question it. I just looked at him, battered and bruised, and I wanted desperately to save him from his future. If the NKVD got hold of him again, they wouldn't stop until they silenced him for good.

"I have to tell you," I said, serious now, "I'm afraid we can't keep you under observation for more than a night."

His eyes drifted around the room again. "It's so clean in here. Like being on a different planet."

"They'll beat you up again."

He gave me a funny look. "Actually, it was two tons of coal."

"What!"

"They dropped two tons of coal on me. From a height. It was *a very unfortunate accident*," he said with a mocking frown.

"It's a miracle you survived."

"A miracle." He pondered for a moment. "I think you might be correct. Even though I no longer believe in a personal deity, I have noticed God still seems to take an interest in me for some obscure reason. You won't believe me, but every time I get into one of my life-and-death scrapes, something happens to get me out of it. I've taken to talking to Him sometimes. I say, 'Good morning, God. It's Ivan the troublemaker again.' And God says, 'Ah. Ivan. You're so amusing. What can I do for you today? Save you from two tons of coal? No problem.'"

"Be serious! Next time they'll kill you."

"How can they? I have a guardian angel now. Ergo, God must have another daring escape planned for me."

I laughed. "You really are crazy."

"Ah ha! I've learned another thing. Angels can laugh."

I gathered up my cloths and basin and turned to leave.

"Will my angel grant me another visitation?"

"If you promise to be good."

"So good you won't recognize me."

I smiled at him and opened the door.

"Final lesson," he said as I went out. "Angels have enchanting smiles."

CHAPTER TWENTY-EIGHT

I stood in the corridor outside the confinement room, my mind in turmoil. Ivan Kovach had blown into Vorkuta like a whirlwind from the steppes of Central Asia, and all the emotions I had worked to control during the last eight years rushed in with him. Anger at the injustice that landed him in the gulag and fear that the NKVD would kill him were the most urgent. Frustration, because I could not think of a solution and was helpless to stop them. Along with these were even more disturbing emotions I had buried. In the last thirty minutes with this stranger, they were all resurrected. Joy. Hope. Excitement. Happiness. Humor. Attraction. Love. No. That was impossible. I couldn't love someone in thirty minutes. I couldn't love someone at all. Love like that was denied me. I wasn't worthy of the love of a good man, and especially not this man. He was a man of honor. If he ever found out who I had been and what I'd done, he would turn from me with contempt. I was so far from an angel it was a joke.

I shook off these thoughts and walked slowly down the corridor. I would talk to Miriam. Maybe she would think of a way we could at least keep him in the hospital for a longer time. Say a week. What would happen when that week was up? I didn't want to think about that. All I wanted was his company, to listen to him talk, to hear about his adventures, to have him tease me and laugh, to talk to him about home. I wanted the resurrected emotions to live on for just a little longer. Was that too much to ask of the God I no longer believed in?

I turned the corner into the administrative end of the hospital and nearly ran into Colonel Baranov, NKVD commanding officer, the man with a reputation for exceptional cruelty. Currently, he was the primary candidate to succeed the commandant if the commandant transferred.

Colonel Baranov was arrogant, tall, well-built, and around forty years old. I looked into his rugged face. A chill ran through me, and goosebumps broke out all over. A deep scar, supposedly from the war, trailed down his cheek, from his temple to his chin. He reminded me of Nazi SS officers, with his neat and clean uniform, his well-shined black boots, the pistol in his belt, and the sinister black baton he tapped impatiently against his leg. He looked me over with disapproval but said nothing. I lowered my eyes and stepped aside.

He continued past me, and I watched him open Doctor Miriam's door, without knocking, and walk in. I was sure he was here to talk to her about Ivan. I tiptoed down the corridor until I was beside the office door. Colonel Baranov must have been impatient to speak to Miriam because he had left the door ajar. I looked both ways down the corridor. No one. I edged as close as I dared and listened.

"Colonel Baranov." Doctor Miriam's voice had an edge I hadn't often heard. "Mr. Kovach was brought here after having received a thorough beating within an inch of his life. He suffered a concussion and was unconscious. There were multiple abrasions and lacerations on his face and torso. Most were contaminated with coal dust. We have not had time yet to assess internal injuries. What did he do to merit such treatment?"

"Prisoner Kovach was transferred here for crimes he committed at his former camp," Colonel Baranov replied, his voice edged with annoyance. "He is a documented troublemaker and saboteur!"

"What you are telling me is that transferring Mr. Kovach to Vorkuta *was* his punishment. Why, then, was it necessary to beat him?"

I was amazed at Miriam's determination to hold her own against Baranov. Her insistence on calling him "Mr. Kovach" instead of "Prisoner Kovach" bordered on insubordination. Papers rattled in the silence of a pause.

"Colonel Baranov, this documentation says Mr. Kovach arrived yesterday. That is a very brief time for him to plan and carry out an act of sabotage here in Vorkuta."

"I would advise you, *Doctor*, to stick to your job of healing the prisoner," Baranov snapped. "You are misinformed. Prisoner Kovach was not beaten. A coal cart overturned. He happened to be under it. It was nothing, really. He was the victim of an unfortunate accident."

I choked down a laugh. It was the same thing Ivan had said.

"Let me drop two tons of coal on you, Colonel, and see how——"

"No arguments! Just tell me when we can have him."

"I have to check him for internal injuries," Miriam replied slowly and deliberately. "This hospital is always overloaded and understaffed. It will take——"

"We will be here tomorrow morning. See that Prisoner Kovach is ready!"

I heard the baton slap and then the scrape of his boots on the floor as he turned to leave. I rushed down the corridor and into the nearest room. When I heard the door slam at the end of the corridor, I went to Miriam's office. She stood looking out the window, arms at her sides, fists clenched. She turned when she heard me enter.

"Celia. Mr. Kovach will be discharged tomorrow morning. You may give him twice the rations of bread and soup."

"Why waste the rations? You know they'll kill him."

"For the sake of this hospital, I cannot afford to get into a fight with the secret police. Even the commandant can't protect us from the NKVD." Her voice softened. "It may not be as bad as you fear. Perhaps they'll just give him a beating."

"Just?"

"Please, Celia," she sighed. "Go back to work."

After she hung the stethoscope around her neck, she gathered a few patient charts and left the office.

I had patients to attend to, so I gathered the necessary supplies and medicines and hurried from the office. Taking care of them took my mind off the problem for a time, but when I had cleaned the last wound and admonished the last patient of the day to eat all his rations, the fate of Ivan Kovach troubled me again. It was Sunday, and I realized I had forgotten I was to get together with Anichka and Branca in the *zemlyanka* by the cemetery. Maybe they would have some ideas. At least I could tell them about my meeting with Ivan. I put on my padded jacket and pants, pulled my *ushanka* down over my ears, and hurried out into the snow.

CHAPTER TWENTY-NINE

As I approached the cemetery, rough wooden crosses, black with coal dust and leaning askew in the permafrost, stood out like tired soldiers against the white of the snow. Bones, blackened with coal dust, protruded from the shallower graves. Someone had stuck a skull on top of one cross, a grisly reminder of the ultimate reality in Vorkuta. The old wooden door to the *zemlyanka* was gone, probably torn off to use for firewood. The wind had blown dry brush against the opening. I moved it aside and peered in. Branca and Anichka huddled by Branca's kerosene lamp inside, whispering. Branca grasped my hand and dragged me inside.

"You're late," she huffed. "We were worried. We're hoping you have something interesting to tell us," Branca said. "We were just complaining about how boring this past week has been since that blizzard brought everything to a halt."

"Oh, Branca, come on," Anichka chided. "It was a blessing for everyone to get a little chance to rest."

"And reduced rations because the supply train was stuck somewhere for two days," Branca grumbled. "And now everyone's got cabin fever. Even the Pissers in our barracks. And that's saying something." She chuckled. "As Comrade Stalin, may he burn in Hell, would have said, 'All play and no work make prisoners dull dogs.'"

"Don't even mention his name." Anichka shivered. "It gives me goosebumps."

"Goosebumps?" Branca laughed. "How can you tell at forty below?"

Anichka ignored her and took my hand. "You don't usually sit quietly like this. You've had some kind of adventure, haven't you?"

"The best of my life," I answered. "I've met the most remarkable man."

"Oh! How wonderful!" Anichka clapped her hands.

"Yes, and tomorrow the NKVD will kill him if I don't figure out how to stop them."

"That figures," Branca said. "The NKVD's job is to destroy anything remotely remarkable. Especially if it's a human being. But go ahead—tell us about this remarkable man who's doomed to die tomorrow."

"How romantic!" Anichka exclaimed. "And tragic."

I told them the entire story. What had happened. What Ivan said and did. What he was like. I tried to hide the feelings for him that still lifted my spirits, but I couldn't help the excitement in my voice. I know they suspected, but I felt I should keep it a deep personal secret. It would just bring bad luck to express it.

"Two tons of coal?" Anichka's blue eyes flashed in the *zemlyanka*'s darkness. She nibbled at a piece of bread Branca had brought for our get-together. "It's so terrible."

"Can't Doctor Eliashvili keep him there for some medical reason?" Branca asked. "Examinations for broken bones, internal injuries, that kind of thing?"

"She tried, but if she doesn't do what Baranov orders, he'll make trouble for her. I don't know what to do. I just *can't* let them kill him."

"It's as clear as day to me," Branca declared. "He needs to get sick. So sick they have to keep him in the hospital. I think something highly contagious would be the best. Even the NKVD won't want to mess with that."

"That would be great," I agreed, "but aside from a few cuts and bruises, he's in perfect health." I sighed. "Too perfect."

"I have it!" Anichka grabbed my arm. "You've learned so much working in the hospital. Can't you think of some way to fake a serious illness?"

"I could fake a rash or something like that, but he would have to have a real fever to fool them. They're not stupid. They'd check."

"But—"

"Shhh!" Branca hissed. "Voices." She extinguished the lantern.

We edged ourselves against the cold earth of the back wall of the *zemlyanka* and listened. The sound of crunching snow, heavy breathing, and a couple of grunts testified that more than one person was approaching. The grunts also sounded like men, not women. I had drawn the branches back across the opening of the *zemlyanka*, but if they'd come here to use our hiding place themselves, we were in trouble. The crunching of their footsteps stopped. We had no idea how close they were.

"Why the cemetery, Boss?" The gruff voice sounded like it was right outside the *zemlyanka*.

"Yeah," a different man whined. "This place gives me the creeps."

There were three of them. The next voice sent a wave of fear through me.

"I wanted to remind you where Prisoner Kovach was supposed to be today if you idiots hadn't screwed up last night."

I couldn't mistake Colonel Baranov's voice. I had just heard it this morning.

"C'mon, Boss," the gruff voice said. "Yefim and I beat him up and dumped a couple of tons of coal on him. It's not our fault he survived."

"Vova's right. How did we know some bleeding-heart prisoners would dig him out?"

"You should have stuck around to make sure they didn't," Baranov snarled. "Now he's in the hospital where we can't get at him. I don't trust that Georgian bitch of a doctor. She's not one of us. She might be protecting him. And the commandant protects her."

"What's so important about this Kovach guy?" Vova asked. "Why not just work him to death? Less trouble than killing him."

"Because, unlike you fools, Kovach has a brain. He's an organizer and a troublemaker. The sooner he's eliminated, the better. Remember what our late Great Leader said."

"No man."

"No problem."

"If the Great Stalin hadn't died, we wouldn't have troublemakers like Kovach," Baranov growled. "Those wimps in the Kremlin have been getting weaker and more compassionate every day."

"You're right, Boss—just causes trouble. Right, Vova?"

"Right. Remember that big prisoner strike here two years ago? That was a bloody mess. Never should have happened."

"We crushed that one good, though. Wiped out sixty-six of the bastards."

"Yeah. Including that Latvian priest. What was his name, Yefim?"

"Mendriks. Vicious viper, that one."

Baranov cut in. "It could happen again. Kovach just led a strike at one camp in Kazakhstan. They didn't put that one down. The Kremlin cowards caved. Met all the demands. Kovach won. And, from what I've heard, he's got some crazy scheme to get all the foreign nationals released. He's a damned saboteur."

"Released?" Vova said. "The foreign prisoners make up a third of our camp."

"Yeah," Yefim agreed. "And they're the best workers."

"Exactly," Baranov said. "Where else do you think they'll get workers for Siberia? Russians won't volunteer. Do you think any of us would be here without kickbacks and skimming off the top? What do you think will happen to you if men like Kovach win and they have to shut down the camps?"

"They can't shut down the camps."

"Sure they can," Baranov said. "What will you do then, Vova? Become a brain surgeon?"

Yefim guffawed. "That's a good one. Vova—a brain surgeon."

"And you, Yefim," Baranov continued. "I suppose you'll take up rocket science?"

"Hey! The State guarantees us a job!"

"Sure it does," Baranov sneered. "As a janitor on thirty rubles a month. That's less than a tenth of what you put together now between your salary and, shall we say, fringe benefits?"

"They can't shut down the camps!" Vova shouted.

"Last time I was in Moscow, that's exactly what those Kremlin block-heads were discussing."

"Yefim," Vova grunted, "we gotta get rid of Kovach."

"They'll turn him over to me tomorrow," Baranov said. "And this time you'd better take care of him. No mistakes. Is that clear?"

They answered in unison.

"Clear as a bell, Boss."

"It'd better be. Otherwise, you'll be looking at new jobs." Baranov paused. "In the mines!"

The men groaned and grumbled.

"Shut up!" Baranov shouted. "You have your orders. Now get out of here. I've wasted enough time with you today."

We listened as the crunch of their footsteps grew fainter, and waited until we were sure they'd gone before we moved the brush aside and looked around the cemetery.

"I have to get back to the hospital," I said. "I don't know what I'll do, but I'll think of something. I'm glad we were meeting today. Without your suggestions, I probably wouldn't have the courage to save Mr. Kovach. I'll figure out how to fake some kind of contagious disease." I shrugged. "I've certainly seen enough faked illnesses by prisoners over the years. I just have to find a way."

"Before you go, I want to give you something for Mr. Kovach." Anichka dug into her jacket pocket and took out a little figure carved out of quartz. "One of the miners found a small seam of quartz in the mine. He gave some to me because he knows I make and sell these talismans. It's really special. Like a diamond, almost."

She handed me the little figure of a crouching polar bear with his nose thrust forward as if he was on the alert for danger. The quartz, milky white with a few clear veins running through it, sparkled even in the dull gray light.

"I can't take this, Anichka," I said. "You could get a lot of money for food if you sold it."

"No! Mr. Kovach needs a talisman. It's the only thing I can do to help. The criminal boss says quartz is powerful." She smiled. "They really believe in magic, the criminals. So strange. They're such brutal, savage men."

"Thank you, Anichka." I hugged her. "I'll give it to Mr. Kovach. Who knows? Maybe your little bear will have just enough power to save him."

CHAPTER THIRTY

The little quartz bear was nestled in my pocket that night when I opened the door to the confinement room. My unsuspecting patient was sitting up in bed, eating soup and bread. He looked like he'd had a good sleep and was in the best of health. Baranov would demand his release for sure. The bruises and lacerations must still have pained him, but he didn't seem bothered by them. A wave of guilt swept over me at what I was about to do to him. I was also afraid. If I made a mistake in the dosage, I could kill him just as surely as the NKVD. He looked up and smiled at me, and my heart turned over. How could he be so cheerful facing death? Either he had enormous confidence in overcoming the forces against him, or he was crazy.

"My angel has returned." He waved his hand in the air. "When they said *Vorkuta,* I assumed Hell with ice demons. But here you are, drifting in like a benevolent spirit." He winked at me. "Never assume."

I felt a bit awkward in his presence this time, and not just because of what I planned to do. This morning, he had still been weak from his wounds and the sedative. Now his energy filled the room, and I felt small and insignificant and shy. I pulled some sheets of paper from under the metal tray I was carrying and held them up.

"You did it! Brava, my angel!"

I went to the bed and handed him the papers along with a pencil. He took them quickly, rolled onto his side, and tucked them under his mattress.

"Tonight, I will write an appeal that will rock the Kremlin." He dunked a piece of bread into his soup bowl. "I don't believe this soup. Real vegetables. And meat! Real meat!"

"Doctor Eliashvili saved the commandant's little boy from typhus. Now she gets anything she wants or needs . . . within reason, of course."

"A commandant with a heart. Maybe there's hope yet." He ate the piece of bread.

I had to get on with my plan. Colonel Baranov would want to get his victim as early as possible. Probably before dawn, so they could kill him in secret. There was no time to lose.

"I wouldn't eat any more of that if I were you," I said, removing the cloth that covered the little tray.

He looked at me suspiciously. "Poisoned?"

"No, but you'll just throw it up."

"For heaven's sake, why?"

"Trust your guardian angel. The NKVD will be here early in the morning, Mr. Kovach."

He smiled again. "Call me Ivan. We're landsmen, remember?"

How I wished I didn't have to do this. That we could sit and talk without fear. I put on a bright smile. "Ivan."

"That's better."

I tried a joke. "You know, I don't think the NKVD are coming to take you to Moscow tomorrow for negotiations with the Presidium of the Supreme Soviet."

He laughed. "Alas!"

"They mean to kill you this time . . . Ivan." I took a large syringe from the tray and held it up. I would not do this behind his back. I wanted to be honest and warn him. "But I think it will be all right, because when I finish with you, they won't want you."

"What kind of guardian angel are you?" He raised an eyebrow at the glass syringe. "That's an impressive syringe. But I'm not a horse. Are you going to tell me what I can expect, or will you surprise me?"

"I tried to think of some way to prevent the NKVD from taking you tomorrow and killing you."

"How do you know they mean to kill me?" He smiled. "You have spies at headquarters, little angel?"

"I overheard Colonel Baranov giving the order to two men this afternoon."

"I've underestimated you. I thought you were a sweet and charming angel nurse, and now I find you're a clever undercover agent. I won't ask how you overheard them. I wouldn't want you to reveal your tradecraft."

"It was purely by accident. And they didn't know I was there."

"Of course they didn't. A clever undercover agent never gets spotted."

"Please be serious. It will be bad. Do you trust me?"

"With those eyes? How could I not? Go ahead. Do your worst, my angel."

"Turn over then and pull down your pants."

"Am I not allowed even a modicum of dignity?"

He pulled down his pants and rolled over onto his stomach. In order to distract him, I asked a question. "What does modicum mean?" I knew he would tell me the definition.

"Modicum is . . . OWW! That wasn't fair!" He rolled over and gave me a look. "Well, Mademoiselle Doctor, now what?"

"Now . . . we wait. I should tell you what I've given you . . . before it takes effect."

"Do. Because I'm already feeling a bit woozy."

"I've given you a shot of arnica."

"Arnica!" His eyes opened wide at that. "Arnica is deadly." He blew out a puff of breath. "I hope you got the dosage right."

"I think I did. I wanted to fake a serious illness that we can claim is contagious in order to fool Colonel Baranov. That will keep you here for at least a week."

"And you're hoping they forget all about me?"

"That would be too much to ask, but we'll see what happens. Anyway, the arnica will make your heart race, and you will develop a rash of red blisters." I frowned. "They will probably itch. I also gave you a tetanus shot to raise your temperature. Along with the arnica, that should give you chills and aches and pains. Oh, and you might become delirious."

"And here I thought I would write appeals to Moscow tonight."

"I doubt that."

He frowned and studied my face. "I suspect you've come under a wicked spell that has transformed you into an evil angel."

"Please don't joke! It was the only thing I could think of to save you."

His eyes softened. "I'm sorry. Thank you. Don't worry, I won't die— no matter what. I promise you. I'm stronger than you think."

He lay back with a sigh. I could see his eyes were already bright and his breath quick.

I was terribly frightened. I sat with him all night, watching the progression of my faked illness. The arnica worried me most. It's a flowering plant that grows wild in Siberia, sometimes called wolfsbane. When applied to the skin, it helps with bruises, joint and muscle injuries, and pain. Taken orally in very small doses, it helps with arthritis, headaches, and general pain. In the wrong dose, arnica is fatal. Too little and Ivan Kovach would not develop the signs of a truly severe illness. Too much and I could kill him.

He made more jokes for a time, probably to calm my nerves, not his. But as the night went on, he stopped joking as the drug took effect. By midnight, his temperature was 102, and he was sweating profusely. His heart rate leaped to 240. Just before dawn, the red blisters appeared all over his arms and torso.

I applied wet cloths to help his fever, but I dared not do anything too beneficial until after Colonel Baranov had seen him and gone away. Ivan became delirious, rolling his head from side to side and moaning. Sometimes he muttered things in a language I didn't know, and several times he cried out in terror. I thought he must have been having visions from his experiences in the camps of Kazakhstan. Each time, I was sure he was dying. He said he was strong, and I hoped he was right.

What would Miriam say when she saw him? I didn't care. My fear for his life was greater than my fear of reprimand. I remembered Anichka's little quartz bear. I took it out of my pocket and held it. It looked carved out of ice and felt cold in my hand.

"I hope Anichka, our *Shamanka*, has carved magic into you," I whispered to the bear as I pushed it under his pillow. "Please make this work."

CHAPTER THIRTY-ONE

"My God, Celia! What have you done to him?"

Doctor Miriam confronted me over Ivan's bed, where he lay moaning and burning up with fever. She had just taken his vital signs and was appalled.

I told her the truth. "I've given him arnica to cause a rash and a tetanus shot to induce fever."

"Are you crazy? His blood pressure is soaring, and his heart is in extreme tachycardia. You could kill him."

"I was very careful in the dosage. It will only last long enough to save his life. When Colonel Baranov comes this morning, he must believe Mr. Kovach is deathly ill. Tell him it's highly contagious and you must quarantine Mr. Kovach to prevent infection of the entire camp."

Miriam glared at me. I reached out and took her hands, desperate to make her understand. "Please, Miriam! They'll believe you."

She pulled her hands away. "If they find out the truth, they could have us both shot. You have put everyone who's working for good here in danger. How could you do this?"

"I can't let them kill him. He's saved people and fought for justice and risked his life."

"I know you admire him, and I understand it. He does have a reputation as a fighter for justice, but this—"

The door flew open and Masha, one of our nurses, rushed in.

"Baranov is here, Doctor," she said in a panicked whisper.

"Thank you, Masha."

Masha turned to leave and ran right into Baranov, who was striding through the door. Miriam grabbed a white lab coat from a hook on the wall and rushed over to him. I guessed what she was going to do. I picked up a strip of bandage and followed her.

"Colonel Baranov," Miriam said, holding out the coat for him. "Please, put this on."

Baranov stiffened and tried to move farther into the room, his eyes on the bed.

"Colonel," Miriam persisted, "I must insist. Mr. Kovach has developed a condition that we don't immediately recognize. If you wish to look more closely at him, you must wear this coat and cover your mouth and nose. It would be irresponsible of me to expose you to what has all the symptoms of a highly contagious disease."

He stood still, frowning at the bed. Then he nodded consent and Miriam helped him into the coat. He tied the bandage around his own mouth and nose, then moved slowly to the bed and peered down at Ivan. I pulled down the sheet to reveal more of the red welts covering his body. Ivan moaned and turned on his side, the side nearest to Baranov, who backed quickly away in alarm and stared suspiciously at Ivan.

"This came on suddenly," he said. "And fortuitously for Prisoner Kovach. What is your opinion, Doctor?"

"It is my opinion that Mr. Kovach was already carrying this disease when they brought him to Vorkuta. He could have contracted it at the former camp in Kazakhstan or in transit. Infectious diseases, such as this appears to be, usually have an incubation period. Now that he's here, I recommend we keep him in quarantine. However, if you want to take him now—"

"No!" Baranov backed away farther. "No. I'm sure you're right. You will inform me of his progress for better . . . or worse."

"I will certainly do that, Colonel," Miriam said. "You'll be the first to hear."

Baranov cast one last searching look at Ivan and left.

Miriam turned to me and whispered, "How much arnica did you give Mr. Kovach? We should induce vomiting, although it may be too late for that."

"He didn't take it by mouth. I knew that would have killed him. I gave him an injection. I wasn't sure if it would result in dramatic enough symptoms, but it was all I could think of."

Miriam sighed in relief. "Injection. Thank goodness. I'm surprised at the severity of his reaction, but I think it will wear off well. It could be the tetanus shot causing most of his symptoms. Our supply is old. We're long overdue for new vaccine shipments."

"Will he have any lasting injury from what I did?"

Miriam put her arm around me. "I don't think so. Make sure he drinks a lot of water today, and check on him often. It should wear off by tonight. The rash will be uncomfortable but useful if Baranov comes to check on him."

"Do you think the colonel will be back soon?"

"The idea of a contagious disease got to him. Even NKVD officers have a healthy respect for germs. I don't think he'll want to spend any time in this room for a good while."

Miriam left me then, and I focused on using wet cloths to cool Ivan. The delirium eased and he stopped thrashing around. He was still very hot, but the fact that he was sweating so profusely meant the fever wouldn't last long. He fell asleep finally, and I left him to see to my other patients.

When I returned that night, I found the fever and aches and pains had gone. He was sitting up in bed, rolling something around in his hand. When he saw me, he held up Anichka's little quartz bear between his thumb and forefinger.

"I found this. I kept wondering why there was a rock in my bed. I fished it out and, lo and behold, it was a little work of art."

"My friend Anichka wanted you to have it for good luck. She carves little amulets and talismans to sell for food and other things."

"Talented girl. It's beautifully carved. Does anyone buy them?"

"The criminal boss is very superstitious—it's funny because he's such a brute—but he gives Anichka protection because of them. He calls her a *Shamanka*."

"A *Shamanka*. What an interesting story." He twisted himself around abruptly and began furiously scratching. Unfortunately, I had been right about the red rash.

"My God, it itches! I've changed my mind. You're a dark angel. And I'm not referring to your lovely raven hair."

I tried to dab calamine lotion on the welts while he twisted and turned. "Stop thrashing!" I ordered. "I can't apply this if you don't keep still. You should be thankful the fever's gone."

"I'd rather have a fever than this torture."

"Concentrate on something else. That will take your mind off it."

"All right. I'm concentrating." He closed his eyes and paused for a moment. "It's still itching," he complained. He went back to thrashing and I applied more lotion.

"Talk to me," I said. "Tell me something about yourself. Or tell me a story . . . anything."

"A story. I have a long history of storytelling. It saved my life."

"When was that?"

"A lifetime ago in Central Asia." He leaned against the back wall and grinned. "In fact, it's a story about another ferocious criminal boss. His name was Kustor Barza."

CHAPTER THIRTY-TWO

The Tale of Kustor Barza

As told by Ivan Kovach

The road to Kazakhstan was long. They loaded me onto a truck with other prisoners destined for the camps of Central Asia. Those camps were to be my home for the next nine years. Unbelievably, I was looking forward to it. After my arrest as an enemy of the State, they shuffled me from prison to prison. The gulags were depressingly similar, as were the interrogations and beatings. I didn't know what the work camps were like, but I figured anything was better than a Soviet prison. With Borodin's beautiful *In the Steppes of Central Asia* running through my head, I bid farewell to western Russia and headed east.

Sometimes a good education can preserve your sanity. Exotic cities—Bukhara, Samarkand, Tashkent—rose in my mind as I imagined myself traveling along the famed Silk Road. Of course, it was nonsense, as I soon discovered. The steppes of Central Asia, unlike Borodin's music, were singularly unromantic. Our caravan of prisoners jolted its hot and dusty way across a vast, lonely steppe through cold sunrise, burning day, bleak sunset, and freezing night. Occasionally, we glimpsed a lone camel, its rider swathed in scarves against the unrelenting heat and dust. Sometimes a yurt appeared with a couple of scrawny goats cropping dry grass nearby.

Some men in my truck had been prisoners for over a decade. I was an interesting newcomer, and they took delight in describing what I was in for as a loyal laborer in Stalin's camps for the reeducation of benighted dissidents.

"Ah, Kovach, you'll curse the day you were born, for sure."

This came from a prisoner who must have been sixty if he was a day. How he had survived this long was a mystery. He was nothing but sinew and bone coated in skin like tanned leather. His pale gray eyes glowed inside deep sockets.

"The bosses rule with a steel fist." He broke into a laugh that was close to a witch's cackle. "What could be more appropriate, huh? *Stalin* means steel. Steel fists for steel Stalin."

"I'm ready to learn," I replied. "Forewarned is forearmed."

"How much contact have you had with criminals, Kovach?"

"Some. I was a lawyer in my former life."

He grunted. "Lawyer. Hah! City boy. Suits and silk shirts. Divorces, petty thieves, corruption."

"Yes," I confessed. "That's about it."

"The criminals in the camps are the worst of the worst. Rape, torture, murder. They kill for entertainment," he said, relishing his story. "They've spent their whole lives in and out of prisons. They're as cold as Siberia." He shook my arm. "What're you here for?"

"I backed the wrong government," I said.

He nodded. "A political. The criminals eat politicals for breakfast. The bastards are illiterate, vulgar primitives. They have contempt for educated men and get off on keeping them in abject terror. They have absolute rule in the camps."

"Why do the camp authorities allow it?"

"Why do you think?" He looked at me as if I was a stupid kid. "The criminals are useful to the commissars because they keep you politicals terrorized and working hard. That means the criminals don't have to work much and the commissars don't have to deal with you."

"Sounds like a nightmare. What can I do?"

He didn't have to think for even a minute. "Entertain them," he said. "They're like stupid children. Any political who can entertain them gets treated with respect and even awe. They'll protect you and get you extra food. It's crazy, but that's how they are."

I didn't believe the old man, but I soon found out the truth of what he said. It was my first great piece of luck.

When our truck finally arrived at the destination, I was shoved out with the other politicals. As the truck drove off to the next camp, the old man waved to me and shouted good luck.

The authorities counted us and signed us into the camp. All the political prisoners stuck together. I guess they thought there was safety in numbers. Anyway, we entered our barracks in a group and were met by a colorful gang of criminals. They formed a ring around us, adorned with all the accessories of their class: grotesque tattoos, piercings in the most disgusting places, jewelry made from found articles such as nails, tin cans, stones, bones. Their sweaty undershirts and torn pants reeked of nonexistent hygiene and unfettered masculine toxicity. They were an impressive bunch. Fear hung in the air like heavy humidity.

A gorilla of a thug, with a pockmarked Mongolian face and a crude cross made of human bones around his neck, shoved his way through the ring. A squat, powerfully built Genghis Khan, he was, and he looked us over with undisguised contempt.

He spat on the floor and said, "I am Kustor Barza! Killer of bulls. Who is your *sarkor*?"

The politicals stood in silent submission. I recognized *sarkor* as the Tajik word for boss, so I translated for them. The politicals muttered among themselves, conscious of the danger we were in and unsure how to respond to this gangster.

Kustor Barza spat again. "*Chuchakoi!*" He turned to the criminals. "Hear that, men? Chicken tonight."

Being called chickens didn't bode well. For some reason, probably because I understood some Tajik language, the politicals looked at me. I gave them a dry smile, shrugged, and stepped forward. I didn't know what I would do if Kustor Barza attacked me. I was not in the best of shape from my recent prison sojourns. He would probably floor me in one blow. I made a point of looking significantly at the wicked knife in his belt, then raised my eyes to his.

"We have no *sarkor*," I said. "We are equals. Men among men."

Kustor Barza spat. "*Harza!* You speak nonsense. You are prisoners. Here, you are nothing." He turned again to his men. "Unless I choose to make you something."

His men growled their approval.

"Like you," I pointed out, "we are prisoners. Unlike you, our minds are free."

Kustor Barza laughed, and the criminals laughed with him. "Hah!" he shouted. "You can keep your minds. We'll see how free they are in a month."

"As you say." I shrugged.

Kustor Barza moved right up to me and looked me over. "You look like you read books."

"I'm a lawyer, so, yes, I read."

"Not laws!" He spat on the floor again. "Stories! Do you know stories?"

Amazing! The old guy in the truck was right. It seemed a good education might save your life. I smiled. "Stories. There you're in luck. I know some of the greatest stories ever written. *The Count of Monte Cristo, War and Peace, Crime and Punishment.*"

Kustor Barza capered, jumping up and down and slapping his hands against his thighs. "You hear that, *vory*! Tonight, thieves, we get entertainment." He brought his face closer until we were nose to nose. His breath smelled like rancid fish. "What are you going to start with, lawyer?"

"Call me Ivan." I smiled.

He grinned, revealing an amazing mouthful of tarnished, silver-crowned teeth.

"Hah! Ivan! Listen, lawyer. You will tell us stories. If we like them, you and your men will eat. If we don't like them . . ." He grinned again and shook his cross of bones.

"Wonderful! The Scheherazade of the Gulag."

"Who is that?"

"A woman who told stories to survive."

Kustor Barza sneered at me. "You are no woman. What will be your story tonight?"

"Gogol."

"Gogol? Who is this Gogol?"

I walked around the circle, being as dramatic as I could, pausing by each thug. "Gogol. The weirdest Russian writer of them all. Gogol. A man of fugitive noses and vindictive overcoats. Gogol. Who believed the devil was stalking him dressed in a frock coat and wearing a pig's snout. Gogol. A lunatic who died with leeches gnawing at his nose. Gogol. The perfect man for the gulag."

The group of politicals laughed nervously, as if they thought I was crazy. I took a chance, walked back to Kustor Barza, and laid my hand on his shoulder. "Gogol will be our guiding star," I declaimed, then raised my other arm toward the ceiling.

Kustor Barza looked coolly at the hand on his shoulder, and then at me. "We will see, lawyer." He brushed my hand off his shoulder. "Tonight!"

He strutted back to join his men, turned, and pointed his finger at me.

"From now on, you will be Ivan *Sarkor*. Kustor Barza has said! So it will be!"

And that's how Ivan *Sarkor* became the Scheherazade of the Steppes. The entire time I was in that camp, I told stories nearly every night to a bunch of hardened criminals who listened like children do to bedtime stories. For this, they gave me protection, and all of us political prisoners benefited from the extra rations and occasional treats of meat, courtesy of Kustor Barza.

CHAPTER THIRTY-THREE

Ivan Kovach finished his story with a flourish and a bow. I was enchanted. I could have listened to his deep, resonant voice for hours and hours. It wasn't that the story was unique, because these things happened in the Vorkuta camps as well. The criminals protected Anichka because of her amulets and talismans and her fairy tales. Those prisoners who could perform at the camp theater also received extra food and special treatment. It was the way Ivan told the story in that fascinating voice of his. He made the whole thing dramatic and even amusing. My heart ached at how much I missed my father telling me stories when I was a child.

"Do you really know all the great books?" I asked.

"Some of them. I read them starting when I was a boy. Some I've read three, four times."

"I've never read them. My schooling was interrupted by . . . the war. I'm not well educated at all. I always wished I could . . . well . . . learn more. About everything, I guess. And like you said, a good education might keep you from going crazy, or even save your life."

"Or, in my case, get you thrown into the gulag," he said with an ironic smile.

"Would you tell me the story of one of those novels?"

"Of course. What novel would you like?"

"Do you know *Anna Karenina*?"

"A very romantic story, *Anna Karenina*."

"Yes. My father gave me the book for my sixteenth birthday. I started it, but . . . we had to move . . . and . . . I lost the book."

"How far did you get?"

"I remember there was going to be a ball. Anna was trying to decide whether to go or not. I don't think she really wanted to. Did she go? I never found out."

There was something new in his eyes as he looked at me, a searching look, as if he was trying to understand something. I felt small and shy again, like an ignorant schoolgirl. I wished so much that I was somebody he could admire, that I was clever and intelligent and had never lived through what I had or been the person I'd been. Then he smiled at me in the warmest way and my insecurities faded away. I pulled a chair close to his bed and sat like a child eager for a bedtime story.

"Anna Karenina did go to the ball." A roguish look came into Ivan's eyes. "And she danced with the handsome Count Vronsky."

"Oh, tell me what happened."

He leaned back and gave himself to the story.

"When Anna arrived at the ball, the room was a swirling sea of sound and light, and a rainbow of color. Dresses in lace and satin, velvet and tulle, floated around the room like exotic butterflies. The colors that season were pastel pinks and yellows and white. A thousand candles in crystal chandeliers blazed over the heads of the dancers. The air was redolent with the fragrance of summer flowers and exotic perfumes."

Ivan's voice swept me into the story as if I were there. Vorkuta and all its ugliness melted away, and I heard the captivating music of a waltz, saw the women in their beautiful gowns, the dashing cavalry officers. I felt transported, like I was one of them, gay and enchanting.

Ivan's voice deepened even more. "Anna, however, had chosen a black velvet dress. The low-cut neckline revealed her white shoulders. She had raven black hair . . . like yours. She piled it high, and the only ornament was a small garland of pansies. The contrast of her velvet black to the gay colors of the other women was so striking that all eyes turned to look at her, dazzling in her classical simplicity. She was twenty-seven and radiated grace and elegance."

"What did Count Vronsky do when he saw her?"

Ivan's eyes changed again, softened. "Ah. He lost his heart to her. Knowing she was a married woman, he had been fighting his attraction to her, telling himself it was wrong, that he would shame himself and her. But when he took her in his arms for the waltz, he knew he was hopelessly in love with her. They whirled around the ballroom with eyes only for each other."

"Oh!" I sighed. "How wonderful to feel such happiness."

"Yes. But their joy was someone else's misery."

"No!"

"Have you forgotten the young Princess Kitty Shcherbatsky, Anna's niece?"

"Oh, yes, I remember her."

"Kitty had pressed Anna to go to the ball, if you remember. It was to be a night of triumph for Kitty. She, too, was hopelessly in love with Count Vronsky and believed him to be in love with her. This night was to be the night he would propose marriage. Kitty was so sure of it that only a few days before, she had refused to accept the proposal of Konstantin Levin, a childhood friend who loved her to distraction. Before she met Vronsky, she had felt she could live happily forever with Levin. Now, watching Vronsky and Anna together, Kitty felt her heart break."

"Poor Kitty. What happened? Did she find love? Did Vronsky give up Anna? Did Levin try again for Kitty?"

"Celia."

Miriam's voice startled me out of my rapture. I hadn't heard her come into the room. I wondered how long she had been standing by the door. I looked at Ivan. He was smiling at Miriam.

"It's time you were in bed, Celia," Miriam said softly. "It's past two and Mr. Kovach needs to sleep."

I jumped up. "I'm coming. I'm sorry. I didn't know it was so late."

"It's my fault," Ivan confessed. "I was telling Celia stories. Forgive me, Doctor. It's been a long time since I've had so charming and appreciative an audience."

Miriam smiled, but her eyes held a worried look. "I understand. However, we still have a hospital to run. Good night, Mr. Kovach. Sleep well."

CHAPTER THIRTY-FOUR

My romantic fancies in such a place as Vorkuta seem strange, but romance had been denied me at the age when a young girl yearns for such things. When Ivan came into my life in Vorkuta, I had experienced all the horrors and hardships of human existence—persecution, hunger, abuse, slaughter of innocents. In all those years, I had never seen a man who touched my heart or reached my soul. That Ivan had lived through these same sufferings yet could laugh, have hope for the future, and fight for justice drew me to him. I was only twenty-nine. Ivan's smile could disarm anyone.

That night, I fell asleep with his mellow voice in my ears. And I had my first happy dream since the Nazi persecution of the Jews began in Bardejov. In my dream, I was transported to that ballroom in *Anna Karenina*. I was Anna, dressed in black velvet, my hair piled high and garlanded with pansies. I felt admiring eyes turn in my direction, but my heart searched only for Count Vronsky. There he stood across the glittering sea of dancers, a dashing *hussar* talking with his fellow officers. He seemed to sense my presence, and when he turned, my heart leaped. Count Vronsky was Ivan. He moved with masculine grace across the ballroom, took my hand without speaking, and led me onto the floor. His arm came around me, he drew me close, and we whirled into the waltz. We danced and danced and never said a word. I thought I would die with happiness.

I woke to the sound of the Arctic wind flinging icy snow against the frosted window. For a moment I lay there, basking in the dream's warmth, holding onto the happiness for as long as I could. I would see him again this morning. Because he was in quarantine, I was the only one allowed to care for him. I dressed quickly and was glad there was no mirror to reveal Celia Klein instead of the beautiful Anna. With the glow of happiness inside, I felt more attractive than I could ever remember.

Even before I opened the door to his room, I heard him thrashing around on the bed and moaning. I set the tray with his breakfast rations on the floor.

"Escape!" he called out. "Go! Go! Escape! Forgive me. Forgive."

I rushed to the bed and shook him. "Ivan! Wake up! Wake up!"

"Escape!" He woke and blinked at me. "Celia? What are . . . ? What time is it?"

"Morning. You were having a bad dream."

He closed his eyes. "I was." He took a few slow breaths. "But it's all right now."

"I brought you some breakfast. Just *kasha* again. And rye bread. I'll try to get some meat for your lunch. You need it for strength." I was chattering to take his mind off the nightmare.

"Thank you. God, I'm hungry!"

"I'll sit with you if you want. I'm in charge of you now. Because of the quarantine."

"That's good. You're like a tonic."

"You were crying out, *Escape.* Were you remembering the camp in Kazakhstan again?"

"No." He focused on his *kasha.* "That was a different escape."

"Was that the time you got a prisoner freed? I've heard stories about you doing that."

"Another story?" He smiled.

"I like to hear about you. We're landsmen, remember?"

"Landsmen," he murmured. "More than that, I hope."

I felt shy again and retreated into my officious nurse role.

"Eat your *kasha*, Mr. Kovach."

"Yes, ma'am." He finished the *kasha* and bread. "Are you as good a cook as the chef here in Vorkuta?"

"I can't cook at all. I never learned."

"Aha! You are a secret member of the pampered bourgeoisie. Now I see why such a nice young woman is languishing in Vorkuta."

"I was not pampered, at least not much. This conversation is silly. Please tell me about freeing the prisoner."

"I was the Scheherazade of the Steppes, and now I'm the Scheherazade of Vorkuta. For my bourgeois angel, I present The Tale of Dima, the Wronged Sergeant."

CHAPTER THIRTY-FIVE

The Tale of Dima,
the Wronged Sergeant

As told by Ivan Kovach

After a few years in the heat and dust of the steppes, I traveled north into the vast Siberian taiga, the largest forest on Earth, to cut timber to help rebuild Soviet cities damaged during the war. Mile upon mile of thick forests of pine and fir grew in soil just above the permafrost. The taiga is one of the coldest areas on Earth. Temperatures in the winter can fall to minus one hundred degrees Fahrenheit—so cold the air crackles. Cold and lonely, even with the companionship of my fellow prisoners. Spring and summer were so short we'd hardly know they existed if it hadn't been for the winged, blood-sucking insects. Mosquitoes and midges swarmed in such dense clouds that they blocked out the sun. We had to work in masks and mosquito netting to protect our faces, ears, and necks from the parasites. We kept campfires burning constantly to drive them away. I swore I would never again complain about the sweltering heat of the Kazakhstan desert steppes.

We woke every day at six in the morning. After breakfast and roll call, we marched under guard into the surrounding forest to cut the wood that would build the Soviet paradise. We worked in teams, a man on each end of a rustic frame saw. These frame saws were so old and weather-beaten that they regularly came apart and had to be reassembled on the job. Single saws would have been more efficient, but so many were stolen, only rusted ones were left, and they were more useless than the frame saws. One day, they teamed me with a new man by the name of Dima, a former sergeant in the Soviet Army. We'd been sawing away for about an hour when Dima stopped, looked around for guards, and lowered his voice.

"They say you were a lawyer before you were arrested, Ivan. Is that true?"

"Yes. Before they promoted me to lumberjack."

"Listen." He looked over his shoulder again. "I need your help."

"Keep sawing," I admonished. "If the guards don't hear the sound, they get nosy. What do you want?"

We began sawing again with vigor.

"I want you to get me released."

I stopped sawing at that. "You're joking."

Dima pulled on the saw again. "No. I shouldn't be here. It was a great injustice."

"It was for most of us."

"Mine is different. I was a good soldier. Loyal to the Party. Loyal to Comrade Stalin."

I felt like telling him why loyalty to the Party and Stalin was a big mistake, but he was young and earnest, and I didn't have the energy to explain it to him.

"I fought well against the Germans," he protested. "I was decorated. And now I'm in prison for twenty-five years. Twenty-five years!"

"Keep sawing! What did you do? Tell a joke about Comrade Stalin?"

"I would *never* tell a joke about Comrade Stalin!"

"Very wise."

"It was ridiculous. I was with my unit. They'd assigned us to clean up an ammo dump. We were taking a break—sitting around, talking, you know, like guys do. We were talking about cars. About what we'd like if we could ever afford one. That kind of thing. And this ZIS rolls by. Some general being chauffeured around."

"And you failed to salute?"

He stopped sawing and glared at me in outrage. "Of course not!"

"All right. Then what was the problem? Keep sawing."

We worked some more. Dima looked around for guards again. "It was a mistake. After the ZIS went by, we started comparing cars. I told my unit I thought the Studebaker was a better car than the ZIS. I'd driven Studebakers during the war."

"Why is a Studebaker better than a ZIS? Besides looking a lot better?"

Dima brightened. "As I told the guys in my unit, a Studebaker is better because when a ZIS sinks into the mud, you can only pull it out with a tank. You don't need a tank for a Studebaker."

"Dima. That's almost as bad as telling a joke about Comrade Stalin."

"I didn't mean it in a negative way," he protested. "But some bastard ratted on me to the NKVD. They arrested me. Said I humiliated Soviet technology and exaggerated bourgeois technology."

We both stopped sawing.

"In their eyes, yes, you did."

"But I didn't! I mean, it's true. About the ZIS, I mean."

"They don't care about the truth. I can't see a case here, Dima." I threw a hunk of wood on the pile. "What's done is done."

"Wait!" Dima dug in his pocket and pulled out a crumpled piece of paper.

"Marshal Zhukov agrees with me. It's in *Pravda*, so it must be true. After all, *pravda* means truth. Doesn't it?"

"That's debatable."

Dima opened the piece of paper, sidled up to me, and read it aloud.

"Today in Uralmash, Marshal Zhukov urges Soviet workers to produce better machines. *We must improve our technology*, Marshal Zhukov says. *We must build better, lighter, stronger. Like in America.*"

"Here. Let me see that."

Dima gave me the paper. "*Like in America!* That's what he said, Ivan. Marshal Zhukov is the most famous soldier in the Soviet Union. He agrees with me. They applauded *him*." Dima kicked the saw, and it broke. "And I got twenty-five years! What kind of Soviet justice is that?"

I read the *Pravda* article. "No justice at all, Sergeant. I think I'll take your case. I'll send an appeal. Directly to Marshal Zhukov."

Later, I wrote the appeal and sent it through one of the camp managers. He and I enjoyed a rapport and had many long talks in the evenings about politics. I would have given much to have seen the look on Marshal Zhukov's face when he got my appeal. As it was, I expected nothing to come of it. However, a month later, I was sitting in the barracks, cleaning the mud off my shoes, when the door banged open, and Dima rushed in. He ran up to me and thrust a telegram into my hand.

"Ivan! You did it! I'm free! Marshal Zhukov sent me a personal apology. Read it." Dima beamed at me. "He calls me a Soviet visionary. Me! And I'm back in the army. And . . . he promoted me to master sergeant!"

I read it, then handed the telegram back to him. "Congratulations, Master Sergeant!"

Dima enveloped me in a bear hug and bestowed three kisses on my cheeks, right, left, right. The other prisoners gathered around, slapping me on the back and cheering. I was glad I'd succeeded, but I didn't realize what it would mean for my future.

After my success for Dima, I gained a terrific reputation. The prisoners called me the Great Czechoslovak Lawyer. Business picked up. Prisoners would come to me with their grievances and ask me to write appeals for them—even the criminals and mafia members. I had to rework those appeals because they always presented their cases with the foulest language. So many prisoners wanted me to write appeals that I had to set up a kind of law office in the middle of the gulag. Imagine that. They paid me with bread, money, even vodka. I had no idea where they got it. And I didn't ask.

My reputation for getting prisoners freed using Soviet law against the Soviets followed me from camp to camp, wherever I was sent. Of course, I didn't free as many as I would have liked. It wasn't easy. Everything had to be just right. The commissars are not as dumb as we think. Still, it felt great to use the skills I was educated for and do some small bit for justice.

CHAPTER THIRTY-SIX

"You make me proud to be a Slovak, Mr. Kovach." I looked at him with undisguised admiration.

"Ivan," he said softly. "Remember?"

"Yes. Ivan." Self-conscious, I lowered my eyes. "It's just that I feel so insignificant around you."

"Insignificant! My dear girl, you saved my life!"

"I had to do that. You've done all these great things—things people here in Vorkuta, so far from Kazakhstan, know and talk about. It's the fact you did them while undergoing hard labor and all the other horrible deprivations of the camps that make them great. Even Doctor Eliashvili called you a celebrity."

"She was probably joking. I was more surprised than anyone when Dima was freed, and I was proud I helped to make it happen. It inspired me to try to free others, but I didn't really accomplish that much. I wouldn't call myself much of a celebrity."

"Well, I do. Even the smallest action that gives hope to prisoners is a great thing." His eyes deepened as he looked at me. Self-conscious, I changed the subject. "But you've finished your *kasha*, and I have other patients that need some attention."

"Time stands still until your return."

"Nonsense! You're an outrageous flirt, *Mr. Kovach*."

I hurried from the room, but I didn't go to my other patients. The happiness I had felt that morning from the dream came flooding back, filling me with such joy, I was breathless. I had to get outside into the fresh air, away from the smells of the hospital, the groans of the patients, the confinement. Impulsively, I ran to the outside door and rushed out into the snow. The wind had died down. Against the leaden gray sky, puffs of pure white snow drifted gently around me. I turned my flushed face up to meet them and savored the cold softness on my skin. Like a child, I spread my arms and turned around and around, faster and faster, until I was laughing from sheer delight.

"Celia!" Miriam appeared out of the snow, breaking the spell. I whirled to a stop, breathless and embarrassed.

"What are you doing out here?" she scolded. "You don't even have a jacket on. You'll catch your death!" She took off her coat and wrapped it around my shoulders, holding my arms for a moment and studying my face. "Come inside. I have something I want to say to you."

She rushed me into her office and sat me in a chair. I was shaking with cold now and awake to the reality of dancing around outside in below-zero weather without my padded jacket or pants. Miriam handed me a metal mug of steaming tea. I cupped my hands around it to warm them while she looked at me.

"What possessed you to do such a foolish thing? If I hadn't been coming back from one of the barracks, you might have been outside long enough to get a serious case of frostbite. It isn't like you to do something like that. It worries me."

"I'm sorry, I don't know what made me do it. I felt hot and stuffy and wanted to get out of the hospital and breathe fresh air. I didn't think. And it felt so good to be out, almost like being free."

"All right. We'll let it go. I have something else I want to talk to you about. I know I put you in charge of Mr. Kovach and it's meant you've been spending a lot of time with him. I've also noticed a change in you since he arrived. It has concerned me."

"I've tried to balance my care of him with my other patients and duties here. It's just that I feel a responsibility to help him, particularly with the terrible itching of the rash, because I'm the one who did this to him."

"Yes, I know." Miriam gave me a worried frown and sighed. "Celia, we can't keep Mr. Kovach in quarantine—"

"No! They can't want him back yet! He isn't well. Tell them—"

"It's not just that. I'm worried you're growing too attached to him. It's natural for you to admire him and to enjoy being with a fellow Slovak, but . . ."

The door opened, and the commandant came in just then. Miriam and I both stood.

"Doctor Eliashvili." The commandant looked at me. "Prisoner . . . ?"

"Klein," I said. "Celia Klein." I lowered my eyes.

"Yes. I remember now." He seemed amused. "The bold young woman who went into the mine to rescue prisoners on her first day here. You had a couple of loyal friends who saved you, as I recall?"

"Yes, Commandant." I looked up. "Anichka and Branca."

He gave me an appraising look. "You've been here for how long?"

"Nine years, Commandant."

"Ah. Well, I'm sure you're an excellent assistant to Doctor Eliashvili."

"She is," Miriam said. "What can I do for you, Commandant?"

"Nothing. I have some news I think you might be interested in. I'm being transferred to Moscow soon."

"Congratulations. You're getting out of Vorkuta. You deserve it."

"I have you to thank, Doctor, for many of the good reports that have impressed Moscow. Fewer prisoners have died since you've been in charge."

"And, consequently, production has increased," Miriam said in a dry tone. "That's what impressed Moscow. I sometimes wonder if I'm doing my patients a favor or not, preserving their lives for hard labor."

The commandant nodded gravely. "I know your problems with the system, Doctor. It isn't perfect. But we do what we can. You're to be commended for your compassion."

"Thank you."

"I came by to tell you that Colonel Baranov will probably take my place as commandant."

Miriam gave a little laugh. "Then you can forget any advance in care at this hospital."

"My position in Moscow will be as the director of all camp hospitals. It will allow me to monitor what goes on here in Vorkuta. Many things have changed since the death of Stalin, our Brave Leader. But I advise you to get along with Colonel Baranov. He doesn't have patience for what he views as insubordination from the prisoners. Try to be nice to him, Doctor. It may mean the difference between life and death for your patients."

Miriam sighed. "I'll do my best. Thank you for letting me know. When will you be leaving?"

"As always, bureaucracies move slowly. I will let you know as soon as I know."

"Thank you. I do appreciate it."

He left without saying anything more, and I turned to Miriam. "Please. You've got to think of something to save Mr. Kovach. If Colonel Baranov becomes commandant, the first thing he'll do is kill him."

"Celia, you must calm down about this. It could be many months, even a year, before they transfer the commandant to Moscow."

"Or it could happen tomorrow," I urged. "No one knows. There must be some way of protecting Mr. Kovach."

"You keep insisting on his being marked for execution. The commandant has implied no such thing to me. Even if the NKVD intended such action, they would inform him."

"No, they wouldn't. Colonel Baranov would do it in secret. I know it."

"What I know is you're desperate to save Mr. Kovach from a fate that isn't at all determined."

"Miriam, I overheard Colonel Baranov order two of his men to kill him."

"You overheard Colonel Baranov? How?"

"I didn't tell you. I was meeting with two of my friends in an old *zemlyanka* in the cemetery. Just to talk and share stories. Please don't tell anyone."

"I won't, of course. But what does that have to do with Colonel Baranov? He wouldn't be out in the cemetery."

"All three of us heard him. He met these two men to remind them of where Prisoner Kovach was supposed to be if they hadn't failed to kill him the night he arrived. These two thugs had dumped the coal on him."

"I did wonder why he was attacked on his first night here."

"Yes. It wasn't prisoners who did it. I don't know whether Colonel Baranov has orders from the NKVD to kill him and make it look like an accident, or what. But he told those two men that Prisoner Kovach was a troublemaker and had to be eliminated. Don't you see, Miriam? It must be because he's been successful at getting prisoners freed, and because he's always writing appeals for justice in the camps. You know how dangerous it is even to possess a pencil and paper, much less write appeals and send them to Moscow. Ivan . . . Mr. Kovach . . . told me that one prisoner he got released had a sentence of twenty-five years. That's the same sentence as yours, Miriam. If he could do that when he was in the camps in Kazakhstan, maybe he could help prisoners here in Vorkuta. Maybe you. Isn't it worth trying to save someone who has the courage to risk his life to help all of us who are falsely accused of crimes we never committed? Crimes that weren't even crimes!"

Miriam remained silent for a long time. She was truly a good person and hated injustice and the entire camp system. But she was also protective of the hospital because it was the only way she could help prisoners. I waited for her to make her decision. If she wouldn't take the risk of defying Colonel Baranov, I didn't know what I could do. I had no power at all to save Ivan a second time.

"I think there might be a way to gain more time," Miriam said. "I can ask the commandant to grant invalid status for Mr. Kovach. It would mean they couldn't send him to work in the mines, but he could work here in the hospital. If he's not in the mines or living in the barracks, then it would be hard for Colonel Baranov's men to get to him. This wouldn't protect him forever. But it's the best I can do."

"Thank you, Miriam." Impulsively, I hugged her. "Thank you so very much. Who knows? Maybe a miracle will happen."

Miriam smiled. "What a change. The Celia I met nine years ago would never have uttered the word *miracle*."

"I *am* different," I said. "I feel it myself. If only . . ."

"What?"

"Nothing."

"Celia, try not to get too involved with Mr. Kovach. I mean, too attached. I don't want you to be disappointed or hurt. You have suffered enough. Keep an emotional distance. It's important."

"Emotionally?" I shrugged. "Don't worry. There's enough of the old Celia left to protect her from that."

"I hope so. Now, we both have work to do. I will go see the commandant. You have patients who need you."

CHAPTER THIRTY-SEVEN

I didn't see Ivan until I brought him his dinner rations that night. When I opened the door to his room, I found him sitting in the chair beside the small metal table, writing. He jumped at the sound of the door opening and thrust the papers behind him.

"You don't need to jump," I assured him as I closed the door. "You're still supposed to be highly contagious. Even Colonel Baranov is afraid to get near you. For now, at least."

"Colonel Baranov?"

"NKVD. He's been asking about your health."

"I can imagine." He took the papers and pencil and stashed them under his mattress.

"What are you writing?"

"Right now, I'd rather you didn't know I was writing anything at all."

"I'm sorry. I didn't mean to pry."

"Not at all, angel. It's just . . . what you don't know can't harm you."

"You really have to stop calling me an angel. Because . . . because it's not true."

"Of course it's true. You saved my life by injecting me with that devilish arnica and getting me declared highly contagious—you get angel status. You're also as beautiful as an angel. So I rest my case."

"Nonsense! Stop this. You make me all mixed up. Anyway, I brought you a portion of fresh bread today. I don't know what got into the cook to prepare such a feast. And there's sausage. I didn't ask what's in it. I hope not sawdust."

"Don't look a gift sausage in the . . ." He laughed. "I don't know how to end it. We'll share it."

"Like a picnic." I unwrapped the greasy paper and handed the sausage to him.

"Ah. I am to be the taster, I see. Very well . . ." He broke off a piece of sausage and ate it. "Ahh! A bit of kielbasa, a little bratwurst, with just a dash of sawdust. Let's call it Vorkutawurst." He broke off another piece and held it out. "Here, try some."

"Thank you, but no. You need it more than I do."

"Hmm. Let's say you're more wise than cowardly."

"Will you tell me another story about someone you saved?"

"If you like. I can tell you a story about an old captive rescued from hard labor. Only I was the villain this time."

"I don't believe you." I handed him a piece of bread. "How could you be the villain?"

"Celia . . . may I call you Celia? Since you object to the more accurate title of *angel*." The smile in his eyes turned serious. "I am not the saintly hero you imagine. I'm just a man with nearly all the faults a man can have, mixed with a few qualities you see as virtues. Like any man, I've done things I'm not proud of. I have yet to atone for them. If I ever get the chance."

I was silent. *Atone*. The word stretched between us like a deep crevasse, impossible to bridge. Whatever deeds he had committed in the past couldn't come close to mine. There would be reasons for his deeds, if not good reasons, at least understandable ones. I told myself there was a reason for mine, but I knew there was no atonement. How can you atone for the dead?

Still, it was as if my soul took a holiday when I was with him. I forgot the past and felt genuine happiness. I wasn't blind to reality. I knew he could disappear from my life at any moment. The NKVD could take him, he could be killed, he could be transferred to another camp. But until that happened, I was determined to be near him as much as I could. To smile, to be happy just for a little while.

"Let's not talk of that now," I said. "You were going to tell me the story of the old captive someone rescued from hard labor."

I was afraid he might want to continue a more serious conversation, but after looking at me with a kind of soft understanding in his eyes, he took up the story.

"We called him Old Vanya." Ivan raised his eyes and gazed at the ceiling. "It all started making mud bricks."

CHAPTER THIRTY-EIGHT

The Tale of Old Vanya
As told by Ivan Kovach

My story unfolds, as most of them do, in a camp in Kazakhstan. Prisoners were arriving daily to help build socialism in the vast steppes of Central Asia. But, alas, there was a severe housing shortage. The authorities could not have the prisoners sleeping outside, because they might wander off in the night, get lost on the vast steppe, and never be seen again. A fate, I might add, more desirable than hard labor and starvation. At least on the steppes, you might disappear long enough to find a life. However, the commissars had made plans for a housing development for us workers, and they were not to be deterred.

They set us to work making bricks to build barracks. Each day, we faced three huge piles of materials: one of clay, one of straw, and one of manure. We would take portions of each, add water, and mix it with our bare hands while standing in the miry clay. This was during the summer when it was so hot the chickens were laying hard-boiled eggs. Not that we had any eggs or chickens. I was working with a prisoner from Georgia called Zurab. He'd been in the camp since he was eighteen because they had arrested his father for disloyalty to the Great Stalin—a grave sin for a Georgian because Stalin was Georgian and expected unwavering devotion from his landsmen. Zurab was guilty by association because of his father. At this point, I had been in the camps for only three years, so I wasn't worn to a thread yet, like Zurab, who'd been there for ten. He was still a handsome young man, though, with dark, smoldering eyes under heavy brows, and a long, thin nose.

My tale begins just as Zurab gathers manure from the pile, throws it into the trough, jumps in, and starts to stomp the mixture to soften it up.

"It's too hard, Ivan. We need more water."

I went to the wooden sled that held the water barrels and dipped out a bucketful. Zurab stopped stomping, and I poured the water into the trough.

"That should be enough," I said, jumping in and joining him in our bizarre dance.

"If I close my eyes and ignore the smell, I can imagine I'm stomping grapes back home." Zurab's expressive mouth curled into a smile. "Have you ever had Georgian wine, Ivan?"

"Once only. With a friend from Georgia who was visiting Prague. We drank all night. I remembered nothing the next day."

"That's Georgian wine! You were in the arms of Lethe, goddess of oblivion. Lucky man. I wish I were in her arms right now."

"I do remember a woman," I said. "She was Georgian. Beautiful! Huge dark eyes. And incredible eyebrows."

"Our women are as legendary as our wine." He picked up a clump of clay and kneaded it with his hands to soften it more. "We've been making wine in Georgia since six thousand B.C. Did you know that?"

"No. That's impressive."

"We still do it the ancient way. We put the wine into enormous earthenware pots and bury them up to the neck in the ground for six months." Zurab held out the clump of clay. "This clay would make great *kvevri* pots. Minus the manure and straw, of course." He threw the clump back into the trough and began stomping again. "Why am I torturing myself with memories?"

Suddenly, his knees gave way and he fell face-down into the muck of clay and manure. I hauled him to his feet again and helped him out of the trough.

"You're too weak today to do this work, Zurab. You know what gets me? It's the inefficiency of this stupid process. We're behind on our quota from weakness, excessive heat, and hunger. The whole workload is on the shoulders, or rather, the legs of starving men."

I looked over at the wooden sled with the water barrels. The horse who pulled it was peacefully cropping the dry grass.

"Old Vanya there has four legs. You and I together have four more. With eight legs we could realize a one-hundred-percent increase in productivity." I put my arm around Zurab's shoulders and turned him to look toward Old Vanya. "Look at him, Zurab. He's living the life of a pampered bourgeois. He makes maybe only three or four trips a day with the sled, and in between he feasts off the bounty of the steppe. He's not doing his share of the work!" I strode over and unharnessed Old Vanya. "Come on, Vanya. Time for you to speed production."

I led him over and into the trough, which was just wide enough. With a bit of encouragement, Old Vanya stomped up and down in the trough. I confess he was probably just trying to get his hooves out of the muck, but his weight certainly improved the quality of the mixture quickly. The three of us stomped for a good fifteen minutes before a guard spotted us and came to Vanya's rescue.

"Here!" the guard hollered. "Halt, you fascists! Who gave you permission to torture this poor animal? It's all in a lather."

"We were just using horsepower to speed production according to the plan," I explained.

"Don't try to worm out of it!" The guard glared at us. "You're exploiting an innocent animal to get out of work."

"It all becomes clear to me now," I said. "Demanding human labor from a horse is exploitation. But hard labor for humans is not exploitation. Why then do we measure workload units in horsepower if we expect a man to hold up longer than an animal?"

"What? You can't talk your way out of this abuse, lawyer! Stop this torture now!"

I patted Old Vanya and helped to guide him out of the trough. "Sorry, Vanya. Go and relax. Maybe they'll make you a commissar and give you a posh stable in Moscow. You can live off the exploitation of the workers."

"One more joke and it's solitary for you, Prisoner Kovach."

And so Old Vanya was saved and prisoners Ivan and Zurab continued to stomp clay, straw, and manure, according to the plan.

CHAPTER THIRTY-NINE

When he finished his story, Ivan raised his head and emitted a loud whinny. It was exactly like an old horse, and I laughed so hard it made my eyes water.

"That's the first time I've seen you laugh," he said.

"I'm sorry." I stopped. "I didn't mean to laugh."

"Please, don't stop. There's nothing wrong with laughter."

"I rarely laugh. It makes me feel guilty. How can I laugh when there's so much suffering and injustice?"

"Don't feel guilty. Humor is often the only way we can get through this nightmare. Even if the laughter lasts only for a moment."

"The idea of Old Vanya as a commissar was so funny. I could see him in a hat and uniform, marching up and down . . ." I started laughing again. "Tell me something serious. What happened then? Did Zurab survive?"

"Barely. Without help from Old Vanya, the men in my brigade grew weaker and weaker. We fell behind in our work quota, which meant we got less food, which made us even weaker still. They worked us and starved us until we became nearly transparent. At that point, the camp bosses decided to get us off their books and send us to a camp for invalids in Spassk. It was known as 'the place of no return.'"

"Why was it called that?"

"Invalids are useless to the State, so the State wastes no resources on preserving them with enough food or drink to restore them to health. What awaited us in Spassk was certain death."

"That's evil. But how did you escape?"

"You know how God seems to take a strange interest in me? Well, the guards loaded us into a truck, and we rode through the vast expanse of the steppes again, roasting by day and freezing by night. After three days, we stopped at a new camp to take on supplies. This camp was looking for carpenters, painters, masons, technical workers. If they decided you could still work, they allowed you to stay in this camp instead of going on to Spassk. This was the village of Saran in Karaganda."

"And you were strong enough to work?"

"Not exactly. But I got very lucky. Again."

"Tell me what happened."

"Another story." Ivan's eyes held mine for a moment with such intensity I shivered and looked down. He took my hand in his. "Remind me to tell you sometime how much more delightful an audience you are than Kustor Barza and his crew. I could tell you stories for the rest of my life." He smiled with a little laugh. "Until you got tired of my performances."

"That would never happen," I whispered.

It was true on both counts. I would never tire of listening to him, but I also knew I could never be with him for the rest of my life. Miriam was right to suggest I should distance myself from Ivan, physically and emotionally, but I simply couldn't.

"Tell me the Spassk story." I shook myself out of my thoughts and smiled at him. "Is there an animal in that story too?"

"Yes! How did you guess?"

CHAPTER FORTY

The Tale of a Lucky Dog
or
Better One Friend than a Hundred Rubles

As told by Ivan Kovach

Saran was in a desolate place. As far as the eye could see, there was nothing but flat, dusty land covered in scrub grass. The sun beat mercilessly down on us as we unloaded from the truck. The few official buildings and barracks were crowded together as if they were desperately trying to be an actual town. When we arrived, a pack of guards and other officials gathered to inspect us and decide who could stay to work and who would go on to the dreaded Spassk. I got down from the truck and tried to look hale and hearty. A man broke from the group of officials and rushed to stand directly in front of me. I didn't recognize him, but he seemed to know me.

"Ivan?" he asked, looking at me curiously.

"I don't think I . . ." I stammered.

"Artur. Artur Mandel," he said. "Mukachevo Middle School. Nineteen-twenty-four."

I couldn't believe it. "Artur! They got you too?"

He enfolded me in a big bear hug. "Afraid so. Never could keep my mouth shut."

I laughed. "I couldn't keep my mouth shut either. I should have listened to Professor Zanoff. *Think befo e you speak, Ivan.*"

Artur gave me a knowing smile and nodded. "But why are you here? Last I heard, you were on your way to a brilliant career in the Czech Parliament."

"That's what I thought too," I said. "But then Prime Minister Chamberlain gave Czechoslovakia to Hitler. Remember? *Peace in our time!*"

"And look where we are!" Artur swept an expressive hand over the bleak landscape.

"In hell. Maybe we deserve it. We always were the class troublemakers."

"Don't despair, Ivan." Artur laughed. "Miracles still happen. Here we are together on the steppe of Central Asia." Artur took my arm. "But you can't be on your way to Spassk, Ivan—that's the end of the line. No exit from that place. You don't look good, but you don't look bad enough for Spassk."

"I'm not. If I could just get enough food and rest for a couple of days in a row, I'd be fit for work."

"You've come to the right place and the right man, Ivan. Believe it or not, I am the bookkeeper here in Saran. I thank our old math teacher for that. You remember how Professor Shapiro mercilessly drilled numbers into my head? Saved my life, the old tyrant. Come with me to administration. I'll sing your praises to Commissar Gavrilov."

We found Commissar Gavrilov at his desk, eating lunch. An old chubby dog sat at attention nearby, staring hard at its master, hoping for a scrap. I looked even more longingly than that dog at the bread and cheese and *kvass* spread out before the commissar.

"What do you want, Mandel?" Gavrilov snapped. "Can't you see I'm eating?"

"It's about that problem we have with the foreign prisoners," Artur said, undaunted.

"Blasted headache!" Gavrilov took a drink of *kvass*. "Can't understand a word they say. They could be plotting sabotage, and I wouldn't have a clue. What about them?"

"This man just arrived on the trucks for Spassk," Artur said, indicating me.

"I can't use any invalids. We're rationed for food as it is." He threw a hunk of cheese at the dog. "Here, Sabachik!"

I licked my lips as I watched the dog gobble up that piece of cheese in one bite.

Artur persisted. "Prisoner Kovach looks thin, it's true, but we need this man, Commissar. He's a polyglot."

"A what?" Gavrilov grimaced.

"He speaks Czech, Hungarian, Slovak, French, and German."

Gavrilov stared at me. "What about Japanese?"

"*Konnichiwa! Sayonara!*" I barked and bowed. *Hello* and *goodbye* were the only two Japanese words I knew.

Gavrilov waved a hand. "Fine. Get him set up. Now, get out of here. I've got work to do." He threw the last crust of bread to the dog. "Here, Sabachik!"

Sabachik snapped up the bread and looked to Gavrilov for more.

"That's all you get, ungrateful cur. You're always hungry. Just like the prisoners."

CHAPTER FORTY-ONE

When Ivan finished the story, I was furious at Commissar Gavrilov and his callous indifference.

"Again!" I exclaimed. "There you are, obviously starving, and the commissar is feeding a fat dog. First it was Old Vanya, who couldn't be tortured with stomping clay, and now a fat dog. Why not the same compassion for humans? It infuriates me."

"Part of the ideology, my dear. Old Vanya and Sabachik are not class enemies. Men and women who disagree with the ideology are dangerous and deserve to be starved, worked to death, tortured. Or killed, when you can't get anything more out of them."

"It's all so hopeless."

"Not completely." Ivan's eyes sparkled. "Commissar Gavrilov didn't know what trouble he'd brought to the Soviet State when he agreed to let me stay in Saran."

"What did you do?"

"What I can't seem to stop doing," Ivan said with a wry smile. "Making speeches. You see, Artur Mandel set me up as a brigadier to oversee the foreigners. He filled me in on who these prisoners were and what I could expect from them. I walked into the foreign barracks and was confronted with a babble of languages. The babble stopped, and they all stared at me. Deeply suspicious. Somehow, I had to convince them I wasn't a spy for the commissars."

"Why would they think you were a spy? You were a prisoner like them."

"Yes, but I came out of nowhere and had the blessing of Commissar Gavrilov."

"Ah, that would be suspicious. How did you convince them to trust you?"

"There were around thirty men from various countries in the foreign barracks. I stood there silent for a few moments, looking them over. Some were sitting on bunks, others on the floor or pacing around the room. They were mostly political prisoners, not criminals, and probably well-educated men.

"I introduced myself. 'Gentlemen,' I projected in my clearest voice. 'The commissars see this foreign brigade as a Tower of Babel and see themselves in the role of God. God divided men by creating all the languages of the earth. He did it to keep men subject to Him. The commissars think if we can't understand one another, then they can keep us as slaves and control us by setting us against each other. To this, I say, We Are One! *Egyek Vagyunk! Jestesmy jednoscia! Nous sommes un! Jsme Jeden! Wir sind eins!*'"

"What did they do?"

"To my surprise and relief, they stood and gave a cheer. When they stopped, I continued. I told them I was chosen as their new brigadier and that I understood how a brigade worked. If the brigade leader is fair, I said, democratic and not arrogant, he can always count on the brigade. It would never let him down. It would stand up for him.

"They translated for each other and nodded in agreement. I told them how the brigade must be able to trust their leader. They must feel he's one of them and has their interests at heart. Their lives may depend on him. 'I am one of you,' I said. 'I will never let you down. I will fight for your rights, whether it's for full rations of food, the meager salary they pay us, or unjust punishment. If we work together, we will survive. If we quarrel among ourselves, if we cheat each other, lie to each other, we will be as dogs fighting over a nonexistent bone. Together, we will survive this hell!'"

"That was really inspiring. Did they accept you?"

"I wasn't sure they would, but when I finished, they rushed up and shook my hand. Some of them gave me bread and a ration of cheese, others a drink of water. These were the only things they had to offer in welcome. I tried to eat politely and not inhale my food like Sabachik."

"I think you enjoyed that speech," I said. "Like being back in parliament."

"Yes, I admit I did. It was a little like that. Fortunately, I didn't have to repeat it in each language. They helped each other out. But you're right. A lawyer's always ready with a persuasive argument. It was exhilarating, I must admit."

"What happened then?"

Ivan laughed. "I'm feeling like Scheherazade again. If only we had a thousand and one nights."

"That sounds like an awfully long time. How many years is that?"

"A little over two and a half. But miracles can happen."

"I don't believe in miracles."

There was a knock on the door, and I opened it. Masha stood in the hall, looking worried. "Hurry!" she said. "They're bringing someone in. I think it's your friend Anichka."

My heart stopped. "Anichka! Please, God. No! I'm coming."

With a last look at Ivan, I rushed out.

CHAPTER FORTY-TWO

I dashed into the corridor and there was Yogush, the criminal boss, carrying Anichka in his arms. Branca hovered behind him. Miriam appeared at the door to her office.

"What happened?" Miriam asked.

"Unconscious," Yogush barked, his ugly, tattooed face a blend of anger and worry. "Found her outside in the snow. Don't know how long she was out there."

"Follow me." Miriam led him down the corridor.

Branca rushed up to me and we followed them.

"What happened?" I asked her.

"I don't know. Anichka went out to take one of her amulets to another barracks. When she didn't come back, I went to make sure she was all right. I found her in the snow halfway there. I tried to lift her, but I wasn't strong enough. I was going to run for a guard when Yogush just appeared out of the snow like a ghost. How he knew is a mystery."

We stopped outside the room Anichka was in.

"Did she just faint from cold or hunger?" I asked. "Was she dehydrated?"

"I'm not sure." Branca leaned against the corridor wall. "To tell you the truth, she hasn't been well for over a week. Frankly, I don't know how she's survived these nine years. She never was strong enough. Just damned determined. But she caught cold last week during the big freeze, and it's like her body just gave up."

"Why didn't she come to the hospital?"

"They increased the quotas in the mines and had to put extra people to work there. Anichka and I got caught up in the recruitment. I protested, but they put two new overseers on who were crazed about the quotas. Anichka was coughing more than ever in the mine, what with the cold and dust and such hard labor. I asked them to send her to the hospital, but they said she couldn't be spared." Branca slammed her fist against the wall. "Bastards!"

"Let's go in. I have to see her."

Miriam was checking a thermometer with a worried frown when we entered the room. Yogush stood next to the bed, staring at Miriam with those strange eyes of his. He tore his gaze away and leaned over Anichka. He brought his face next to hers and whispered in her ear. He blew a breath over Anichka's face, then, while muttering something in a strange language, he removed the *Shamanka* necklace he had given her as a badge of honor. Miriam opened her mouth to say something, but Yogush stretched a hand over the bed and grabbed Miriam's wrist.

"You cannot save her," he growled. Then he let Miriam go, turned, and walked out the door.

I rushed to the bed. Anichka had blankets piled on top of her. She looked so tiny and frail. I took her hand, fighting back tears. Her eyes opened, blue as a summer's day.

"Celia." Anichka smiled at me. "It's good to see you."

"You too," I said. "You're in the hospital now. You can rest. We'll make you well."

"Rest." She tried to take a deep breath, which brought on a fit of coughing. "Rest. That's nice. I'm so tired, Celia."

"I know. You don't have to do anything here. Just sleep and eat and get your strength back."

"Strength." She sighed. "I tried to do the exercises you taught me. To be strong. But it was hard after working all day in the freezing cold. I just . . ." She coughed again and closed her eyes.

"Shh. Don't try to talk."

"Don't go into the mine." Anichka's fingers tightened around my hand. "There are rats. And it's so . . . cold in the mine."

"You'll get warm here."

I looked up at Miriam. She looked away. I could tell Yogush was right.

A guard appeared in the doorway. From the look on Branca's face, I figured he was one of the new overseers. He moved to the bed and looked down at Anichka.

"When will she be out of here?" he grumbled. "We've got a quota to—"

"I'll let you know," Miriam snapped, cutting him off.

The guard turned to Branca. "You! You're needed at the mine. Come on!"

"She stays until I examine her," Miriam said. "This could be contagious."

"We've got a quota—"

"You will never reach your quota if all your miners get sick. I'll send her back when I've finished."

The guard stomped out, muttering to himself.

"I feel fuzzy," Anichka murmured. "Is Branca still here? She forced them to bring me."

Branca looked at me. "The bastards wanted to send her back to the barracks instead of bringing her here."

"Branca's here, Anichka," I said.

Branca moved to the other side of the bed and took Anichka's other hand.

Anichka closed her eyes for a moment and smiled. "Remember when we rocked the car, and the train almost went off the track?"

I squeezed her hand. "Of course I remember. You were great. You kept everyone going."

"It was fun," she whispered. "We were the Pissers. Strong." Another coughing fit shook her. "Fuzzy." Her eyes swept my face. "You're hazy, Celia."

"Rest. Don't talk. You're going to get well."

"I tried . . . I tried to . . . I guess . . . I just wasn't a very good miner."

"You were a great miner, Anichka. The best at everything."

I watched her face soften into another little smile. She sighed and closed her eyes.

Miriam checked Anichka for a pulse. Branca sucked in a quick breath, and I lifted my eyes to Miriam. She shook her head. I gazed back at Anichka's sweet little face, remembering how her eyes lit up at anything funny, the way her smile radiated warmth in the coldest place on earth. Anichka. My Anichka was gone.

My eyes burned with tears I could not stop. Branca was crying, too, but her expression looked like she wanted to murder someone.

"Anichka makes eight," Branca said through clenched teeth.

"Eight?"

"The Pissers. Eight are gone now. Worked to death."

— ★ —

I couldn't bear to see them take her body away. I couldn't bear to think of her boxed and buried in the frozen tundra of Siberia. I had to be alone. I hurried out and shut myself up in the tiny isolation room we had for prisoners who became violent. The room had no windows to let in light, so I sat in the dark and gave way to my grief, rocking back and forth. For nine years, Anichka had been a small but glittering light in the darkness of Vorkuta. The cruelty and bestiality of the camp had never destroyed her quiet gentleness. She moved through this hell like a celestial spirit, always understanding, always helpful, always kind. Even the criminals sensed it and protected her. She was like a living amulet, radiating hope just by existing.

I heard the door open. Miriam had guessed where I was. I said nothing, just continued to rock and stare at the floor.

"I'm sorry, Celia. I know she was a friend."

"It should have been me." I couldn't keep the bitterness out of my voice. "I should have been in that mine with her. I should have been working with them all this time."

"You can blame me if you want to," Miriam said. "For playing God and keeping you from hard labor and death."

"I don't blame you. You couldn't know I wasn't worth saving."

"Won't you tell me what it is that still torments you? I don't judge, Celia."

"Confession?"

"It can be a path to atonement."

I stood up then and faced Miriam in the darkness. "Atonement is impossible for me. Not in a million years of punishment." I went to the door and opened it. Light from the corridor streamed in. "You're too good to understand, Miriam." I turned and walked down the corridor. Better she never know the darkness inside the person she had worked so hard to save.

CHAPTER FORTY-THREE

I didn't go to Ivan's room until late afternoon the next day. I had to come to terms with my anger and grief. I didn't want to burden him with my problems. I knew that if I told him about Anichka, I would break down and he would comfort me and that would lead to the intimacy I was afraid of. I had worked hard to keep as much emotional distance from him as I could. Each time I was with him, it became more and more difficult.

He stood by the window, looking out at the leaden sky. "It seems I have some bodyguards watching my window," he said with humor. He gathered his papers and put them under his mattress.

"I have your dinner," I said. "It's early, I know. I wanted to get some meat for you before it was all gone."

"You're too good to me." He turned and looked at me. "What's wrong?"

"Nothing."

He took the tray from me and set it on the bed. Then he took my chin in his hand and lifted my face. "You've been crying."

I shrugged. "Just another death." I dug my teeth into my lip to stop the lump in my throat from turning into tears. "I knew her."

"I'm sorry." He stroked my face so gently. Like soothing a child.

I backed up, straightened my shoulders, and looked away. "I'll get over it. Eat your dinner."

I could feel his eyes still on my face. "Shall I tell you a story?"

"Sure."

I knew I was being curt, keeping a distance, but I had to or I'd fall apart. Ivan didn't comment on my manner—just continued as if there was nothing unusual in the room's atmosphere. I knew I should leave, but I didn't want to be alone, thinking about Anichka, about myself, about what was and what could not be.

"*Anna Karenina?*"

"Yes. You never told me what happened to Anna."

"First let me tell you what happened to Kitty."

"Right. I always forget about Kitty."

"So did Vronsky. When he rejected Kitty, she fell ill for quite some time."

I let the sound of his voice and the world of the story take me once again outside reality and out of myself. I was beginning to understand the healing power of stories. Through the sufferings and joys of fictional characters, paths opened from despair to peace. They say misery loves company. Maybe that was why I craved these tales.

Ivan's voice, soft and low, caressed each word. "Levin waited, hoping against hope the love they'd shared before would return. He was afraid to see Kitty. Afraid to ask her again to marry him. Afraid she would refuse him. So Kitty's family stepped in. They invited Levin to a large dinner party they were giving. Levin was unsure, but he went. The moment he had been longing for, and dreading, arrived. Kitty saw him across the room. She smiled. Not a formal smile this time, but a smile of true love."

"And they married?"

"They did. And they lived and worked together on his estate in the country. They took joy in the seasons, the farm, the quiet beauty of the countryside. They raised a family and lived as happily as any two people can."

I didn't respond, and Ivan let the silence hang comfortably in the air.

"Is that what you'd do?" I asked. "If you ever got out of here. Live in the country?"

"I once thought country life would be like Marx said, idiotic and boring. Now, I think it would be heaven."

"Heaven. That's just a story too."

"Not always." His voice was so calm, so deep and comforting.

"What happened to Anna?"

"Ah. Anna. There was no happy ending for Anna."

"Why? What happened to her?" Maybe it was my depression over Anichka, or that I was so emotionally drained, but I had a feeling Anna Karenina was another tragedy.

Ivan gently continued the story. "Anna was madly in love with Vronsky, and he was madly in love with her. But Anna was married and had a small child. Her husband refused to give her a divorce. She left him and her child, and ran away with Vronsky. For a time, they lived a life filled with passion and romance. But the guilt Anna felt, especially for deserting her child, grew stronger. All her friends turned their backs on her. She felt even Vronsky didn't love her. How could anyone love someone who had done such a selfish thing? But she couldn't stop herself. She lied to herself. Told herself it wasn't her fault. It was fate. But she knew the pursuit of her own desires was at the expense of the happiness of her son and husband. And in the end, she came to hate herself for what she'd done."

As I listened, I saw myself in the story. Not the romance of the love affair with Vronsky, not even the desertion of Anna's child. The selfishness was the connection. The sacrifice of others for Anna's own desires. The lying to herself, telling herself it was fate, and she was helpless to do anything else.

"How did she live with that?" I really wanted to know, even though it was fiction.

"She didn't. In the end, she committed suicide. She threw herself under a train."

He said it without emotion. Like it was inevitable. Expected. Necessary.

"Then it isn't a story about love at all. It's a story about guilt."

"It's a story about choices," Ivan said. "Some good. Some bad. And what we make of them."

I had to get away. The air in the room had become so close I felt I could not breathe. "Thank you for telling me the story. Your dinner is cold. I have to go." I stood and walked to the door.

"Celia." Ivan came to me and put his hand on my shoulder. "I shouldn't have told you. Not after the death of your friend."

"It's all right." I didn't look at him. "There's no connection. I'm tougher than you think. Good night."

I opened the door to escape, but I had to turn back. He was looking at me.

"I wish you a night with no dreams," I said, then left.

CHAPTER FORTY-FOUR

I had to get outside. My head was swimming with memories and disturb-ing thoughts. Thoughts of my friends working at hard labor. Thoughts of Ivan and his kindness to me. Thoughts of Anichka's death. Thoughts of Anna Karenina's suicide. I dressed in my padded clothes, pulled my *ushanka* with the earflaps down tight on my head, and left the hospital. For a time, I stood still, listening to the sounds of the mining machinery and watching the lightly falling snow. The snow was black today. Black snow often fell when there was so much coal dust in the air. It mixed with the snow as it formed in the clouds. I walked in the black snow until darkness descended, then turned back, knowing I had patients to attend to and reports to fill out for Miriam. I was just entering the side door when Branca walked out of the darkness.

"Celia! You'll freeze out here," Branca scolded.

"Not any more than you. It's good to see you, Branca."

"You too. I've brought you a birthday present."

"Birthday?"

"Funny. Anichka said you wouldn't remember."

"Anichka remembered my birthday?"

"Yes. And this present is from her. She was going to bring it to you, but . . . so I'm bringing it. Anichka made it for you." Branca handed me a bundle wrapped in newspaper. "*Pravda*'s not very cheerful wrapping paper, but it's all I had."

I unwrapped the present. It was a statue of a nude woman carved out of coal. Both her arms reaching for the sky, her hands clenched into fists, and her chin lifted in defiance.

"It's wonderful," I said. "So powerful."

"It's supposed to be you. Anichka always admired how strong and tough you were on our journey to Vorkuta. How you got us to be a team. How you saved us all those times on the train."

"I always loved the little amulets and talismans she carved." I turned the figure in my hands. "But this is a genuine artist's sculpture. She had such talent. It's so awful that . . ." My throat constricted, and I brushed away tears.

"She liked carving things out of the coal." Branca reached out and ran her hand over the carved figure. "Said she liked the blue-black shine of it. Wanted to make it into something nice, so it wasn't just a symbol of suffering in the mines. That was our Anichka—always looking for beauty."

"Thank you, Branca. I'll treasure it."

"I've got to get back. Curfew. Happy birthday, Celia. Take care of yourself."

"Stay safe."

"Don't worry about me. I'm as hard as coal now."

Branca disappeared into the rapidly falling snow. I hugged the statue and let the tears roll down my cheeks, freezing into tiny pearls of ice on my skin. I hadn't realized it was my birthday. I had banished birthdays from my life years ago. Now, I thought of home and how gay and bright birthday celebrations had been when I was a child. Presents wrapped in pretty paper with ribbon bows. My mother and father always telling my sisters and me how proud they were of us, what wonderful daughters we were. A family party, cake, ice cream, toasts to the birthday girl. And love—gentle, unconditional love—wrapping me in a secure cocoon of happiness.

Standing in the bitter cold of Vorkuta, I felt empty. I could see no beauty or light anywhere, only ugliness and darkness. Even the snow, which was supposed to cover the world in a blanket of white, was black. I was like Anna Karenina, alone and outcast, trapped forever in hopeless desolation. I shuddered with cold, and an overwhelming desire for human warmth and affection swept through me.

I rushed back inside to my little room in the hospital. I tore off my outdoor clothes and put on the dress I sometimes wore as a nurse in the summer. It was a faded blue and had a long row of mismatched buttons down the front. The hem had frayed from years of wear and washing on a rough board. But it was a dress. I felt like a woman in it, not just a prisoner with a number. I didn't know if I'd have the courage to do what I planned, but I knew I had to try. Today was my birthday. I was twenty-nine. If not now, then possibly never.

I walked quietly down the corridor and opened the door to Ivan's room. It was in total darkness. He was asleep. I could hear his breath rising and falling in a peaceful rhythm. I stepped inside and shut the door as softly as I could. For a time, I just stood there in the darkness, watching him sleep. I couldn't do it. I felt stupid for even thinking I could. I turned to leave, and he must have sensed I was there since I had made no sound.

"Celia?"

"Yes." I turned back. "It's me."

"Is something wrong?" He sat up.

"Not really."

"Just a visitation from an angel, then?"

I could feel his smile.

"It's my birthday," I whispered.

"How wonderful," he said. "I've learned something new. Angels have birthdays." He moved to sit on the edge of the bed. "I wish I had a present for you. Unfortunately, I'm all out of champagne."

I waited in silence for so long that I was afraid he'd be alarmed, but he seemed to know I was trying to come to a decision, and he said nothing.

"Would you . . . ?" I stammered. "I have no right to ask, but would you . . . ?"

He stood and came over to me, put his hands on my shoulders and looked into my eyes. "Celia. What is it?"

I answered him in a rush, my heart pounding, my voice unrecognizable even to myself. "Would you make love to me?"

He stepped back at that, but he kept his eyes on mine. His eyes were dark, but there was light in their depths, like embers of coal in the dark room. He didn't smile, not even with his voice. "With pleasure. But . . ."

"I want to know what it's like," I said with determination.

He took a pause. "Are you saying you've never had—"

I cut him off. "Sex? I've had more than enough. If that's what it really was. But I've never had what they call making love. I've wondered what that was like. If it was really something . . . pleasant."

He let out a long breath. "It can be much more than that. Especially if two people love each other."

"I don't know about love either."

"And I don't know what it's like to make love to an angel." He came close and took my face in both his hands. "Now," he said softly, "I am longing to find out."

CHAPTER FORTY-FIVE

That night, I knew I loved Ivan more than anything, and I would love him forever, even if we could never have a life together. I was sure they—the gods, the State, Fate—would never grant us that happiness. His gentleness with me, his compassion and tenderness, were the most precious gifts I could ever have.

Morning came too swiftly. I woke from a dreamless sleep to a strange feeling of happiness. Usually, I woke to the realization of another day in Vorkuta, another day in a bitter life that would never end. But this morning I woke to the feeling of arms around me, embracing me, protecting me, assuring me that I was loved. In the pale light I saw that the snow had fallen so thick during the night that it covered the window. The room was bitter cold, but I was warm. I longed to stay this way forever, but a noise in the corridor alerted me to reality. Apprehension drove me quickly to fling myself into my clothes. I would be late for my duties. Others would be in the corridor and would realize where I had spent the night. Miriam would know and disapprove. I would be reprimanded.

Ivan stirred, and I quickly left the room before he could wake up. I almost felt more nervous confronting him than anyone else. I rushed down the corridor and into Miriam's office.

"I'm so sorry, Miriam," I breathed. "I overslept. I don't know what happened."

She looked at me curiously but only said, "You've been up quite late for several nights recently. You should try to get to bed a bit earlier. We can't have you getting sick. There are too many patients needing care. Another pneumonia case came in late last night." She picked up a sheet of paper and handed it to me. "I've made a list of the most pressing duties for you today. I want you to complete them all before you spend any more time with Mr. Kovach. He's much better and doesn't need constant care now."

I looked her in the eyes and hoped mine didn't betray the elation I felt from the night before. "Yes," I said. "I've noticed how much better he is. I'll leave him to his own devices until dinner rations."

"Good. You may go now, Celia. As always, let me know of any important changes in your patients."

I turned toward the door and froze. Colonel Baranov came striding in, unannounced, as usual. I couldn't leave with him blocking the door, and I didn't want to say anything because he looked so fierce. I could have been invisible—he paid no attention to me, nor did he order me to leave. I backed away, kept my head down, and stood still. He strode to Miriam's desk and confronted her, annoyance in his tone. Miriam didn't even stand up at his entrance. Reckless of her. But brave.

Baranov got to the point. "It has come to my attention, Doctor, that you have assigned Prisoner Kovach invalid status. I told you to let me know when he had recovered. He is a saboteur and an enemy of the State. As such, he is the property of the State and is to be subjected to due punishment."

"He is also my patient." Miriam's tone stood firm. "I have the authority to decide when he is fit for release."

"You have *exceeded* your authority, Doctor Eliashvili. It is my duty to report your insubordination to the commandant. He will decide what punishment to prescribe for you."

"Colonel Baranov, the commandant himself signed the order for invalid status for Mr. Kovach. You must not have read to the bottom of the page. That was careless." Miriam shrugged. "Still, it is your solemn duty to confront the commandant on his ill-advised decision. I look forward to his response."

"The commandant will be transferred to Moscow soon, Doctor," Baranov said with obvious smugness. "I will be taking his place. There will be changes. Security and discipline have been deteriorating since the death of Comrade Stalin, our Devoted Leader. *That will b rectifie .*"

"I have no doubt, Colonel." Miriam gave him a tight little smile. "However, you are not commandant yet. Now, if you will excuse me, I am terribly busy trying to make order out of the chaos you so abhor."

Baranov slammed his fist on Miriam's desk. "Attitudes also will change, Doctor," he snarled. "Good day."

He turned sharply and marched out the door. A few seconds later, the entrance door slammed. I looked at Miriam.

"Well," she said. "We had a nice fight."

"I'm sorry for causing you so much trouble. I want to thank you before I go, for getting invalid status for Mr. Kovach. I was afraid it would be impossible. Now, he'll be safe. Won't he?"

"For now, yes. For his sake, we must hope the bureaucracy in Moscow is as slow as the commandant thinks it might be. From my experience, it could take at least a year."

"I hope so. Anything might happen in a year."

Miriam raised her eyebrows. "I don't usually hear optimism from you, Celia."

"I don't know why I said that. Nothing ever changes."

"Except the arrival of Mr. Kovach." Miriam's eyes questioned mine.

"Yes. That was different," I said blandly. "I'd better go."

★

I had only spoken the truth when I said nothing ever changes. Vorkuta was a place of soul-destroying inevitability, death by starvation, or overwork taken for granted. Brutality and abuse formed the framework of everyone's lives. You fought back when you could, succumbed when necessary. Your mind focused solely on the essentials of survival. When treated like animals, men *behaved* like animals. Though I was spared hard labor in the mines or clay pits, I saw the gruesome results of life in the camp every day.

And yet, Miriam was right—today everything had changed for me. A simple act of intimacy had complicated my life in a way I never imagined. I had learned what it was to love, and I also knew it could never last. Like Anna Karenina, I had made choices, and those choices destroyed lives. That had been years ago now, in a different hell. Many still alive knew what I was and what I had done. But not here in Vorkuta. At first, I saw Vorkuta as my punishment. Horrible as it was, it seemed *just*. Until Miriam altered its severity. Then Vorkuta had been a place to hide. I never spoke of my past to anyone. Maybe no one would really care in this barbaric place. I didn't know. Still, I believed if Anichka and Branca had known the truth about me, they would not have wanted to have anything to do with me. Miriam might have tried to help me come to terms with my guilt, but even she could not have forgiven me. Not that I wanted forgiveness. I didn't deserve it.

And now there was Ivan. It was as though I'd been living in a dark prison cell, and he opened the door, and outside, the sun was shining on a beautiful garden. He held out his hand for me to leave the prison cell, but just as I got to the door, it slammed shut. No. Ivan was the last person on earth who I wanted to know about those choices I had made all those years ago. I would have to go on pretending and deceiving until Fate took him away.

When I took him his dinner rations later that day, he was sitting at the small table again, looking over some sheets of paper, reading and making corrections to what he'd written. I felt so awkward and shy after last night. I stood there in silence until he sensed my presence.

"I'm interrupting you," I said. "It's just some soup. I'll leave you to . . ."

He jumped up, grabbed the tray, and set it on the table. "Leave? I've been waiting for you all day."

He took my hand, raised it to his lips, and kissed it. Then he drew me into his arms and kissed me tenderly, then long and deeply. Holding me at arms' length, he said, "There's that angel blush again." He took my face in both his hands. "My darling girl. I feel like I could take on the entire Soviet Army and defeat them single-handedly. You . . ." He kissed me again. "You have given me the fire I needed to finally take action."

"What action?" I still felt awkward.

He snatched the sheets of paper off the small table. "See these? Letters, Celia. Letters I hope will get us home!"

"Home? Letters? How?"

"Letters to the Americans, the British, and the Supreme Soviet."

I felt a cold rush of fear. "If I inspired this craziness . . ."

"Inspiration to action, not craziness." He lowered his voice, guided me to the bed, and sat me down. "I've been waiting to tell you, but after last night I've decided not to wait any longer. Listen. The United Nations passed a resolution. All foreign prisoners are to be sent back to their home countries. Even the USSR has signed this resolution."

"I don't believe that. How do you know?"

"That is a story you will love. But before I tell you, I want to ask you to help me. I've written letters to remind the powers-that-be about the foreign prisoners who the Soviet authorities haven't released yet. The UN resolution authorizes their immediate release. But the prisoners in the remote Siberian camps, like Vorkuta, have *not* been released yet. Even Moscow might not know we are still here. The camp commissars want to hold onto these foreign prisoners, namely us, for as long as they can. Remember, the foreigners are the best workers. If they let us go, they will never meet their quotas."

"It sounds wonderful. But how can I help?" I smiled a bit ruefully.

"Here's the plan. I would like you to give these letters to Doctor Eliashvili to put in the mail pouch. She has the authority. That pouch goes by air. Imagine! Those letters could be in Moscow in a day. In a day, Celia!" He held me with his eyes. "Will you do it?"

"Of course! Give me the letters." I would do anything for him.

"I'll put all three into one envelope. It's going to a friend of mine in Moscow who will get them to the appropriate embassies and to the Supreme Soviet."

He folded the letters, put them into an envelope, and sealed it. I took the envelope from him and put it in the pocket of my lab coat.

"But how did you find this out?" I asked. "It surely wasn't in *Pravda*."

He laughed. "That is an incredible story, and one I still have a hard time believing myself."

"Another story!"

He drew the chair up to the bed where I sat and faced me. "Do you have the time? I don't want to get you into trouble. I know I'm not your only patient."

"Just my most fascinating patient." I smiled softly into his eyes. "Don't worry. I've finished all my duties for today. Tell me. I love your stories. They take me out of Vorkuta for just a little while."

"If my letters succeed, I will take you out of Vorkuta forever." He turned my hand over and planted a kiss on my palm.

"You certainly don't lack confidence," I said lightly, covering my conflicting emotions. "Even when the odds are impossible."

"Not impossible! Who knows? God may find it amusing to help me yet again."

"Just so you'll stop pestering Him?"

"Exactly."

He released my hands, and I felt a sudden sense of loss.

"What's your story this time?"

"It's a bizarre one. About a forbidden radio and an abandoned outhouse."

CHAPTER FORTY-SIX

The Tale of the Outhouse Radio

As told by Ivan Kovach

It was the winter of '54, the coldest winter in memory in Kazakhstan. On a bitterly cold day, a truck rolled into the camp in Saran. More foreign prisoners to replace the ones who had died. The door to the barracks opened and in walked a man I hadn't seen since my days as a graduate student at Saint Elizabeth University in Hungary. His name was Jura Horvat, and when I saw him, I could hear the gypsy music at the old Twelve Apostles restaurant where we went to escape the tedium of books and papers. Jura was a Yugoslav, one of the many foreign students given scholarships by the Hungarians. An engineering major and a tinkerer, his tiny, rented room was crammed with what he called his tinker toys: handmade clocks, electric toasters and heaters, a pocket camera. Pieces of wire and metal were everywhere. You had to be careful when you sat down.

When Hitler conquered Yugoslavia, Jura left school and returned home to join the resistance. I thought he was dead. But here he was in Saran. Even though his tall frame was emaciated from hard labor and lack of food, the old fire still burned in his dark eyes. They put the two of us to work, laying bricks for a building foundation. We looked like a couple of Bedouin nomads with rags wrapped around our necks and heads against the fierce wind and blowing dirt. Our bare hands were blue-white from the cold. Still, we fell easily into our old camaraderie.

"We're wasting our time out here, Ivan." Jura scooped up another handful of the mud mixture we used in place of mortar. "Bricklaying is a mindless endeavor."

I spread some more mud on a line of bricks. "I've tried to explain that to our overlords, Jura, but it doesn't penetrate."

"In other words"—he slapped another brick in place—"you came up against a brick wall."

"Exactly. They have no concept of brain power."

"You're wrong there, Ivan. Brain power got me expelled from my last camp."

"Let me guess. You were tinkering again."

Jura's eyes glittered in the small slit between the rags covering his chin and those wrapped around his head. "They overreacted. It was a ridiculously small rocket."

"A rocket! You crazy fool!"

"You're behind the times. Rocket technology is whizzing along. There's talk about sending a satellite into space. My brain should be in a lab in Moscow."

"Sure"—I slapped some more mud on a brick—"and I should be Secretary General of the UN. Tell me about your ridiculously small rocket."

"You know how lax things have gotten since Stalin died. It's amazing how these *apparatchiks* need a tyrant to tell them what to do. Well, things went to hell in my last camp. I think the commissars were getting just as tired of snow as I was. They didn't care what bits and pieces of various materials I picked up. And I became friends with the commandant's little boy. Cute kid. Around eight, I think."

"It takes a kid to know one."

"Yeah. Little Misha was crazy about rockets. Talked about them constantly. So, I told him I'd make one for him. It was our secret. Until he set it off inside the commandant's house."

"What!"

"Blew a hole in the roof. It was stunning!"

"I'm surprised they didn't shoot you."

"The commandant thought about it. But little Misha threw a fit. That kid was spoiled rotten."

"And so, they sent you to Kazakhstan."

"Yeah. Figured I couldn't do as much damage in this wilderness. But I've got the itch to tinker again, Ivan. You in for a bit of fun?"

"You're like a tonic. What trouble do you want to get me into?"

"Listen, I smuggled some bits and pieces here with me. If you could come up with a few more, we could build a radio."

"A radio!"

"With a short wave, we could listen to Voice of America. Not that it would help us, but we might pick up a little jazz to warm our long, cold, lonely nights."

"I'm in. Tell me what you need, and I'll see if I can come up with it."

"Terrific! We also need a place to build it that won't be suspect."

"How about the old, abandoned outhouse that's too polluted for even us to use?"

"If you can stand it, I can."

The abandoned outhouse stood in an area near the perimeter of the camp. Possibly someone desperate used it in the summer months, but in the depths of winter, no one would venture that far. Even the arc lamps, spaced every fifteen yards, seemed to pass over it. It was easy for Jura and me to make the occasional excursion to it at night under the cover of a snowstorm or the polar mist that descended at random.

We were fortunate it was winter because it made our remodel of the outhouse much easier. Everything was frozen solid. We hacked at the frozen excrement with our picks and threw it out into the tundra. Then we covered the hole in the floor with boards we liberated from those destined for the barracks building we were laying bricks for. When we finished, we had transformed the outhouse into a snug, if occasionally smelly, retreat.

We transferred all of Jura's bits and pieces and began work on constructing our taboo radio. Jura dubbed it *Radio Free Gulag*. He was as excited as a kid to try to get transmissions from Voice of America.

"They're broadcasting from ships floating in the Mediterranean," Jura said, unscrambling a bird's nest of wires. "Targeting us in the Soviet Union. It's a miracle! Do you realize, Ivan? If this works, we can listen to American jazz. Think of it! Louis Armstrong. Duke Ellington. The Top Ten."

One night, I stealthily left the barracks to join Jura and continue our work on the radio. We had made amazing progress thanks to Jura's scientific genius. A hazy moon shone dimly on the ice-covered outhouse. I stopped and listened. The infectious rhythm of American jazz drifted across the frozen steppe. As I got closer, the outhouse seemed to shake to the beat of a loud thumping sound. I opened the door and there was Jura dancing up a storm in the cramped space. When I stopped laughing, Jura grinned at me.

"We have Comrade Stalin to thank," he said. "He died to set our feet free."

"You're right there, my friend. We never would have gotten away with this in the old days. But tamp it down. You'll tip over the outhouse."

"I'm the Fred Astaire of the Steppes!" Jura executed a spin and a slide.

The song changed to a Russian tango. We both had danced to it in our youthful days of wine, women, and romance. Moved by the rhythm and memories, Jura bowed, took my hand, and we danced with each other while we sang along.

CHAPTER FORTY-SEVEN

Ivan seemed to forget telling the story and began humming a lilting tune, eyes closed, his thoughts far away in that outhouse. He opened his eyes, focused on me, and a smile lit up his face. He stood and made a formal bow.

"Miss Celia Klein." He held out his hand. "May I have this dance?"

I took his hand, and suddenly I was a young girl again, the girl I was before the war, before Auschwitz, before Vorkuta, before men and nations embraced insanity. Ivan's arm came around my waist, pulling me close, his cheek against mine, the tune vibrating in his chest as he guided me into the tango. Romantic dreams from years ago drifted around me while he hummed the sensual tune so popular before the war. We melted into each other's arms, and I knew I was falling deeply in love with him.

It was foolish. We were prisoners in one of the worst places on earth. Only the hopelessly naive imagine love blossoming in hell. Love looks to a future. Love resurrects hope. Ivan was marked for death. I couldn't save him again. They would kill him. Hope would die, and I would be left with a heart full of unbearable pain.

I had cast reality aside and basked in the happiness Ivan had brought into my life in such a short time. I loved his kindness, his humor, his passion, the way he spoke to me as if I were his equal. That was foolish too. I was not his equal. He had no idea who I was.

To him, I was Celia Klein, a young woman who ministered to the sick and dying in a world of hopeless suffering. He had no idea I carried the shadow of another young woman inside. Little Cilka, once her father's joy, had become a creature of the Nazis. Cilka, whose mistreatment of the sick and dying would never be forgotten. I had denied her on the train to Vorkuta. I denied her as I worked to heal the prisoners under my care. I denied her each time I smiled and laughed with Ivan. Cilka, the cynical young woman with a heart of stone. My other self. I wanted her buried deep in the ashes at Auschwitz. God knew my soul was buried there.

Miriam might say being sent to a labor camp in Siberia was punishment enough. But Miriam had no idea what I had done. I never spoke of it. I knew even Vorkuta could never erase such terrible things. And those I had wronged were dead. I could never atone by making amends. I would never have the chance to stand before them, confess my wrongdoing, and beg their forgiveness. Ivan saw an angel. I knew I was one of the devils. How could I have the gall to fall in love with a man of honor?

Still, while I danced with him, my whole being longed to love and be loved in return. So, I denied Cilka once again, closed my eyes, and melted into Ivan's embrace.

He brought our dance to an abrupt end. I opened my eyes and saw Miriam standing in the doorway. She carried a pair of pants, a shirt, and a white lab coat in her arms. I wondered how long she'd been watching us. Her expression was difficult to read as her eyes shifted between Ivan and me, but when she spoke, her tone was casual.

"You've made a miraculous recovery, Mr. Kovach."

"Physical therapy, Doctor." Ivan smiled and raised an eyebrow. "Works wonders."

Miriam's eyes drifted back to my face. "For nurse as well as patient, I see."

I moved away from Ivan and stood up straight, hands clasped behind my back, waiting for a reprimand. Instead, she turned to Ivan.

"I've asked the commandant to give you invalid status, Mr. Kovach. That should keep you out of the hands of the NKVD for a while longer. However, as I am sure you understand, there are no guarantees."

"Certainly not on this earth," he said. "As we've all learned."

Miriam handed him the clothes. "You can help around the hospital now. You've been altogether pampered."

Ivan glanced at me. "You're right, Doctor, and I'm happy to do anything I can to help."

"Good. The white coat is for working with patients."

His eyes laughed. "So they don't feel like the inmates are running the asylum?"

Miriam smiled. "Something like that. When you've changed, come to my office and we'll discuss your new duties. And Celia, you will come with me."

She left the room. I walked to the door, then turned back. Ivan gave me a smile and an encouraging nod. *For heaven's sake*, I thought. *If this man can brave violent criminals and vicious NKVD officers I can certainly take a reprimand from Miriam.* I smiled back and walked down the hall to Miriam's office.

She was studying some papers. I waited in the doorway, my conscience nagging me. I had been so wrapped up in my own emotions and needs that I'd forgotten my job and what I owed to Miriam. It was selfish. And what must she think of me, dancing the tango in a hospital in the gulag? I was behaving like a lovesick schoolgirl. She had every right to forbid me contact with Ivan again.

"Celia." Miriam looked up, a worried look in her eyes. "Close the door. I want to talk to you before Mr. Kovach gets here."

I closed the door. "I'm sorry for my behavior, Miriam. It was inexcusable, and I . . ." I stared at the floor.

"Sit, please. I'm not angry with you."

I sat in the chair by her desk and wondered what she would say.

Miriam's eyes softened. "You've suffered for so much of your young life. You've had family, friends, hope itself torn from you. Now, through no fault of your own, you're trapped in a nightmare in a foreign land. I understand the attraction. Mr. Kovach is from your homeland. Just to speak your Slovak language again is comforting. In the time you've been nursing him, I'm sure you've talked about places you both remember and love. I have a feeling Mr. Kovach is a wonderful storyteller. He also seems to have a certain amount of charm. But we know little about him. They have formally declared him a saboteur, an organizer of strikes, a dangerous enemy of the State."

"We are all enemies of the State." I couldn't hide my frustration. "You, of all people, know that. How can the accusations of such a corrupt government weigh with you at all?"

"They don't. It's just that Mr. Kovach has no future now that they've got him cornered here, and I don't . . ." Miriam leaned forward and held my eyes. "Celia. Are you in love with him?"

The question startled me. What could I answer? I had only just admitted the truth to myself. Did my face and manner betray my feelings? I dropped my eyes and stared at my hands in my lap.

"I see." Miriam sighed.

Ivan knocked on the door.

"Come in," Miriam called and gathered her papers together.

"How do I look?" Ivan held his arms out to model the new clothes. "Will your patients take me seriously?"

"Once they find out who you are, they certainly will," Miriam responded.

"Vorkuta is a long way from Kazakhstan."

"The prisoner network is amazingly fast, Mr. Kovach. I'm sure all of Vorkuta knows of your presence here . . . and why." Miriam sat back. "Theories and conspiracies are prison entertainment, and the blending of fact and fiction creates heroes and villains who often bear little resemblance to reality. I have heard stories and received documents declaring you a saboteur and an organizer of strikes. However, even State documents may be subject to exaggeration. Colonel Baranov can be, shall we say, overenthusiastic. I like facts. When I can get them. I would like to hear your story from you."

Ivan closed the door and leaned against it. "Colonel Baranov is right, Doctor. I am a saboteur. If you can call someone demanding justice a saboteur. They made me the leader of our foreign brigade at my camp in Kazakhstan. It was an honor I didn't take lightly. It was well-known throughout the Kazakh camps that the foreign prisoners were the best workers. Our brigade became the most productive in the camp. I don't take credit for this. The men in my brigade were honest and hard-working. Our increase in productivity pleased the commissars. They even praised us. A rare occurrence, believe me."

"Am I wrong to think your leadership had something to do with it?" Miriam asked.

Ivan placed a hand over his heart. "I think it was more that I worked as hard as all the men in my brigade. We shared the suffering and the work equally. But even though the praise from our commissars was heartening, I didn't trust it. It was out of character for them."

Miriam's eyes held a question.

Ivan shrugged. "The Scheherazade of the Steppes?"

I couldn't help laughing.

Miriam frowned. "Scheherazade?"

"You said you thought he was a storyteller," I said.

"Doctor. Would you like to hear the story of the strike in Karaganda?"

"Very much."

CHAPTER FORTY-EIGHT

The Tale of the Karaganda Strike

As told by Ivan Kovach

I was sure the commissars' enthusiastic praise for our increased productivity had a secret motive. I suspected they were stealing supplies and lining their pockets with the profits, so I did some undercover investigating. The supply trucks always arrived at the camp by night. I hid in the shadows nearby and watched as two trucks drove in and began unloading. A few guards stood around, watching. Soon, a couple of commissars joined them. They took two truck drivers aside, and I saw money pass hands. The commissars got into those two trucks with the drivers and drove off to a different area. I followed.

They parked by an old, unused shed. I watched them unload the trucks and put two loads of goods into the shed. For five nights, I watched this process repeated. Two or three truckloads of bricks, sand, and roofing would disappear into the old shed every night. Somewhere, they had a middleman to fence the stolen goods.

Soon, we noticed our rations of bread and *kasha* seemed smaller than before. I walked into the foreign barracks one day at mealtime. The prisoners and the other brigadiers were lined up, getting their rations from the guards. The prisoners passed them around and went to the long tables. A low grumbling was heard.

"Ivan!" Sasha waved me over to a group from my brigade.

"What's going on?" I asked.

Sasha held up his bread. "Is it because I'm always hungry, or does this hunk of dry bread look smaller?"

Kolya examined his meager lump. "I thought I was the only one who noticed. Sasha's right. Look, Ivan."

The piece of bread was significantly smaller.

"It's not just the bread, either." Kolya held up his cup of *kasha*. "I made a mark on my cup where the *kasha* came up to a week ago. Look! It's a good inch less."

Other prisoners gathered around and began comparing rations.

"Brigadier Kovach!" Slava, a prisoner from another brigade, came over. "Something's screwy. Either there's less of both *kasha* and bread, or we're all crazy."

I examined the cup of *kasha*. "You're not crazy. I've been wondering about it myself. Looks like somebody somewhere is skimming off the top at our expense."

"Stealing supplies and shorting us on food and pay!" Sasha slammed his fist on the table.

"Yeah!" Slava grumbled. "And now they've increased our quotas again."

"And this is the coldest winter in memory," Kolya said. "We can barely meet the quotas now. They're using slave labor to line their pockets!"

"What do you say, Brigadier Kovach? You're a lawyer. Is that fair? Is it legal?"

"Legal?" Slava laughed. "You think they care about legal? The whole system's corrupt."

"True," I said. "But it may not go all the way to the top. If we can bring it to the attention of the authorities, they might put a stop to it. They don't want trouble with Moscow."

"Sure." Sasha shrugged. "But how are we to do that?"

"I propose we strike," I said.

Another brigadier joined us. "Strike? You're crazy, Kovach. They just had a strike in one camp up north. Over sixty prisoners were killed and more than a hundred wounded."

The grumbling grew. "Bastards!"

"It's true. Several revolts were brutally put down," I said. "But since Stalin died, the commissars have lost some of their confidence. And the authorities in Moscow don't want trouble. Dead prisoners are dead workers."

The other brigadier looked at me. "How do you propose we go about this strike?"

"Look," I suggested, "I'll write to the Department of Justice in Moscow, lay out our just case, and present all the evidence of corruption in this camp."

"Lawyers! Hah!" Slava laughed. "Who'll pay attention to a prisoner lawyer?"

"Well, they've paid attention before," I pointed out. "And this is a much worse injustice."

My fellow brigadier clapped me on the back. "Then I propose we elect Ivan to be strike leader. He can take the fall."

"They'll put you in solitary lock-up!" Kolya shivered.

"Probably," I said. "When that happens, all the prisoners have to go on strike until they meet our demands."

"You're willing to do that? Suffer solitary with no guaranteed end?" Slava looked horrified. "It's as damn cold in there as it is in Lenin's Tomb. Colder, maybe."

"Because it is so harsh, they'll think my being locked up indefinitely will intimidate the rest of you. This plan will only work if we stick it out. I'm willing. But you must refuse to work until they meet our lawful demands. They won't shoot you if you don't march on them or do any violence. Just refuse to work. Don't show up."

The other brigadier raised his fist. "I say, let's do it."

"Yeah," the prisoners shouted. "We are One!"

CHAPTER FORTY-NINE

Miriam looked at Ivan and shook her head. "Did they put you in solitary?"

"They did." Ivan gave her a crooked smile. "It was a five-foot underground cell. They chained me to the wall. Every other day I got a miserable ration of dry bread and water. The worst was I didn't know if my comrades were striking. If they broke, my situation was hopeless. They might never let me out. I felt like the Count of Monte Cristo."

"Who's that?" I asked.

Miriam smiled. "A wonderful book, Celia. I'm sure Mr. Kovach will tell you the story sometime."

"With pleasure," Ivan said.

"But what happened?" I wondered. "Did the prisoners continue to strike?"

"They did. It took great courage from each of them because they were all put on punishment rations. But they held fast. What happened next surprised us all. My letter to the Department of Justice in Moscow was read and, to our amazement, got results. The prosecutor of the camps in Kazakhstan got a phone call from Moscow demanding that he investigate the charges of corruption and injustice. He came. I was released and ordered to accompany him during his investigation."

"That's quite extraordinary," Miriam said.

"Not as extraordinary as the results of his investigation. He gave the order to fulfill all our demands. The shoe was on the other foot. He said if our demands were not filled, the camp commissars would go to jail. It was an incredible victory for the rule of law. Especially since it was Soviet law."

"You must have been very proud," Miriam said.

"I was enormously proud of my brigade and all the prisoners. They risked their lives for justice. When I returned to the barracks to announce our victory, the prisoners gave out a huge hurrah and threw me up into the air. Three times. The last time, I touched the ceiling!" Ivan smiled. "It was one of the happiest days of my life in the camps."

After a long pause, Miriam asked, "Then why are you in Vorkuta, Mr. Kovach?"

Ivan's ironic smile returned. "A secret radio. A conceited lawyer. And the Voice of America."

Miriam stared at him, wide-eyed. "You had a radio? In the camp?"

"He did, Miriam! He and his friend Jura built it. They listened to jazz music. It was amazing!"

Miriam gave me a look I couldn't figure out. "Ah," she said softly. "So that was what prompted your physical therapy session."

Ivan held up his hands. "Guilty as charged, Doctor. I should not have corrupted this charming young woman. As we all know, jazz is a bourgeois opiate of the people."

"As are many things," Miriam agreed. "But I'm curious about the radio."

"The radio was incredible!" I raved. "You won't believe what they heard."

I had such a fierce desire for Miriam to finally know what an amazing man Ivan was. She hadn't heard all the stories he'd told me. I was so proud of him. Proud to know him. Proud he liked me. I knew my heart was in my face and voice, but I didn't care.

"It wasn't only jazz we listened to in that outhouse, Doctor," Ivan said. "At times, when the authorities weren't jamming the radios, we could get Radio Free Europe and Voice of America. On one particularly cold night, I heard a broadcast that astounded me. The UN Security Council had passed a resolution. All the countries on the Security Council, the Big Five, were to release whatever foreigners from the war they still held and send them back to their home countries."

Miriam frowned. "If what you heard was correct, then all the foreign prisoners here in Vorkuta should go home. They are free."

"That's what I thought." Ivan's expression darkened. "Until I figured out why I was still in Kazakhstan and not on a train back to Slovakia."

"Why?" I asked. "Why aren't we all on a train back to our homelands?"

"Labor, my dear." Ivan sent me a little smile. "Foreign prisoners are a prime labor force. I should have guessed it right away. I saw it in all the camps I've been in. The foreign prisoners are smarter and worked harder than the Soviet prisoners. To release them would mean the Soviets would have to hire replacement workers. That would not be too much of a problem in the western part of the Soviet Union. But the pay they could offer hired workers wouldn't be enough to tempt people to go to places like Siberia and Kazakhstan. Vorkuta and Karaganda and Magadan would lose their best workers."

Miriam sighed. "And then they wouldn't meet their monthly quotas."

"And they couldn't steal as much from the workers as they do," I added.

"Absolutely correct," Ivan said.

Miriam shook her head. "Am I right to suspect that you got yourself involved again after finding this out?"

"Yes. And this time, it was my undoing. Coming off the success of our strike, I was puffed up with my own importance. Not the first time in my life, I assure you. Anyway, I decided to try again. I wrote another letter. This time to the prosecutor of the Kazakh camps, pointing out the UN resolution and demanding the release of all foreign prisoners in Kazakhstan."

Miriam covered her eyes.

"Yes, Doctor." Ivan nodded. "It was stupid. But I thought I was on a winning streak. Why shouldn't the walls of Jericho crumble under my trumpet blast?"

"I think Joshua had a bit of help," Miriam said with a little smile.

"He did. What I had was an overdose of pride and unbelievable naivety for a man of my age and experience. Of course, Commissar Gavrilov intercepted my letter, and it never reached the prosecutor. Gavrilov was fed up with Prisoner Kovach and saw his chance to take revenge. He pulled a very old trick. You'd think I would have been smarter."

"What did he do?" Miriam asked in the voice of an exasperated mother.

"He gave me one of his old suits." Ivan grinned.

"What?" Miriam and I said in unison.

"Sorry to joke, but in retrospect I was so naive. Gavrilov called me into his office and said my letter had reached Moscow and they wanted to talk to me about the problem. He looked me over, standing there in my prison clothes, and pulled a suit from a closet in his office. I should have suspected something was wrong when he held the suit up to me like some salesman checking if it was the right size."

"'Can't have you looking shabby for the prosecutor,' Gavrilov told me. His smile was a little too broad, but I was focusing on the feel of the suit after so long in rags. He told me I was to leave right that day, by the next train, and ushered me outside. He had gathered a significantly large contingent of foreign prisoners to see me off. They shouted greetings of good luck and encouragement. I smiled and waved. What a fool!"

Ivan cast his eyes up to the ceiling before continuing. "A black ZIM-12 limousine pulled up and stopped. An officer got out and held the door open for me. You can imagine how proud I felt with everyone slapping me on the back and shaking my hand. I got into the car and waved from the window as it drove off into the steppe toward the station."

"Who was in the car with you?" Miriam asked.

"Two officers and the driver."

"Didn't that ring some alarm bells?"

"Sadly, no. I was so confident in my role as the brilliant Lawyer of the Gulag that I thought the three officers were there as a guard of honor to impress the prisoners with the sincerity of their surrender. Just before the station, we stopped by a sidetrack. I looked out the window and the only train in sight was a locomotive with a single cattle car. Still, I didn't get it. One officer got out and opened the door for me. The driver and the other officer followed. I looked around. 'This isn't the station,' I said. 'You got that right, Prisoner Kovach,' the officer said, and then he punched me in the face. 'You're taking the VIP Express.' All three of them jumped me and knocked me to the ground, kicking and punching me. They ripped the suit off me and threw my old prison clothes on top of me as I lay there, amazed at my stupidity."

"You're lucky they didn't kill you right there," Miriam said.

"I've always wondered why they didn't. Anyway, they dragged me to the cattle car and threw me inside. 'Enjoy the trip, Ivan,' the driver said. 'Give my best to the prosecutor.' Then he slammed the door shut, and the last thing I heard before I passed out was their laughter. Five days later, I was under two tons of coal in Vorkuta." He looked at me. "And saved by an angel."

"That's quite a story," Miriam said. "My advice, as your doctor, is to give up these crusades and make yourself as inconspicuous as possible for a time. In my experience, you can only push them so far."

"I'm sure you're right, Doctor," Ivan said. "I'll try to follow your prescription."

I watched Ivan. His expression showed nothing but calm, but his eyes were dark. I remembered the letters I was supposed to give Miriam to put in the mail pouch. I was sure she would never do that without making me tell her exactly what they were about. I couldn't lie to her—she would know. Once I told her Ivan was writing not only to the Supreme Soviet in Moscow but also to the Americans and the British, she would probably tear the letters up to protect us all. Her priority was the hospital. She wouldn't jeopardize that, even to get freedom for the foreign prisoners here in Vorkuta. But I could not let Ivan down. I realized I would have to get those letters into the mail pouch myself.

"Oh my!" I jumped up and rushed to the door. "I didn't realize how late it is," I said, turning back. "I have to go take care of my patients."

CHAPTER FIFTY

The corridor to the commandant's office was so dark I had to run my hand along the wall to find my way. There were no windows here to allow even the frosty light of the arc lamps to seep in. I knew the office would be empty. The commandant always went home to his family at night. No guards hung around the corridor. There was one outside door at this end. The guards watched that door, more concerned about a breach of entry from outside the office than inside. I crept quietly but quickly toward the commandant's office.

I wrapped my fingers around the ice-cold doorknob, afraid to turn it and find it locked. Fortunately, the knob turned easily and quietly. Was this the one lucky day that someone had cleaned the commandant's office and forgotten to lock the door? I almost laughed with relief. Ivan would say the gods were with him in his quest for justice. If that was so, I guess I was part of their plan. I shut the door and stood for a moment, listening. My heart raced, and my breathing was amplified in the quiet of the room. I held it to hear better. Silence.

The commandant's office had one window to the outside. Ice and snow blocked it as efficiently as any shade or curtain. Dim light from the lamps outside penetrated the ice to lend a ghostly glow to the room. It was enough.

I searched for the mail pouch that was always kept here. There it was, in a corner by a bookcase. I started for it and froze. Somewhere, a door had closed. Which door? The door outside? I searched the room, frantic. Where could I hide if someone came in? The commandant's desk had drawers on the side but was open in front, so I couldn't hide under it. There was no place. I waited, listening. Nothing happened. I heard no footsteps in the corridor. I took a deep breath and moved to the mail pouch. I had to get Ivan's letters inside and get out of there.

The pouch was firmly closed by a leather strap tied into a tight knot, ready to be shipped out in the morning. I fumbled with the knot. The leather was stiff with the cold, and I seemed to be all thumbs struggling to untie that knot. I forced myself to be calm. Finally, the knot gave way, and I opened the pouch. As I pulled the envelope from my pocket, the door to the office opened and my heart stopped. Colonel Baranov's imposing figure filled the doorway. He flipped the switch for the single overhead light.

"What are you doing here?" Baranov demanded.

My mouth was so dry I had to force my tongue to move. I held up the envelope. "Dr. Eliashvili asked me to be sure this letter went out with the pouch to Moscow," I said, trying to give some authority to my voice.

Colonel Baranov stared at me in silence. I stared back at him, hoping he couldn't see the terror in my eyes. When he spoke, ice could not have been colder.

"Only the commandant, Doctor Eliashvili, or I may put mail into this pouch."

"It's not her fault," I blurted out. "She was terribly busy. I said I would do it for her. She trusts me."

Baranov made a sound like a low growl. "I, on the other hand, do not trust anyone. Give me that envelope!"

I had heard prisoners in the camp talk about moments of such fear their blood turned to ice in their veins. I'd felt it many times before in Auschwitz. And now, that familiar wave of ice engulfed me once again. The fate of three people lay in my incompetent hands. I had failed. Baranov would force the envelope from me and see what Ivan had written. He would take him out and shoot him. No doubt they would shoot me too. They would strip doctor Eliashvili of her rank in Vorkuta and probably send her to work in the mines.

Colonel Baranov began to move. Like a trapped animal, I instinctively backed farther into the corner, nearly falling over the mail pouch.

"Celia!" Miriam's voice stopped him. "Haven't you mailed that letter yet? I have been looking all over for you. I need you back in the hospital right now."

Baranov turned. I felt so weak with fear and relief that I braced myself against the wall so I wouldn't sink to the floor. Colonel Baranov took two steps toward Miriam.

"This is against regulations, Doctor. She is not allowed in this room."

"If the hospital weren't as understaffed as it is, I wouldn't have to go against regulation, Colonel," Miriam said. I could hear both anger and tension in her voice.

"What is this letter?" Baranov demanded.

Miriam walked over to me and took the letter from my nerveless hand. "This is a request to Moscow for special medicines for the commandant's son." She held the letter up. "Do you wish to keep it back?"

Colonel Baranov frowned. "Well . . . no," he hedged. "If that is the truth."

"If you doubt my word, I suggest you go to the commandant right now and ask him about this. His son's condition is not something he discusses with every officer in this camp. It is a chronic illness that is constantly aggravated by the miserably severe weather here in Vorkuta and the fact that the child never sees the sun for half the year. The medicine will help relieve some symptoms that plague him. Unfortunately, it will not cure him. But if you want to go into all that with the commandant, please go now, because this request must be on tomorrow's plane."

Colonel Baranov glared at Miriam. "I will not bother the commandant this evening. The letter may go with the mail. However, in future you will follow strict regulations, Doctor."

"Certainly, Colonel. As I have always done. Now, if you will excuse us, we have important work to do. Good night, Colonel."

Colonel Baranov took a last look at me and at the mail pouch before turning on his heel and leaving the room. I slumped against the wall and took a deep breath. Miriam held the envelope in her hand, looking at it.

"Miriam," I said in little more than a whisper, "how did you know?"

"Mr. Kovach told me what he had asked you to do. He was worried when you left so suddenly that you would take it upon yourself to put the letters in the pouch so as not to get me into trouble. I was so angry with him for putting you and the entire hospital in jeopardy with his insane scheme, I told him instead of freeing the foreign prisoners, he would probably get you shot. Fear doused the flame of heroism in his eyes." She shook her head. "But not for long. He nearly made it out the door to rush to your rescue before I slammed it shut to stop him. I would have been here sooner if I hadn't had to waste time explaining to him why it was better I dealt with this." Miriam slapped the envelope against her other hand in frustration. "What is wrong with men? Why can't they see beyond the crusade? Why does the glory of the cause blind otherwise intelligent men to the consequences?"

"I'm sorry, Miriam," I said. "I only wanted to help . . . I . . ."

"I understand." Her tone softened. "Don't cry. You've fallen in love with Mr. Kovach. It's not so surprising. Perhaps this is the first time you've ever been in love. I don't know. Perhaps he's in love with you. I don't know that either. And love is another of those emotions that blinds us to consequences. Vorkuta is not a healthy place for such a fragile thing as love." Miriam sighed. "Being a human is so very hard sometimes."

She held the envelope, studying it with an expression I couldn't read in the dim light. I knew she was trying to decide what to do. I could imagine how conflicted she was about this issue. Miriam was such a noble, caring person. A decision like this, between two right goals with different consequences, was something I wished she didn't have to struggle with. If only I had been quicker. The envelope would have been in the pouch, and I would have been gone before Colonel Baranov ever knew anything about it. Now the decision was Miriam's. I held my breath. Would she put the letters in the pouch?

"I'm as insane as he is," she whispered.

She opened the pouch, put the envelope inside, pulled the strap, and tied a tight knot.

CHAPTER FIFTY-ONE

The next morning, I slipped into Ivan's room, eager to tell him his letters were safely in the mail pouch. Almost before I had shut the door, his arms were around me, crushing me to his chest.

"You little idiot!" he whispered in my ear. "I don't scare easily, but when I knew you'd gone to put those letters in the pouch yourself, I was terrified." He pulled away and held my face. "Why didn't you ask Doctor Eliashvili to mail them like I told you?"

His voice was harsh with anger, but his dark eyes held mine with a look I couldn't name. Gentleness? Compassion? Need? Some emotion I had never felt before stirred inside me. I tried to look away, but he turned my face back.

"Tell me! Why did you go yourself?"

"I didn't think Doctor Eliashvili would do it." My eyes pleaded with him to understand. "It was so important. It meant going home again, and I knew it might be our only chance. Miriam is dedicated to this hospital, as she should be. I didn't want to put her in danger. If they arrested her, the hospital would be shut down."

"And if you were caught, you would have been shot!" He flung his head back and groaned. "God! I thought I'd lost you."

He drew me into a tighter embrace, his lips caressing my forehead, my eyes, my face, until he reached my mouth with a kiss of desperation and relief. My whole being gave an enormous sigh of release.

"I love you, Celia," he whispered hoarsely.

I gasped. As though someone had thrown me into ice water, my body shuddered with cold. Love me? He couldn't. Images of Auschwitz and Ravensbrück filled my mind. Lines of women and children walking to the gas chambers, young girls returning from the hospital with deformities from Mengele's experiments, women writhing on the filthy floor of my block while rats ran over them. And me, Cilka, watching it all. Ivan Kovach loved *me*? He didn't know what he was saying. I pulled myself from his embrace and walked to the window, my back to him, staring through the filthy glass. Icicles hung from the roof outside like crystal stilettos. I wrapped my arms around myself, digging my nails into my sides, trying to hold back the despair sweeping in to destroy the only happiness I had known.

"Celia." Ivan spoke softly from across the room. "If we get out of this, I'd like you to come with me." He waited for me to say something, and when I didn't, he continued to talk about an impossible future. "I don't say it will be easy, my love. To the Communists in Czechoslovakia, we'll still be under suspicion. They will likely put us in prison for a time, I don't know. No doubt they'll also forbid us to have jobs, but it doesn't matter. That will pass. My brother has a *dacha* we can go to. It's just a little wooden house by a lake. But there's room for a garden. We can grow vegetables. I'll write as many appeals as it takes to whomever will listen. In time, we'll be rehabilitated and get work permits. Think of it, Celia. I'll read to you at night, and you can finally get the education they denied you. Like Kitty and Levin, together we can build a new life. Maybe find some peace at last. Come with me. I love you."

The icicles seemed to melt and run down the dirty window as tears warped my vision. I had to tell him how impossible it was, this future he saw for us. I longed to accept it, to lie to him, to pretend I was the woman he thought he knew. But there would be no hiding the truth in such an intimate relationship, and when he discovered who I really was, the lie would be far worse than the truth. I couldn't face him, couldn't bear the look of shock and disappointment in his eyes, the disgust. So, I continued to stare at the window and forced myself to say the words that would damn me in his eyes.

"You know nothing about me. You think you love an angel. If you really knew what I am . . . if you ever knew . . ." I fought to hold back the tears and lost.

He was beside me in an instant, turning me to him, holding me while I sobbed uncontrollably. He stroked my hair like a father would soothe a child. When my sobs subsided, he walked me to the bed and sat me down, taking a place by my side, holding me close.

"Celia," he murmured. "I know about Auschwitz."

I shuddered and pulled out of his embrace.

"Doctor Eliashvili told me. It doesn't matter—that nightmare is finished. You were an innocent victim. Terrible things were done to you. You were never at fault. You did nothing to deserve that."

I moved to the end of the bed, as far away from him as I could, crouching against the wall, pulling my knees up to my chest and holding them there with my arms.

"But I did! I did horrible things. Things I can never . . ." I wanted to explain, but my mouth wouldn't open to say the damning words.

"What could my angel possibly have done? A young girl thrown into hell like that."

"I can't tell you. You would hate me, and I couldn't bear that. You were a victim, too, but you did fine and noble things. You risked your life to save other prisoners, you stood up to the monsters, you—"

"Stop. You're making me out to be some sort of hero. Believe me when I tell you I'm not. I've asked you to come with me if we're ever released. I love you. I'm not wrong in believing you also feel something for me. However, I don't want you to have any illusions about the man you'd be committing your future to. I am not a hero, Celia. I'm just a man like other men, a medley of strengths and weaknesses, honorable one minute, prideful the next, brilliant at times, woefully stupid at others. The fact I'm aware of this is to my credit, but it doesn't mean I haven't made many mistakes in the past or that I won't continue to make mistakes in the future. I gather you carry some guilt concerning your time in Auschwitz. I can't imagine what that might be, and you don't have to tell me if you don't want to. It doesn't matter to me. But I won't let you think I'm something I'm not or that I am guiltless. The guilt I carry has been with me since the day I was arrested. What I did follows me like an evil shadow and haunts my dreams. In truth, Celia, I'm an egotistical and stubborn man who destroyed his family through his own pride and conceit."

"Destroyed your family?" What was he talking about?

"I was a married man. Long before I was arrested, I had a wife and child . . . my son." His voice deepened, becoming hoarse. "Their fate was my doing."

"You were married?"

"Yes. And I didn't live up to my responsibilities as a husband and father." He paused, holding my eyes. "How to explain it? You say I was a victim like you—"

"You were!" I almost shouted at him. I didn't want him to make himself into something he wasn't just to make me feel better. "You were a victim of the Communists."

"I was, yes, but through my own actions, I turned my wife and child into victims as well. Victims of my overwhelming ego and stubbornness."

I shook my head. "I don't believe that. You would never willingly destroy anyone. Whatever happened, it wasn't your fault."

"It was my fault and my fault alone. Listen. After the war, during the time after you were released from Auschwitz and sent here, the Communists pushed for control of Czechoslovakia. Repeatedly, my wife, Galya, warned me the Communists would take power. She knew what she was talking about. Her family fled the Bolsheviks in 1918, just after the Russian Revolution. History would repeat itself, she said. I told her she was paranoid, that Czechoslovakia was a democracy. That it could never happen there." He ran his hands through his hair and sighed. "She saw the future clearly. I was blinded by my ambition."

"Was it ambition to have faith in your country?"

"Ah, Celia. A noble excuse for what was a very selfish act. I wasn't stupid. I could see what was happening to all the surrounding countries. One by one, they fell. I refused to listen to Galya, to take my wife and son out of harm's way. Why? Because I was ambitious. I clung to the dream of a political career. I envisioned myself in parliament, a brilliant young politician. And to be honest, I was afraid of starting over in the West where I didn't even speak the language, afraid of being a nobody, when I should have been afraid for the future of my wife and child."

"You would never be a nobody," I whispered.

"You're looking with romantic eyes, my dear, just as I did when I imagined my brilliant future. Galya was a realist, and she wasn't fooled. She told me I couldn't keep my mouth shut if the Communists took over. That I would speak out anywhere and everywhere for democracy in Czechoslovakia despite what was obviously the end of that dream. You see, by that time, she knew exactly what kind of man I was. Proud and stubborn. She said they would arrest me. She asked me what would happen to her and our child when that happened."

"She must have been terrified."

"Yes, but I didn't want to think about that. I was a self-absorbed man with a head full of visions of glory. My fantasy stretched all the way to prime minister. What an idiot! While the people in Prague leaned more and more toward accepting the Soviets, I walked around composing brave and stirring democratic speeches in my head. Galya told me I was the most stubborn man she had ever seen. She was right. Even after the Communists took over, I refused to leave. I hoped it would all change, that it was only temporary. And then one day, when I was walking to work, two strange men stopped me and asked if I was Ivan Kovach. A simple question, but I knew right then I had made a terrible mistake. They arrested me that very day. No crime. No charge. Just prison. I left Galya with no one she could rely on. All our good friends turned their backs on her, afraid to associate with the wife of an enemy of the people."

"What did she do?" I didn't know her, but my heart ached for her. I had seen the fear in the eyes of so many women with small children at Auschwitz, women abandoned by the world.

"Galya." Ivan sighed the name, and his eyes softened as he looked back. "For years, in prison and the camps, I didn't know what had happened to her and our son. Like most prisoners, they confiscated any letters to me. The few that got through were so heavily blacked out they were useless. I convinced myself of the worst, believing Galya was either sent to the camps and my son to an orphanage, or they were both dead. I tormented myself with guilt over what I'd done. Then one day I received a letter from my mother with news of them. Why that letter got through, I didn't know, but it was a blessing." He smiled at the memory. "My mother told me Galya had escaped across the Iron Curtain with our son. I always knew she was clever and courageous, but to organize a successful crossing of the Iron Curtain with our four-year-old child was something I never imagined. As usual, I underestimated her."

"How did she do that? They must have been watching her."

"Yes, they were. We both knew they would be. When she came to say goodbye to me in the prison after I was arrested, I forced her to agree to divorce me. She didn't want to, but she understood the danger of being the wife of an enemy of the people. Maybe divorcing me was why they didn't pay close attention to her for a few months, just long enough for her to avoid arrest and arrange for someone to smuggle the two of them to the border. They escaped into Germany and spent a year in a DP camp. My mother told me Galya worked all the time at any job she could get while our four-year-old son ran around the camp or waited in line for a mug of gruel. Galya never gave up. Eventually they got to Canada and freedom."

"I'm so glad they were saved!"

"With no help from me to my eternal shame. Celia, when I compare my own actions with those of my wife, I do not appear as any kind of hero. She wasn't afraid to leave Czechoslovakia behind. She wasn't afraid to cross the border. She wasn't afraid to start over in a country where she didn't speak the language. Can you imagine? Galya spoke five languages, but English wasn't one of them. She had a law degree, but after she got to Canada she had to work as a cleaning woman. She barely supported herself and our son while she learned English to get a better job. She did all this alone. No husband to protect her, provide for her, care about her. And while I am here, writing what may be useless letters to Moscow, my son is growing up without his father. I carry that guilt with me every day, and at night, it haunts my dreams."

"You called out, *Escape!* That time I shook you awake. It wasn't the camps, was it?"

"No."

"Are they waiting for you? Your wife and child?"

"No. I soon realized my time in the camps of Siberia had no definite limit. Oh, they gave me a sentence of ten years, but I didn't believe them. And even if they released me, there was the reality of the Iron Curtain, which had closed forever. I sent a letter to Galya through my mother. I told her I had no future. She should find someone to marry, give our son a father." Ivan sighed and looked away to the window. "A boy needs a father."

I studied Ivan's profile, a face that had grown so dear to me. I knew I could never be with him, that the happiness of sharing a life with him was impossible for me, and the thought of his wife and son, who were surely waiting for his release, was further proof I was right. And yet, even as I gave him up, I wanted desperately to know if his wife had married again. If he was free.

"Did she find someone?" I couldn't imagine anyone taking his place.

"Not only did she find someone to replace her woefully inadequate first husband, but she has reunited with her first love! The man she was in love with at age eighteen." Ivan laughed. "A real fairy-tale ending." He turned to me and took my hands in his. "So, you see, I'm not a hero and I'm not a martyr. I brought Siberia on myself. What punishments I have endured, I deserved. Have I atoned for what I did? Who can say? I've tried to use what skills I have to bring a modicum of justice to my fellow sufferers in the gulag. Am I proud of that? Definitely. Am I still ambitious? For justice, yes. Am I a man who still needs love? Yes. We may go free, Celia, if we are lucky. But I have no desire to face that freedom alone. Not since I found you. I want to marry you. I want to care for you and bring you peace and happiness. If you'll have me. Say you will, my beautiful guardian angel."

I longed to say yes. It would be so easy to lie, to pretend I was the woman he thought he knew, to face the future with this wonderful man. Oddly, his honest confession of guilt for what he did gave me the courage to tell him the truth.

"I can't." I tried to hold back the tears, to fight against the past, to shut out an impossible future. I avoided his eyes and stared down at my clenched hands. "How can I make you understand why it's impossible? You talk about how peaceful our life will be, how we will live in a cottage and work in our garden. How you'll write, and at night by the fire you'll tell me stories, and we'll love each other . . . and it will be forever. Like Kitty and Levin. But it won't be like that, Ivan. It can never be like that. Because I will always know what I have done. Such things, Ivan. Such terrible, evil things."

He took me in his arms again and held my head against his chest, rocking me gently and softly stroking my hair. "What could a sixteen-year-old girl in the hell of Auschwitz possibly do that's worse than a thirty-four-year-old man abandoning his wife and child? You were a child. How could you ever be evil?"

He was so kind. Something broke inside me, and the imaginary life I had been living since Ivan arrived fell into pieces. I was an impostor—worse, a deceiver—wantonly pretending to be someone I knew was false. I was not, and could never be, anyone close to the woman Ivan saw. It was evil to let him go on planning and dreaming of a future together. I had to be hard, make him see the truth, make him understand why there was no happy ending to our story. I pulled out of his embrace, threw myself off the bed, and turned to face him.

"All right!" I nearly shouted. How easy it was to become Cilka again. My voice, loud and harsh, my eyes cold. "I'll tell you exactly how a six-teen-year-old girl can be evil. You'll hate me, but that will make it easier for both of us. I was not just an innocent young girl in Auschwitz. I was a block leader, Ivan. Do you know what that is? That's not a brigade leader like you, who looks after his men. A block leader is a collaborator. A prisoner who works for the enemy in order to live a better life in hell. Auschwitz and Ravensbrück were hell on earth and your angel was one of the devils."

"Celia—"

I covered my ears with shaking hands. "Stop! I don't want to hear you apologize again for me because I was young and scared and facing extermination." I pulled my hands down and continued in a rush. "All of that was true, but it doesn't change what I did. I don't know why they chose me over other sixteen-year-olds who went to the gas chambers, but I do know they picked out the young ones like me because we were more desperate to live and easier to bend to their will. The SS officer who recruited me said I would get more food, better clothes, a room of my own if I did this work for them. I was a fool to fall for it. Or maybe I was just a frivolous young girl, although how I could have been after watching my mother and sisters go to the gas chambers, I will never understand. Their deaths made me profoundly guilty for being alive. And deeply afraid to die."

"Any person, young or old, would feel the same, Celia. You must—"

"Don't interrupt me! I don't want excuses. I want you to know who I was and still am. The SS officer said all I had to do was keep order in my block, make sure the women were clean, keep them in line and ensure they worked. It seemed all right to me. I even thought I could help the women by preventing trouble, getting the weak some extra food, keeping them alive. You will say I was naive. I wasn't naive, Ivan. I was simply ignorant of how much cruelty I was capable of."

Ivan held up his hand to stop me. I glared at him but let him speak.

"We all would do things to survive in hell we wouldn't dream of doing outside."

I laughed, a sound without joy. "Things? Let me tell you the *things* I did. One of my jobs was to make up the lists of those women in my block who were to be gassed. When I was first told this, I refused. Two SS men took me to a room, beat me, and locked me in. Later that night, two men came and raped me. Several times. I don't know who they were. I doubt they were SS because I was Jewish and that was forbidden. They called me a whore and a bitch. No one had ever said such things to me. Done such things. The next morning, an SS officer released me. All he said was . . . *Remember*."

Ivan's face expressed so much compassion I nearly broke down. I turned away so as not to look at him.

"After that, I made up the lists for them. I knew if a woman was sick, or too weak to work, she would either be sent to the hospital for Mengele to experiment on, or she would be gassed. I put the names of those miserably wretched women on the list. I told myself it would happen anyway. I told myself I was saving them from torture or from the torment of living in constant fear of the gas chamber. Talk about excuses! The truth was it was to save my own neck, and I knew it." I turned back to face Ivan. "The women in my block were always hungry, always tired. I'd been told to keep order, keep them in line, keep them working. I had a choice: Do my job, or become one of them. I chose to harden my heart and do my job. I shouted at them, dragged them to their feet when they fell. The block was always dirty. We were never given soap or disinfectant. I was terrified of the next SS inspection. Terrified I'd be raped again or shot for failure to do my evil job. So I made them scrub the floors with dirty water. Wash out the latrine with their bare hands. If they slumped from exhaustion, I would shout at them to stand up straight. If their ragged dresses were sloppy on their emaciated bodies, I would make them dress and undress over and over. If they cried, I would shake them and slap them until they stopped. When they got sick from the filth and vermin in the block, they went on the list. Oh, I was a very *good* block leader."

Ivan's silence told me I was getting through to him. I wanted him to despise me, to realize what living with me for the rest of his life would mean. I wanted him to understand the immense difference between us—that I was nothing fine and good and he would be better off alone than trapped in a relationship with me.

"They all hated me," I continued. "I didn't blame them. I hated myself. But I didn't know what else to do. Evil had taken over my soul. I knew well what my punishment would be if I didn't follow orders from my SS masters. I would be turned over to the very women I was tormenting, and they would beat me to death. Poetic justice."

I paused. Suddenly, I felt extremely cold. I wrapped my arms around myself and stared unseeing out the dirty, ice-covered window. "I survived. I shouldn't have. I should have been struck dead by the God I no longer believed in for the evil I had done. I didn't know who I was anymore. I had become a stranger to myself. Tough, bitter, and mean. When I returned to Slovakia after liberation, the NKVD arrested me as a spy. The people who wanted my family home framed me. What they didn't know was that I was guilty of something worse." I turned and looked Ivan in the eyes. "Vorkuta was exactly what I deserved."

He said nothing—just watched me silently for a time with his arms crossed and a stern expression. Like a lawyer contemplating a new client. Or, more likely, a judge ready to pass sentence. Well, whatever the punishment, I deserved it. I waited in silence, fearing his rejection, yet wanting it so we could put a period to this ill-conceived romance.

"In Czechoslovakia, after the war," Ivan said, "I knew of the existence of the Nazi concentration camps. But it wasn't until I ran into a Soviet soldier in my camp in Kazakhstan that I learned something about the extent of the atrocities committed in Auschwitz. This soldier had been with the Red Army on the day of the liberation of Auschwitz. When he returned home to Kiev, he was arrested for protesting the arrest of his own brother, who'd been a prisoner of war in Germany and who was later sent to the gulag as punishment for getting himself captured." The corner of Ivan's mouth turned up in a twisted smile. "Stalin seems to have been an admirer of the ancient Spartans. *Come back with your shield, or on it.* Spartan mothers used to say that to their sons going off to battle. Stalin's take on it was, *there are no prisoners of war, only traitors.* But that's another issue. My Red Army prisoner friend said the things he saw in Auschwitz turned his stomach, and he had seen his share of battle horrors. He described body parts strewn around the cremation pits, barracks encrusted with human excrement, survivors who were nothing but skin and bones, frostbite, gangrene, typhus. He told me they found storerooms filled with shoes, piles of eyeglasses, masses of prosthetic legs and arms. It was pitiful, he said. But the most horrific thing for him was the piles of toys taken from the children they had murdered. If he hadn't seen it with his own eyes, he would never have believed human beings capable of such depravity."

"It's one thing to observe the depravity of human beings," I muttered, "and another thing to find depravity in yourself."

Ivan held up his hand. "Let's not blur the difference between the criminal and the victim, Celia." His expression changed to curiosity. "Tell me. Did you ever do an act of kindness in Auschwitz?"

I stared at him in confusion. Why was he talking about kindness? I'd just confessed to multiple acts of cruelty and indifference carried out over nearly three years, increasing in frequency and harshness. How could he not understand that?

"It is a simple question," he persisted. "Did you ever do an act of kindness at Auschwitz? I don't mean the acts of cruelty you say you excused as kindness. I'm asking about incidents where you did something generous or charitable for another person. Think back and answer truthfully."

I had blocked out those moments. They were so few, and they didn't fit with the overall portrait of Cilka the Monster I'd painted for myself. But Ivan's question had to be answered. There had been times I gave my extra food to pregnant girls and assigned them to lighter work. Why I wanted to help a baby be born into that hell, I never knew. Sometimes I broke up fights among the women over water or food and tried to portion it out fairly. I thought of the times I told stories to comfort young girls who, like me, had lost their mothers. How I sometimes kept women off the death list who had a sister or mother still alive in the camp. And then there was Leah, the only real friend I had then, and how I bullied her into survival. I guess Ivan would consider them acts of kindness.

"Yes," I murmured and kept my eyes on the floor as I related them to Ivan. "But those acts were too few to matter."

"They are examples of empathy and compassion in the face of your own personal physical and mental suffering. Considering your age, they do matter." There was an edge to Ivan's voice. "You had just turned six-teen when they sent you to Auschwitz and forced you to become a cog in the Nazi machinery. You think, what? That you should have killed yourself?"

I raised my head and confronted him. "Yes! Rather than help those monsters torture, maim, and kill women like me? Yes! But the truth is I didn't. I wasn't just weak in the face of evil. I *embraced* that evil to survive."

"You've chosen to condemn yourself. If you had been an adult in a normal world, your actions would make you guilty. In the distorted, nightmare world you experienced as a child, conventional morality was no longer black and white but an ever-shifting gray."

I threw him a look of defiance. Let him try to white-wash my past. I knew the truth. Ivan looked back at me with raised eyebrows.

"Do you think children should be judged the same as adults?"

I shrugged.

"If someone holds a gun to the head of a child and tells that child to commit a crime or be killed, who is responsible for that crime? Because that is what happened to you. The Nazis gave you an impossible choice for a sixteen-year-old girl—do as they commanded, or die. It is human nature to want to live, particularly when we're at the beginning of our lives. You did not choose to do the terrible deeds that torture your soul. Fanatical sadists forced them on you. No doubt they took perverse pleasure in coercing innocent victims to commit cruel acts." His eyes softened, and he smiled. "The past can never be erased, but it is finished. You've suffered enough, Celia. It's time to forgive yourself. You deserve a chance at happiness."

"You're wrong. I deserve nothing but shame. There are too many victims of my abuse, living and dead. They would not forgive me, and I have no right to forgive myself. As long as I can remember what I did, the past is never finished. My soul is scarred forever, and I see no way to heal it. Maybe I don't even want to. I deserve punishment. I didn't deserve to survive Auschwitz and Ravensbrück. I didn't deserve Doctor Eliashvili's protection and care here in Vorkuta. I don't deserve happiness. And I can never deserve your love, Ivan. Never! Understand me. I don't deserve anything good."

"What about the good you've done here? What about the patients you've saved? I'm one of them. You risked your life for me. What of those whose suffering you've eased? What about the friends you brought comfort to in this hell? I see no devil when I look at you. I saw an angel my first day here, and I will always see an angel." He took a step toward me, his voice soft and low. "If those letters work, we may go home, my darling. It won't be easy even then, but it will be much, much better if we have each other. We will never speak of these things again. We can't erase the past, that's true, but we can overcome its pain in our mutual happiness. Let me love you, Celia. Redemption is that simple."

"Redemption?"

He smiled. "Grace. Atonement. Forgiveness. Love."

"Why can't you understand?" Tears trailed down my face. "I'm not worthy of any of those things. I would ruin your life."

Ivan put his hands on my shoulders. I could not look at him.

"Don't I have any say in what would ruin my life?" He took hold of my chin and raised my head, forcing me to look at him. "You've been so long in your circles of hell you've lost the ability to hope." His hand caressed my face. "But I haven't. I rest my hope in you. My angel. I need you." His arms went around me in a tight embrace.

"Oh, God! Don't!" I choked on my own tears. "Just . . . don't." I pushed him away. "Please! I . . . it's impossible!"

Stumbling, my eyes blinded by tears, I backed toward the door and ran from the room.

CHAPTER FIFTY-TWO

For the next few days, I avoided Ivan as best I could. It was difficult since he continued to help in the hospital, and it was impossible not to encounter each other sometime during the day. At first, I would see him down a hallway and quickly dart into whatever door was nearby. I knew it was foolish and cowardly, but my thoughts were so chaotic I couldn't trust my reactions. One minute I was angry with him for being stubborn and not accepting what I knew was best for his future. The next minute I longed to feel his arms around me, hear his deep, calm voice assuring me his love was all I needed to heal my tortured soul. Gradually, I stopped hiding from him and simply passed him in silence, avoiding his eyes. He didn't stop me or try to talk to me. At first, I felt he must have thought over what I said and come to understand how wrong he was about me.

But one day I opened the door to the supply room while Ivan was on his way out, and we ran into each other. I stumbled, but he caught my arms to steady me, and I forced myself to look up at him. The warmth of his smile reached his eyes, and I caught my breath. He released me, sliding his hands down my arms and giving my fingers a gentle squeeze. Then he silently stepped aside to let me pass. The message was clear. He had said all there was to say. It was up to me to decide whether I would allow myself a future with him or not.

I wasn't given many days to brood over that decision. Ivan's letters reached Moscow, and the response was swift. He was not the only one in the Soviet Union who was aware of the violation of the order to release the foreign prisoners still in the remote camps of Siberia. The fact that his letters also reached the British and American Embassies brought the violation to the attention of the outside world. It was an embarrassment to the Soviet authorities that could not be swept under the rug. Six days after my confrontation with Ivan, Miriam called me into her office.

"I have good news!" Her smile lit up the dreary day. "You're going home!"

For a moment, I just stared at her, speechless. "The letters reached them?" I had trouble believing it. "They were accepted and read? Not thrown away? You're sure? How do you know?"

"I just had a meeting with the commandant. It's official. All foreign prisoners are to be released immediately. You are free, Celia!"

Free. I should have been overjoyed. What I felt was a deep sense of insecurity and, unbelievably, fear. I had been a prisoner for thirteen years of my life. Even before Auschwitz, in 1938, when I was only twelve, the fascists had brought their repressive fist down on us Jews in Bardejov, taking away our homes, our livelihood, our right to assemble freely. We were outcasts in our own town, watched, harassed, vilified. And then I became a prisoner of the Nazis. Liberation freed me for a few short months, only to become a prisoner once more, this time of the Soviets. Thirteen years of persecution. Thirteen years of living in fear and in the shadow of death. Thirteen years of never thinking for myself but always waiting for orders. Prisoners make no choices in the everyday business of living. They eat what they're given when they're given it. They wear what they're told to wear. They live where they're assigned. They go nowhere without being watched. They're constantly ordered to line up, march, be silent. Even their bodies are not their own. They are slaves, or sex objects, or subjects for medical experiments. Someone else's property. How would I ever function as a normal human being in the outside world?

"Celia?" Miriam touched my arm. "What's wrong?"

"Nothing." I forced a smile. "It's wonderful. Do you think they'll allow you to go back to Georgia?"

Miriam's eyes shifted from mine. She moved away and sat on the edge of her desk. "I've decided to stay in Vorkuta." She held up a hand to silence my protests. "No. Listen, Celia. I didn't choose this profession lightly. I chose it at first because the study of medicine fascinated me. Gradually, the knowledge and skills I learned gave me the ability to help heal the sick and injured. This gives meaning to my life, especially in a place such as this."

"Of course!" I couldn't keep silent. "But you can heal the sick back in Georgia just as well as in this hell. And you will have much better facilities. You won't have to scrimp and work with inferior equipment. You'll have a proper hospital, a professional staff. You can't stay here, Miriam. It's crazy!"

"You're not thinking this through. Georgia is under Soviet rule. I am still a criminal in the eyes of the authorities. Do you think they'll forgive and forget? No. If I'm not put in prison on my return, I will surely be forbidden to work again as a doctor in Georgia. The punishment for criticizing the State is everlasting. If I'm allowed to work at all, it will be in the most menial of jobs. Why should I scrub floors for the rest of my life just to return to my home country?"

"They couldn't do that," I protested, even though I knew in my heart she was right. "They need doctors. Especially good ones like you! You're valuable to them."

"You know as well as I how little they value people over power. Well, I value my work as a doctor over a dubious freedom. Vorkuta is more than the camps. There is also the town. And I believe many released prisoners will elect to stay here because, like me, they have nothing to return to. The mines will continue. The difference will be that the miners will no longer be slaves but paid workers, however meager their salaries. They will marry and raise families in this place. Odd as it seems"—Miriam gave a little laugh—"I've established a *practice* in Vorkuta. Who knows? With Stalin dead, things may change in the camps for the better." She smiled. "I belong here."

My heart revolted against the truth of what Miriam said, the cruelty of her choice which was no choice. I thought of what she had told me about the beauty of Georgia, the rugged mountains, valleys of blossoming peach trees in the spring, ancient cities perched on deep gorges carved by rivers of cold, sparkling water. And the warm hospitality of a people determined to keep their heritage despite Soviet power. She would never see it again.

Thoughts of my home in Slovakia rushed in, but with those thoughts came the memory of my return after Auschwitz and the anger and resentment of the people I had once called neighbors. Slovakia was Soviet now as well. Like Miriam, I would probably be looked on as a criminal there.

Ivan had already said we would not be allowed to work. It would be hard enough for him to survive under such circumstances. To be burdened with a second mouth to feed, another person to worry about, wasn't fair to him. He had been through enough. I had no doubt he'd build a new life for himself in Slovakia. He had relatives, old friends, people who would remember him from before and welcome him home. I had nothing to return to. My family was dead. And the resentment and prejudice against Jews ran deep. Ivan would say it didn't matter, but I knew it did. Slovakia had actually paid the Nazis to take the Jews off their hands in return for the promise they would never come back. I didn't think the end of the war had changed that. Jews would still be despised in Slovakia, and Ivan didn't need to be saddled with one of them.

Thinking it through, I realized Miriam had again solved a dilemma for me. She saved me from death-by-hard-labor on my arrival in Vorkuta. Now she could save me from a spiritual death.

"If you think I can be of use, Miriam, I'd like to stay here with you."

I hoped I didn't look as desolate as I felt. She didn't protest immediately, just looked at me in silence, tiny frown lines at the corners of her eyes. I straightened my shoulders and lifted my head to give myself courage.

"There is nothing left for me in Bardejov. I'm sure my father is dead, and I have no other family. My town is now a town without Jews, and I doubt the rest of Slovakia has changed its thinking about us. They weren't happy to see me return in 1945, and I don't think they'll kill the fatted calf for their prodigal daughter after her ten years in a Soviet labor camp. I have too many strikes against me to find employment. And even though I've gotten used to very little food," I risked a jest, "I'd rather be hungry and useful here with you than hungry and desolate in a place without friends." I took a deep breath. "I know I've been enthusiastic about the return of the foreign prisoners, even risking you and the hospital to get those letters to Moscow. For that, I apologize, even though I'm proud I played a small part in the eventual success. But my happiness for others does not include myself. I want to belong to something, to be useful, to have . . . worth. Like you, I found more of a purpose here than I ever thought possible. I've learned useful skills and your guidance has helped me become, in part, a better person." I lowered my eyes and studied my hands, which had twisted in a knot. Somehow, I had to make her understand it was best for me to stay without bringing Ivan into it. "Please, Miriam. Help me to stay. I don't think I have the courage to face freedom alone."

Silence filled the room with unasked questions I didn't want to answer.

"And Ivan?" Miriam said.

"What about Ivan?" I hedged.

"Do you have the courage to force him to face freedom alone?"

"What do you mean? I would never force him to do anything."

"Ivan came to my office yesterday. This was before we heard the good news about the foreign prisoners. We had a long talk, and I was glad to get to know him. We spoke about politics and the tragedies in our respective countries. He also told me about his life and how he came to be arrested and sent to the gulag. He's a rather remarkable man, although he would deny that. He has a fascinating, stubborn optimism that defies reason or even common sense. Yesterday he had no idea whether his letters even reached Moscow, much less that the foreign prisoners would be released. He knew if they were not released, and things stayed the same in Vorkuta, his life would be forfeited. Colonel Baranov would finally seize him. Ivan's latest open resistance to the rules would be added to the long list of his perceived offenses over the years in the Kazakhstan camps. He thought these letters would probably be the last straw. Oddly, he didn't look troubled. When I asked him why, he said he had managed to escape by the skin of his teeth so far, and if he'd learned anything in the camps, it was to take each day as it comes because torturing yourself over the unknown was a waste of energy. That brought us to the real reason Ivan came to see me. You, Celia." Miriam fixed me with a pointed look and raised her eyebrows.

Cold gripped my heart. I had never told Miriam what I'd done in Auschwitz. How much had Ivan revealed? I couldn't believe he would betray my trust. He said we would never speak of those things again. Still, he might have felt Miriam was a sympathetic soul who wouldn't judge. He was right about her, but how could she, a fellow Jew, ever forgive such treachery? Worse, knowing what I had done, why would she ever want to keep me as an assistant here in Vorkuta? Another ray of hope flickered and died. When I didn't answer, Miriam continued.

"Ivan told me he asked you to go back to Slovakia with him if the foreign prisoners were released, and you told him you couldn't."

"Did he tell you why?"

"He said you were harboring an overpowering sense of guilt because you had survived Auschwitz when so many were sent to their deaths. That is understandable, Celia. Your family, your friends, and everyone you loved were murdered by the Nazis. Any feeling person would ask, why them and not me."

"I don't ask that question because I know the answer. The *best* did not survive."

"I assume that means you count yourself among the *worst*. Forgive me, but I fail to see how being one of the few survivors in a group of discriminated people targeted for complete annihilation makes you a bad person. I also am sorry to hear you label yourself as *the worst* of all those who have survived what I have come to understand was one of the most viciously sadistic acts of genocide imaginable. Survival is not a crime, Celia."

"What you *do* to survive can be."

"That depends. Ivan didn't go into the details of what you told him. I don't know what you did, and I don't want to know. I've been a doctor here for a decade and a half. The Soviet concentration camps are also vicious and sadistic. My job as a doctor goes beyond healing the sick and wounded to also helping wounded minds and souls. Even here, guilt creeps in like a thief to rob many well-meaning prisoners of their peace and sanity. Did they do something to get another person killed? Did they fail to do something to save another? Did one stronger, starving person take food from another weaker, starving person? The robust feel guilty in the face of the frail. The healthy are guilty to have escaped illness. It haunts their dreams, fills them with anxiety on top of their already daily fear of death. It is another way our Soviet masters win. They are the guilty ones—not their victims."

"Even victims can do terrible things," I whispered.

"Celia." Miriam gave a sigh of exasperation. "You had just turned sixteen! You were a sheltered child, thrown into hell to watch her family go to the gas chambers! For some reason, sick fanatics plucked you from the jaws of death and used you for purposes known only to them. You did nothing to deserve that. No! Look at me! Over the last ten years, I have watched you grow from a bitter, tormented young girl into a caring, compassionate woman. You told me once that you deserved Vorkuta. I tell you now that your time here has atoned for anything you think you did in Auschwitz. You have been cleansed by fire, Celia. Auschwitz was not your fault. Vorkuta was not your fault. What *will* be your fault will be destroying the rest of your life because of your past. Don't use your guilt as a shield to protect you from facing the future and living the life that was stolen from you. For the love of God, don't let happiness pass you by. Seize it! Hold onto it! Make happiness your shield to weather any storm you may face."

There was a desperate passion to her words, forcing me to listen and understand myself. Miriam had been like a mother to me, guiding my fearful footsteps, teaching me how to give of myself to others, building in me a sense of worth. My soul knew she was right. Ivan didn't care about my past. He said he loved me, and I believed him because he was not the kind of man to take love lightly. I knew I loved him and always would. Was I being unfair to him, diminishing his future happiness by refusing to let him be with me? I didn't have the courage to face freedom alone, but I was telling him to do just that. Instead of seeing myself as a burden to him, someone who would ruin his life, maybe I was just the opposite, someone to give purpose and meaning to what was sure to be a difficult future for him. Maybe it was time I stopped living in my wretched past. Maybe Ivan was right, and love was the path to redemption.

Miriam came to me and held me by the arms. "Do you love Ivan?" she asked, searching my eyes.

"Yes."

"Then tell him. Go with him and experience happiness. You both have suffered enough. You deserve to be loved and so does he. Choose life, Celia."

The ice around my soul melted and warmth flooded in. "Yes. I will." Tears filled my eyes and rolled slowly down my face. "Thank you, Miriam. Just . . . thank you."

I wrapped my arms around her, and she hugged me close. There was no need for more words. Miriam had saved me again. This time, from myself.

CHAPTER FIFTY-THREE

They ordered the foreign prisoners to be on the train the next day. Word had spread throughout the Vorkuta camps, and now the authorities expected trouble from the Soviet nationals who were not being released. If we lucky ones were not around, excited to be getting out, the authorities hoped things would get back to normal quickly.

Ivan. I still had not seen him since my talk with Miriam. I rushed to find him right after, to tell him I wanted nothing more than to be with him for the rest of our lives, but he was nowhere around the hospital. I worried that something had gone wrong. Had Colonel Baranov taken him into custody before he could get on the train? Could it be possible that Ivan had been somewhere in the camp last night and was killed in an ambush by the two guards who worked for Baranov? Was he lying dead, even now, covered in coal in some ditch or deep in a mine? I tried to shake off the thoughts, but when freedom and happiness were close to becoming a reality, fear that something would ruin it was quick to surface.

I gathered the few belongings I had. The guards gave civilian clothes and some essentials to those of us who were leaving. Stuffing everything into a small suitcase, I pulled on the wool coat they gave me, tied a scarf around my neck, and ran through the hospital corridors. I searched every room for Ivan. He was nowhere. I ran into the corridor and nearly collided with two hospital workers assisting a disabled patient. Even the wounded or handicapped foreign prisoners were ordered to go.

"Have you seen Ivan?" I asked one man.

"Ivan who?" He gave me a surly look which told me he was one of the Soviets not being released.

"Prisoner Kovach. Have you seen him?"

"Ah!" His face darkened. "The saboteur! Is he one of the lucky ones?"

"He's a Slovak, so yes, he will be leaving."

"I doubt it." He shook his head. "He's a thorn in their sides. The NKVD doesn't forget."

My heart lurched at the thought. Colonel Baranov must have grabbed him as soon as he heard about the release of the prisoners. That had to be why I couldn't find Ivan. Where was Miriam? She might know something. She might have been in contact with the commandant. I raced out of the hospital and into the freezing morning. It was just starting to snow again. I ran first to the barracks where my friends were. Maybe Branca heard something about Ivan from Vlad. In a flash of thought, I realized Vlad would not be going. He was a Soviet. I wondered what Branca felt about it. Vlad had been her protector for a good eight years. She never said he was anything special to her, other than that he kept other men away and wasn't an absolute brute. But eight years is a long time to have an intimate relationship with one person, even if it was simply out of necessity and not of the heart. I put it out of my mind. Branca would deal with it. She was going home, and Vlad would fade into her tragic past for good. Branca wasn't one to get sentimental over a prison guard in Vorkuta, anyway.

"Celia!"

Four of the Pissers, faces bright with smiles, waved at me as I approached the barracks. I ran up to them, and they swept me into enthusiastic hugs. Branca appeared in the barracks doorway with Vlad carrying her small suitcase. Only Branca could train a Soviet prison guard in the art of gentlemanly behavior. Vlad's face, with its coarse features and broken nose, had the expression of a mongrel dog being left behind by his master. If I weren't so worried about Ivan, I would have laughed.

"Pissers!" Branca shouted. "We have an escort to the station." The girls cheered, and Vlad grimaced. "Vlad says tensions are running high against our good fortune, and he wants to make sure we aren't molested on the way." She rolled her eyes at Vlad. "You would think he knew by now that no one messes with the Pissers."

Another cheer rang out. Branca came over and gave me a hug. "At last, Celia, we're going home." She took me by the shoulders. "Don't look so worried. Everything will be all right. You'll come to visit me in

Bratislava, and we'll go to that little pastry shop that makes the most incredible strudel." She closed her eyes and breathed deeply. "I can smell the scent of cinnamon and apples already." She put her arm around me. "We'll sit in the café and eat strudel and drink coffee with cream. Imagine, Celia. Real coffee! Not ground up burnt bread crust floating in greasy water. And real forks—silver, with the imprint of the café on them. And real china cups, and a white tablecloth, and linen napkins. We'll be in heaven, Celia."

"Yes," I agreed. "It will be wonderful." I approached Vlad. "Have you seen Prisoner Kovach? I've been trying to find him for two days now. Do you know anything about him?"

Vlad scratched his head. "Prisoner Kovach?" The light of recognition came over his face. "He's the saboteur who's been in hospital. That right?"

"Yes, but he's a Slovak and is supposed to be on the train today. I can't find him, and I don't want him to miss the train."

Vlad shrugged. "Wouldn't know what he looked like. Never met the guy."

I gave a sigh of exasperation. "I wonder if you've heard anything about a foreign prisoner being arrested by the NKVD in the last couple of days."

Vlad looked wary. "I don't mix with that crowd. Can't help you." He nudged Branca. "We've got to go, Branc. Train won't wait."

Branca turned to me. "I'll look out for Ivan. If I see him, I'll tell him you're looking for him and he should stay by the train and not go looking for you." She raised an eyebrow at me. "You two made up?"

"There was nothing to make up," I said. "I just came to my senses, that's all. Now I've got to find him and let him know everything is all right. I just hope . . ."

"Branc!" Vlad grabbed her arm. "Let's go!"

"See you on the train, Celia." Branca laughed as Vlad dragged her away.

I was frantic now. I couldn't dash all over the camp, hoping to find Ivan. I had to get to the train if I was going to leave with everyone else. But, if Ivan would not be on that train, if he were a prisoner still, or dead, then I didn't want to go. I couldn't imagine a life without him. I didn't *want* a life without him. For the first time, I knew how wonderful love felt. I also knew how painful love could be when it was taken away. I gave myself a mental shake and refused to despair. I also had to find Miriam to say goodbye. I ran back to the hospital. She was just coming out with the last of the patients for release.

"Miriam!" I must have looked stricken because she came quickly.

"What's wrong? Why aren't you at the train?"

"I can't find Ivan!" I could feel the tears brimming in my eyes. "Have you seen him? I haven't been able to find him since we talked. I'm so afraid Colonel Baranov has him. He swore he would get him." I grabbed Miriam's arm. "I'm sure Baranov has killed him. Oh, Miriam," I sobbed, "what will I do?"

Miriam told the hospital orderlies to go on with the patients. She drew me aside and put her arms around me. "Don't cry. I haven't seen Ivan, but I have one piece of good news. I saw the commandant earlier this morning. They have arrested Colonel Baranov for theft, sabotage, and crimes against the State. He's being sent to Moscow, probably to Lubyanka Prison, to stand trial."

"Good!" I drew a hand across my eyes to wipe away the tears. "I hope they don't shoot him but send him to the worst of the worst camps and make him work in the mines for the rest of his miserable life."

"That would be the best poetic justice. As for Ivan, I think the commandant would have said something to me about him if he knew anything. The time to panic is when the train is leaving, and Ivan isn't on it. Until then, don't question fate. Trust that Ivan will find you."

"But he doesn't think I want to go with him. I never found him after I talked to you. He still thinks I rejected him. I never got the chance to tell him I love him." Tears came again.

Miriam took me by the arm. "I'll walk you to the train."

I had to go with her. There was no way I could search the entire camp. Yet I still couldn't get rid of the awful feeling that Ivan was dead. They say if you love someone deeply, you will know if something terrible has happened to them. I figured two souls would have to join for that kind of intimate premonition. I hadn't been in love, real love, for long enough. How long did it take for souls to join? I didn't know. Maybe I was sure he was dead because it fit in with the disaster my life had been. Every time hope had risen in my heart, something killed it. Well, if Ivan wasn't at the train, at least I knew what my future would be. I would stay in Vorkuta.

The train that would take us away from the hell we'd known for years waited like a smoking behemoth at the long platform that passed for a station. Steam rose in noisy bursts from the ice-encrusted engine, swirling in and around the falling snow. If my heart hadn't been so heavy, I would have felt the scene was magical. Miriam and I found an almost carnival-like atmosphere by the train. The foreign prisoners were a much larger group than I had expected. They rushed in and out of the cars, shouting to friends to come and see the inside.

"There are real seats! It's not a cattle car!" A woman stuck her head out of the window of one car farther along. "There's a sleeping car! With pillows!"

"Did you see the dining car?" two young women sang. "There's a big samovar, and lemon and sugar for tea. Real tea!"

One man stumbled down from the third car with tears in his eyes, waving little pieces of paper. "They have toilet paper! Thank the Lord!" The group near him cheered.

"From slaves to honored guests in the blink of an eye. Such is the magic of the People's Paradise," Miriam said in amused irony. She turned to me. "This is goodbye, Celia. I must get back to help with the last of the patients being released."

I threw my arms around her. "I will miss you more than you know. You took a bitter young woman and taught her the skills and courage to be a kinder, more caring person."

"You did that yourself." Miriam smiled that gentle smile I'd grown to love. "All I did was give you the chance to find that person. She was always there."

"I wish so much you were going too. It's so unfair. This is such a terrible place to spend the rest of your life."

"Don't worry about me. Someday we may all be free. Who knows? Good could triumph. Stranger things have happened." She kissed me on the forehead. "I'll always feel you were the daughter I never had. I wish you the very best of luck. Be happy, Celia." She caressed my face with her fingers, turned away, and left me. I watched her until she disappeared down the road to the camp and the hospital.

An announcement came over a loudspeaker. "This train will leave in ten minutes. Anyone not on it will remain in Vorkuta!"

Ivan! Where was he? I rushed down the length of the train, in and out of the cars, searching each one. I knew he would call to me if he were inside any of them. He wasn't there. I walked back to the front of the train and stood near the engine, looking down the tracks leading out of Vorkuta. There was so little time left.

"Five minutes!" The loudspeaker startled me, and my heart raced in time with the chuffing of the engine. "Foreign prisoners! Board the train. Now!"

I couldn't go. Wouldn't go. Without Ivan, freedom meant nothing to me. I looked down at the tracks again.

"Anna!"

I was hearing things. The voice was so like his. A burst of steam enveloped me. I closed my eyes.

"Anna Karenina." Again, that hint of humor I knew so well. "Don't do it!"

I turned around slowly, afraid there would be no one there, that it was only my imagination. I opened my eyes. The steam swirled, dissipated, and there he was. I stared at him. They'd given him a suit. I could see it under the heavy overcoat he hadn't taken the time to button. His raven black hair, dusted with snow, fell in an unruly wave over his forehead. He looked distinguished. The lawyer from Prague, dropped by fate into Vorkuta. And then he smiled, and my heart turned over. He held out his arms, and I rushed into his embrace.

"I love you, Ivan! I'm so sorry . . ."

He stopped me with his mouth on mine.

Of all the kisses that people have shared in parting and greeting over all of time, the kiss we shared that last day in Vorkuta carried an everlasting promise. Our trials were not over, but we would never face them alone again. Our pasts were not forgotten, but they could not tarnish our future. We were free beyond our release from the prison camps of the gulag. Love had freed our souls from the burdens they had carried for so many years. Ivan was right. He was my redemption, and I was his. It was that simple.

Epilogue

The Long Road to Freedom

By George Kovach

The first stop for my father and stepmother was not freedom but the infamous Butyrka Prison in Moscow. It had long been a place for brutal interrogation of political prisoners and a transfer point for those sentenced to the gulag. However, for the foreign prisoners released from Siberia in 1955, it was a holding pen where they were fattened up, given new clothes, sorted, and documented before being sent on their way home.

In September 1955, my father and stepmother, along with a large group of other Czech prisoners, were led on foot through the border zone between the USSR and Communist Czechoslovakia. Guards with guns at the ready formed two lines. Each Czech citizen was called by name and had to pass through this gauntlet. The first called were those who had received amnesty. They were given gifts and souvenirs and whisked away on buses like tourists. Unfortunately, the Communist Czech government still viewed sixteen others, including my father and stepmother, as dangerous. They were hustled into black prisoner transport vans equipped with a row of tiny cells on either side of a narrow corridor. The cells were so cramped the prisoners could only sit or stand hunched over. Inside each cell was a bench that could be transformed into a toilet. A peephole in the door allowed the guards to spy on the prisoners at any time. In this way my father and stepmother were transported to the Ruzyne Prison in Prague, where they would spend most of the next year. They were still viewed as "enemies of the Czechoslovak State."

When brought before the prison procurator to be interrogated, my father demanded again to know the charges against him. He had never been told. He had never received a trial. He had never been allowed to present a defense. Now that he had the chance, my father confronted the procurator with the question that had burned in him all during his time in the gulag. What right did the Communist Czech government have to hand him, a Czech citizen, over to the NKVD, the secret police of the USSR? Didn't the Czech government recognize the lawlessness and arbitrary tyranny of the cult of Stalin? My father then vividly described the degradation and humiliation of his slavery in Siberia. The procurator, not knowing what to say, tried to calm him down. After that meeting, my father was never called again during his entire time at the prison. The Communist Czech government, of course, did not have a leg to stand on in my father's and Celia's cases. They had not convicted my father of any crime when they arrested him in 1948. They had simply turned him over to the Soviet NKVD to use as a slave in Siberia. The Communist Czech government, even under its own constitution, knew it did not have the right to hand over my father or stepmother for slavery in Siberia. But now, once again, the Czech authorities didn't know what to do with them. Finally, on June 1, 1956, my father and stepmother were released from the prison in Prague.

They never did get answers to their questions.

Ivan and Celia shortly after their release from Vorkuta, 1958.

Though my father and stepmother were freed, they still carried the stigma of being "enemies of the people." This meant they could not get a work permit or go to school, and were not allowed any of the rights of their fellow citizens. They were, in effect, impoverished non-persons.

My father's brother, Vasili, came to their aid and gave them the use of his one-room *dacha* in the country near the town of Kosice. There, they grew vegetables on the acre of land around them. The physical work at their own pace was relaxing after the gulag. In the evenings, my father would write more appeals to the government and read Russian classics to Celia. It was not quite Kitty and Levin from *Anna Karenina*, living on a country estate, but it was also not a Siberian concentration camp. After so many years in overcrowded and contentious barracks, it was a relief to have solitude, privacy, and the joy of love.

Starting a new life was complicated. My father and stepmother spent over a year in the country. They were still under surveillance by the secret police. Their freedom of movement was curtailed because the authorities were always suspicious that they might try to escape the Socialist Republic of Czechoslovakia.

In 1956, Khrushchev, the new leader of the USSR, shocked the Communist world by denouncing Stalin and his gulag system. Consequently, Communist states of Eastern Europe slowly and reluctantly granted rehabilitation to their former political prisoners. For two years my father kept badgering the Czech Communist authorities with appeals for rehabilitation for him and Celia. Rehabilitation meant they would be pardoned. Only then would the normal rights of citizens be restored to them.

In 1958, the Communist Czech government finally rehabilitated my father and Celia. The bureaucrats in Prague probably breathed a sigh of relief now that they could get rid of the annoying ex-lawyer who had bombarded them with so many appeals for so many years. The government actually admitted its errors, restored full rights of citizenship, and paid my father and Celia a small sum for the time they spent in Czech prisons. The Soviets, however, never paid Celia or my father one kopek as reparations for their long years of slavery, "building socialism" in Siberia. Now Celia and Ivan could finally get married, find jobs, and stop growing vegetables.

However, what were they to do now? My father, after what he had experienced, would never agree to work or be able to work as a lawyer in a Communist legal system. Therefore he decided to utilize his great love of Russian literature. Here, he was in luck. Since Communist Czechoslovakia was a puppet state of Russia, there was always a great demand for teachers of Russian, and my father's Russian was impeccable. He became a professor of Russian language and literature at the University of Kosice.

Celia could now go back to school and get the education she had been denied because of Auschwitz and the gulag. She became a government accountant. She was so exacting in her work and so incorruptible in a corrupt system that she worked her way up in the bureaucracy quickly.

Celia and Ivan enjoying a middle-class life in Kosice.

Celia was valued highly, the commissars said, because she would never take bribes. For this reason, the government businesses whose books she audited also feared her. The unbelievable cruelty and torment she had suffered and survived under the two most vicious regimes of the twentieth century had left Celia with an intense fervor for justice, truth, and honesty.

Gradually, their lives changed for the better, and by the late sixties, they were able to save enough to buy a small, one-bedroom apartment. They could now live a modest lifestyle in Kosice.

Celia and Ivan had endured the worst that the evils of the twentieth century could inflict on them, and they had survived to find peace and happiness. Their bond of deep love and respect for each other endured until the end of their lives.

FATHER AND SON: REUNION

I was three-and-a-half years old when my father was arrested by the Communists. I didn't see him again until I was twenty-two. We had to meet in Hungary because I, too, was considered an "enemy of the people" and forbidden entrance into Czechoslovakia due to my "treacherous escape" at age three-and-a-half. My father always carried a deep sense of guilt for not leaving Czechoslovakia when my mother begged him to, thus causing her and his son years of suffering, even though he suffered the most for his decision. He knew if he had only listened to my mother, and we had all left Czechoslovakia before 1948, our lives would have been very different. I would not have grown up without a father, the whole burden of supporting a family would not have fallen on my mother, and my father would not have suffered in the gulag for eight years. It was a guilt for which he would never forgive himself. When I met him in Budapest in 1967, the first thing he did was apologize for the terrible decision he had made in 1948.

I assured him no apology was necessary. To me, my father was a hero. Whatever my mother may have felt, she never spoke of my father in a negative light. As far back as I can remember, she always spoke of him as courageous and honorable, a man condemned to years of cruelty and suffering simply because he stood in opposition to a rigid, intolerant, totalitarian regime bent on destroying all individual freedom of thought and action. It was nothing new. Our family had been running from communism ever since the 1917 Bolshevik Revolution, when my

George and his father meeting for the first time since Ivan was arrested in 1948. Budapest, 1967.

grandmother and grandfather, with my mother (age two), were driven out of Russia. They, too, were declared "enemies of the people," not for anything they had done but for the crime of belonging to the "wrong" class. My family had endured and survived the ideological frenzies of the twentieth century. I had grown up *living* history.

When I met my father, I was eager to hear his story, to live through history with him. I was rewarded beyond measure. We stayed up all night while he told me of his time in the camps of the gulag. He was a magnificent storyteller, and I felt I was there with him. What most impressed me was his ability to find humor in the most awful situations. At twenty-two, I was a serious young man when it came to the evils that had plagued my family. However, during that long night of stories, I had never laughed so much in my life. My father taught me a vital lesson: Humor can often get you through the worst of times.

Three generations together in Budapest, 1984.

I first met Celia in 1984 when my wife and I brought our six-month-old son to see his grandfather and step-grandmother. It was a three generations reunion. Again we met in Budapest because I was still forbidden entrance into Communist Czechoslovakia.

Celia's joy and touching affection for baby Peter moved me deeply. She was such a warm-hearted and loving woman. And I knew, from what my father told me, she had always wanted children, but because of the horrors she'd suffered, she could never have them. My six-month-old son rarely took to strangers. He was wary and suspicious of them. To my amazement and delight, he took to Celia right away. In his six-month-old wisdom, he trusted her and knew instinctively that she was kind and genuine in her affection for him. The photos of the two of them together, smiling and cheerful, still bring me happiness.

Baby Peter and Celia, wearing matching outfits that Celia knitted.

In the eighties and nineties, I traveled to Europe often and always stopped by to see my father and Celia. The more time I spent with her, the more comfortable she became with me and opened up about herself. Since my father was no longer in good health, I would go shopping with her or just sit and talk with her in the park. Mostly, she spoke about my father. I, of course, asked her to tell me about her extraordinary life. Celia wished to bury that past life. She didn't want anyone they knew, or might meet, to know of these things.

"How could I live in this town if people knew I was in Auschwitz and the gulag?" she said. "What would they think of me? What could I say to my friends? How would they look on me, knowing these things? I would be strange to them. I would probably lose friendships I've been fortunate to have."

My father had told me of her terrible sufferings both in Auschwitz and the gulag. Celia was one of the few people to have been imprisoned in both those hells. Past prejudices and fears remained with the older generation. Celia was afraid that if people knew her history, their prejudices and fears would taint her reputation and friendships. Also, during her years working as a state accountant, it was vitally important that her past remain a secret. She told me she knew trust was fragile. It could be destroyed by rumors and lies. Even if they were proved false, doubts

Ivan and Celia wedding photo

might still exist. Somehow, friends, neighbors, and colleagues might suspect she was sent there for a legitimate reason.

But she came to trust me because she knew my admiration and affection for my father was sincere. This was the most important thing to her. Because I loved and admired him as she did, it meant I wouldn't reveal family secrets. I told her I would never do anything to bring her or my father pain. She knew I had a fascination with history—especially the history of my family. So during our times alone together, she told me many things about her life.

Always, as we talked, she would go back to the deep love and admiration she had for my father. She wanted me to know how grateful she was that Fate had brought him to her, how he had saved her from the memories of her dark past, and how their life together filled her with a happiness she never imagined she could have.

Why we wrote this book

By George Kovach

Love and Redemption was born out of grief, love, and the desire to restore my stepmother's tarnished reputation.

Celia Klein/Kovacova, my stepmother, whose extraordinary story of survival and courage you have just read about in this novel, was originally misrepresented in two global bestsellers: The *Tattooist of Auschwitz* and *Cilka's Journey* by Heather Morris.

I was not aware that anyone was writing books about my stepmother. Ms. Morris had not reached out to me before starting these books. In 2019, she did finally contact me, asking for photos of Celia and my father, and even requesting I write an afterword for *Cilka's Journey*.

When I read her books, I was stunned. In those novels, Celia appears under the name "Cilka," a character portrayed as a dazzlingly beautiful young woman who survived Auschwitz by becoming the mistress of not one, but two SS commanders, and later portrayed as a drug thief in the Siberian Gulag. While marketed as "based on a true story," these characterizations bear absolutely no resemblance to the woman I knew.

I felt not just sorrow but outrage at Ms. Morris's portrayal of my stepmother. This wasn't simply creative license, it was character theft in service of sensationalism. Because Celia was deceased and not my blood relative, she had no one to protect her.

So, my wife Julia and I wrote *Love and Redemption* under our pen name, Julia George. We did not intend to compete with Morris's fiction, but to rescue my stepmother from that fiction and restore the memory of the woman we knew. We based our account of my stepmother's story on my in-person conversations with Celia, my father's memoirs, and family records. What you have just read is not a salacious tale "inspired by real events." It is a son's effort to bring light to what was darkened by some else's imagination.

Fiction has power. But so does Truth.

If you would like to read a more detailed account of my struggle with Heather and her publishers, you can find it on our website (juliageorgeauthor.com) under the Facts Behind the Fiction section — *Why We Wrote Love and Redemption/A Son's Struggle to Redeem the Memory and Character of his Family.*

About the Authors

Julia George is the pen name of a husband and wife writing team.

Their first novel was the award-winning cozy mystery comic *Galya Popoff and the Dead Souls* (Best of 2012 in its category on *Kirkus*). This was followed by *Blood into Wine*, a traditional detective novel set in Napa Valley. *Kirkus Reviews* called *Blood into Wine* "A great vintage, with an edge of barbaric murder, a hint of romance, and the smooth aftertaste of justice served." *The Mars 7* is Julia's science fiction novel for young adults.

They both graduated from UC Berkeley and went on to create the Berkeley Shakespeare Festival. George was also a resident director at the Berkeley Repertory Theater. George and Julia worked in numerous regional theaters both on the West Coast and in Chicago and New York. George had a brief stint as a talent agent in New York, and then commercially produced Broadway shows in San Francisco and Chicago.

George also spent a fascinating year in the Soviet Union working for the State Department. He traveled all over the USSR, met thousands of people, and handed out thousands of "forbidden" books, *gratis*. The following year he returned to film a documentary in Siberia. George was the first American allowed to film actual gulag camps at Kolyma which, because of their location above the Arctic Circle, are still in-tact.

Julia and George live in Northern California where the sun always shines and the absurdity never stops.

Printed in Dunstable, United Kingdom

71735161R00170